Tyrsa's Choice

Book 2 of The Jada-Drau

Sandie Bergen

Mature Content Disclaimer:
This book contains some sex and violence.

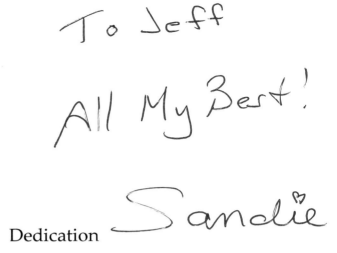

To Jeff

All My Best!

Sandie

Dedication

This book is dedicated to Charlie, my husband and soul-mate, who's put up with my foibles for the last thirty-three years. You are my rock, my lighthouse, during the shipwrecks of life.

TYRSA'S CHOICE

Edited by Sandy Fetchko
Cover art, design and layout by Stephen Blundell.

Published April, 2012 in print & Kindle Ebook

Print ISBN: 978-0-9850052-0-7

Marion Margaret Press
Headquarters:
1312 16th St
Orange City, FL 32763
Business Office:
PO Box 245
Hebron, NE 68370

email: publisher@marionmargaretpress.com

www.marionmargaretpress.com

Acknowledgments

First and foremost, I'd like to thank Steve Shumka, my friend, massage therapist and the man who taught me how to kill and maim people. He is a wonderful inspiration and does a fantastic job of keeping me on track with my writing. His knowledge and insight is invaluable.

To my children, Amanda and Aaron, thank you for your love and support. I am *your* biggest fan!

Thank you to the following people for their input, suggestions, helpful reviews and general support: Diana Cacy Hawkins, Sharon Partington, Sandy Fetchko and Sheila Hanson.

Hugs to you all!

Characters and Pronunciation Guide

Jada-Drau – (**jay**-da-**drow**) – the child of prophecy

Bredun

Artan – assassin, apprentice to Snake
Iridia – (ear-**rid**-i-a)Saulth`s daughter by Saybra
Islara – (Iss-**lara**) – mother of the Jada-Drau and Saulth's concubine - deceased
Meric – (**mare**-ik) – Saulth`s son by Saybra
Petrella – Saulth`s second wife
Rymon – (**rye**-mon) – Saulth's councillor
Saulth – (**sawlth**) – lord of the principality of Bredun
Saybra – Saulth`s first wife - deceased
Snake – assassin
Tajik – (**tay**-jik) – Guard-Commander of Bredun

Dunvalos Reach

Aleyn – (a-**lain**) – captain of the station at the foot of the trail leading to Eagle's Nest Pass
Cenith – (**ken**-ith –like Kenneth) – lord of the principality of Dunvalos Reach
Daric – (**dare**-ik) – former mercenary, Cenith`s councillor
Elessa – (eh-**less**-uh) – Daric`s wife
Ifan – (**eye**-fun) – Cenith's father - deceased
Ors – (**oars**) – Guard-Commander of Dunvalos Reach
Tyrsa – (**tear**-sa) – illegitimate daughter of Saulth and Islara, wife to Cenith, the Jada-Drau

Daric and Elessa`s Children

Kian – (**key**-an) – Killed by an assassin at age 20

Avina – (ah-**vee**-nah) – 18

Jennica – (**jen**-i-ca) – 17

Talon and Varo – 15, twins

Mina – (**meen**-a) - 12

Nani – (**naw**-nee) – 8

Chand and Chayne – 5, twins

Rade – 9 months

The Lady's Companions

Jolin – (**jaw**-lin) – captain

Jayce – lieutenant

Trey – (**tray**) - lieutenant

Barit – (**bare**-it)

Buckham – (**buck**-am)

Dathan – (**day**-than)

Ead – (**eed**)

Fallon – (**fa**-lun)

Keev

Madin – (**mad**-in)

Varth

Yanis – (**ya**-niss)

Others

Urik – (**oor**-ik) – lord of Amita

Jylun – (**jie**-lun) – lord of Kalkor

Esryn – (**ess**-rin) – lord of Sudara

Lorcan – lord of Mador

Rigen – (**rye**-gen) – last king of Ardael, split the kingdom into six principalities to stop the squabbling of his sons; reset the Ardaeli yearly reckoning to year one.

The Ardaeli Pantheon

Maegden – (**meg**-den) – father of the gods, lord of the sky

Talueth – (ta-**lu**-eth) – goddess of hearth and home

Keana – (key-**anna**) – goddess of agriculture and commerce

Shival – (**shiv**-ull) – goddess of death

Aja – (**aw**-juh - the 'j' is soft) – god of luck and thieves

Tailis – (**tay**-liss) – god of water

Siyon – (**sigh**-on) – god of war

Ordan – god of fire and smithing

The Calleni Gods

Cillain – (kill-**ane**) – god of sky and earth

Niafanna – (nee-a-**fan**-na) – goddess of all that`s living

Principalities and Countries

Dunvalos Reach – (dun-**vah**-los reach)

Bredun – (bray-**dun**)

Amita – (a-**meet**-a)

Sudara – (soo-**dar**-a)

Mador – (**may**-dor)

Ardael – (ar-**dale**)

Syrth – (**seerth**)

Tai-Keth – (tie-**keth**)

Callenia – (ka-**len**-i-a)

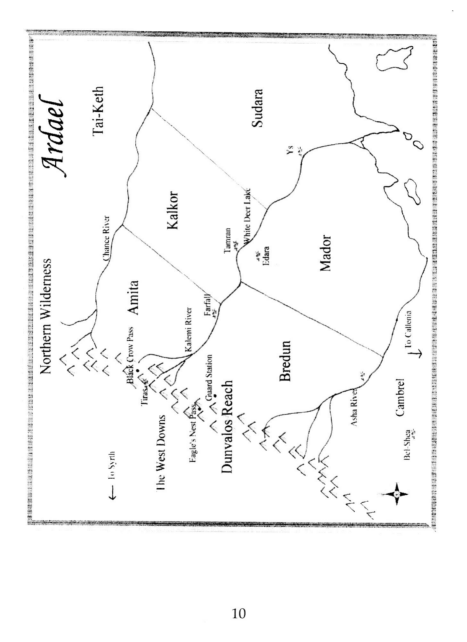

Ardael

Tai-Keth

Sudara

Ys

Northern Wilderness

Chance River

Kalkor

Tamran

White Deer Lake

Edara

Mador

Amita

Black Crow Pass

Kalemi River

Farfall

To Callenia

Tirasa

Guard Station

Bredun

The West Downs

Eagle's Nest Pass

Dunvalos Reach

Asha River

Cambrel

Bel Shea

To Syrth

10

Chapter One

Cenith, blocked the bedroom door, arms crossed, legs apart. "No. Baybee stays here."

"I need Baybee!" Tyrsa clutched the doll to her chest, her lower lip stuck out in a pout—an expression she must have picked up from one of Councillor Daric's younger girls. There was little light in the bedroom, only the small patch of sunlight that shone through the glass in the balcony doors and leaked into the room through the open door. Assassins had broken their tall bedroom windows and boards now kept the weather, and the sun, out. Despite the lack of light, he could easily see her glare.

Cenith stood six-foot-four while Tyrsa barely reached five feet; nonetheless, she glared up at him in utter defiance; sad behaviour for the wife of the Lord of Dunvalos Reach.

Despite his brutality, Lord Saulth, Tyrsa's father, had only beaten her stubborn nature into hiding, not out of her completely. Once she realized no one in Tiras Keep would hurt her, it had come charging to the forefront.

"You didn't need Baybee during Kian's funeral. Or several times since." Only ten days had passed since the death of Cenith's best friend and talking about him still hit a raw nerve. "That tells me you don't need to have her all the time." He kept his voice calm, but firm, putting a lie to the tension coursing through him. Lunch churned in his gut, adding to the stress; just what he needed on his first day running the annual Dunvalos Reach council meeting.

"You are Lady of Tiras Keep and my wife. None of

the other girls your age carry dolls around with them. We're going to meet the dukes and you are *not* bringing Baybee with you. Understood?" Their unexpected, and swift, marriage hadn't allowed them much time to adjust to each other, though Cenith doubted he'd ever get used to his wife packing a doll around.

Most of the girls Cenith knew would try using tears or beg with large, luminous eyes if they didn't get their way. Tyrsa, growing up alone and in the dark for almost sixteen years, knew none of those antics. Cenith almost wished she did. Daric had told him about the performance she'd pulled when he wouldn't let her go to him at the station at the foot of Eagle's Nest Pass, when Cenith almost died.

Tyrsa had healed him that night and suffered a great deal of pain because of it, but now her entire body trembled, her jaw set against him; and it had nothing to do with healing. He steeled himself, preparing for the tantrum building within her; the hitting, kicking, wildcat Daric had described.

"Listen to me," Cenith said, hoping to make her see reason before she erupted. "It's time to grow up, Tyrsa. I don't want you packing your doll around the keep anymore. You can cuddle Baybee anytime you want when you're here, in our rooms." He relaxed his stance and took her by the shoulders. "Leave her here. You can come back later if you need to."

Jerking away from him, Tyrsa strode to the table beside their bed. She set Baybee carefully near the unlit candle and smoothed the doll's pretty blue dress, the tiny white flowers bright against the darker material. Then she made sure the white apron covering it was also suitably arranged. The yellow yarn hair, loose like Tyrsa's own, partly covered one blue button eye.

Cenith released a long breath and stepped away from the door. "Thank you. Shall we go? We're late." He held his hand out to her.

Tyrsa refused it and stomped out of the bedroom. Not waiting for him, she yanked open the outer door. Cenith's long legs caught him up fast. Fallan and Buckam followed her down the hall, leaving the other two guards outside their door to protect an empty suite, a necessity since the invasion by assassins ten days previous. Tyrsa tramped toward the stairs, her head high, both hands clutching the sides of her dark green overdress as if it might try to escape. He waved the two Lady's Companions back, answering their silent question while they descended the stairs.

"She's in a mood, so watch her closely. I want to keep this as short as possible," Cenith said, staying far enough behind that Tyrsa couldn't hear—he hoped. "When I've finished introducing her, take her to Elessa." Perhaps Councillor Daric's wife might have some luck with her.

"First fight, My Lord?" Fallan's dark grey eyes danced with humour and he struggled to maintain the bland expression adopted by all soldiers when on guard duty.

Cenith scowled. "Good guess." He took the main stairs down two at a time, reaching Tyrsa before she arrived at the second floor. The Companions followed two steps behind. He removed Tyrsa's left hand from her dress and, holding it tight, pulled her into the second floor hall. Just before they reached the Grand Staircase, he tugged her to a stop. The Companions halted a discreet distance away.

"Look what your anger is doing to your dress."

13

Cenith tried to smooth the wrinkled cotton.

Tyrsa's scowl eased. While growing up in Saulth's storeroom, she'd had little in the way of clothes and those were ill-fitting and old. Her dresses were almost as important to her as Baybee. She released her grip and copied him. Together, they managed to work most of the creases out. Taking her chin in his other hand, Cenith forced her to look at him. The frown may have lessened, but anger still added sparks to her eyes.

"We don't have time to talk about this right now. Please be nice to these men. They're important to the principality and I need them to think well of you. Understand?" Cenith released her chin. She nodded once. "Can you please try to smile? You look much prettier."

Tyrsa blinked. Though she still refused to speak, her features relaxed to the point where she appeared merely annoyed. The lingering anger tinged her pale cheeks red, improving her looks.

Close enough. "When I introduce them, all you have to do is nod. You don't have to talk if you don't want to." Perhaps she might, just to spite him. Tyrsa could be difficult to read at the best of times. They'd only been married six weeks, but right now it felt like six years. "Once you've met them all, Fallan and Buckam will take you to Elessa. Maybe playing with the children will put you in a better mood."

She flashed him a glare. Putting her hand on his arm and holding it there, Cenith escorted her down the Grand Staircase. It was the last day of Sixth Month and though the day was warm for the mountains, the keep retained some of the spring's chill. The two massive fireplaces flanking the Hall radiated a pleasant heat, as well as aiding the chandeliers, torches and narrow windows in lighting the dim hall.

Thirty-four of the mountain principality's dukes, ranging in age from early twenties to late sixties, stood when they appeared. Four were absent and had sent birds explaining why—one due to illness, another had broken his leg, while two had neglected to allow themselves enough time and would arrive the next day.

Cenith's councillor, guard-commander and Master of the Treasury completed the council, bringing their number to forty-two, including Cenith. A cleric sat next to the councillor's chair, though he had no say in matters; he simply recorded the proceedings. Councillor Daric and Guard-Commander Ors would miss their first council meeting in their new positions, but that couldn't be helped. Daric had left on a mission assigned to him by Lady Violet, Tyrsa's other persona, while Ors escorted the assassin Snake to the border and wasn't due back for another four days.

A double row of tables had been pushed together to accommodate the council. Pewter goblets sat at each place and servants had set flagons of wine, ale, and water at regular intervals.

Cenith led Tyrsa to a spot near his chair at the head of the tables situated in the middle of the large hall. Avina, Daric's oldest daughter—and now his oldest child since the death of Kian—stood in for Daric and would read the guard-commander's report as well. A small, neat, sheaf of parchments waited for him in front of his chair.

Each council member bowed when introduced to Tyrsa, while she stood stiff as a board. When they finally reached Avina, to Cenith's right, she managed a small smile. He doubted Tyrsa would remember even one of the dukes' names, let alone all of them, but propriety was observed and that was all that mattered. He motioned to the Companions and they accompanied Tyrsa back up the staircase.

Cenith sat in the high backed chair, hiding his sigh of relief. The nobles took their seats and waited for him to start the meeting. He spent a moment shuffling through the stack of parchments, more to gather his thoughts than to read what he already knew was written there.

He cleared his throat. "This year's opening session will be different in more ways than one. First, the death of my father and Councillor Halen has affected us all." Months had passed since an avalanche swept his father away, but Cenith felt his death as keenly as Kian's. He waited until several of the newly arrived spoke their condolences.

"I sent messages so you all know I appointed Daric as my councillor and Ors as guard-commander." He watched their faces for any sign of discontent. Most nodded, their expressions showing agreement. A few, those from the farthest reaches of the principality, kept their features bland. Cenith could see no open objection, though each of them had given Avina at least one questioning glance.

Ramos, Duke of White Deer Valley, raised his hand to be recognized. "My Lord, have you recovered the bodies yet? We've had no word."

Spring thaw in the mountains was long in coming, particularly this year. "There's a search party out now. I expect them back any day. With luck, we can hold the funeral the day after this meeting ends so you can all attend." Cenith's words brought on murmurs of appreciation. Halen's and the guards' bodies would be returned to their families. "Father kept me apprised of all that happened in the principality. Nonetheless, Daric and I went through his and Halen's papers. For those of you who sent Father messages before his death, we are aware of your concerns and they will be dealt with...but not today."

A few grumbles met that remark. Cenith set the parchments down and plowed on. "Next, Councillor Daric's absence. He's on a trade mission to Mador and won't be back for at least two weeks." A blatant lie, but a necessary one. "Daric's daughter, Mistress Avina, is filling in for him. She has been invaluable to me over the last several days." He hoped that put an end to the glances.

"You all want to know exactly what happened here last week." When Cenith had made love to Tyrsa for the first time, she'd screamed in pain, her eyes had turned violet and she'd glowed white. That was only the beginning of a very strange night that had also seen her creating the ash symbols that were now a permanent addition to the hearth in his suite; the invasion of the keep by assassins who'd tried to abduct his wife and stole a piece parchment that had hung around the keep for four hundred years; and the death of Kian, Daric's son and Cenith's best friend. The dukes wouldn't hear all of it though.

Cenith rested his folded hands on the table. "That tale is long in the telling and I'm sure will take the rest of the afternoon. It started in Edara and hasn't ended yet. Gentlemen and Mistress Avina..." He nodded in her direction, "fill your cups and sit back. We're going to be a while."

* * * *

A woman's face swam before Artan's bleary eyes. Not his mother. No, she'd died nine years ago. The woman set a cool cloth against his forehead. She looked older than his mother, her face veined with fine lines, her brown hair streaked with grey. *Would Mother have looked similar if she'd lived?* His vision, and his head, improved enough for him to realize he had no idea where he was.

Artan forced his thoughts back to his last clear memories—stealing the parchment; seeing his dead comrades lying on the ground outside Tiras Keep; waking up in a narrow depression in a mountain, his throat sore, his head stuffed; trudging through the mountains, fearing with every step that he'd be discovered. He vaguely remembered sneaking past the Dunvalos Reach soldiers at the end of the pass and the relief he'd felt once he'd made it to the Bredun Main Road.

A village...an inn...one of his stolen gold coins in exchange for a hot bath, a warm bed for a few days and food. His gold. *The parchment!* Artan sat upright, startling the woman seated next to the bed. He looked around the room, finally spotting his pack leaning against the wall near the door; his suspiciously empty looking pack. Making a fuss over it now might alert the woman to something wrong, so he decided to wait until she left.

"Are ya ready for a bit t' eat then?" she asked, reaching for something beyond his vision. A wooden bowl.

If it held food, Artan couldn't smell it. His nose didn't even allow air past. His head swam and he had to concentrate on the woman's kind, brown eyes to steady it. "How..." That brought on a coughing fit.

"Perhaps some water first," the woman said, exchanging the bowl for a cup.

With her help, Artan swallowed all the water. "How long have I been here?" His voice cracked when it didn't come out as a whisper.

"Since yesterday. Yer still sick, so I hope yer not plannin' on goin' anywhere soon. Yer not th' sickest boy I've seen, but if ya don't take care, this could get into yer lungs and then ya will be in for a right time o' it." The woman picked up the bowl again and handed it to him, making sure he didn't drop it. "Drink this. 'Tis broth with herbs to help yer head and throat. I think it's all ya can handle right now."

Artan nodded his thanks before sipping the broth. His hands shook while he drank. The liquid tasted bland, despite the herbs the woman said were in there, but that might be his throat's fault and not the cook's.

"Yer clothes and blankets are still dryin', but they'll be ready long before ye're fit for travel agin." The woman took the empty bowl from him and stood. "There's more water there on th' table within easy reach and th' chamber pot's under th' bed, but ya should try t' sleep now. As I said, ya don't want t' make it worse."

Artan nodded rather than try to force more words past his sore throat. He settled back against the pillows and watched her leave. Stairs creaked outside the door and he waited until they fell silent before leaping out of bed. He landed in a crumpled heap on the floor.

My gold! The parchment! Artan crawled to his pack. The wooden frame, the piece of scroll still in it, lay on the soggy remains of the food he'd packed in the cave. Artan clutched it to his chest, reassuringly cold and damp against his naked skin. He looked down at the rest of his body. The woman had taken all his clothes, even his small breeches. No matter. Other than a water mark at the left edge, the parchment was safe. Even if she'd taken the rest of his gold, this was worth more than the coins he'd stolen.

Artan's vision blurred, sweat dampened his forehead and cheeks. Had the woman drugged him? He set the parchment against the wall and shoved the old food in the pack aside, a foggy memory driving him on. Underneath the sodden mess, something clinked. He pulled out a wet, dirty cloth tied into a bundle heavy with gold. Now he remembered hiding it there before entering town.

His head reeling from the herbs, the illness and relief, Artan crawled back to the bed on his elbows, parchment in one hand, coins in the other. He slid the framed treasure under the bed, leaning it against the wall. The coins he stashed beneath the pillow.

Artan sucked breath past his stinging throat and dragged himself back into bed. Sliding his hand under the pillow, he clutched the cloth with the gold and let himself sink into sleep.

* * * *

Capturing Snake proved no challenge, not after the torture he'd suffered. Daric simply rode up beside the assassin, pulled him off his feet by the back of the old shirt they'd given him, and tossed him across the front of his saddle.

The man yelled about 'freedom' and 'border' and other things Daric ignored. Every now and then Snake's legs twitched. The damage done to his nerves the week before still bothered him and watching him try to walk across the scrubland of western Bredun had been quite entertaining. Daric wished the pain could last forever, but that would mean letting the bastard live and that couldn't be allowed.

Nightwind thundered east over the ridges of the rocky scrubland and onto the green plains. The sun shone warm, a pleasant break from the rain that had almost flooded the entire principality of Bredun. The horse's hooves still sent up a spray of water from time to time. Nonetheless, the trip was pleasant, disturbed only by Snake's mutterings.

After an hour's ride, Daric slowed the bay to a canter, then a trot, cooling the horse. A short walk brought them to a copse of small, mixed trees that proved an ideal spot for what he had in mind. He guided Nightwind into a small clearing with a brook trickling near it. Leaving Snake where he lay almost unconscious, Daric removed the rope from his saddle and tossed it at the base of a sturdy elm. He measured several lengths, cutting them with his dagger.

Snake cried out when Daric hauled him off Nightwind and tossed him on the ground. He let him writhe and moan for a few minutes before dragging the assassin to the tree and propping him against the trunk. Too groggy to resist, the man sat while Daric looped a length of rope under his arms. Holding the ends of the rope and moving behind the tree, he reached around and hauled Snake to his feet. He tied the rope at the back, then brought both ends forward and bound the assassin's hands. Soon, Daric had Snake tied at the waist, knees and ankles as well.

Snake roused enough to continue his verbal barrage. "What happened to mountain honour? Lord Cenith promised me my freedom!"

Daric turned his back on the assassin. Striding to

Nightwind, he removed the saddle and bags and set them near the center of the clearing. The blanket he hung from a nearby tree branch. Turning his attention to Nightwind, he took his time brushing the horse down; removing a few mats and burrs from the bay's mane and tail. He also spent it completely ignoring Snake's protests.

"You're doing this without Cenith's permission aren't you! Why? I told you what you wanted! I signed that document!" Snake struggled against his bonds, to no avail. "Can't I at least sit down?"

Leading Nightwind to the stream, Daric let him drink his fill then tied him opposite the glade from Snake to graze. Now he allowed time for himself. Scanning the clearing and nearby brush, he found rocks to form a fire pit. Long days of sunshine had dried enough twigs to allow him a fire. Another search provided him with bigger branches to keep it burning.

"What are you doing? You can't kill me. Your lord promised me my life!"

While water heated for tea, Daric found part of an old fallen tree to use as a seat and dragged it over by the fire, placing it so he could keep an eye on Snake without looking at him directly. He stretched out his legs and rubbed his right thigh. It had been split to the bone years ago by a Syrthian soldier and ached from time to time. His fiftieth birthday lay only a few months away and sometimes he felt every one of those years. Daric ate a cold but delicious meal of roasted beef, cheese, a couple apples and a chunk of fresh bread, all provided by the women of the station at the base of Eagle's Nest Pass.

"What about me? Don't I get anything to eat? I'm hungry too, you know." Snake wriggled and squirmed.

Daric allowed himself a smug smile. Snake's legs

had to be hurting from the nerve damage he'd suffered when Daric tortured him several days earlier.

The smile disappeared as Daric stared at the fire, stretching his aching fingers. Had it only been ten days since he'd cut them on an assassin's sword? Only ten days since he'd held Kian while his son breathed his last? It seemed just yesterday.

He hadn't told Elessa everything he'd planned for this trip. His wife knew about Saulth's scroll and that Tyrsa had asked him to retrieve it. That worried her enough. She didn't need to know about his slide into the darkness of his old mercenary life. In the days since Kian's death, he'd thought and dreamt of only one thing.

Revenge. *Violence feeds violence and I am a shining example.* No truer words had he spoken that night with the men who would become Tyrsa's Companions. He'd told them a valuable truth, but he'd also spoken a lie.

"Daric." Snake sneered his name. "All the tales of your honour and courage are nothing but chaff. Lies borne down the mountain by fools and churls. You have no honour and neither does Cenith." The assassin spat, but Daric sat too far away.

Killing his mother's murderer had been worth it. The long years spent learning how to kill; the satisfaction of watching life leave the man's eyes while he was bound and gagged in his own tent, his blood splattered on the walls, the blankets, the fancy clothes Daric had cut off him; the knowledge that the man would never hurt another woman again; the resulting two months in prison was all worth it...for one, brief, instant.

"Shival will have her revenge on you!" Snake struggled against his bonds. Pointless. "She won't just drag you to Char, she'll burn your soul personally! And those of your wife and children, too! From what I hear, you've whelped enough of the brats to keep my Dark Lady busy for an eternity!"

Daric glanced at Snake. Another of a similar ilk. *Violence feeds violence.* If Saulth hadn't hired Snake, Kian would be alive and Daric wouldn't ache with the burning need for revenge. Only now it wouldn't take fourteen years to accomplish. Of necessity, the merchant's death had been brutal, messy and quick. Daric could take his time with Snake. He pulled out his dagger and sharpening stone.

* * * *

An endless barrage of questions followed hard on the heels of Cenith's tale. He'd answered them all, working his way around a few to avoid telling the council about Tyrsa's strange abilities—not even Avina knew. He mentioned nothing about Tyrsa's arms trapped in the bank of the ravine or the healing of Varth's wound and played down his own injury. More important, he reassured his dukes that he'd gained her trust enough that an heir was probable.

Most of the dukes were family men and took the story of Tyrsa's nightmare life—living in a dark storeroom, suffering Saulth's beatings—with various levels of shock and horror. Saulth's deception, attempted theft, aborted kidnapping and ensuing violence had them leaping from their chairs in anger.

The announcement of the formation of the Companions to protect Tyrsa was met with both approval and disapproval. Duke Orman of Warbler Ridge voiced his concern over extra cost. Cenith reassured him the pay scale would remain the same as the rest of the guard. The only ones with raises were the officers. He deliberately avoided mentioning the new uniforms; they shouldn't arrive until after the council left for home anyway.

Cenith was right when he figured it would take some time to complete the story—dinner waited. When he judged the council satisfied with his answers, he held up his hand to halt the murmurs and whispered conversations.

"Many of you have brought your wives and some your entire families," Cenith said. "I realize your women will want to meet Tyrsa and that's fine. Just be aware that they should approach singly or in pairs. As I'm sure you noticed earlier, she's nervous in crowds and not likely to say much. Tyrsa's picked up quite a bit of our language in the six weeks we've been together, but she's hardly fluent." He hoped this would forestall any problems during and after dinner, especially if Tyrsa was still in her 'mood'.

Cenith pushed back his chair. "Dinner awaits and I'm sure my staff would like to rearrange the hall. Tomorrow's meeting will see a return to regular format." He stood, the council following suit. "I will be available in my study for two hours after dinner if anyone wishes to converse privately. Dismissed."

He spun on his heel and strode to the Grand Staircase, taking it two steps at a time. Tyrsa's 'mood' lay heavily on his mind and he didn't want to be delayed by small talk. Moments later he knocked on the door to the nursery, the most likely place Tyrsa would be if she'd stayed with Elessa. The Companions weren't in sight, but they could be in the room with Tyrsa. Nani, the seventh of Daric's ten children, answered the door, giving him a clumsy curtsy. Noisy children filled the background.

"Please come in, My Lord."

"Thank you, Nani."

Elessa smiled her approval at her daughter's improving manners—just a few months ago eight-year-old Nani greeted Cenith by trying to jump on his back for a ride. He was surprised to find he actually missed it.

"I assume you're looking for Tyrsa," Elessa said, her smile fading.

"And I see she's not here." No wife, but a lot more children than usual. It appeared some of the dukes' wives had taken advantage of the nannies helping Elessa with the horde. Cenith couldn't help but wonder why they didn't leave their small children at home. As a councillor's wife, Elessa could have left her abundant offspring in the care of the nannies, but she preferred to raise them herself.

"She left not long after she arrived." Elessa's eyes glanced to Chand and Chayne, the youngest set of twins, playing a rough and tumble game with some other young boys in the far corner of the large room. Even with two extra nursemaids, this tribe would be difficult to supervise. "She seemed a bit...off...today. Angry and petulant would be a good description."

Cenith sighed. "I was hoping if she spent some time here she'd get over that."

Elessa brushed back a strand of hair that escaped the bun perched on the nape of her neck. "I assume you two had a fight?"

"Is it that obvious?"

She laughed. "First fights are never easy and making up even harder." A wistful look crossed her delicate features. "I remember our first fight, back when we lived in town. Daric had tracked mud across my just cleaned floor. It had been a long day for both of us and I let him know just how bad mine had been." Elessa deepened her voice. "'And how am I supposed to get the wood to the fireplace, woman?' The fight was on."

A shadow replaced the wistful look. With one finger, Cenith lifted her chin. "He'll come back, Elessa. Daric's too tough not to." At six-foot-eight and broad as a bear, the former mercenary took tough to a high height. Cenith lowered his hand. Elessa's worry mirrored his. She'd lost Kian. To lose Daric now…

Elessa nodded and the shadow disappeared. "Might I recommend you smooth some ruffled feathers? Tonight will be rough enough for Tyrsa, meeting more new people who'll want to talk to her. At least her table manners have improved to the point where she won't embarrass you."

The twinkle returned to Elessa's light brown eyes and Cenith laughed. "Speaking of tonight," he said, "you might want to leave this pack of cubs and get ready yourself. If I could prevail upon you to take Tyrsa in hand, I would appreciate it. I promised the first two hours after dinner to hold private conversations with the dukes."

"Of course I don't mind. My own children are noisy enough, but this lot…" Elessa blew out a breath. "I'll enjoy the time away." She set a hand on Cenith's arm, concern now shading her eyes. "You realize Tyrsa will probably never be the lady you expect.

"Frankly," she continued. "I'm surprised she's adapted as much as she has. Your mother could charm a mountain cat to eat out of her hand. She worked through the dukes' wives to help Ifan make them see reason. Tyrsa can't do that for you. She's so afraid of crowds and new people, to hear her say 'hello' is reason to rejoice. I know you want her to grow up and be a proper wife, lady and mother. I'm just warning you that may not happen, especially in light of her…other talents."

"She seems to have progressed well under your tutelage." Now that they'd shared the marriage bed, setting Tyrsa aside was no longer an option unless she proved barren. Even then, Cenith doubted he could do it. Despite this morning's antics, and her mysterious powers, he cared for his wife.

"She has, but we work alone. Tyrsa's grown comfortable with me. If I understand Daric correctly, she spent her life living in the dark with just Rani's few months of teachings to guide her. We're lucky that brave woman defied Saulth, otherwise I doubt Tyrsa would have been so receptive to you. You seem to be able to get her to do things no one else can." Elessa clasped her hands in front of her. "These are just my thoughts and she may surprise us. She certainly has already. Just don't expect too much, too fast."

Cenith was five when his mother died of a fever. When Daric and Elessa had moved into the keep all those years ago, they'd brought little Kian with them. Only a few months older, the dark haired son of a mercenary rapidly became Cenith's best friend and Elessa a second mother. Her advice had proved sound in the past and he had no qualms about accepting it now.

He nodded, took his leave and almost ran to his suite. Tyrsa had to be there. Two of the Lady's Companions, Dathan and Keev, stood outside the door with the two regular soldiers. He'd guessed right this time. Nodding to the guards, he entered. At first glance, the sitting room appeared empty. He made a move for the bedroom, then caught sight of part of Tyrsa's dress at the edge of the chair Daric usually sat in.

She lay curled up, sound asleep, Baybee clutched to her chest. Cenith crouched beside her and slid the hair back from her face. Tyrsa didn't move. Keeping her anger up all afternoon must have exhausted her.

Cenith tugged the doll out from under her arm and stuffed it in the corner of the chair. Taking her in his arms, he sat in his chair and settled her in his lap. She was so small, and thin as a promise. He thought about what Elessa had said, and, using that advice, how to approach this problem. Rather than wait for her to rouse on her own, he kissed his wife awake. Tyrsa responded, then pulled away, her pixie face a comical mixture of confusion and forced anger. He couldn't help but laugh.

Tyrsa's brow furrowed more. "I thought you were mad at me."

"I wasn't really angry, only very frustrated. Especially when you wouldn't talk to me." Cenith kissed her cheek. "Listen. We had our first fight. It's not a big tragedy. Husbands and wives argue, so do brothers and sisters, parents and children. It's a fact of life. My father once told me the secret is to not let the arguing take control. You have to talk without arguing. That's the only way the problem can be solved. Understand?"

"I think so."

"I need you to be brave when you're outside our rooms. Now in particular. There are a lot of people visiting that you don't know. Some you met this afternoon, others you'll meet tonight. They're going to want to talk to you and I can't have you carrying your doll with you when they do. It's just not acceptable at your age." At almost sixteen, she should have put her doll away several years ago. He had Saulth to thank for that.

"But she helps me feel…safe."

Cenith smiled. "You don't have her now."

"I don't need her when I'm here with you. But you're not with me much anymore. You're away a lot." The pout put in a reappearance. She turned her face away.

"I told you several days ago I can't be with you all the time. As Lord of Dunvalos Reach, there are things I have to do. That's why you need to make friends, like Elessa, Avina and Jennica. They'll keep you company when I'm busy. I know you're not used to a lot of people, but I know you can be brave." Cenith set a gentle hand to her cheek and forced her to look at him. "Mara and Laron will be here soon to help us dress for dinner. We won't be eating here tonight, but in the Hall with everyone else. Like we did at Kian's funeral."

Fear widened Tyrsa's eyes. Her body stiffened.

"I'll be with you while we eat," Cenith stressed. "But then I have to go for a while after dinner to talk with some of the dukes. Elessa will stay with you so you won't be alone. The Companions will be near as well. I know you're not afraid of them." He hugged her to him. "I'm trusting you to act like the Lady of Dunvalos Reach, not a lonely little girl locked in a room. You aren't that girl anymore. Elessa has taught you what to say and do. Stay with her. Trust her. She likes you. Don't be afraid to ask her questions if you need to. Understand?"

Tyrsa's head rested under his chin. He felt her nod.

"And Baybee stays here. Right?"

She nodded again and Cenith hugged her tighter, relieved that problem was solved.

Chapter Two

"Food. Parchment. Gold. Clothes. Cooking supplies." Artan ran over everything he'd stored in his new pack. No one had removed the food from his old one and after four days the soggy remains had become a part of the leather, the odour unbearable, even through his still stuffy nose.

He sat down on the bed and leaned on the headboard, tired and weak from his illness, despite the rest and the woman's herbs. Ill or not, he couldn't wait any longer. *Here it is, the last day of Sixth Month. I've been away from Valda for a month and a half!* Amazing, for someone who'd never left the city before this mission. *I hope never to leave it again.*

Eager to be off, Artan had ventured out that morning for the first time since arriving. He'd purchased his new pack, another set of clothes and a horse. Now he could travel quickly and, with the gold, in comfort, staying in inns along the way instead of sleeping on the ground.

Gathering what strength he had, Artan stood and shouldered the pack, staggering under its weight. Neva, the woman who tended him, had turned out to be the innkeeper's wife. She'd insisted on stuffing half his pack with food for the journey, clucking at him about his health and that he still wasn't well enough to travel. He'd played the part of a wandering merchant's son wanting to go home to his family. It also explained his speech. Snake had insisted all his assassins speak like merchants, though they could affect common speech if it was required. She seemed to buy it.

Artan took a last look around the tiny room,

nothing more than a simple wooden bed, a wool stuffed mattress, a small table and a plain wooden chair, all of which had seen newer days. He couldn't fault the cleanliness though. Neva didn't possess fancy new furnishings, but she cared for what she owned, giving the room a homey feel he hadn't known since... A pang of regret and a flurry of forgotten memories surged through him.

The modest room almost felt like home now; ridiculous, when he thought about it. He'd lived in Snake's hidden lair for two years. Before that, Artan had avoided 'home'. After his mother died, his father wanted little to do with him, seeking solace in the taverns and neglecting his job on the docks. Whenever the old man managed to find his way to the house, he needed little excuse to beat and belittle his only child.

Artan trudged down the narrow stairs to the tavern room, his mind still in the past. The streets of Valda had proved entertaining, educational and profitable. He'd brought home the proceeds of his first theft, hoping to help pay the rent, and left with more bruises than he had coins. Life on the streets turned out to be safer and happier.

All Artan wanted was to go home. The lair would still be there, but the assassins, except possibly Snake, wouldn't. Between the two of them, perhaps they could start again. The gold Saulth provided for the scroll would certainly help. If Snake wasn't there...

"All set then?" Neva's gentle voice broke into his musings. She stood behind the long wooden bar, wiping wooden mugs. "I still think ya should rest a few more days."

Not yet noon, the tavern chairs stood empty, waiting for patrons to fill them. Bright sunlight shone through old glass to highlight the gouges and nicks on the thick oak tables. Neva's touch showed here as well. No dingy windows, few stains decorated the tables, and the only odours came from the kitchen, the fireplace and the fresh straw on the floor.

"Thank you for your concern, Good Mistress," Artan said. "But I'm anxious…to be home." Most of his voice had come back, though it tended to crack from time to time.

Neva's kind smile pulled at his heart, long forgotten visions of his mother haunting him. Artan attempted a smile in return.

She set down her cloth and the mug she'd worked on. "My husband totalled everything, yer meals, the room, bath and laundry. The gold ya gave us was too much." She reached into her apron pocket and pressed several coins into his hand, some copper, most of them silver.

Artan's mouth opened and closed like a brothel's front door. Everyone he knew in Valda would have kept the money regardless of the amount of the bill. He snapped his jaw shut.

"Thank you, and, ah…" Artan picked a half silver coin from the pile in his hand. He stared at it a moment before giving it to her. *Did I just do that?*

"And I thank ya, kind sir," Neva said, giving him a small curtsy, her smile widening.

Artan nodded in return, stuffed the remaining coins in his pocket and hurried out the door before he did anything else foolish.

* * * *

The first day of the council meeting had resembled

picking daisies when compared to the last three. Cenith resisted pounding his head on the table. Most of the rest of the council rolled their eyes or leaned their heads on their hands, trying to stay awake.

"The boundary runs one mile east of Waen's Rock." Von of Bear Creek Valley stabbed the table with every word. An older man, with a touch of grey in his chestnut hair, he had the size and strength to make the table shudder with every jab of his thick finger. "It always has and always will. Boundaries don't grow legs and move on their own!"

They do if there's a just discovered gold mine at stake. Not that it mattered to Cenith. The principality would receive its tithe regardless of who owned it.

He rubbed his eyes and thanked Maegden that Von's adversary, Orman of Warbler Ridge, sat on the right, near the end, while Von sat on the left, five chairs from the head of the tables. The confrontation might turn violent. Two guards stood at the main doors. Cenith caught their eye and they both gave him a short nod. They would be ready if needed.

"It runs three miles to the west! This map proves it!" Orman shook a rolled parchment at his opponent. Of an age with Von, he was shorter, and pudgier, though no less powerful of voice.

"The ink isn't even dry on that fake!" Von jumped to his feet, his chair clattering to the floor, jerking the sleepy nobles upright, one or two snorting as they woke from a less than restful nap.

"Sit down, Von," Cenith said, struggling to maintain a calm tone to his voice.

"But, My Lord…"

"Sit. Down." Remembering how his father handled

these situations, Cenith tried his best stare on him.

Von picked up his chair and plunked himself in it, broad face red, his full mouth set in a grim line, his normally brown eyes almost black with anger. With a huff, he folded his arms across his chest. He looked more a pouting child than the duke of one of the oldest, and most important, holdings in the principality.

Cenith held his hand out. "Orman, let me see that map. Why didn't you bring it yesterday when this dispute was first scheduled?"

Stiff legged with indignation, Orman delivered the map himself, then adjusted his velvet tunic; a deep blue, trimmed with gold thread, it let everyone know just how prosperous his duchy was. "I didn't think I needed to, My Lord. I thought my word would have been enough."

I doubt it. Both his father and Daric had warned him about this duke. Greed sat high on Orman's list of vices. Cenith waved him back to his place before examining the parchment. One scan and he wished for the hundredth time over the past three days that Daric was here. Just having him in the room tended to make people see reason.

Abryn, the young clerk assigned to record the meeting, had spent the previous evening in the library trying to locate documentation of the original boundary. A clear record of Bear Creek Valley and Warbler Ridge couldn't be found. Odd, considering the meticulous records Cenith's ancestors had kept. Odder still that Orman 'happened' to have a copy when it looked like the situation had turned against him.

The parchment, brown and crumbling at the edges, appeared remarkably pristine in other places. Cenith rubbed one corner between his thumb and forefinger. Crisp, as if it had been burned, it flaked easily. He waved Orman back to his place.

"Avina, would you bring me a lit candle, please?"

"Of course, My Lord."

While she retrieved the candle from a nearby sideboard, Cenith begged a clean sheet of parchment from Abryn. Orman squirmed in his seat. The other nobles shared puzzled glances. Avina set the candle on the table in front of him. Careful not to hold the parchment too close to the flame, Cenith watched a corner of it turn the same shade as Orman's copy.

Laying the papers side by side, Cenith took a closer look at the ink on Orman's. Von was right. Ink on a paper over four hundred years old should have faded. Despite the attempt at aging the document, the ink stood out dark.

"Orman, did you really think you could pass this off as an original?" Cenith tossed the fake parchment back down the table. It slid a few feet before stopping near the center.

"My…My Lord!" Orman said, affecting a surprised expression. "I had no intention of such a deceit! My clerks assured me this was our copy of the original."

Cenith fixed him with a glare. "Then I suggest you hire new clerks or find someone to train these ones in the finer art of forgery."

The room burst with laughter, Von's the loudest. He slapped the table and guffawed until he couldn't breathe. Orman clenched his jaw and met Cenith eye for eye.

Never back down, son. You back off once and they'll have your nuggets in a clamp the rest of your life. Ifan's words rang no truer than now. Cenith refused to budge, not moving a muscle until Orman finally gave up, shifting his gaze down.

Cenith held his hand up for quiet. "Unless legitimate proof can be brought to me saying otherwise, I declare the boundary between Bear Creek Valley and Warbler Ridge to run one mile to the east of Waen's Rock. To be fair, I will have Daric look into it when he returns. He may be able to locate the missing document."

Von sat back, a satisfied smile adding more creases to his already lined face. Orman scowled at the table, embarrassed, but hardly subdued. Cenith didn't dare let this go, but the matter would have to be dealt with in private. *Tomorrow, after the funeral.* That would allow him enough time to think of something.

Why did there have to be controversy over every item on the agenda? The council had applauded his deal with Urik and the gold mine bordering Amita, until Timron of Sunset Vale voiced his concern that the actual location of the boundary would be found out eventually. Others pointed out that if it hadn't been discovered after four hundred years, the chances of it happening now were slim. The argument had lasted half an afternoon. Thereafter, every agreement Cenith had made in Edara that spring came under scrutiny.

The need for new recruits resulting from the Lord Council's demand for more men on the Tai-Keth frontier had been met with cries of outrage. The recruiting of men from the villages and towns meant less to work the mines and farms. Doubling the guard at the passes and the twenty-six lost in the assassin's raid hadn't helped. Neither did removing the Companions from regular duty to protect Tyrsa. Saulth had made it very plain that he wanted her back and Cenith would do everything in his power to prevent it.

Petty slights, real or imagined, predominated every day. Right of way, trade deals between holdings, even bride prices for marriage arrangements had been argued. Two hours had been spent trying to decide how to divide the cattle from the Amita mine deal.

Cenith couldn't help wondering if the unusually long, cold winter had deranged his dukes. He didn't remember past council meetings as contentious as this one, but then his father had run them. Perhaps the council sought to test his mettle; perhaps they thought a nineteen-year-old too young for a lord's duties. It made more sense than the mine tailings he'd been forced to listen to for the past three days.

On top of all this nonsense, two other concerns lay heavy on Cenith's mind. Tyrsa, for one. Her mood had improved little since their talk the first night of the meeting. According to Elessa, Tyrsa spent the mornings with her while she entertained the duke's wives and older daughters. Tyrsa said little and most of the women had given up making conversation. Understandable, since he doubted she'd comprehend half of what they discussed or care about the other half. Cenith hoped she'd observe and learn how they behaved and interacted with each other.

However, after lunch, instead of accompanying Elessa, Tyrsa headed back to their rooms and refused to move from in front of the fireplace, Baybee held tightly to her breast. No amount of coaxing from Elessa or Jennica, Daric's second oldest daughter, could move her.

Of necessity, Cenith had to spend the evenings socializing with the nobles and their wives. Where Tyrsa could refuse Elessa's wishes, Cenith stood firm and forced her to accompany him. She rarely smiled during her ordeal, but neither did she scowl and they both persevered.

The second matter weighed heavy on Cenith's soul. His father lay in one of the physician's rooms. Even now, Garun prepared his body for tomorrow's funeral. The search party had returned late yesterday, bringing the missing men home. Cenith had declined to view the bodies, especially his father's. It had spent several months buried in snow at the bottom of a deep ravine, then endured a spring thaw. He had no intention of remembering him that way and had already left instructions that the entire funeral would be held with a shroud covering the man who had sired him…raised him…loved him as no other.

"I believe there is one more matter on the agenda, My Lord." Avina's quiet voice brought Cenith back to the matter at hand. "Tithes."

He cringed inside. Another fight. *Just bull ahead and make my position firm from the start.* "In light of the floods, tornadoes and other problems occurring in the rest of the country, certain trade goods have risen in price, grain and hardwood in particular. The caravans slogging over and around flooded roads take more time and, therefore, more money. Although we prefer to purchase goods from our own country, Daric and I have taken the liberty of ordering extra grain from Syrth and the West Downs. We simply can't rely on sufficient supplies from the plains. Other than what has already been negotiated, we can pass on the oak and maple for a time. People will just have to do without their fancy new furniture. We can use our aspen for the important things, but the grain we'll need for winter."

The ensuing nods and murmurs of agreement he'd expected. Considering the flow of the rest of the meeting, his next words might well cause a real uproar.

Cenith had spent most of the night rehearsing how he'd approach this. "To compensate, I should by all rights raise the tithes, but…" He lifted his hand and those about to speak closed their mouths. "…that would mean you gentlemen would then raise the taxes on your lands, bringing harder times on the ordinary folk. As you heard from Zev's report, the principality's treasury is stable. We can handle a short year, perhaps even two. I know most of you were counting on a reduction. However, we dare not risk backsliding. Therefore, I have decided to keep the tithe rates the same. I assume you will advise your thegns that their towns and villages will have to make do with last year's budget."

Scowls and grumbles ensued, not the uproar Cenith had expected. Had reason finally prevailed over pettiness and greed? He scanned the faces around the table, meeting each man's eyes.

"Do I take it then that we are agreed?" Mumbled assents met his disbelieving ears. "Is there any other business?" Could this actually be over?

"Nothing on the agenda, My Lord," Avina said, looking as worn out as he felt.

The council members sat silent.

"In that case, the funeral for my father will commence at noon tomorrow. Orman, I'd like to see you afterwards." The errant duke gave a start, but only nodded as way of acknowledgement, his heavy brows dipping in a deep frown. "As usual at the end of a council meeting," Cenith continued, "music and entertainment will be provided after dinner tonight." That announcement cheered the room, though Cenith hardly felt like celebrating, even the ending of this meeting. Nevertheless, tradition had to be observed. "I officially declare the Dunvalos Reach Council Meeting for 426 finished and done. Thank you gentlemen and Mistress Avina."

Before anyone could trap him, Cenith made a dash for the Grand Staircase, hoping for a little peace in his suite before dinner. Mara met him at the top.

"My Lord, Mistress Elessa would like to see you in her rooms." The maid curtsied and hurried on her way.

Cenith groaned. *What has Tyrsa done now?* He ran up the main staircase to the third floor, where Daric and Elessa's suite was situated. He nodded to the guards outside the door, one of whom knocked for him. Normally, the only guards were on the stairs leading to the various floors. With Snake's revelation that Saulth wanted Daric dead, Cenith had no choice but to post them here as well.

Elessa greeted him, baby Rade in her arms. "Thank you for coming, My Lord. The meeting is finally over?"

Cenith nodded. "Do I want to know what happened?"

She sighed. "Please sit, we'll both be more comfortable."

No fire burned in the sitting room fireplace. The balcony doors hung open, letting a late afternoon breeze waft through the room. The councillor's suite was laid out similar to his own, though smaller, and the tapestries covering the walls gave it a cozy touch.

When settled, Rade on her lap, Elessa sighed again. "I finally discovered the reason for Tyrsa's moodiness. Her moon cycle started this morning, not long after you left."

Cenith's cheeks warmed. His father, in lieu of his long dead mother, had explained the workings of a female's body when Cenith's own had begun to change, but the subject still left him uncomfortable. "I've never seen you act like that."

A little smirk lifted the corner of her mouth. "I'm better at hiding it than others, though Daric might say otherwise, and Tyrsa doesn't know to act in that situation. To make a complicated subject simple, it's been over six weeks since she left Valda. Everything she's seen and done has been strange and new. Her days and nights have been completely turned around and it's all upset her body's natural rhythm. My best guess is that she should have had her moon cycle at least two weeks ago. Because it's so late, she's suffering more pain and discomfort."

"Not to mention moodiness."

Elessa nodded.

"So what did she do?" Cenith sat forward and clasped his hands between his knees. Elessa wouldn't have asked him here just to discuss Tyrsa's female problems.

"Mara said Tyrsa went back to bed after breakfast, not coming out until lunch," Elessa said. "She ate with the rest of us and seemed no different than the last few days, moody and quiet. I thought she'd gone back to her room for the afternoon, but according to Mina she came to the nursery a couple of hours ago. She had Baybee with her for the first time in days."

Cenith's clasped hands tightened. "I'd told her she wasn't to take that doll out of our rooms."

Elessa grimaced, bouncing the active nine-month-old on her knee to keep him amused. "I'd thought as much. Tyrsa set Baybee on one of the chairs so she could play with Nani. Rade found Baybee, decided the doll would make a good snack and chewed on her arm. When she saw him, well…Mina said she'd never seen Tyrsa so angry." Elessa took in a breath, worry creasing her eyes.

"She hit Rade."

Cenith jerked upright, gripping the arms of the chair. "She did *what*?"

His reaction startled Rade, whose face screwed into the beginnings of a bellow. Elessa clutched him to her breast, rocking him until he calmed. Her next words poured out in a rush, unusual for her. "He's all right. She hit him until he cried. Left a red mark on his arm, but it's gone now. As soon as he let go of the doll, she ran out of the room. Mina brought Rade to me and explained what happened."

"This is ridiculous." Cenith rubbed the back of his neck. "I think the time has come to take that doll away."

"If you want my opinion, that's not a good idea. I think it'll make matters worse." She smoothed Rade's ruffled black hair and kissed his forehead.

"How could it make it worse? The Lady of Dunvalos Reach packing a doll and hurting a baby because he didn't know better than to chew on it? Elessa…"

"Remember our discussion the other day?"

Cenith nodded, though with all that had happened during the days of the meeting, that talk seemed weeks ago.

"Tyrsa may look like the Lady of Dunvalos Reach, but less than two months ago she was an abused, lonely girl with no one to talk to…no one to love…except that doll. Never having seen how children grow and mature, Tyrsa has remained a child in so many ways. She remembers her short time with Rani and bases everything on that. When Rani was killed, Baybee became mother, sister and best friend to her. Go slow." Elessa's rich, dark brown hair was pulled back in its usual bun and she brushed an errant strand from her forehead. Rade resumed his threat to fuss and she rocked him again.

Cenith leaned back into the chair and stared at the ceiling. "I see your point. Tyrsa's always so concerned when anyone is hurt. I never thought she'd deliberately hurt someone."

"It's all she knew for most of her life, beaten for doing things others perceived as bad, even though they weren't. And her moon cycle certainly hasn't helped."

"A baby of her own might settle her down. I'd hoped she'd be pregnant by now. That's obviously not the case." Cenith blew out a long, frustrated breath before standing. "Well, thank you for telling me. I'd wanted to spend the time before dinner relaxing, but I guess I'll be having another discussion with my wife."

Elessa rose to her feet, shifting Rade to her hip. He had his thumb stuffed in his mouth, content for the moment. "Good luck,' she said, with a wry smile. "Apparently she's locked the door and won't even let the Companions in."

Cenith rolled his eyes and took his leave of Daric's wife. A quick sprint saw him up another level and in front of his door.

"She won't let anyone in, My Lord," Yanis said, shrugging his shoulder. "Not even Jolin. He tried a little while ago."

Cenith rapped on the solid oak. "Tyrsa, unlock this door. Now. I'm tired and I don't want any of your nonsense."

He waited a couple minutes and was about to pound on the door when he heard the bolt slide back. Tyrsa didn't open it. After a moment, he turned the knob, leaving instructions they were not to be disturbed. Cenith leaned against the closed door, composing his thoughts, running through his mind what Elessa had told him, both times.

Tyrsa's pale ivory gown spilled across one of the arms of the stuffed chair they usually shared. He pushed himself away from the door and crouched to her right. She'd buried her face in the crease where the back met the arm. Black hair tumbled down her shoulders. They shook and he realized she was crying, something he'd rarely seen her do. Thinking back, the only times he could remember were when she hurt from the beating or thought Baybee lost.

Baybee. The doll's cloth legs stuck out from under her arm. Cenith didn't even try to take it away. He slid his hands under Tyrsa, lifting her from the chair. She didn't resist. He sat, cradling her while she cried, waiting for her to make the first move. Then it struck him that not only had he rarely seen her cry, he'd never heard her laugh, not even when she played with the children at the station. A girl who never laughed. It didn't seem right. How could he fix that?

Tyrsa's crying eased. She sniffed a few times until she stopped, but kept her face hidden between his shoulder and neck. "Are you going to hurt me?"

Cenith blinked, not expecting that question. "Of course not. I'm not Saulth. I'm upset you think I would. Why would you think I'd hurt you?"

"I hurt Rade. I shouldn't have done that." She sniffed again.

"No, you shouldn't have. I'm glad you realize it." Maybe he could make some progress now. "You see why it's better that Baybee stay in our rooms?"

She nodded.

Well, that was easy. I just hope it wasn't too easy. I

thought we'd had this resolved before. Perhaps Elessa was right when she said he could talk Tyrsa into things others couldn't.

Cenith decided to push a little more. "Elessa told me your moon cycle started today. I know you hurt and are uncomfortable, but that's no reason to be mean to other people. Especially babies. Rade is too young to know what he's doing."

Another nod.

"How bad is Baybee hurt?" *Am I really asking this?*

Tyrsa sat up, strands of fine black hair clinging to her tear damp face. She showed him the arm Rade had chewed. A large wet spot marked the place.

After a pointedly thorough examination, Cenith stated, "Other than a little sogginess, I don't see any damage. I think she'll recover."

With a little sigh, Tyrsa laid her head on his shoulder. "Elessa is mad at me."

Elessa hadn't mentioned seeing Tyrsa herself. "How do you know that?"

"I would be mad if she hurt Baybee."

That made sense, of a sort. "She's not happy, but you could make things better if you apologized."

Tyrsa sat up again. "What's that?"

"It means saying you're sorry for what you did. That you know what you did was wrong and won't do it again."

"I'm sorry, I did wrong and I won't do it again," she repeated. "I tell her that and she won't be mad?"

Cenith brushed aside strands of hair so he could kiss her cheek. "Elessa's had ten children. She understands. You apologize, and mean it, and all will be back to normal. Are you better now?"

Tyrsa shrugged. "I still hurt. In my back."

"Lean forward." Cenith rubbed her lower back while he talked, hoping it was the right thing to do. "I hope you're up to dinner with the nobles."

She groaned. "Again? How many times?"

"Tomorrow night will be the last dinner, then there's the official leave-taking the next day. And after dinner tonight the Story Teller will come and there'll be music and dancing."

"Music? Dancing? Like at the station?"

"Yes, but even better."

When bringing Tyrsa home to Dunvalos Reach, they'd been attacked by bandits and forced to spend some time at the guard station at the foot of Eagle's Nest Pass so Cenith could recover from a serious injury. The night before they left, anyone who could play a pipe or drum, or even keep time, joined in for a farewell party. Trying to teach Tyrsa to dance had been a real chore; the poor girl had no sense of rhythm. Stories, music and dancing played a large part in mountain life, keeping the old tales and legends alive, bringing families and communities closer together. That she had been denied it was almost unthinkable.

Cenith kissed her. "You'll see. Tonight will be fun," he said, surprised to find he now looked forward to the festivities. Tomorrow still loomed large in his mind, but perhaps, for a little while, he could set his worries and grief aside.

* * * *

Daric examined the edge of the dagger he'd sharpened. The same one he'd used to split Snake's nose two days earlier. He'd let the assassin stew for an entire day before actually carrying through with the threat he'd made in the storeroom where he'd tortured him.

During that time, Snake had alternated between railing at Daric's and Cenith's dishonour, making threats of his own or calling down every curse from any god he thought might listen. Daric ignored all of it as he went about his daily business, which made his prisoner even angrier.

Eventually Snake passed out from exhaustion, hunger or pain. Daric gave him water occasionally, but, except to tighten his bonds, that was the only attention he paid to the man until he'd cut him. He'd held the assassin's head still with one big hand, then maintained his silence while he split the skin from between Snake's eyes to the base of his nose. For all his bravado, the man had passed out before Daric finished. He then peeled back the skin and stitched it to Snake's cheeks with needle and thread from his field medical kit.

He glanced at the assassin. Snake slouched in his bonds, asleep or unconscious, it didn't matter. Flies had come to do their part and now maggots performed their macabre dance, crawling in and out of the wound. Some fell, catching on the ropes binding him to the tree or landing on the ground to wriggle and squirm until they died of starvation. Daric had chosen not to follow through with the second part of the threat he'd made in the keep storeroom; slicing into Snake's innards would have been messy and pointless.

Daric learned years ago that pain played only a part of torture. Toying with a victim's mind in conjunction with physical suffering produced better results. During his later years as a mercenary, Daric could have a man telling him his life's story and not shed a single drop of blood. He'd accomplished it with Snake back in Tiras, though more blood would be spilled in the end. Kian had to be avenged.

When Cenith agreed to set the assassin free, Daric thought he'd be denied that retribution. Thank Niafanna he hadn't been too lost in his anger and need for revenge to realize what Cenith offered him, the chance to do what he wanted, when he wanted, with no witnesses.

The nerve damage Daric had inflicted on Snake in the storeroom still tormented the assassin. Supporting his weight for the last three days hadn't helped. Snake slipped in and out of consciousness. When lucid, he'd raved about lack of honour and exacting revenge; other times he talked to his dead comrades, whimpered, begged or babbled nonsense before passing out again.

The assassin groaned. A few minutes and he'd wake once more. Daric slid the edge of his dagger over the stone one last time. His eyes lifted to the sky. *Almost noon, on the last day of the month. The sun is shining, the birds are singing. A good time for a man to die.* Much as he would enjoy dragging this out, he had an errand to run for Tyrsa.

Dagger in hand, Daric strode to his prisoner. Snake's head lolled on his chest. He grabbed him by his greasy, grey hair and yanked his head upright. The action pulled on Snake's facial wound and he bit off a cry of pain.

"Do you still wish to know why?" Daric asked, his deep voice breaking the silence of the glade.

Snake's eyes, lucid for now, drilled into his. "It speaks. I thought you'd lost your voice, or your stones. The *honourable* Daric. The Calleni who keeps his word. Horse dung. You're nothing but a worthless, lying demon-futterer who serves a double-crossing spoiled brat of a goat-turd. Yes, I want to know why."

Daric touched the tip of the dagger to Snake's throat apple. "To set things straight, my lord promised you safe escort to the border of Dunvalos Reach. You know he has no jurisdiction past that point. He kept his part of the bargain. It's not our fault none of your lord's men were there to greet you. Nor is it our fault that your own men couldn't rescue you. If you hadn't chosen to attack us, they'd be alive."

Sharp steel caressed Snake's throat. "I was merely doing my job," the assassin said through clenched teeth. Beads of sweat dripped down his lined forehead into his wound.

"Do you have a son?"

Snake tried to frown at Daric's question. He sucked in a breath when the action disturbed his damaged flesh. "Several. I've never kept track of them. That's their mothers' problem, not mine. I don't have time to coddle whelps."

Why should I be surprised? Men like Snake only cared about themselves.

Realization flickered in Snake's eyes. "Your son was killed in the raid. This is revenge. If he looked anything like you, I didn't kill him. I'd remember."

Daric's dagger stopped at the soft spot at the base of the assassin's throat. "No, you didn't. I killed the one who did. You might remember him from our visit outside the keep. He was the one missing most of one arm. The one with his chest sliced in half."

"Edge." The word escaped Snake's lips as a mere whisper.

"Appropriate. He took my edge well." Daric removed his dagger from Snake's throat and flicked a couple of maggots off the man's chin.

"I didn't kill your son. You have your revenge. Let me go."

"I don't see it that way. You brought Edge to my home. You chose to attack. You hold responsibility."

The dagger shifted to the vein in Snake's neck. A little nick produced a slow, steady rivulet of bright red blood. Daric used Snake's filthy shirt to wipe the small stain off the dagger. With a quick flip, he sheathed it.

"I had no choice! Saulth hired me. I can't afford to turn down a job offer, especially from my lord!" Snake squirmed against his bonds. His ruined face could show little emotion, spread open like that, but his eyes...Snake appeared to know fear after all.

"There is always a choice," Daric said, keeping an eye on the flow of blood from the assassin's neck. "If it's any consolation, Saulth also holds responsibility. Someday he will pay."

Daric sauntered over to the fire. He picked up his sword from where it lay against the log and drew it from the sheath. The metallic ring widened the assassin's pain-wracked eyes. Daric made a show of examining the edge before returning to the assassin. After all Snake had suffered, it was nothing compared to the loss Daric would have to live with for the rest of his life. "My son's name was Kian. A finer man you could never meet." He slid the length of the blade between his thumb and forefinger. Snake's eyes never left it. "Smart, brave, kind. Loyal to his principality, his lord, his family. With the potential for so much more."

He centered the tip of the great sword on Snake's chest, then moved it an inch to his victim's left. "Kian died from a thrust, right here. I think it only fitting you do too."

One solid push, until the tip of the sword struck tree—driving a sword through a man's flesh and bone wasn't as easy as some people thought. A whoosh of fetid air gushed from Snake's mouth. His eyes widened. Daric yanked the weapon free.

The assassin grunted, sagging into his bonds. He sucked in as much air as he could. "May Shival hold your son's soul in her hand and squeeze for all eternity!" Blood followed the words, red and frothy.

"Curse all you want. Kian's soul is safe with Niafanna. Your dark goddess has no hold on me or my family." Daric placed the tip of the sword on the ground, resting his hands on the crossguard. He smiled.

Snake tried to cry out. Gurgles of blood and strangled mewling resulted. The light died in the assassin's eyes. His head lolled once more on his chest.

Daric stood for a moment, finding solace that another perpetrator of the deed had met his end. *One left. But that one will take time.* Using his dagger, Daric increased the size of the cut to Snake's neck vein. Blood oozed out, now that the heart had stilled. He waited for the flow to stop, thinking about what he'd do to Saulth if he ever had the chance.

He took hold of Snake's oily hair, lifting his head high enough that one good swing of the sword removed it. Daric knocked the head against the tree twice, dislodging most of the maggots, then hung it from a low branch. He took up his seat by the fire to clean and sharpen his weapons before replacing them in their sheaths, then changed out of his old black clothes into newer ones, just as non-descript. Nothing he'd brought showed where his allegiance lay.

He saddled Nightwind and re-stowed his

belongings except for one item, a burlap sack—a new home for Snake's head. He hung the bag and its grisly contents from the back of his saddle, placing his old cloak over it. With one last look at the body still tied to the tree, he guided Nightwind out of the copse.

The afternoon sun beat down on man, horse and plains. Daric set Nightwind's head toward Dunstown, the first village on the Bredun Main Road, and let the bay run himself out.

Justice has been served. Another part of Kian's vengeance has been achieved. No one else has to die by Snake's hand.

Daric repeated the words like a mantra, then again and again. Just before dark, he walked the bay into the small village. A dozen buildings lined each side of the road, the largest displaying a sign advertising the only inn. He stabled his horse in the public livery next door, paying extra for good food and a proper rubdown.

Rolling the burlap bag in his cloak, Daric took it and his saddlebags with him. Coins exchanged hands. While the cook fetched his dinner, he carried his things to the small room given him and stored the sack as far from the bed as space permitted.

Downstairs once more, he sat at an old oak table in the farthest corner. A pleasant, middle-aged woman brought him his meal. "Ale please, and keep it coming." He cut off a chunk of beef with his eating knife and stuffed the gravy laden meat into his mouth.

"Certainly, sir," the woman said, with a kind smile. "If ya need anythin', just call. I'm Neva."

Chapter Three

Tyrsa the child. Tyrsa the enigma. Tyrsa the woman? Cenith folded his hands behind his neck and, resting his feet on the desk, leaned back in the study chair he still thought of as his father's. He found it hard to believe Elessa might be right and Tyrsa would never grow up enough to assume the duties his mother had performed.

Tyrsa had stood beside him during his father's funeral, clutching his arm like a terrified child in a thunder storm. Too many people; but he'd asked her to be brave and she'd stayed with him afterwards while the guests ate and chatted. Some of the dukes even managed to coerce a smile from her.

She'd enjoyed herself at the banquet the night before, so long as Cenith didn't stray too far. Tyrsa desperately wanted to learn to dance, so he took her off into a corner and tried his best with no more success than at the station. *Maybe if she relaxed and didn't try so hard.*

The evening had ended, for Cenith and Tyrsa at least, when the nobles took the opportunity to wish them the best for their life together. They hoisted them in the air, startling Tyrsa, before depositing them at the top of the Grand Staircase. Traditional cheers and songs followed them down the hall and up the main stairs. Someone had hung a wreath of wild flowers on their door to keep the evil spirits away, a distinctly mountain custom.

The Companions finally had to chase the last of the

well-wishers away. Tyrsa's moon cycle put an end to the other part of the proceedings. *Do I feel more married because the ritual has finally been observed? Hard to say.*

Cenith twisted the ugly black ring encircling the middle finger of his right hand. No jewel decorated it, no engravings redeemed it. *Where in Shival's hells is Orman? He's not improving matters by dawdling.*

He'd lain awake half the night deciding what to do with the errant duke. This ring represented only part of it. Nothing more than a thick, rough, iron band painted in black enamel, Cenith had thought it fascinating when nine years old. He'd spotted it in an armoury while out with his father and pestered him until he purchased it. Too large for any finger, he kept it on his thumb, holding it there so it didn't slip off. He'd almost lost it several times before losing interest. It had spent the last ten years in the bottom of a drawer in his old suite. What made him think of it last night he couldn't say, but it was just what he needed.

He undid the top fastenings of his black tunic and the tie on the grey silk shirt, the same outfit he'd worn to Kian's funeral. The study backed onto the storage tunnels on the first floor and had no windows. Holes had been cut into the ceiling along the rear edge and covered with fine wooden lattice work. They brought a little fresh air into the room, though Cenith had no idea how. Whoever had built the keep had done a remarkable job. This deep into the rock, the room always remained cool which was nice in the summer. Keeping the fireplace lit helped alleviate it in the winter.

Giving in to his restlessness, Cenith left the chair to pace in front of the cold hearth. The black slate had no god symbols glued to it, unlike the one in their sitting room, a result of Niafanna and Cillain, the Calleni gods, teaching

Tyrsa about the different gods and the Old Ones.

Tyrsa had learned so much in the time they'd been together, disregarding what happened the night the assassins attacked. *Tyrsa is improving. She's smart and curious, and stubborn. She must be capable of more.*

Lady Violet displayed a maturity that held hope. *Lady Violet.* Tyrsa's other persona hadn't put in an appearance since the night they laid Kian to rest, and gave Daric an impossible mission—to retrieve Saulth's scroll and the Bredun councillor with it. Cenith rubbed his neck. If it wasn't one worry it was another, all sitting above him like a ripe avalanche. A knock sounded at the door.

A guard's face appeared in the half open doorway. "Duke Orman to see you, My Lord."

"Let him in." Cenith returned his attention to the fireplace, twisting the ring on his finger. He could feel Orman behind him, the man's beady dark eyes boring into his back. At least he had the decency to remain quiet.

Cenith spun on his heel, catching the sneer on Orman's face before the man could school his expression. "You're late."

Orman bowed, his lips stretching into a smile as thin as the hair on his head. "My apologies, My Lord. I was delayed…"

"You try my patience." Cenith strode to his desk, though he remained standing.

The duke eyed the chair across from him, the smile fading.

Cenith motioned for him to sit. He folded his hands behind his back and paced the length of his desk twice before gripping the back of the chair. "You have left me with a problem I'd rather not have. First you lie in council, then provide false evidence to support that lie."

Orman showed his empty palms to Cenith, an old Ardaeli sign for truth-telling. "I explained that, My Lord. It was my clerks…"

Cenith's fist hit the table, startling the duke. "I find it hard to believe your clerks would take it upon themselves to forge a document without your knowledge!" He stood straight and stared directly into Orman's eyes. "This is nothing short of treason. I should have you hauled off to the dungeon to await trial. The rest of the dukes aren't leaving until morning, I'm sure we could convince them to stay over for the proceedings."

Orman's mouth opened and closed faster than a whore's purse strings on the keep guards' payday. Cenith also kept an eye on the duke's still open hands; the man's dagger hung too close to them. He didn't think Orman foolish enough to try it, but desperate men sometimes attempted rash acts. Cenith resisted the urge to tap his own dagger on his belt.

He let Orman stew over the charges before he sat. He clasped his hands and rested them on his belly, feigning a calmness he didn't feel. "Frankly, I'd rather not waste the time."

The duke's mouth snapped closed. He placed his hands on the table, gripping the edge with his thumbs.

"Instead, I have a proposal for you."

"A proposal?" Suspicion supplanted fear in Orman's eyes.

"I don't want to have to replace you. With you not having an heir, it's too much trouble and we have enough of that right now."

Under Ardaeli law, none of Orman's five daughters could inherit and his only son had died as an infant. Though two of the daughters had attained marrying age, neither seemed inclined to find a husband and, by all reports, Orman didn't seem to care. Training someone else, even a man of Cenith's choosing, would take time.

Cenith held up a finger. "But, I can't have one of my dukes trying to trick another out of a gold mine. When you took your father's position as Duke of Warbler Ridge, you swore to work for the benefit of your holding and your principality, and to remain loyal to your lord. What you did was for personal gain only, in complete disregard of that oath." He sat forward. "To make amends, I offer you this…support me in everything I do for five years and a day starting today."

Orman frowned. "What are you planning that you need my support?"

Cenith sat straight and shrugged. "I don't know yet."

"That's all?" The duke's eyes narrowed further.

"Not quite." Cenith pinned him with what he hoped was a hard gaze and removed the black ring from his finger. "You will wear this ring at all times. For the rest of your life." He tossed it on the table. It rolled before toppling to settle a few inches from the duke's splayed hands.

Orman sat rigid, his eyes studying every inch of Cenith's face. "Why?"

"To remind yourself that you are a traitor. You should be hanging from a gibbet. By my graces, you not only breathe but remain in control of your lands."

Orman's eyes looked like they stared into Shival's deepest hell. "What will I tell anyone who asks?"

Cenith flashed him a cold smile. "I don't care. This is between you and me." Which wouldn't remain strictly true. Though Ors had returned in time to catch the last of the funeral, he didn't need to know unless something went wrong. Daric, on the other hand… "And I will find out if you don't comply."

Orman blinked. Suspicion joined fear in his eyes. Planting the thought that Cenith had spies in his holding couldn't hurt. Perhaps word might pass around and he'd have less trouble with all the dukes. *And if wishes were gold nuggets, we'd all wear silk.*

"As I said in council, I'll ask Daric about the original map when he returns. If it proves you right, I will apologize, burn the document, you can return the ring and the proposal ends."

Orman said nothing, studying him with his shifty eyes.

Looking for a way out? "It's not as if you have much of a choice here, Orman."

The duke nodded, slow and deliberate, a scowl twisting his features. "I accept your proposal."

"Good." Cenith pulled a parchment out of the right hand drawer, one he'd drawn up and signed that morning. He placed it in front of Orman.

"You expected me to agree." Orman's scowl deepened.

Cenith dipped the quill in ink and passed it to him. Tight lipped, Orman read the document, thoroughly, and signed it. Cenith melted two red blobs of wax at the bottom and had Orman press his signet ring into one while he used his ring, three stylized mountains in a circle, on the other. He replaced the parchment in the drawer. Orman's eyes followed it until the drawer closed.

I'll have to move it to a safer location. And keep a guard at the door until he's left for home. Cenith mentally shook his head, a sad thing when one your own dukes couldn't be trusted a finger's span. "You'll be leaving in the morning with the rest?"

Orman nodded. "Too late to go now. I hope you don't mind a few more for dinner." Pleasant conversation in strained tones.

"Of course not. Now that we've set matters straight, you're welcome at my table." Cenith smiled, a genuine one this time. "My lady wife and I look forward to visiting with Miryl and your daughters."

Orman sagged into his chair, all attempts at posturing gone. He sighed. "I had hoped to offer one of my older girls to you in marriage. I waited too long and that opportunity has passed."

Cenith tried to hide his surprise. *You old weasel! Sought to control me through your daughter, did you? No wonder neither appeared eager to marry.* He thanked Aja for rolling the dice in his favour, odd favour though it turned out to be. *And I'd thought Tyrsa a burden?*

"Too bad," Orman said. "I think either girl would have been a fine match. You would have had good-looking children. Just an observation, Lord Cenith, but your lady wife is small, not built for bearing the heir you need. My daughters are strong. If anything...unfortunate should happen...well, please keep them in mind." The duke stood and straightened the lace sticking out of his dark blue tunic. "I'll see you at dinner then, My Lord." He bowed and almost slunk out of the room.

I think I'll have good looking children regardless, he thought, miffed that Orman would suggest otherwise.

A marriage with one of Orman's daughters? Not something Cenith would have considered on any day. Both Orman and his wife had been attractive in their younger years, but their two eldest had inherited their worst aspects, and not just in looks. He shuddered. Tyrsa, with all her faults and peculiarities, appealed to him far more, whether she could bear children or not. As for something happening to Tyrsa…Cenith forced those thoughts from his mind.

Later that night, restless from the day's events, Cenith watched his wife sleep. He pushed strands of fine hair back from her face, still pale despite the days spent outside at the guard station. At least she no longer looked like she lay on death's door. He kissed her forehead, unconcerned about waking her. Once asleep, she had every intention of staying that way until her body said it was time to wake up or he kissed her awake.

"Now that all this council nonsense is over, I'm going to spend some time with you," he whispered. "We're going riding, every day I hope. Get you out in the sun. I want to show you more of your new home; the forests, the rivers, Canyon Falls."

Cenith lay back, pulling her close to him. He closed his eyes, slipping into memories of his father, hunting the forests, fishing the rivers, and marvelling at Canyon Falls.

* * * *

The rasp of steel on whetstone echoed in the rafters of a small room at the back of Snake's den. Artan sat cross-legged on a mat next to his bed and slid the dagger along the stone again before testing the edge. Satisfied, he wiped it down and slipped it in the sheath at his waist.

Snake only ever had nine men, eight skilled and one apprentice. Technically Artan now replaced Ice as second-in-command and was entitled to his spacious room near the front of the lair. He doubted Snake would allow a seventeen-year-old to fill that responsibility…if he ever returned.. With enough room for a single bed, a chest for his belongings and a mat between bed and door, his room left little space for sharpening a sword. Nonetheless, this was home and he needed to be here.

After four days of steady riding, Artan had arrived late in the evening of the previous day, just as the gates closed for the night. He almost ran down several wandering refugees in his haste to be home. A cold, silent lair awaited him.

Artan glanced at the parchment lying on the wooden chest, still in its thin frame. As leader, it was Snake's job to take it to Lord Saulth. *And if Snake never comes home? Are you just going to hang onto it forever?* Enough of the stolen gold remained to keep him comfortable for a while, but Artan realized he might have to admit Snake may not have survived. *Not today. I'll wait one more day.*

Taking the parchment to Saulth would then fall to him. His heart quailed at the thought. All the stories of the lord's quick anger and tales of him gone mad…perhaps that's all they were, stories; but maybe they weren't. *Tomorrow. If Snake doesn't come, maybe I'll go tomorrow.*

Artan lifted one butt cheek, then the other, bringing some life to his nether regions. He reached for his sword, resting against the bed, and examined it for non-existent nicks and scratches. Not surprising since Snake refused to allow him to use it when not training.

Needing something to keep him occupied, Artan spit on the whetstone and ran it lovingly along the edge of the weapon. The repetitious motion soothed his soul, allowing him to clear his mind and retreat to a peaceful, quiet place.

* * * *

Daric rolled his cloak in the dirt, shook it out, and placed it over his shoulders. He pulled the hood as far over his face as possible. The other side of a low ridge flanking the Main Bredun Road hid him from curious eyes while he affected the changes required for his plan. He hadn't shaved for the past few days and the salt and pepper scruff added to his disguise. Wiping sweat from his brow, he rubbed his tired eyes before scanning the view in front of him, his memory drifting back to the last time he stood on this ridge, the day Saulth thrust Tyrsa on Cenith.

Valda was half drowned in river water then. With less rain in this area of Bredun, the winding Asha River had receded enough to allow workers to repair the bridges and docks and reclaim most of the flooded part of town. Gold and green banners that had snapped in a brisk wind now hung limp from sunlit poles. If the weather held, the fields might have half a chance of yielding a crop before it rotted.

People still flowed in and out of the gates, though not as many and fewer appeared to be the homeless looking for a new life. Little else had changed. Most important, the city remained the fortress he remembered.

Three days of steady riding had ended in a small village with the anomalous name of Big Bend; the road ran straight through a town of less than a dozen buildings. A day's walk from Valda, it was the last village on the Bredun Main Road before the city itself.

Daric wrapped the lower half of his old battered scabbard in an worn cloth from his pack and tugged his cloak tighter around his shoulders. Hunching over, he used the scabbard, sword inside, as a crutch. Satisfied the ruse would work, he slung his pack over his shoulder and the bag containing Snake's head over the other. Though the thick burlap did little to contain the ripening odour of the assassin's remains, it would help keep people from coming too close.

Affecting a limp, Daric made his way down the ridge, back to the main road into Valda, easing his way into the crowd. The early evening sun beat down on his head, shoulders and back, heightened by the battered wool cloak and his already overheated body. Sweat trickled down his face, his back. There had been a time when he could have made the walk from Big Bend to Valda while carrying a bigger load and in greater heat. The years had stolen it from him.

The long ride had been tiring enough, the lack of good sleep made it worse. Daric had slept in comfortable beds, but couldn't prevent the dark dreams haunting him every night, the faces of men he'd betrayed...tortured...killed; all at the whim of the men who'd paid him, visions he'd thought long buried. They hadn't bothered him then. Not then. *I'm just like Snake.*

Elessa! I need you! Her love, her touch, forced the visions back to the corner of his soul he swore could never be cleansed, merely hidden away; but she wasn't here. She didn't lie beside him at night working her sweet magic with just with a touch, a soft breath. Would she understand? That he'd had to do it? Had to avenge Kian?

Daric bumped into a man, one almost as ragged as he. The man opened his mouth in a prelude to a snarl. Daric moved close enough to allow him a good whiff of what hung in the bag over his shoulder. A grimace replaced the snarl and the man backed off. So did several others around him, leaving him a twig floating alone, surrounded by a throng of leaves flowing with the current of the stream.

He paused to rub his back. Riding would have been easier, but a ragged peasant with a horse like Nightwind would have attracted more attention than a naked whore in a barracks. Daric had balked at stabling Nightwind in Big Bend, in the small livery attached to the inn. One would think the few stalls it held easy enough to keep clean. Instead, he found the straw filthy and damp. He planned on staying in Valda only a few days, but that would be enough for thrush to set in.

Daric had forced the young man in charge of Nightwind to clean a stall properly, then withheld half the cost. The threat he left the stable owner with paled both their faces. With a sigh, and a hope he'd still have a healthy horse when this was over, he rejoined the rush.

By the time he reached the gates, the sun sat half above, half below the horizon. The crowd hurried now, cramming the gate. Keeping his affected posture, Daric, with his smelly companion, forced his way through to the guard, wishing only to put an end to the day.

"Here now," one of the soldiers said to him, when a man complained. "No need for shovin'. What's that you've got in th' bag? Perhaps it needs lookin' at."

Daric chuckled and pulled the sack off his shoulder. "Open it if ya'd like t' see, sorr." A dry throat cracked his voice, making him sound older. "'Tis all that remains of a dear departed friend. I'm bringin' 'im 'ome for burial. Bin on th' road for a few days, though." He held the sack out for the soldier to take.

"Gah!" The guard backed off, holding his nose, and

waved him through. "On yer way!"

Replacing the bag, Daric trundled into the city. Keeping to the shadows, he headed straight for the Waddling Duck, praying to Niafanna the bartender would remember him and what had been said that night in Fifth Month when he'd paid gold for information about Tyrsa.

Once in the city, more changes came to light. Refuse lined the once clean streets, human as well as other. The alleys, crowded in Fifth Month, crawled with people trying to make a home. Different coloured canvas blended with wool blankets to form crude shelters. Children cried or sat quietly at the edges of the alley, those with food the objects of envy to those without.

Eyes followed him, guards, merchants, refugees, even the few nobles and ordinary folk out and about. As he walked, the sun sunk lower in the sky, briefly tingeing the spires blood red. The merchants closed their shops, expected for that time of night. The refugees thinned, disappearing into alleys and ramshackle buildings no one else would live in. The nobles and townsfolk seemed to vanish—not expected—and the guards watched him until he passed from their sight.

I've done nothing, why would they watch a crippled old man? From beneath his hood, Daric studied the guards. No more than he remembered, nor were they armed differently. Yet, they acted unusual. They didn't keep an eye on just him but all the refugees on the street, hands on sword hilts, as if they expected trouble. He didn't remember this behaviour from his previous visit.

It's quiet. Too quiet. The night people should be putting in an appearance. On such a warm evening, the tavern doors should be open, spilling laughter and light onto the sidewalks and streets. Instead, most of the taverns were closed, their windows dark. Those standing open expelled dejected patrons who hurried on their way. *Something's up.* Daric decided to keep his head down and do nothing to attract attention, just concentrate on making it to the Waddling Duck; around the castle and half way to the docks, just as he remembered.

Warm, friendly light illuminated the open door, though the noise of pleasant conversation and the lute player were absent. Daric hobbled in, keeping his disguise. A quick glance showed just three patrons seated near the cold fireplace, all draining their mugs in rapid fashion.

The bartender wiped the counter, his eyes fastening on Daric. "Yer too late. We're closin'."

Daric remembered him from Fifth Month and moved closer to the bar. He raised his hood just enough to allow the bartender a good look. At the man's widening eyes, Daric put a finger to his lips and gave a quick nod in the direction of the men preparing to leave.

"I guess I can give ya one, if ya drink it fast."

A small mug of cold ale appeared in front of Daric, who drowned it in one gulp. Each of the three men eyed him as they left. The bartender waited a few minutes, before striding over to the door and bolting it.

"Tis good t' lay eyes on ya, Yer Excellency. I 'adn't expected to see, or smell, ya again." He crinkled his nose, the salt and pepper moustache wriggling like a caterpillar. "What is that foul odour?"

Daric straightened, stifling a groan. Walking hunched over for so long had added to the ache from Snake's bouncing head. He pointed to the bag on his shoulder. "Necessary, I'm afraid. A tale long in the telling. I need a bath, food and a room. And Lacus. I have a favour to ask that he may not grant, but I have to try."

67

"Bath, food and room I can provide, but Lacus'll have t' wait 'til mornin'. Saulth imposed a curfew three weeks ago. That's why I 'ave t' close so early."

"Curfew?" That explained much.

The bartender poured him another ale. "Too many people in the streets with nowhere t' go. The guards claimed they were causin' trouble at night, breakin' into people's 'omes, murderin' others for a spot to sleep in an alley." He shrugged. "Don't know if it's true or not. I never saw anythin', only 'eard o' it from those I know." He leaned closer to Daric, then caught a whiff of Snake and jerked back. "Rumours say he's afraid o' an uprising. The folks 'ere ain't 'appy with their lot. Saulth 'as no control over th' weather, but some relief would 'elp and nothin' comes but more taxes."

Daric let both pack and bag drop to the floor, then leaned his sword against the counter before downing the second ale. He licked the foam from his upper lip. "All those people who entered with me aren't going to find a place to hide from the guards. Not tonight."

"Alleys are considered safe, 'cept they're all full. Those poor folk'll be caught on th' streets and taken t' th' dungeons." The bartender scratched his balding head, a disgusted look on a face with more lines than a Cambrellian poem.

Harsh, but Saulth always needs to be in control and doesn't care how he does it. Any threat to his position would be dealt with in a swift and decisive manner. "What about the regular folk? The merchants and nobles?"

"Curfew applies t' all, though us with jobs don't get tossed into th' dungeon, just escorted 'ome. Same for nobles. They ain't 'appy 'bout it either. Particularly th' young roustabouts. Puttin' a wrinkle in their raunchin'."

"The dungeons must be crowded by now."

"Heard rumours there too."

"Willin?" A woman's voice shouted from somewhere beyond the door behind the bar. "Ya still got someone out there? They're gonna get nicked!" A chubby, red face bordered by a halo of silver grey hair peeked around the doorway.

"Tis all right." Willin waved her out. "He's one 'o those who 'elped that poor girl in th' castle. He'll be stayin' th' night."

A short, rotund body filled the doorway. Her smile crinkled her eyes almost shut. "Well, now. In that case, yer welcome."

"Councillor Daric, this 'ere's Hadera, my wife."

She gave him an awkward curtsey. Her smile faltered. "You be needin' a bath, and right now, Yer Excellency. That smell ain't all you, is it?"

Willin laughed. "No, 'tis comin' from a bag on th' floor."

Hadera tsked. "Give it t' me and I'll get rid 'o it."

Daric shook his head. "Can't do that, I'm afraid. It has to be disposed of properly and I'm the only one who can do it. If you show me my room, I'll take it up there and open the window."

"Just a minute." Hadera disappeared back through the doorway, emerging a few minutes later with an empty sack. "I sprinkled some herbs on th' inside. If ya put it in 'ere, it should be less…offensive."

Daric thanked her and put Snake's bag in the sack. It did seem to help, but it might just be that he'd grown used to the smell.

"Willin," Hadera said, on her way out of the tavern room. "Show 'im to 'is room while I prepare a bath." She

69

winked at Daric. "And then we'll feed ya up right proper."

Daric returned the wink, adding a smile. He picked up bag, pack and sword and followed the bartender, now innkeeper, up the stairs. "How many others are staying here?"

"Just one, and 'e's at t'other end 'o the hall from ya. Most people comin' 'ere these days just don't 'ave th' money t' spend on a room and we can't be affordin' t' give it to 'em for free."

"Understandable."

Three short halls, lit by fancy brass wall sconces, branched off the stairs. Old, but well maintained, carpet lined the freshly painted corridors. Willin led Daric down the left one and stopped in front of the first door. He pulled a set of keys from his pocket, slid one off the ring and opened the door. Passing the key to Daric, he said, "This 'ere's our biggest room. Two full silvers a night, including bath and meals, but for you, one."

Daric held up his hand. "No, I'll pay two, just like anyone else. You've already been a great help to me."

Willin grinned and led the way into the room. Spacious and clean, a large bed took up the wall to the right of the door. An oak wardrobe, six feet wide, occupied a portion of the wall to the left. Straight ahead, two open windows showed him the street, a long wooden chest nestled between them. A desk and chair hid behind the door. Everything sat on a woven carpet in patterns of red, green and blue.

The innkeeper strode to a door on the right. "Ya even 'ave yer own privy." Willin opened the door and stood back, revealing a privy as large as the one in Daric's suite in Tiras. Besides the usual facility, a fancy table held towels, a large washing bowl and jug of water with space for the guest's personal toiletries. A gilded mirror hung above it and a picture of a rural scene decorated the opposite wall.

"Very nice." As Cenith's councillor, Daric would be offered the best. It was more than what he needed, but how could he say no?

"Hadera should 'ave yer bath ready shortly, Yer Excellency. We always 'ave water on." Willin headed for the door. "Th' bath room is off th' kitchen, so come down anytime. Soon as yer clean, we'll feed ya. And then we can talk some more." He lost his smile. "I'm sure ya will be interested."

Daric nodded and the man closed the door. Herbs or no, he dealt with Snake's head first. He tied off the double sack and using the other end of the rope attached it to his sheathed sword before wedging the weapon under the window frame. He flipped the head out the window and closed it. After a moment's thought, he closed the other as well. The result might be a stuffy room, but an errant breeze wouldn't send the odour back at him.

Tossing his pack on the chair, he pulled out Buckam's parchments. Satisfied they'd come to no harm, he replaced them and removed his extra clothing, except the armoured jerkin and leather trousers. Of the three sets he'd brought, one remained clean. He set those aside and wrapped the dirty ones in his cloak.

Daric's gut reminded him he'd eaten lightly at noon. He gathered both clean and dirty clothes, as well as his shaving kit, and headed for the bath, locking the room behind him.

Willin paused from sweeping the floor and directed him to the bath. A young man, who took after the innkeeper's wife in looks, emptied a large pot of hot water in a long wooden tub; steam rose from the surface, only a few inches from the top. Hadera appeared in the doorway and shooed her son away.

Daric held out his cloak-wrapped dirty clothes. "For a few extra coppers, could I impose upon you to do my laundry?"

Hadera laughed. "O' course! Tis no trouble. Toss those yer wearin' out th' door and I'll do them too."

He sincerely hoped Hadera could remove the smell from the ones he wore, Snake's disgusting odour permeated everything.

* * * *

Clean and fed, Daric drained his mug and held it up for more. The innkeeper brought over a large jug and an extra cup. He filled both mugs before sitting down across the table from Daric. Willin's son had extinguished the chandelier and most other light, leaving one candle on the table and two in nearby wall sconces. No fire warmed the hearth, no moon backlit the windows. Only a few shadows danced to the tune of the candle wicks.

Willin emptied half his cup in one draught and sucked the foam from his moustache. "Not a bad brew, if I do say it m'self."

Daric chuckled. "Your own recipe?"

"Yep. Passed down through eight generations." Willin glanced around the tavern room. "As has this inn."

"Then here's to eight more generations of fine ale, food and hospitality." Daric raised his cup to Willin's and they drained the mugs before slamming them on the table.

Willin wiped his mouth on his sleeve. He refilled the cups, his gaze flashing to the bolted door before returning to Daric. "As I was sayin' earlier, there's some things I think ya should know."

"About the refugees in the dungeons?" Daric leaned against the wall, settling in for a tale.

Willin nodded. "Now these are just rumours mind and I'm not usually one for passin' 'em on unless I think they 'ave somthin' to 'em."

"I understand."

"Well, you asked the same question many o' us 'ave asked. How many more people can Saulth fit in 'is dungeons? First off, I ain't got no idea how big they are. For all I know, they could spread out under th' entire city. But I doubt it. Ain't been much cause over the last four 'undred years to 'ave dungeons that big. But guards 'ave been pullin' people off th' street for three weeks, so those people 'ave t' go somewhere.

"Some o' th' refugees 'ave found work cleanin' up the docks and rebuildin' bridges," Willin continued. "And that's fine. Honest work and bein' paid for it. But some folks 'ave come in from outlyin' areas with tales o' women and children just showin' up in Saulth's fields. No one knows who they are. Ain't local. Tend t' keep t' themselves. Don't say much."

Daric watched the candlelight flicker in a water ring made by his mug. Could even Saulth stoop so low as to force his own people into slave labour? "Are they being paid?"

Willin shrugged. "Haven't 'eard one way or t'other. These days, anythin's possible."

"Has anyone seen cartloads of people leaving the city?"

Willin shook his head. "Not as I've 'eard. If anyone 'as seen anythin', they ain't talkin'." He scratched his chin.

"If they're taken out at night, though, wi' th' curfew, who would see?"

Daric drummed the table with his fingertips. He didn't have a problem with putting the people to work, so long as they were paid a fair wage and young children were exempt. Although, Willin had said 'women and children'. Nothing about the men. "You said it's only women working the fields?"

"Yep. And children. Young ones too. Th' women can't afford to 'ire someone t' look after 'em, so they bring 'em along."

"What happens to the men?"

Willin leaned closer. "Now that's th' part I'd thought ya'd be most interested in. And this ain't no rumour. Lacus says the barracks are overflowin' with new soldiers and most of 'em don't look like they want t' be there."

Daric sat up straight. "Saulth's recruiting the men?"

Willin nodded. "And lads. Anyone fifteen and older fit enough t' train."

"Why does he feel he needs a bigger army? More guards to patrol the streets?" Using refugees to contain refugees? It did make sense of a sort.

"Possibly," Willin said. "But I 'aven't noticed an increase in th' guard."

"It's only been, what did you say? Three weeks since he started the curfew?"

The innkeeper nodded.

"Not enough time to train them. Keep your eyes open. I wouldn't be surprised if you saw an increase somewhere around the end of the month." Daric emptied his cup and shook his head when Willin offered him more.

"Thing is," Willin said. "The number o' people comin' in 'as decreased. The weather's improved. No reports o' tornadoes nearby in th' last month or so. Why would Lord Saulth need more guards?"

"From what I heard on the way here, the tornadoes haven't stopped farther north."

Willin harrumphed. "We've been lucky 'ere then. Maybe those guards will 'ave someone to 'aul away when those 'omeless arrive."

Daric stared at his empty cup. In Dunvalos Reach, when people were left homeless by avalanches, neighbours, or even those from the next village, took them in. Everyone gathered together and could build a small house in a few days. *But those unfortunates didn't usually lose their livelihood.* The mines remained and, once the snow thawed, the land was still usable, though it might need clearing. These folk hadn't just lost their homes. Floods destroyed farmland and rain rotted crops.

"If ya don't mind my sayin," Willin said. "Ya look all done in. I can 'ave Lacus 'ere first thing in th' mornin'."

Daric nodded. "That would be wonderful. Thank you, for that and all you've done."

"My pleasure."

When Daric reached his room, he breathed deep. No smell of decay came through the windows. He lay awake longer than he wanted; thoughts of why Saulth felt he needed a larger army kept wandering through his mind—one in particular, a memory from the Lords' meeting two months earlier.

Saulth wanted to be king of Ardael. A desire that could only end in war. The other lords had made it obvious they wouldn't submit to him and Daric already knew where Cenith stood. Five principalities against one.

75

Saulth couldn't win, regardless of his increased army.

The man had to have something else hidden in his cloak. Was that where Tyrsa, with her mysterious powers, came in? If so, why give her to Cenith? What did the scroll have to do with it? Questions he'd asked before and still without answers. Perhaps soon, after they knew what the scroll said, some of those questions would be resolved.

Before Daric fell asleep, he decided to advise Cenith to step up their own recruiting and training. It never hurt to be prepared.

Chapter Four

Daric scooped the last of his eggs into his mouth, cut another slice of the sharp yellow cheese Willin had provided and bit it in half. Lacus sat on the other side of the table, a steaming mug of tea in his hands, Willin beside him, sipping a tankard of breakfast ale.

Lacus tilted his head and narrowed his eyes. "If ya don't mind my askin', just what are ya plannin' on doin' once yer in the castle? That kitchen is my livelihood. 'Tis how I feed my family. What yer askin' is treason. I could be hung for it."

"I'm aware of that and if you don't want to do it, I understand. I'll find another way in." Daric jammed the last of the cheese into his mouth and waited for Lacus' response.

The cook's tongue curled around a drooping moustache that made Willin's look like glued on sticks of straw. He sucked on it while he thought, studying Daric thoroughly. "Depends on what ya want I 'spose. Talkin' 'bout the girl was one thing…"

Daric had figured he'd have to tell him, even though his life depended on Lacus' decision. Trusting a man he'd only met once rubbed Daric's fur the wrong way. Trust was something earned, not given. *It's not like I have a choice.* "I plan on stealing Saulth's scroll. The one he keeps in the library."

Lacus blinked several times, then burst out

laughing. "The scroll! Lord Saulth's precious scroll?"

Willin's heavy brows dipped in a confused frown.

Lacus waved a meaty finger at Daric. "That…now that would be somethin'. Those pieces of tattered parchment mean more t' 'im than this principality. Maybe wi' them gone, 'e'll go back t' bein' th' lord 'e once was." Lacus shook his head, suddenly sober. "It's bin bad 'ere of late. The gods don't listen no more. People say they've up 'n left us 'angin'." The cook leaned closer, though no one else was in the room. "Tis said many 'ave turned t' foreign gods, like yours, in 'ope o' gettin' 'elp from them." He leaned back and tapped his nose.

The head cook sniffed and twitched his moustache before leaning forward again. "If Saulth didn't 'ave that parchment takin' up all 'is time and thinkin', 'e could put more into fixin' up 'is lands and 'elpin' people like 'e used to. Bein' rid o' it would be good for the people. So, if I 'elp you, I'm 'elpin' everyone. It ain't treason if yer 'elpin' yer principality." He looked to Willin, who nodded his agreement. Lacus made a stab at the air in front of Daric's face. "You 'ave to promise me that ya don't intend t' commit murder." He squinted, his eyes fixed firmly on Daric's. "Your Excellency."

Daric returned the gaze without flinching. "I have absolutely no intention of killing anyone, including the guards, which is why I need your help."

Lacus slapped the table. "Then I think I can get ya in, but yer gonna 'ave t' do some actin'. Ya do tend t' stick out in a crowd."

"It won't be the first time."

"Don't know what yer gonna do once ya get in there. Lord Saulth's got guards everywhere." Lacus blew on his tea before trying it.

Should I tell them? Daric stared at the steam rising from the fragrant cup he held. *Could it cause trouble for Saulth?* He almost grinned. "If you can get me to Lady Tyrsa's room, I can use the hidden tunnels to move around without being seen."

"Tunnels?" Willin's tankard stopped halfway to his mouth.

"Lady Tyrsa?" Lacus asked at the same time.

Which one to answer first? "The girl needed a name. Lord Cenith chose to call her Tyrsa. She likes it."

"Huh. Never heard it before." Lacus slurped his tea.

"It's Calleni. There's a series of tunnels in the walls of the castle." Daric spoke to Willin now, but watched Lacus.

The head cook's eyes snagged his. "And how would you know that?"

Daric smiled. "A little inside information. And a map. I gather it's no secret to you."

"Tis to me," Willin said, his frown still firmly in place.

"We've suspected for years. Sometimes th' staff 'ears noises in th' wall. Never could find a way in, though. Not that I've spent a lot o' time lookin', mind." Lacus grinned. "Would be interestin' t' know how to use 'em. I assume ya know?"

Daric nodded. "I do, and I would have no problem showing you."

Lacus' grin widened. "Now this could be fun."

Willin shot him a disgusted look.

Daric had a feeling he didn't want to know what kind of 'fun' the cook referred to. "What do I need to do?"

Lacus swallowed some tea, then leaned forward.

Willin did too. "There's a shipment o' grain comin' in this afternoon. Ten wagons. I need men t' unload 'em, but can't spare my regular staff. So, I go t' Bastra's Square. Anyone needin' a bit o' work goes there in th' mornin', and someone like me 'ires 'em." He stabbed the table with his finger.

"Now, don't go t' th' square 'cause you'll stand out like a black cat in a pack o' white dogs," Lacus continued. "Wait 'til noon, then make yer way t' th' back o' th' castle. Hide in th' last alley and ask to join as we go by. I'll 'ire ya on th' spot. Th' guards at th' gate won't be any that saw ya last time, so ya should be able to walk right in with us."

Should be able to? "Are you sure about the guards? The soldiers in the hall and on the gates got a good look at all of us."

Lacus nodded. "I'm sure. The ones at th' back don't rotate wi' those on th' front. There's only a change if someone's sick, promotes or retires. Regulars are on this mornin', so no worry."

"And when I don't leave with the others?"

"Shift change 'appens before th' wagons'll be done. You'll 'ave t' work while t'other guards are on, but only a couple o' hours, if ya don't mind." Lacus flashed him an apologetic look. "Your Excellency."

"I've only been a councillor for a few months. It hasn't made me soft yet. I'm not afraid of a little hard work."

Lacus grinned. "Good. Tis all settled then." He drained his cup and pushed himself up from the table. "I'll see ya this afternoon…Your Excellency."

Daric nodded and the cook left. He swallowed half his now warm tea.

"By the time ya 'ave t' go, yer clothes should all be

dry. Do ya want t' leave yer stuff 'ere while ya do what you're doin'?" Willin asked.

"No, I doubt I'll be able to return. I suspect I'll be making a fast exit from town. Not sure how to take it with me, though."

"I'll 'ave my son, Kalden, take it t' Lacus this afternoon. Kinda concerned 'bout that smelly bag, though." Willin stroked his moustache. "Might 'ave Hadera add some more herbs to it."

"Wrap it in my cloak as well. Hopefully it will be enough. Have your son drop my things off just after the guards' shift change. That way I can take them into the tunnels with me." Excitement coursed through Daric's veins. He smiled to himself. It had been years since he'd attempted anything like this. *Strange. I thought I was done with all that.* He felt alive in a way he hadn't in over twenty years.

"You goin' in those clothes?" Willin asked, intruding on his thoughts. "They're old enough, but look a mite clean for th' fellows that 'ang 'round Bastra's Square."

"I'm sure I can find some dirt to fix things up."

"Turns out I 'appen to 'ave some fine quality stuff out back. Would work just fine."

Daric laughed.

Willin winked. "I also 'appen to 'ave a large floppy 'at I don't use no more. Too old and ragged, but it would 'elp 'ide yer face…just in case."

"Sounds like a plan to me." Daric finished his tea.

"Now, we've a couple o' hours before ya need t' get ready. Mind tellin' me all this stuff 'bout scrolls and tunnels? And that stinky bag?"

Daric held up his cup. "More tea and you have a deal."

* * * *

The roar of Canyon Falls pounded in Cenith's head, clashing with the ring of steel echoing in the wide meadow. He caught the edge of the sword flashing toward him on his hilt. Quick as the water rushing nearby, he grabbed his adversary's right wrist, preventing him from breaking away.

Mustering his strength, Cenith pushed his aggressor back. One foot, then two. Sweat dripped from his brow, bare chest and back. With a sudden wrench, his opponent twisted out of the grip and broke off, skipping several steps to the side. Laughter surrounded him.

"Almost got him there, My Lord!" Yanis called.

"Almost don't count! My foot stayed in th' circle!" Jolin grinned as he slid behind Cenith, forcing him to turn and face the Companion.

Now Cenith stood too close to the edge of the game boundary scratched into the ground by hard boot heels. Breathing hard, he tried dodging to the side, as Jolin had done, but the captain charged, a hellish grin on his sweaty face. Just before Jolin made contact, Cenith ducked low, diving at the Companion's knees, sending him sprawling.

"Hand and half an arse outside the circle!" Barit called. More laughter followed from the nine Companions standing around them.

"Siyon's…balls!" Jolin said, between gasps for breath. "Now that…was some mighty fine…*cheatin'!*"

Cenith sat on the ground in the circle, sucking in air and holding his side where he'd hit Jolin. He glanced at Tyrsa sitting on a blanket nearby, hoping she didn't hear her captain's lack of decorum; she had her hands over her eyes, not her ears. Tyrsa had watched Dathan and Keev fight, hiding her face against Cenith's chest half the time. Both Companions ended up with some scratches and she said she didn't want to see Cenith hurt.

He turned back to Jolin, still trying to catch his breath. "Tough to cheat…in a game with one rule." Cenith waved his sword at him. "*You* left me no choice. With a charge like that…you'd have blasted both of us out of the circle!"

Jolin fell back on the grass, his chest rising and falling like a bellows. His panting turned to chuckles, then laughter. Cenith's breathing eased enough to allow him to join in.

Tyrsa put her hands down, a disgusted look on her face. Cenith struggled to his feet and planted his sword in the center of the circle. He staggered over to her and dropped to his knees, still chuckling.

She waved her hand at him and turned away. "You don't smell good."

Cenith laughed harder. "The point of the game isn't to smell good. It's to win. Which I did. As my lady, you are supposed to be proud of me and bestow upon me your favour. A kiss."

"Keev didn't ask for a kiss when he won." Tyrsa's pretty brow dipped in a frown.

"Because you're not Keev's lady. You are mine." He stabbed his chest with a finger.

Cenith leaned down, cupped her face in his hands, and stole his favour. She tried to push him away, then gave up. He resisted the temptation to crush her to him; the sweat from his body might stain her pale blue dress. Tyrsa's lips tasted sweet and he made the reward a long one.

Sniggers and muffled laughs told him what the Companions thought of his stolen favour. *Time to quit.* Today all the Companions but two had chosen to accompany them on their daily excursion, giving up any free time they may have had. Varth and Ead remained behind, sleeping for the night shift.

Cenith grinned at the look his wife gave him; a confused combination of annoyance and pleasure on a face that now glowed with natural colour—alabaster with a hint of blush instead of dead white; odd for a girl whose parents both had darker complexions, even with her growing up without sunlight. Cenith doubted she'd ever tan like he did and took precautions to ensure she didn't burn.

The past few days proved beneficial to them both, spending time in the forests and valleys. Good for the body and the soul. He hadn't felt this relaxed since before his father died. The fresh air and warm sun had banished the last of Tyrsa's moodiness, and, though she still hadn't laughed outright, a giggle had escaped when Barit and Yanis held a face making contest. She smiled a lot and seemed happy. That was enough for now.

"M'lord." Jolin had found his feet and bowed to Cenith, holding out his hand, his grin immeasurable. "Ye must surely be breathless after that. Join me at th' pool and we kin wash away th' sweat that offends our dear Lady Orchid." Eloquent words for Jolin.

Cenith accepted his hand and the captain pulled him to his feet. He glanced at the sun as they walked. *An hour until noon. Close enough.* "Have the others bring out the food. I'm hungry enough to eat the arse out of a bear."

Jolin snapped out the orders and several of the remaining Companions ran for the far end of the meadow where the horses were tied. Cenith strode to a small, deep, water-filled depression carved from the rock at the edge of the gorge. Six feet separated him from the Kalemi River where it thundered over the three hundred foot precipice.

Sunlit mist curved into a rainbow that disappeared the closer he came to the falls. The rainbow had fascinated Tyrsa; the falls, on the other hand, overwhelmed her with the noise and sheer volume of water. The spray billowing from the gorge clung to Cenith's hair and skin, cooling him. He stood in front of the pool and performed the pattern of stretches Daric had shown him years ago. As always, it helped calm him and ease overworked muscles.

"'Twas a good fight, m'lord. Nice t' know married life ain't made ye soft." Jolin imitated Cenith's stretching positions.

Cenith grinned and glanced back at Tyrsa. She sat like an imperial queen of old while her Companions set up lunch around her. "My wife may be small, but she's energetic. Soft is not a problem." Jolin's roar of laughter almost drowned out the falls. "And if we don't get back to her, she and the rest of the Companions will eat everything in sight."

Jolin stepped back, allowing Cenith full access to the pool. He lay down, leaning over the water, dunking as much of his upper body as possible. The sun had warmed the water somewhat so it wasn't the shock it could have been. Nonetheless, a few seconds was about all he could handle.

A muffled shout filtered down through the water. When Cenith tried to lift his head, a large hand clamped onto his neck, holding him down. His eyes flew open. Sunlight streaked the glacial water. *Jolin! What in the three hells are you doing!* He struggled but couldn't find the fingers that held him. Cenith flailed with his hands until he clutched a solid rock ridge. Leaning over so far interfered with the leverage, making his attempts at freedom feeble. He tried to duck deeper, wriggle out of the strong grip. It didn't work.

Other hands pulled at his legs. Shouts and a deep roar reached Cenith's ears. *Maegden's balls! This isn't funny, Jolin!* It also wasn't the captain's type of humour. The thought of Jolin trying to kill him should have been incomprehensible. *Loyal to a fault Jolin?* But that was all that stuck in Cenith's mind. *Why? And what the bloody hells are the other Companions doing?*

Someone kicked him in the side. The shock of it forced what air he had out of his lungs. Cenith struggled harder. His chest burned; the need to breathe warring with the cold of the water that chilled him to the bone. White stars exploded before his eyes. *I'll have your rank for this! And your balls! Then your head!*

Black replaced the stars. Anger changed to dark fear. *I'm going to die!*

Hands grabbed Cenith's arms, pried his fingers from the rock. Warm sunlight hit his face. Someone hauled him backwards for a distance before laying him on the ground. A hand touched his neck and he sucked in air.

"Thank the gods! He's breathin'!" a voice said. He knew it, but couldn't put a name to it.

Cenith coughed up water and someone rolled him on his side. Black turned to blurred green and yellow. *I'm not going to die.*

"I'll leave him t' you!"

Jayce! Cenith gulped in air, resulting in more coughing. His vision cleared. Green grass and yellow buttercups stared back at him.

Shouts and cries filled the air. "Goes right through! Watch…left! Can't touch…!" Different voices, and nothing made sense.

Cenith lay on his side, gasping until he could breathe at a more normal rate. Someone massaged his back. He cranked his head around enough to see. Jolin knelt behind him, soaking wet.

"Jolin!" Anger surged, but another round of coughing hit him.

"Take it easy, m'lord. Yer safe now, though I'm goin' t' have t' move ye."

Cenith found his voice. "What in the hells were you doing? You almost killed me!"

Jolin's green eyes widened, reflecting the hurt and horror on his face. "T'wasn't me m'lord! Look!"

The captain helped Cenith to a sitting position. Now the words he'd heard fit. He blinked and took a few deep breaths to be sure it wasn't lack of air making him see what had tried to kill him. The creature fighting the Companions could only have come from a bad dream.

"Water? It's a man made of water?" Cenith could only see half the thing, but judging by that half it had to be twelve feet tall.

It clung to the cliff with one hand and swiped at Barit with the other. The Companion dodged while Buckam tried a double slash with his long knives. They passed through the creature like…swords through water.

"Aye, m'lord. It jus' popped up over the top and pushed ye under. I had no weapon and tried to pull ye back 'til the others could git here." Jolin nodded in the creature's direction. "Ye kin see what affect we have on it. Madin's arrows don't work neither."

"This isn't one of your backwoods sprites, is it?"

Some 'sprite'.

"Nay, m'lord! Ain't heard o' anythin' like it."

"I still don't believe what I'm seeing." Cenith closed his eyes and shook his head. Stars shot across his eyelids and he opened them. The creature remained.

Its hair flowed like a water fall, ending at its shoulders. Strange and hypnotic, the water always rippled down, never up. Cenith forced himself to look elsewhere. The creature's eyes moved like any man's, as did the arms, its muscles, but it was all water, reflecting the blue of the sky as would a mountain tarn. As he watched, tiny white wavelets formed on its massive chest, then disappeared.

"Jolin, I apologize for thinking you could kill me."

"Gladly accepted, m'lord."

Swords had no effect on the creature and yet its hand had been solid enough to hold Cenith down. "How did you get me free?"

"Trey attacked its face. When his sword passed through th' creature's eyes, it jerked back and let go. No damage was done, but it didn't like it." Jolin pointed to a red mark on Cenith's left side. "Hope that doesn't hurt too much. Trey tripped o'er ye."

That explained the kick. Cenith turned his attention back to the nightmare fighting his men. Madin had given up his crossbow and pulled his sword. Both he and Fallan attacked the creature, one from each side. The water-being folded its hand into a fist and punched Madin in the chest. Cenith expected the blow to pass through him. Instead, Madin flew backwards, landing close to the edge of the cliff.

Cenith counted Companions. Only seven fought where there should have been nine. "Get them back!"

"M'lord? We can't let it get t' ye!"

"Get them back! Now! Someone's going to go over the side! Draw it out! Fight it back here!" *Who's missing?*

In order to be heard, Jolin had to leave Cenith. He returned before Cenith's still swimming head could identify the missing Companions and hauled him to his feet. "I'm gittin' ye t' safety."

"Tyrsa!" Cenith spun to look where she'd been sitting. Saddlebags and food were all he could see. A wave of nausea hit and he staggered.

"Dathan and Keev took her into th' trees." Jolin steadied him. With an arm around Cenith's waist, the Companion almost dragged him away from the meadow. "An' that's where I'm takin' ye."

So much for feeling relaxed!

* * * *

The noonday sun shone straight down on the alley, the last one before the castle. Odours of cooking food, unwashed bodies and too many people in too small a space assailed Daric's nose. He leaned against the wall just inside the alley, his arms folded. One old man who had his refuge set up beside him tried to force him to move on. One frown from Daric and the man decided to return to his own business.

Daric didn't have to wait long. He heard someone whistling a popular tune called 'Sunset O'er the Mountains'. A peek around the corner showed Lacus striding up the sidewalk, his hands stuffed in his pockets. He stopped whistling and turned to the men behind him. "Step lively there! Lots o' work t' do!"

Six dirty men followed him. Only half looked like they really wanted the work. Daric stepped out of the ally, positioning himself so he blocked the path. "Lookin' for some 'elp, sorr?"

Lacus almost ran into him before stopping. He lifted his head to meet Daric's gaze. "I 'ave 'elp, right 'ere." He jabbed his thumb at the men behind him.

"Huh. Ya call that 'elp? I can 'aul more than any o' them."

The cook rocked back and forth on his heels while he 'thought about it', one hand still jammed in his pocket. "Guess ya might be able to at that. All right, come along and prove yer boast."

The other men scowled. Another man meant less time to do the job and less money for them. It couldn't be helped.

"Thankin' ya, sorr. I won't disappoint ya." Daric waited until the line had passed before tagging onto the end. On impulse, he limped, favouring his right leg, injured in the assassins' raid over two weeks earlier along with his right hand. It didn't bother him anymore, but faking it might be useful.

The guards at the back gate leaned against the open doors. Daric could swear they were asleep until one spoke.

"Afternoon Lacus. Wagons comin' in t'day?" The man talked as lazy as he looked.

"Yep. Five o' them. Should be here any time."

The other guard, younger and slightly more alert, stood straight and gave Daric a solid going over. "Ya got a big one 'ere, Lacus. Might be a good prospect for th' recruiter."

The recruiter? With my grey hair? Then Daric remembered the hat hid more than just the top part of his face. Guard-Commander Tajik would take one look at him and gut him on the spot. Keeping his roving gaze casual,

90

he searched for places he could run.

Lacus scowled. "He's a worker. Ya know th' rules. He ain't wanderin' at night. If ya take all th' good workers, we'll get nothin' done, includin' yer dinner!"

"Besides," put in the older guard. "Didn't ya see 'is limp?"

Lacus' eyes widened. "Limp?"

"Course I did," the other guard said, though his expression said he hadn't. "Could be fakin' it."

Daric thought fast. "I ain't fakin'. I was cut by a useless turd who didn't know 'ow t' use a scythe. Want t' see?" He undid his belt. Daric had enough scars that if they actually wanted to look it wouldn't be a problem.

"No!" Both guards voiced their opinion. The older one waved them through. Lacus tried hard not to laugh.

"This limp ain't gonna interfere with ya workin', is it?" The cook had to ask the question. The other workers, not to mention the guards, would expect it.

"I can do th' work. I just can't walk on it all day, so's I can't join th' guard. Won't be no problem, sorr." Fortunately his hand was almost healed and he'd removed the bandages a few days ago.

"See that it ain't." Lacus stomped to the front of the line.

Daric grinned as he passed the guards. "Have a good afternoon, sorrs."

* * * *

"Cenith!" Tyrsa struggled to reach him.

Keev's arm around her waist prevented her from running to him until Jolin brought him into the trees. She hugged Cenith tight, not caring about his wet body. His skin felt too cold against her cheek, but his chest pounded as hard as hers. He didn't die, like Kian, and that was all she cared about.

She had come. The one Cenith called Shival. She'd knelt at his side, smiling up at the water man. The bottom of her tight black dress, the same colour as her long hair, flowed into the ground. When Tyrsa had tried to go to Cenith, Dathan picked her up and carried her here. She told him she had to keep Shival away from Cenith, but he wouldn't listen. Shival didn't look happy when the Companions took Cenith away from the water man. Tyrsa hugged him tighter.

"Dathan, Keev," Jolin said. "Git into yer armour, but stay here and guard m'lord and m'lady." He ran out of the woods to where they'd put the horses.

Dathan left first, then Keev after he'd come back. Tyrsa looked up at the man who'd become more important to her than anything. Though Cenith held her as tight as she did him, he watched the Companions fight the water man. Tyrsa turned her face so she could watch too. She didn't see Shival anymore and that made her happy.

The water man bothered her, though. She knew him, just as she knew the Companions couldn't defeat him. Jolin had found his sword and the hard clothing Cenith called an armoured jerkin. He ran to fight with the rest of the Companions. The water man would kill him and the others, and then Cenith; but it wasn't them he wanted. It was her.

What can I do? Tyrsa thought hard about the first time she went to the cliff. The Mother and Father told her lots of things, but she couldn't remember them. She needed help. The other Tyrsa agreed.

She let herself retreat, though she didn't move her

body, only her mind. The other Tyrsa came forward, the one who would know what to do, the one who knew how to use the power. As she passed herself, two became one.

The first time she'd done this had been the day of Kian's funeral, the day the other Tyrsa told Daric she needed the scroll. Her other self had come forward and showed her how to change. It had felt strange then to hear herself say things that she didn't think of. It felt strange now.

Her other self looked out at the meadow. Four Companions lay on the ground. Two didn't move. "They cannot win." She let go of Cenith, looking up at him. "They need my help."

Cenith's eyes widened.

"Lady Violet!" Dathan cried.

Cenith gripped her shoulders and leaned down. "You're not going out there. That thing will kill you!"

"I have to. I am the only one who has a chance to defeat him." She pulled out of his grip. "It is us he wants, not you or the Companions. He only fights them because they are in the way. He will come and he will kill you to get to us. I have to do this."

Cenith didn't look pleased. He stared into her eyes for a long time. "What are you going to do?"

"Use our power, the only way I can."

Tyrsa caught a glimpse of the plan. Fear gripped her, but she couldn't run. She had no control over her body. *No!*

We have to do this. It is the only way, her other self said.

I'm afraid! It'll hurt!

You must work with me or we are all dead.

"If you go, I go," Cenith said.

"My Lord, no! Ye have no armour and yer sword is out there!" Keev pointed at the game circle and the sword standing like a steel tree in the center of it, too far away.

"Swords are useless anyway. We all go." Cenith took her hand.

Tyrsa tried to calm herself. She needed to be brave. For herself, for Cenith, and for the Companions. When they reached the edge of the meadow, the other Tyrsa pulled Cenith to a stop.

"I do not need to go closer," she heard herself say.

Tyrsa pretended to grit her teeth, make her body rigid, prepare for hurt the way she had all the times Saulth beat her. Her body didn't do what she wanted, but it helped ready her for the pain and struggle to come.

The other Tyrsa put her hands on her stomach. Deep inside, the white ball that was 'her' pulsed. "Stand behind me," she said to Cenith. "Do not let me fall."

He did as she asked. Dathan and Keev took up positions on either side of her.

"Ahhhh!" The water man knocked Fallan out of the way. "You have come out to play, little insect." His voice sounded like the waterfall, a loud, watery roar.

She reached inside herself, through her clothes, her skin, into her very core, and pulled out the glowing ball holding her power. Gasps of astonishment from the three men around her told Tyrsa this was something they hadn't seen before. Neither had she before that night on the cliff. Now came the hard part.

Five Companions lay on the ground. Jolin tried to attack the water man's eyes while Trey dodged the hand reaching for him.

Think of all the bad things. All the times he *hurt you. The pain, the loneliness*, her other self said.

I will lose control again!

You must! We will worry about control later.

"Dathan, Keev! Go help them!" Cenith ordered.

Dathan gripped Cenith's shoulder. "My Lord! We can't leave you!"

"You have to keep it away from Tyrsa. She needs time. If you don't, we're all dead. Go!"

And we are all dead if you *don't,* her other self said. She held the glowing ball in front of her, waiting for Tyrsa to unleash the pain, the hurt, the lonely dark days.

The two Companions ran to join the fight. Tyrsa shed imaginary tears, dragging hurtful memories from the corner of her mind where she'd locked them away. Her chest ached with loneliness. Rani had gone and not come back. She cried and no one came. Tyrsa felt every beating anew, each blow as if Saulth had only just delivered it. She sobbed and would have collapsed if she had control of her body. *It hurts! Mother! Father! It hurts!*

The ball, the size of the palm of her hand, dimmed, shedding its bright white light for a pink hue that rapidly changed to a deep, burning, angry red. The other Tyrsa spread her hands, making the ball grow larger. Trey went down, then Jolin. Only Dathan and Keev stood between the water man and Cenith. Even as she watched, first one, then the other fell to the water man's blows.

The water man looked at her and grinned, a smile as nasty and evil as Shival's. "Little insect. You are mine." He strode toward them.

Cenith! The biggest hurt of all—when Shival almost took him from her. Now the water man would kill him and Shival would take the most important part of her life.

With that final, devastating thought, the other Tyrsa released the angry red ball.

Chapter Five

Tyrsa grit her teeth against the pain beating in her head, pounding like the horses hooves on their ride to the falls. Agony throbbed and burned inside her. The other Tyrsa collapsed against Cenith and he held her tighter.

Flaring like an angry sun, the red ball shot straight toward the water man, hitting him in the chest. It buried itself in the centre, pulsing, blazing brighter than before. The water man took a stride and the ball glowed strange, moving like her reflection in the pool that morning.

"Maegden…protect us,' Cenith said, his voice rough and broken.

"No!" the other Tyrsa cried. "Do not pray to him!"

The water man lost his grin. Another stride and a look of surprise rippled across his liquid face. The water surrounding the ball steamed, then boiled. "I will kill you!" He took another step.

The burning heat of the orb spread to his stomach and neck. Steam rose into the air. The water man screamed, his mouth opening wider than anyone's should. His arms, legs and head all bubbled like the stews the Companions had made on the trip to Tiras.

Behind him some of the Companions stirred. Jayce sat up. He had blood on his face. Buckam rolled to his knees, clutching his right side. Both their jaws dropped when they saw the water man. His entire body boiled with violent, popping bubbles.

"You're too close!" Cenith called to them. "If he bursts, you'll be burned! Move as many of the men away as you can! I'm taking Tyrsa back into the woods!" He picked her up and ran.

The other Tyrsa peeked back over his shoulder. The water man had fallen to his knees, his hands on his head. He twisted and writhed, screaming in agony. Tyrsa cried out her own pain, throbbing in time with the pulsing ball in the water man's body. No one could hear her.

Cenith stopped and set Tyrsa on her feet. "I hope we're far enough away."

"I do not know." Her other self leaned against him, her strength almost gone and he put his arms around her. "His power is waning and that is all that matters."

"I wish I could help the Companions," Cenith said. "They have armoured jerkins and leggings, but their faces and hands aren't protected."

"Neither are you."

Jayce and Buckam each grabbed an arm of another Companion and dragged him away. Madin, Barit and Yanis struggled to their feet and helped them. The water man's bubbles grew in size, then popped, growing larger each time they formed, his body expanding and shrinking in different places at the same time.

"Father!" With a final scream, the water man burst.

Tyrsa's view whirled, making her stomach feel sick, as Cenith spun her around, sheltering her with his body. Boiling water flew by and Cenith cried out. Hissing in pain, he jerked back, releasing her. The other Tyrsa, now steadier on her feet, resumed watching the meadow.

Only the ball remained where the water man had knelt, throbbing its anger and pain. Tyrsa's agony matched it, but she forced herself to concentrate on the

Companions. Those who could move had protected the faces of the ones who couldn't. Two more stirred, though they didn't get up. The last two remained still and Tyrsa feared for them.

Cenith picked her up and strode to the pool, his jaw clenched, his upper body rigid. He set her down and lay on his stomach, just as he had before the water man tried to kill him. "Splash water on my back!"

Several red blotches marked where boiling water had hit. The other Tyrsa knelt beside him and scooped as much water as she could onto the red marks.

Jayce appeared on his other side, his right cheek bleeding from a cut beside his crooked nose. "M'lord, are ye a' right?"

"I will be. Did we lose anyone?"

"No, but there's plenty o' injuries. Every one o' us is bloodied somewhere. Jolin's got a head wound and can't see straight. I think Buckam's got broken ribs. Keev's arm's broke for sure. Dathan and Trey are still out. We're all goin' to have some lovely bruises. Lucky that thing didn't have anythin' sharp."

Tyrsa sighed in relief. At least the men were alive.

"You can stop, Lady Violet. It's going to hurt regardless." Cenith sat up.

Her other self leaned back, resting her hands on her thighs. Tyrsa tried to concentrate on what Jayce said. It helped her control the pain.

"Ye'll not be wantin' the sun on those burns, m'lord. I'll git yer shirt." Jayce strode to the blanket where Cenith's shirt, and the now ruined meal, lay.

Tyrsa didn't want food anymore, she just wanted the pain to go away.

Cenith lifted her chin, examining her eyes. "What

was that thing?"

"Tailis."

Cenith froze. "You killed a *god*?"

"No. Gods cannot die, at least not as you understand it. But he has no power here anymore. I sent him back where he came from," her other self said.

Cenith blinked. "Where did he come from?"

"Tai-Keth, when your people invaded this land three thousand years ago."

"Tai-Keth! We came from Tai-Keth?"

"Yes. I have to go. I am very tired."

"Will any more of the gods come?" Cenith asked. "I doubt we could fight another."

"I do not think so. They are not a typical family. I must go."

"But I have more questions," he said, his brow wrinkling into a frown.

"I have no more answers. Not now."

Jayce returned with Cenith's shirt and put it over his shoulders.

"Go help the others," Cenith told him, then turned back to her. He lifted her hand and kissed it. "Thank you, Lady Violet. You saved all of us."

"You are welcome. Your Tyrsa is in pain from the orb. Help her. I do not have the strength."

Concern and worry creased his brow more. "What do I need to do?"

"Whatever she requests."

As her other self retreated, Tyrsa asked, *They call you Lady Violet. Should I call you that?*

If you wish. Do not let Cenith touch your power. She faded into a quiet corner of Tyrsa's mind.

Physical pain joined emotional, searing through her

entire bod like fire. Tyrsa cried out and fell against Cenith. *No wonder Lady Violet is tired! How could she stand this?*

Cenith pulled her onto his lap and wrapped his arms around her. "What can I do?"

"Hold…me," she gasped. "I need to face the ball…so I can call it to me. Don't touch it. It will hurt you."

Cenith helped her turn so she could face her next fight. She sat between his raised knees, leaning against his chest. He held her shoulders to keep her steady. His body was still cold from the water, but she felt his warmth anyway. Tyrsa called the ball. It resisted at first, but she concentrated harder and it flew back to her to float red and angry between her open hands.

Starting with her feet, Tyrsa repeated the method of removing the physical pain she'd learned on the cliff when the Mother and Father taught her how to control her power. It retreated faster this time, now that she knew what to do. The agony slowly left her feet, her legs, then her arms, retreating to her belly. With one final concentrated effort, she banished it to the red ball. When the pain in her body fled, she allowed herself a moment of relief before attacking the next part—her emotional hurts.

Tyrsa tried to bring the good memories forward. She had more of them now, thanks to Cenith, Daric and Elessa. Stubborn as baby Rade, the red ball resisted.

"I need your love." Tyrsa could only manage a whisper.

Cenith kissed her cheek. "You will always have that, dearest."

He spoke of his love for her—how he adored her blue eyes, her pixie face, and the way she slept, like an innocent child—all whispered in her ear, broken only by kisses. The red ball shrunk, growing brighter and more angry as it fought her control. Tyrsa focused on the times spent with Cenith, both in bed and their quiet moments in front of the fire, on what she felt for the man holding her. There'd been a time, not very long ago, when she'd been afraid of men. Cenith and his friends changed that. She added the laughter, smiles and friendship of the Companions to Cenith's love.

The red faded, changing to pink, then to blazing white. The hurt, pain and loneliness fled to its corner of her mind, far from Lady Violet. Tyrsa slammed the door.

She put the white light back where it belonged, deep inside her. It felt different somehow, stronger. Gasps and cries of wonder echoed around her. Startled, she looked up. All the Companions sat on the ground near them, some holding arms or other parts where they hurt, even Dathan and Trey were awake and staring. They watched her open-mouthed, astonishment mixed with awe on their bloody faces.

Cenith wrapped his arms around her. "Do you still hurt?"

Tyrsa shook her head and shifted so she could relax in his arms, her head resting on his chest. "I'm just very tired."

"At least this time you won't sleep for two days." He paused. "Or will you?"

"I don't think so. But I do want to go home." Tyrsa didn't care how long she slept, she just wanted sleep. "I'm sorry I can't heal your burns right now."

"Don't worry about it. Did anyone check the horses?" Cenith asked the Companions.

"I did, My Lord," Buckam said. "The water came close, but not close enough. They are fine."

"Good." Cenith stood and picked Tyrsa up. "Is

anyone not capable of riding?"

"I'm worried about Jolin, My Lord," Keev said, holding his left arm. "He doesn't remember what happened."

"Neither does Trey," Barit said. "Dathan's got a nasty head wound and can't see straight."

Jolin rested his head against Keev's unhurt shoulder. Blood matted his black hair and smeared the right side of his face where someone had tried to clean him up. He had a large red mark on his jaw. "I'll be a' right. Jus' gimme a few minutes."

Keev held two fingers in front of Jolin's face. "How many do you see?"

"Four."

"Jolin, you're riding with Jayce," Cenith said. "Dathan and Trey will ride with someone else as well. All three of you probably have concussions. Jayce, you're in command of the Companions until Jolin can resume his duties."

"Aye, m'lord."

Concussions? Tyrsa didn't see them with anything different. If they had concussions, whatever they were, they must be hiding them somewhere.

Cenith set Tyrsa on her feet, and, with Jayce's help, put his shirt on properly. His burns looked bad and Tyrsa wished she had the strength to heal him and the men, but she could barely stand on her own.

Some of the Companions cleaned up the blanket, kept what they could of the food for the trip home and threw the rest over the cliff. Others brought the horses. Jolin leaned against Keev until Madin and Fallan could get him up on Jayce's horse, tying him to Jayce like they did Varth when he was hurt. Dathan rode with Madin, Trey with Barit.

Cenith insisted Tyrsa ride in front of him instead of on her pony. He'd taught her how to ride a few days ago and she liked having her own horse and the special saddle to allow for her dress, but she was glad to be in Cenith's arms. She snuggled close to him, her nose full of his strong, comforting scent and drifted into sleep.

* * * *

Artan sat on the edge of the fountain in Castle Square, head down, hands between his knees, the parchment hidden under the new tunic he'd bought that afternoon. People passed by, busy with their daily affairs; merchants calling their wares from under colourful awnings, servant women chatting as they scooped water into jugs and balanced them on their shoulders to take them back to the fancy houses where they worked. He ignored them.

He'd had breakfast at the Eye of the Yellow Cat…three fried eggs, fried bread, a large chunk of sharp white cheese and strawberries with fresh cream. A mug of breakfast ale topped it off. He'd never eaten like that before. At home it was always porridge, with sausage on Maegden's Day, at least until his mother died. After that, he had to find his own meals. Snake believed in a simple diet, porridge every morning.

After stuffing himself to the point of discomfort, Artan had come here to stare at the castle gates; to gather his nerve, he'd told himself. All he had to do was go up to the guard and announce that he had something Lord Saulth needed, something from Snake, who couldn't come himself because… That's what halted him. Why? Could he say the words? Did he dare? He didn't have the girl. Would Saulth take his anger out on him?

Lunch had been at the Donkey and Crow—chicken stew, with actual identifiable pieces of chicken in it, along with thick cut vegetables and rich gravy. Dark brown bread accompanied it, as well as a tasty yellow cheese. Artan ate until he thought his stomach would burst. Two mugs of a light ale washed it down. The afternoon sun found him back here at the fountain. The water trickling from the mouths of giant fish did little to soothe him.

The guards hadn't changed, though they would soon. Maybe the next lot wouldn't seem so intimidating. Artan had spent the last few years avoiding the guards. The idea of walking up to four of them, and actually *talking* to them, chafed like burlap on burned skin. Then some futtering child nailed him with a dog turd. The kid vanished before he could get a good look at him.

Artan didn't dare go before Lord Saulth stinking like a sick dog. Finding a new tunic took longer than planned, the colour wasn't quite right or the style didn't suit him. Once he had the tunic, new trousers were in order; they just didn't match. Neither did his boots, but the new ones wouldn't be ready for a couple of days, so he'd have to make do.

By that time, his stomach felt ready for dinner, at the Oak and Lamb this time. Slabs of beef floating in gravy, soft fluffy turnips and roasted vegetables coated in herbs. Thick white bread with creamy butter topped it off, along with three pints of a dark ale Artan had never had before.

The new lot of guards looked meaner than the old ones. Artan didn't feel very good now anyway. His gut ached, his head swam, and his hands shook. He couldn't go before Lord Saulth in that condition. Artan looked up at the sky. *Where did the sun go?* The square had grown quiet. Few people were about. Dark clouds heralded a thunder storm worthy of Maegden's wrath, not to mention the approaching curfew. *Curfew. What a stupid idea.* The thieves continued operating, curfew or no. Rain hit the cobbled street in front of him, forming rings in the fountain. *It'll ruin my new clothes.*

I have to go home. Artan stood. His head reeled, so did he. *I think I'll have porridge tomorrow.*

* * * *

Daric dropped the last sack of flour on the pile in front of him. He limped down the hall and out the kitchen door. By the time he reached the last wagon, all the sacks had been taken. Instead of quitting after the guards' shift change, Daric had decided to avoid arousing the suspicion of the other workers by finishing the job. He stood true to his word and toted two sacks, one over each shoulder, to the others' one, keeping up his limp.

Lacus paid them a few copper pieces and the kitchen staff provided food. Daric lingered over his until the last worker had left. He wandered into the busy kitchen, catching Lacus' eye.

"Got a privy I can use?" he asked.

Lacus nodded and waved him out of the kitchen into a hall with bare stone walls lit by dripping candles in wall sconces. Several ordinary wooden doors lined the right side. Daric had used each of them several times during the afternoon. All of them had been locked when the unloading was finished. The cook stopped at the first and unclipped a ring of keys from his belt. He checked for anyone watching before inserting one into the lock.

After motioning Daric in, Lacus closed the door, plunging the room into utter darkness. "Just a minute."

One sniff told Daric his belongings had arrived. He stayed where he was while Lacus fumbled with candle and striker, blinking away spots when the light flared. Barrels lined the walls. Sacks of grain leaned against them or lay piled in front or on top. His shoulders and back ached at the thought of moving them. At least he could drop the limp.

"Kalden put yer stuff there." Lacus jutted his chin to the right. Pack and bag sat on one of the barrels in the near right corner. "Now then, 'bout this tunnel…"

"If my source is correct, one of the entrances is behind those barrels and sacks." Daric pointed to the far left corner.

Lacus groaned. "Did ya 'ave t' pile so many sacks in front o' it?"

Daric jerked his thumb to the right. "I piled mine over there. Unfortunately, I wasn't in this room much." He removed the floppy hat, tossing it on top of his pack, and scrubbed his sweat damp hair.

"Well, they ain't gonna move themselves." Lacus picked up one end of a sack, Daric the other.

They'd shifted five sacks and two barrels when a shout came from the hall. "Lacus? Tillen needs you!"

"Talueth's tits! Can't that man do anythin' by 'imself?" Lacus motioned Daric behind the door before opening it. "I'm busy! Tell 'im t' figure it out 'imself!" He slammed the door. "I just know I'll get back there and find everythin' burned. Idiot. Just what I need. Lord Saulth's already in a foul mood."

"Any idea why?"

Lacus shook his head. "He don't need much o' an excuse these days. Burned dinner will send 'im on a right proper binge."

Two more barrels and Daric had enough room to manoeuvre. *Nine bricks up, three to the right.* He pushed the corresponding brick and a three-and-a-half by two foot section of wall slid back, silent as a desert cat stalking a spotted lizard. Daric hoped all the entrance hinges were cared for as well.

Lacus raised his eyes to Daric's and patted his ample stomach. "Neither one o' us is goin' t' find it easy gettin' in."

"A tight squeeze, but I've squirmed into smaller places." Daric retrieved his belongings from the corner, giving the hat to Lacus. "I don't need this anymore. Maybe someone around here could find a use for it." He dug in his pocket for the coins Lacus had given him. "Give these to Kalden. He deserves them for bringing that sack."

Lacus shrugged, stuffed the coins in his pocket and set the hat on a barrel. "I'll see he gets it. Are ya goin' straight for th' scroll? Lord Saulth's probably in th' library now. If ya wait for dinner time, 'e'll be in th' Main Hall."

"Will he go back to the library after dinner?"

Lacus stroked his moustache. "Hmmm. Good chance."

"Then I think I'll wait until late tonight. I need the time to find a way out anyway." Daric bent down and tossed the pack and bag into the tunnel.

Lacus frowned. "I'm not goin' t' be able to 'elp ya there. Won't be around. Ya can walk out o' th' kitchen, but gettin' past th' guards could be interestin'…especially after curfew."

"Don't worry about me. I'll think of something."

Daric crouched down in front of the door and duck walked through, hunching his shoulders inward. The wound in his right thigh pulled and he winced. Lacus passed him the candle. Daric raised it above his head, standing slowly, until he could see the ceiling.

"How is it in there?" Lacus asked.

"I can stand straight, surprisingly enough, though my hair touches the roof." His shoulders brushed the sides of the narrow tunnel, but few were as big as him. "There's a shelf here with a torch and striker, and another torch on the floor. I'll leave one for you if you'd like." He passed the candle back to Lacus.

"Nah. Take 'em both. You'll probably need 'em. How do ya close th' door?"

"Push on it. There's a lever on the left to pull it open from this side." Daric slung his pack and Snake's head over his shoulder. He picked up the torch and lit it. Only a small amount of smoke rose to the ceiling; a good thing, since he couldn't hold it above his head.

"I doubt I'll see you again before I leave, friend Lacus." Daric crouched and held his hand out the opening. Lacus shook it. "Thank you for everything. If I can get the scroll back to Tiras, it will help us, and Lady Tyrsa, a great deal."

"Yer welcome, Yer Excellency. I just 'ope with it gone, 'is lordship will return t' th' business o' bein' a lord."

As do I. Daric stood and pushed on the door. A tiny light on the wall showed a peep hole he had to duck to look through. Lacus stood for a moment, hands on hips. He harrumphed, shaking his head; turning, he blew out the candle and left, shrouding the room in darkness once more.

Daric strode away from the kitchen, stopping to

peer into any lit holes he could find. Most were single rooms for the staff, the rest storage rooms. He came to an intersection and decided he should have a better look at Buckam's maps. Sitting with his legs stretched out, Daric held the torch between his feet and pulled the rolled up maps out of his pack.

Judging by how far he'd walked to the intersection, Daric could get a good estimate on how long it would take him to reach the places he needed to go…the library, the Main Hall, Rymon's and Saulth's suites. One spot on the map of the first floor intrigued him. It showed the beginning of a tunnel that went nowhere.

When Daric had asked the former Bredun guard about it, Buckam said he'd drawn as far in as he could see. The young man said that particular tunnel had always been off limits, on threat of death. Daric made it his first priority.

Turning left at the intersection, he followed the map. Not long after, a glitter of light reflected up from the floor. A gold cup with four emeralds decorating it sat with a few rings and a broach. No dust covered them. Buckam had mentioned nothing about people stashing precious items in the tunnels and Daric suspected this was a recent occurrence. It appeared either the guards were helping themselves to whatever they found handy and hiding them here or someone else knew about the hidden hallways. Judging by the layer of dust on the floor, no one had used this particular tunnel in a long time, except for hiding valuables. A moment's search revealed a lever near the floor—another entrance, this one close to the loot.

The whole thing hardly surprised Daric. Given half a chance, many people would supplement their wages with a little pilfering. On his way to the mysterious tunnel, he found two more stashes and wondered if all the guards who'd watched Tyrsa had sticky fingers. Perhaps even Tajik had a hand in it.

Once Daric reached the unmapped tunnel, he found a sign nailed to the right of the entrance. 'Off limits'; right where it was supposed to be. Tyrsa's words rang in his ears. 'Buckam's heart is true…' and she was right. *So far anyway.*

Fifteen feet into the tunnel, Daric almost fell down a short flight of stairs. Steep and shadowed, he didn't see them until the last second. If he wanted to continue exploring this tunnel, he had no choice but to go down. Once at the bottom, Daric had to hunch over to walk, the smoke from the torch stinging his eyes. This tunnel was cooler and a little damp, probably a result of being deeper into the earth. It was also festooned with spiders' webs that shriveled to almost nothing from the heat of the torch. No footprints disturbed the dust. No one had been through here in a very long time. Another twenty feet led him to a right turn and a lever on the wall in front of him. He crouched and looked up at the outline of a trap door.

Sounds echoed above. Dishes clinking, voices, footsteps—the familiar noises of staff clearing up after a meal. *Must be the Main Hall. And this has to be a bolt hole.* It had to have been built at the same time as the original part of the castle. *Saulth does come from a long line of paranoids.*

A slow smile slid up Daric's face and he set Snake's head in the corner, still wrapped in his cloak. *I will definitely be back this way.* Despite the herbs and double bag, the disgusting contents of the sack churned his gut and he was glad to be rid of it for a while.

Three torches sat on a shelf in the corner. Daric jammed them into his pack. Only one path lay ahead, to the right, and he took it. Several yards later, the tunnel bent left.

After what he judged to be an hour's walk, his torch flickered low. He lit another before putting out the first. Daric dropped to his knees and rolled his aching shoulders. Working all day and then walking hunched over had done his body no favours. As he stretched his sore muscles, he pondered just how far he'd walked—a long way, even for a castle. When he'd worked out most of his body's complaints, he dug through the pack for his canteen and some food Hadera had given him.

While he ate, Daric thought about turning back, but curiosity ruled him and he had time. He tucked the canteen away and carried on. Another long walk brought him to the end of the tunnel. Small piles of chaff littered the floor. He shoved the torch closer to the ceiling. The flames burned away a remarkably solid weaving of spider's webs. It also revealed a wooden door over his head and a lever in the lower left corner of the wall. He set his ear against the door.

Several noises sifted through; muffled thumps, the whicker of a horse, a pig rooting, a cow lowing and the sad bleating of a sheep. No sound of human activity. *A barn, then.*

Daric set his pack down and placed the torch in a holder on the left wall. He pulled the lever and a metallic click sounded from the door. The noises didn't change. Lifting the door a few inches, Daric stood up straight and peered out. Just as he thought, a small barn with no one in it except a few animals.

He opened the door all the way and pulled himself up. The livestock, in pens or stalls, ignored him. Rain battered the old roof, dripping in a few places. Wind rattled grey boards and sang a lonely song in the rafters. Cracks in the walls showed a dark sky, not all of it due to the lowering sun. He crept to the barn doors and opened one a crack. The single horse, old, swaybacked and rheumy-eyed, whickered.

Heavy clouds coated the sky, leaving a gap between them and the distant mountains on the horizon. The sun perched in between, igniting the dark undersides of the clouds and the snowy tips of the peaks in a blaze of reds, pinks and oranges, and highlighting the pouring rain. A spectacular view, but one Daric couldn't take the time to enjoy.

A large wooden house sat several yards away, a tiny light flickering in one window. Another barn, larger and newer, could be seen on the other side of the house. Not wishing to be spotted, he closed the door and glanced around. Another, smaller, door sat opposite. He strode to that one and peeked out. Fields full of hay, cut and ready to be gathered, spread as far as he could see. Daric glanced at the clouds and the rain pelting those fields. He couldn't help but feel sorry for the farmer and sent a prayer to Niafanna to put an end to the onslaught.

Left or right? Daric chose left and crept out the door, keeping close to the wall of the barn. He snuck a peek around the corner. The town of Valda crouched dark against the grey clouds. *About five miles...that feels right for the time I walked.* Daric couldn't keep the grin from his face. *Not only a way in, but a way out. Could it really be this simple?*

Buckam is turning into a large asset. I wonder how Tyrsa knew we needed him as a Companion? If they'd left the young guard in the kitchen, he wouldn't have been available at that meeting to draw the maps. *He's made my mission a whole lot easier.* Daric had to admit, when Barit asked him how he planned on retrieving the scroll he'd had no idea. Buckam's maps not only made the attempt feasible, it made it easy.

The first lord of Bredun had been afraid of something, that much was obvious. The tunnels let him spy on his dukes, nobles and staff. The sheer mass and construction of the castle would intimidate the most ambitious enemy and this route would have been his last resort in case of total disaster.

I wonder if the farmer knows it's here? How could he not? Perhaps it was a secret handed down from father to son. Judging by the fine house, it was a paid secret. Then Daric wondered if the farmer would know someone had been here, the straw over the door had slid off when he opened it.

Daric spun and entered the barn. He lowered himself into the tunnel and pulled the door down, leaving it open enough for him to reach around and push straw back onto it. His unusual height and long arms did have their advantages. Hoping his attempts had been sufficient, Daric hunched over and closed the door, taking note of another point of interest—all the doors he'd found so far had torches and strikers. This one didn't. *A rarely used route, and not from this direction.* Better for him. He picked up pack and torch and started the long trek back to the bolt hole in the Main Hall.

Quiet, and Snake's head, awaited him. Daric paused and thought about what to do next; check out more of the castle, go for the scroll or deal with his smelly companion. *Check out the castle, then get the scroll. The head I can take care of on the way out.* It would be later then and he'd be less likely to be seen, both inside and out.

Digging out Buckam's maps, he headed for the

southeast tower and the narrow, circular steps that led to the other floors. He started at the fourth floor, and Saulth's suite.

No peephole here. The ruling lord would hardly want someone spying on him, but would still need an escape route. The hidden door's lever sat at waist level, beside the fireplace wall. At least he didn't have to worry about someone seeing the torch. Daric listened to a woman humming a simple tune, but no sound of Saulth. He stayed a few minutes longer, then decided to pay a visit to Rymon's rooms.

Daric had just reached the third floor when he heard someone coming up the stairs. Doubting it was Lacus, he extinguished his torch and pressed against the tunnel wall hoping whoever it was turned the other way. Niafanna protected him. A large figure, carrying a torch, headed left. Daric decided to follow. After a few minutes, the man stopped and looked backwards. Daric recognized him and his heart raced. Tajik grunted before moving on. Not long after, Bredun's guard-commander set the torch in a bracket, took a few more steps, then stopped. He set an eye to a hole in the wall and Daric wondered who he was watching so intently.

Daric didn't dare come close enough to listen to what interested Tajik. He marked the wall with soot from the extinguished torch, determined to come back this way to see what was so engrossing.

Tajik's torch had burned low when he finally picked it up and headed back…towards Daric. Using all his stealth abilities, Daric made for the stairs and the tunnel beyond, praying the guard-commander only wanted the stairs. Niafanna heard his prayer. Tajik headed down and when Daric could hear no more sounds, he relit his torch and found his way to the mark and the peephole where Tajik had stood.

A chubby, middle-aged, half-dressed nobleman sat in a bedroom, alternately sipping wine and kissing a scantily clad young woman perched on his lap. Both bore the flush of recent lovemaking. Daric knew Tajik to be a tough, ornery bastard, but not a pervert—unless he gathered information for Saulth to use against that noble. Daric shook his head and returned to the task at hand. Rymon's room was next.

The councillor's suite lay directly under Saulth's. This one had a spy hole. The Lords of Bredun didn't even trust their councillors. Rymon's furniture reflected the nature of the man, elegant simplicity and only what her needed. A fire crackled near the peephole, odd for this time of year, but Daric could see no sign of Rymon, even after waiting several minutes in case he was using the privy.

Next stop, second floor and the library. They'd either be there or, perhaps, Saulth's study on the first floor. Another trip down the stairs, a longer, convoluted one through the tunnel, and he heard voices. Daric identified Saulth before he reached the library. No spy hole here, either.

"How much longer do I have to wait?" A fist hitting a table echoed down the tunnel.

"I've heard Cenith has doubled the guard at the station. Perhaps he's increased it elsewhere and they're having trouble escaping." Daric recognized Rymon's voice. He wished Ardael's gods could have arranged for Rymon to be Lord of Bredun instead of Saulth.

"If he doesn't turn up soon, I'll have to assume he failed and think of something else."

Daric froze. *I truly hope they're not talking about the assassins. The apprentice must have made it back by now.*

After a moment's silence, Saulth said, "I'm going to my room. I need to think."

"I bid you goodnight then, My Lord. Pleasant dreams."

A door opened and closed. Daric heard a sigh, then the slow shuffle-thump of an old man walking with a cane. After Rymon left, he waited several minutes before opening the hidden door disguised as a narrow bookcase beside the fireplace. It swung out on quiet hinges. Rymon had snuffed out the candles and fragrant smoke lingered, smelling sweet after the dust of the tunnels and Snake's foul remains.

The torch showed Daric the cold fireplace, the shelves heavy with books, the delicate tables holding candles with their still smoking wicks, and dark green velvet drapes adorning tall casement windows spotted with rain. It also lit up a large table with pieces of a scroll carefully laid out under a thin sheet of glass. Four pieces of old parchment; Cenith's part glaring in its absence.

Shock gripped Daric's heart, making it skip a beat. *It's not here! I've failed my lady!*

Chapter Six

"We spent four hours making a return journey that should have taken less than two," Cenith told Ors, wrapping up the strange tale.

The guard-commander scratched his bald head. "Not that I think you're lying, My Lord, but I'm having a hard time believing all this." He sat next to the fireplace in Cenith's suite, in the small chair meant for use at the writing table.

"So am I, and I saw it with my own eyes." Cenith perched on the edge of his usual chair, too sore to lean back. He wore nothing on his upper half except the honeyed salve Garun, the keep physician, had spread on the burns.

Tyrsa occupied the other big chair by the fireplace, her bare feet curled up under her dress. She had slept the entire trip home, but woke when they arrived in Tiras, much to Cenith's relief. Unusually quiet, she stared at the hearth and the symbols glued there.

Cenith had heard all about her first experience on the cliff with the glowing ball she called her power. He'd put it down as a dream...until today. *A god. Tyrsa fought, and beat, a god.* Not just Tyrsa, it had taken Lady Violet's help as well. Two Tyrsas in one body, another concept he found difficult to handle.

"Garun is keeping Jolin, Dathan and Trey in the infirmary," Ors continued. "All have concussions, as you suspected, though Jolin's is the worst. The last thing he remembers is riding out this morning. Garun doesn't want him to return to duty for a month. Dathan and Trey should be back in two weeks or so. Keev and Buckam will both be out for six weeks. The rest have various cuts, bumps and bruises, so I'm giving them the next two days off."

Cenith nodded. They deserved it. The Companions had fought like demons to protect them. That left just Varth and Ead, who wouldn't put in an appearance until midnight. "The regular guard will just have to fill in."

"I've already adjusted the roster. Did Garun accept your reason for the burns?"

"I don't think so, though he didn't come right out and accuse me of lying."

The people of the town had stared in shock at the sight of their lord leading a battered group of men to the keep. Rumours would fly. Cenith and the men had tossed around some ideas on their journey home. After much debate they finally settled on bandits.

The story said Cenith and the Companions had surprised the thieves at their camp. They made it five bandits to one Companion and the bandits were armed with bludgeons; a ragged, but desperate, group that had wandered in from the plains looking to steal whatever they could find. Cenith had been burned in the confusion when one of them threw a pot of hot water at him. He told Garun the tall tale lying on his stomach while the healer applied the salve, so he didn't have to look him in the eye.

"Will Garun say anything?" Ors asked.

"He won't. I asked him not to." Bandit attacks were nothing new, but for a group to cause that much damage to armed soldiers sounded off, even five on one. Cenith couldn't think of anything better though. He held up a finger. "One thing I realized on the trip home…if Tyrsa continues to fight creatures like that, the Companions need more protection. If they'd had shields, breastplates and helmets, they'd have taken fewer injuries."

Ors harrumphed. "That's a problem easily fixed. I'll order them tomorrow."

Cenith gave him a wry smile. "Complete with fairy orchids?"

Ors chuckled. "What else? And speaking of uniforms, the tabards came in today."

"Figures, with almost half the Companions unable to wear them. Keep them for now. We'll bring them out when everyone's back on duty. Maybe we can hold a proper ceremony."

Cenith glanced at Tyrsa. She hadn't taken her eyes off the hearth. A tiny frown creased her brow. He'd have to wait until Ors left to find out what bothered her. Sometimes her answers were best left to his ears only.

Ors cleared his throat. "If you don't mind, My Lord, I know you're tired and in pain, but I think we should discuss the consequences of what happened today."

"Speak your mind, Ors."

The older man leaned forward. He rested his forearms on his thighs and tapped his fingers together for a moment. Taking a deep breath, he said, "First of all, I want it understood that I am loyal to both you and your lady. I don't want this taken the wrong way. I will always honour my oath and protect the both of you to the best of my abilities, even if it requires I die to achieve it."

Cenith had never suspected otherwise. Still, Ors' speech moved him. He took a moment to respond. "I'm aware of that. I've never doubted your loyalty."

Ors nodded once. "Then there will be no misunderstanding. What I wish to say is conjecture. I'm thinking like an ordinary person, a miner, a farmer, a merchant; those who go about their everyday business where nothing much changes from day to day. They wake up, go to work, come home, pay homage to the gods, go to bed and repeat everything the next day."

"Understood."

"If Lady Tyrsa really did defeat Tailis," Ors continued, "I have to assume that's why she's here, to destroy our gods."

My Tyrsa? Cenith's eyes shifted to her. She still stared at the hearth. How could anyone so tiny, so innocent, defeat the gods of Ardael? Yet, how could he deny what he'd witnessed today? Lady Violet wouldn't lie about who the creature was…that Cenith knew, though he couldn't say why.

"I've grown up with these gods, as has everyone in Ardael," Ors said, dragging Cenith's attention back to him. "When this news gets out, there'll be trouble on a grand scale. Even if our own people don't revolt, the rest of the country will be on us. You don't mess with people's gods. In view of that, why would we let her do it?"

Cenith's first thought was, *How do I stop her?* They both looked at Tyrsa. Her gaze remained firmly on the symbols, but her frown had deepened. Another thought hit him.

"I wonder if that's why Saulth gave her to me." Cenith's heart skipped a beat. "I'm assuming he knows what she's supposed to do from the scroll. She banishes the gods, sending Ardael into civil war. Saulth could then convince the other lords to set him up as leader of the army sent to destroy us. He's the only one of the lords, besides me, who's capable of leading a military force. Once he'd wiped us out, it wouldn't take much to declare himself king."

Ors eyebrows shot up. "You took that one step further than I did. I figured we'd be on the losing end of a war, but Saulth as king?" He shrugged. "I could see him going for it. Either way, the question remains. Why would we let her destroy our gods?"

Tyrsa leapt out of her chair and almost ran to the balcony doors. Guilt washed over Cenith. They shouldn't have talked in front of her like that.

"You don't understand." She flung the doors open.

Dark clouds replaced the warm sun they'd ridden home under. A breeze, cooled by rain, struck Cenith's burned back sending a shiver through him. Another eddy passed in front, low to the ground, brushing his bare feet.

"Look!" Ors pointed to the hearth.

The wavy ash lines representing Tailis swirled up into the eddy and vanished. Cenith stared speechless at the hearth. So did Ors. No amount of scrubbing could remove those symbols and now a mere breath of wind had obliterated one but left the others intact.

Tyrsa appeared at Cenith's side. "I don't understand it, either." She looked at the remaining symbols, her pixie face sad. "I do know that these gods are not good." She pointed at the ones representing Maegden and the rest of his brood. "They don't help you when you need it. They stopped helping a long, long time ago. The ground hurts because of them. Your gods have grown lazy and arrogant. They take your worship, but don't give back."

Cenith had never heard her speak like that or for that long, nor did he realize she knew some of the words.

121

Despite the seriousness of the subject, he felt proud of her, then wondered if Lady Violet had a hand in those words.

She walked to the bedroom door and opened it. "You told me that storms, floods and big waves have ruined parts of Ardael. The people prayed and gave Tailis things, but he did nothing to stop them. Remember, Tailis attacked me first." Tyrsa closed the door behind her.

Cenith looked at Ors, who blinked several times. "She has a point."

"About the gods doing nothing? Or Tailis attacking first?" Ors asked.

"Both, I suppose." Cenith rose and stepped over to the hearth. He scraped the symbol for Aja with a fingernail. The pair of dice depicting the unpredictable god remained hard and immovable. He shook his head. "If Tailis came after her, I have to assume the others will."

"Now there's a frightening thought." Ors had never looked so grim. "I doubt putting an entire square of regiments in and outside your rooms would help. Not that they would fit."

A square. Fifty regiments of fifty men each. After watching Tailis batter his men about like insects, Cenith doubted numbers would matter much. He glanced at the bedroom door, his heart thudding with a rhythm that had nothing to do with lovemaking. *How can I protect her? How can anyone?*

"It sounds like we don't have a choice," Cenith said. "Either she defeats the gods, or the country continues to suffer. A few more years of this and there'll be no prairie left to grow crops. Gold and jewels won't buy what isn't there. Famine and plague will kill thousands. We'll be easy pickings for not only the Tai-Keth, but anyone else who has half a mind to take what isn't theirs." He

122

scrubbed his face with one hand, tired but needing to think. "When it comes down to it, the number of guards here won't make much of a difference. This is Tyrsa's fight. We'll just have to be watchful and do what we can to help her.

"As far as the people finding out what's happening," Cenith continued. "The Companions are sworn to secrecy and I know you won't talk. If we can keep it quiet, I doubt people will notice anything different. Tyrsa's right. The people and priests are praying and offering everything from food and expensive spices to gold. Nothing's changed. If anything, it's grown worse. Maybe if she's able to defeat them all, daunting as it sounds, it will be easier to convince the people that the gods have failed them."

"Then what do we do?" Ors asked. "People need gods. I know men who wouldn't be able to cope without knowing there's someone with a greater power to praise in times of plenty and blame when things go wrong."

"We could continue the secret. Just say nothing and let people carry on as before. As I said, I doubt anyone would notice they're not here." Cenith reflected on his conversations with Daric and how adamantly he'd defended the gods who now wanted to kill his wife. He never dreamt he could even contemplate his next thought. "On the other hand, the scroll mentions Niafanna and Cillain. They're worshipped not only in Callenia, but in the West Downs, Syrth, and Cambrel, under different names. We just join in."

Ors flashed him a sceptical glance. "I didn't know that."

"Daric told me years ago. I'll admit, I'd always wondered why we didn't worship them until today when

Lady Violet said we'd brought our gods from Tai-Keth."

The guard-commander made a rude noise. "Another thing I find hard to believe. Tai-Keth has been our enemy for longer than we've had written records. For that matter, if we and the horse lords worship the same gods, why are they always trying to take over Ardael? You'd think the gods wouldn't allow it."

"More room, better climate, a chance to kill, loot, and rape. What other excuse would they need? And if the gods don't care...do I have to say more?"

Ors grunted again. Hands clasped behind his back, he stared at the hearth. "I think I need time to absorb all this. The whole thing rubs me the wrong way, but I'll follow your orders, My Lord." Ors stood and stretched. "Now, if you'll pardon me, I'll take my leave and go find some dinner. Yours should be here shortly."

No sooner had the words left his mouth than a knock sounded at the door. At Cenith's request, one of the guards outside opened it and a servant entered pushing a table on wheels. The rich aroma of beef and spiced vegetables wafted through the room, borne on a breeze from the open balcony doors.

"I bid you a good evening, My Lord," Ors said, adding a bow.

"And you." Cenith closed the balcony doors against the storm, retrieved Tyrsa from the bedroom and sat her at the table. Once the servant left he said, "I'm sorry for talking about you like that. We got carried away in our discussion."

Tyrsa shrugged. "Is it better to talk about someone when they're not there?"

A difficult question to answer. "Actually, it's considered rude to talk about people behind their backs, but it's done all the time. Especially in cases like this, where the principality could be in danger."

Tyrsa poked at her mashed turnips. "I didn't mean to cause trouble."

Cenith reached across the table and took her hand. "You had no choice. That thing would have killed all of us if you hadn't beaten him. We owe you our lives."

She peered up at him through long lashes. "I think I'm going to have to do it again. Tailis' brothers and sisters won't like what I did."

"I know." Cenith squeezed her hand before releasing it. "Ors, the Companions and I will help you as much as we can. Just let us know what you need."

Cenith turned his attention to filling his stomach. Jarven had outdone himself and he dug into his full plate with relish.

Tyrsa poked at her food for a while before cutting a piece of beef smothered in rich, dark gravy. "Cenith?"

"Yes?"

"Can we stay home tomorrow?"

Cenith laughed. "Gladly."

* * * *

Tyrsa sat hunched on the bed, her arms wrapped around Baybee. Sleeping half the day meant no sleep now, but that wasn't the only reason she was still awake. Something troubled her, though she couldn't say what. It was as if she had tried to do something but it had gone wrong. All she had done after dinner was talk with Cenith about Tailis and then Garun had come with more salve for Cenith's back and a drink to help him sleep. The fight, though bad for Cenith and the Companions, had gone right for her, despite facing her pain again. She pushed the strange feeling away, not knowing what else to do with it.

Tyrsa laid her head on her knees so she could watch Cenith, sprawled on his stomach, taking up most of the bed. The drink Garun gave him had worked quickly. His burns looked as red and angry as the ball that had held her power earlier that day. White spots, 'blisters' Cenith called them, had formed. It all looked so painful, but he refused to let her heal them. He said she was too tired from the fight.

I'm not tired now. Maybe it'll make me tired. Setting Baybee on the pillow, Tyrsa knelt beside him, careful in her movements. Garun said Cenith would sleep until morning, but she wasn't sure about his 'potion'. Tyrsa could find no place to lay her hands flat without touching a burn, so she used her fingertips, hoping it would work. This was still so new to her, but then, so was almost everything now.

She reached for her power, pulsing quietly within. It had felt different when she finally brought it under control earlier that day. Stronger. She felt that strength now. Tyrsa channelled her power to her hands. A warm, white glow flowed down her arms, lit her fingers and spread over Cenith's back.

Deep in her mind, the hurts, the pains she had suffered, tried to escape, rattled at the door, but she had locked those away. She didn't need them this time. Tyrsa knew what to do, from the time she'd accidently healed Varth and then when she'd saved Cenith's life. She still felt pain, hissing as Cenith's agony became hers. Under her gentle touch, the white blisters flattened, the red faded, until nothing of the burns remained.

Tyrsa lay back on her pillows, her glowing hands

resting on her lap. She closed her eyes, centering her power to remove the pain. Bad as this was, the agony she had to control earlier had been far worse and the whole experience was much easier than when she'd healed Cenith at the station. Making use of her new strength, she opened the door to pain, forced this one inside and slammed it shut.

She let out a long breath. Reluctant to release her power so soon, Tyrsa relaxed and let it wash over her. It calmed and soothed. Maybe she could sleep now. She started to pull her power back to the glowing ball inside her. A voice sounded from a far corner of her mind.

Not yet. We have work to do, Lady Violet said. *Let me come forward.*

As they passed, Tyrsa said, *I thought you were tired.*

I was, but I have rested sufficiently for what we have to do. It is about your strange feeling. We have to talk to Daric.

Daric? *But he isn't here.*

We are going to him. That new strength you gained today will help us. It is important. Lady Violet took control of Tyrsa's body. She walked to the bedroom door and opened it, closing it quietly behind her.

Where did that strength come from? I didn't have it before.

Lady Violet glanced at the hearth and the space where Tailis' symbol had sat. *It is Tailis' strength. We took his power when we defeated him. You can control water now. Spend some time practicing with it, but only use a small amount and do it when no one is watching.*

I didn't know we could do that, Tyrsa said. *It's a good thing.*

It is fortunate that we took his power. We will need it in the future. This is only going to get worse. Her other self walked to the balcony doors and opened them.

The wind blew rain in. Tyrsa's body shivered. Lady Violet gripped the iron railing with both still-glowing hands and spread her feet apart. Dark, swirling clouds had swallowed the mountain peaks. Tiny dots of light showed where people in the town were still awake. No one wandered the rain soaked courtyard except the guards on duty, cloaked against the storm.

Now then, Lady Violet said. *I am going to separate from you, but I will not have a solid body. I need you to stay here and concentrate on your power, just as you did a few minutes ago. Center on it, let it flow, and I will be able to use it to travel to Valda, and Daric.*

That's easy. Tyrsa took a few deep breaths and concentrated on the glowing ball inside her belly. The cool wind and hard rain made it harder than she thought. Thunder boomed in the distance and she jumped.

It is only noise, Lady Violet chastised. *Force yourself to ignore the storm. And keep your eyes open. I need you to see what I see. It is the only way you can learn.*

Tyrsa concentrated, shoving aside the roar of thunder that followed another flash of lightning. The air in front of her shimmered and her other self appeared. She stood on the opposite side of the railing, floating like her ball of power. It was like looking at herself in Cenith's big mirror, except Tyrsa could see the town, mountains and clouds through her, and her body didn't stop the rain.

No one but you can see me unless I wish otherwise. This is not as easy as you think. I have a long way to go and you must concentrate on your power the entire time I am gone. If you do not, I will be lost. Now I must be off. With that, Lady Violet rose into the air and headed east toward the town. She didn't walk, nor did she fly like a bird. Lady Violet just floated.

Through her other self's eyes, Tyrsa watched mountains shrouded in cloud and valleys blanketed in soft fog pass under her feet. They ended abruptly at the guard station, changing to scrub covered ridges, with their thick bushes and scraggly trees, and the rolling plains she had travelled over to get to her new home. Memories of those days with Cenith, Daric and the Companions drifted along with her. So much had happened since then.

No moon shone on the fields, making them dark and uninteresting, a patchwork of greys and black. Soon, a town larger than Tiras appeared. *This is the city of Valda,* Lady Violet said. *This is where you were born.*

Valda looked very different from Tiras. Tyrsa didn't remember it. She only remembered fighting Daric and then waking up with Cenith and the Companions, surrounded by trees.

This town had a lot more streets and the buildings were made of both wood and stone. Saulth's keep didn't look like Cenith's either, other than it was also made of stone. Rain fell here too, running down the streets in rivers. People huddled in the spaces between buildings, trying to keep dry and sleep at the same time. The people of Dunvalos Reach didn't live in these spaces. *Why don't they live in houses like the other people?*

They do not have the money. Bredun is not like Dunvalos Reach. Talk to Cenith about it. We do not have time.

Lady Violet floated down, past the outside gates to the stairs leading up to the main doors. The guards standing there didn't see her. She carried right on through the doors, as if they weren't there. A momentary darkness, and they stood in a large, candlelit room with hallways leading off the sides. Lady Violet paused, tilted her head as

129

if in concentration, then drifted through the open doors in front of them to a larger room, passing two more guards.

I know this place. Her old room lay not far away. Tyrsa had no desire to see it. It felt odd looking at this room again. For one thing, she could smell nothing. This room had always had its own particular smell, of smoke, old wood and men. Though few candles were lit, there should still be the smell of beeswax.

Her other self floated to a place behind the big chair Saulth had been sitting in when he gave her to Cenith. Lady Violet looked down and sank into the floor.

* * * *

Daric sat in the corner of the narrow stone tunnel beneath the main hall. He rested his arms on his upraised knees and leaned his head against the wall, staring at the wooden bolt hole. His pack and Snake's head lay next to him. A torch, flickering in an iron holder, cast wavering shadows in both tunnels.

I've failed. How can I possibly track the assassin down? The man could be anywhere between here and Tiras. Perhaps he'd found out the others were dead and had gone into hiding. He could show up tomorrow, next week or never. Should he wait? Did he have the time? Daric had to get back to Tiras. Who knew what other attempts Saulth might make, not realizing Cenith no longer had the parchment?

Daric well remembered the last time he'd failed on a mission. He'd been eighteen years old. His master at the time, a Cambrellian earl named Zayden, had wanted a Syrthian rival assassinated. Incorrect intelligence and a bad call on Daric's part had resulted in him barely escaping with his life. He'd been lucky that Zayden only dismissed him. The man hadn't tolerated failure. Since then, Daric didn't either. Not in himself.

He regretted leaving Zayden's service. Besides teaching him fighting and stealth skills, the man had insisted he learn how to read and write Cambrellian and Syrthian as well as his own language. How much more knowledge could he have gained? The experience had taught Daric to do his own intelligence and make contingency plans.

Perhaps he could make a few discreet inquiries about the location of Snake's hideout. He could pretend his 'master' wished dealings with the assassin, but that would take valuable time

A wisp of cloud drifted down through the bolt hole and hovered in front of him. He closed his eyes and rubbed them. *I'm tired, that's all, but I have to do something with this head.* Much longer and the stink would leach through the entire castle.

Daric opened his eyes. Tyrsa stood in front of him, the shadows cast by the torch visibly dancing through her. She resembled what he'd always pictured a ghost would look like. *I'm seeing things. I must be more tired than I thought.* Then he noticed her eyes. He leapt to his feet, and banged his head on the ceiling. "Lady Violet!"

"No, please sit. You will be more comfortable."

Daric did so, rubbing the injury. "How…"

"I'm using Tyrsa's power. I do not have much time, but there is much to say."

"Is there a problem in Tiras?" Daric listened, first in dismay, then with pride for both Tyrsa and the Companions as Lady Violet told him an incredible story. He resisted the temptation to interrupt with his many questions until she'd finished.

"Has Ors arranged for replacements for the Companions?" Daric's first concern lay with his lord and lady's safety.

"Yes. I cannot discuss this matter with you any further. I grow tired and still have the return journey to make," Lady Violet said. "There is a more important matter to discuss."

"The scroll." Daric sighed, disappointed his other questions would have to wait. "I'm sorry, My Lady. I've failed you. The assassin hasn't returned with our section. Either he's chosen to keep the thing or he died somewhere on route."

"I do not know why he has not turned it over to Saulth, but I do know he is alive, in Valda, and will come tomorrow." She held her hand up as Daric opened his mouth. "I cannot tell you how I know, only that I do. Be patient. Try again tomorrow night, then hurry back to Tiras. You are needed."

Hope flared in Daric's heart. "I will do as My Lady commands."

"I must go. We grow weary. I..." Lady Violet gasped and her eyes widened in first surprise, then fright.

Daric rose to his knees. "Lady Violet! What is it?"

"Someone..." She screamed, twisting like the wraith she resembled, as something pulled her through the ceiling. Her cry echoed through the tunnel.

Daric dove to grab her legs, but his hands passed right through her and she vanished. He landed hard on the floor of the tunnel.

"Tyrsa!" Daric stared at the roof, his heart pounding. He stood and released the catch on the bolt hole. Lifting the trap door, he peered over the edge. The back of Saulth's chair stood in front of him. No guards

132

were in sight, neither was Lady Violet. He pulled himself far enough out of the hole to see the main doors and the two soldiers standing there. Fortunately, they faced the other direction, oblivious to what had just occurred in the tunnel.

Daric took a last look around before ducking back into the hole, resigned to the fact that he could do nothing for Lady Violet except complete his mission and return home as quick as possible. Cenith and the Companions would have to deal with this. He sent a prayer to Niafanna and Cillain.

Chapter Seven

Tyrsa gasped as Lady Violet flew backwards through Saulth's big chair, past the guards and out the door. Whatever had hold of Lady Violet pulled her out of the castle much faster than she had entered.

What's happening? Tyrsa cried.

Something has hold of me! But I do not know who, or what. Is there anyone on your end interfering?

No!

Can you follow the link back? her other self asked.

I don't know.

Tyrsa tried to pull herself away from Lady Violet, concentrate on the iron railing under her hands, the rain lashing at her cold body, but Valda flashed by in a dizzying blur of shadowy greys and browns to be replaced by fields and wet country lanes, muted by the darkness of the storm. She closed her eyes, but that only made her stomach churn and she thought she'd throw up.

Lightning lit the swirling clouds, turning them, for an instant, from black to silver grey. Tyrsa focused on the vanishing town instead. It helped, until it disappeared from sight. Nausea watered her mouth, turned her tummy sour. She gave up trying to follow the link; it took all she had just to keep her dinner down. A boom of thunder rolled across the shallow hills of the plains, adding to the terror.

Somewhere between Valda and Tiras, Lady Violet

slammed into something hard. It bounced twice, as a bed did if you jumped on it; except a bed didn't stick to you like this thing did. Lady Violet tried to move her arms and legs, with no success, and looked down, allowing Tyrsa to see what had trapped her other self.

Thick green ropes, woven from grasses, crisscrossed in a pattern Tyrsa had seen many times. Little creatures Cenith called spiders made them, but she'd never seen a web this big or this colour. She also didn't see what the ends attached to; they just disappeared into the dark night.

Lady Violet hung several feet above the ground, arms outstretched, just as Tyrsa had done the night the Mother and Father talked to her. *Could this be them?*

No. I do not feel their presence. Lady Violet struggled to free herself. Her legs weren't loose like Tyrsa's had been; they spread as far as her nightgown would allow, her feet stuck to the web. The sticky green ropes held her fast, even her hair. *This is someone else.*

Fear gripped Tyrsa's heart as tight as the web holding Lady Violet. *Could it be one of the gods?*

I suspect so. Lady Violet sounded tired. *If it is, we have a problem. A big one.*

Before Tyrsa could respond, a double fork of lightning shattered the night sky in front of her. White spots danced against a black curtain and a rustling noise sounded from below just as a roll of thunder shattered the night.. A dark shadow separated itself from the rain flattened grasses beneath her. As the spots faded, the shape resolved itself into that of a woman.

At first Tyrsa thought it might be Shival. Another flash revealed not the dark goddess' pale features, but skin of nut brown and hair the colour of ripe grain, waving like long grass in a gentle breeze. She wore a sleeveless, plaited dress of green and gold grasses that blended into the field below, and a nasty smile.

Lady Violet knew her. *Keana!*

How can she see you? Tyrsa asked.

I am not quite in the real world. She and the other gods live in this realm. I was hoping I was too small to notice.

"Shival was right. You are nothing but an insect. And now you are caught in an insect's trap." As she spoke, Keana's wide mouth moved in an odd way. Her lips seemed to ripple like grain in the wind. Like Tailis' hair, once it caught the eye, it didn't want to let go.

Pay no attention to her little tricks, Tyrsa!

Lady Violet's stern voice snapped Tyrsa alert. She dragged her attention to the rest of the woman's face, lean and hard, with edges as sharp as a knife. Eyes the colour of rich earth glared back at her. The storm raged around them, the rain beating the ripened stalks to the ground and drowning new shoots. Yet the goddess remained dry.

"You have been a naughty girl and must be punished. What you did to Tailis was unforgivable. Not that I like him, but he is my brother." Keana ran her hand through the grain waving at her knees, collecting several stalks. "You just happened to catch Tailis off guard. He's stupid anyway. Nothing but water for brains." She laughed. Tyrsa didn't. "With you stuck like that, you cannot use your pitiful magic against me."

The goddess hummed a tune while she plaited the ends of the stalks together. Tyrsa watched what took shape, panic throwing her mind into confusion. *No hurt!*

Once again, Lady Violet's thoughts broke into hers. *Tyrsa! Do not give in to your fear. Fight it! Stuck like this, I cannot use your power as I did with Tailis. You are going to*

136

have to do this on your own.

Without warning, Keana drew back her arm and swung the three-stranded grass lash at Lady Violet. It tore through her thin nightgown as if it wasn't there. Her other self screamed; so did Tyrsa, who shared every bit of the pain. She felt the cuts open on Lady Violet's skin, her skin. Blood from the three stripes across her chest and stomach stained her nightgown.

Memories of another lashing beat at the door Tyrsa had built to hide them. She fought to keep it closed. The lash came down again, across her legs this time. Both Tyrsas screamed in unison. The door rattled and shook. *I can't do this!*

I will try to take your pain. Lady Violet said. *You concentrate on defeating her. Do not forget to keep feeding me power.*

How can I beat her? Without her glowing ball, there was no way of reaching the goddess.

The lash fell a third time, catching Lady Violet's chest, right arm and face. She cried out in agony. The cuts opened, but this time Tyrsa hardly felt them. Despite the hurts clamouring behind it, the door to her painful past remained tightly shut.

Think of something! Her other self's voice already sounded weak and tired. Again the lash struck. Keana's wicked laugh drifted on the storm, distorted her face.

Without access to her power, what could she do? Tyrsa thought back to that morning and the fights she had seen between Keev and Dathan, and the one with the water man. She thought on what the Companions had done. Tyrsa had no weapons, as the men had, and no way to reach Keana even if she did. Her pain and fear gave way to anger and resentment. *How dare you! We beat Tailis! We can beat you too!*

Her thoughts blurred—Keev and Dathan, the little she had watched of Cenith's fight with Jolin, the water man most prominent—blending with rage that she could think of nothing to put an end to the pain. Tailis holding Cenith down, beating back the Companions… Frustration added its flavour to the mix. Tyrsa's mind whirled until she wanted to throw up.

Lady Violet's concentration remained on Keana and the goddess' arrogant features, but Tyrsa could look anywhere in her other self's view. Odd movement behind Keana caught her attention. Everywhere the rain pelted down, except just past the goddess where it bent inwards, collecting into an already existing pool. The water moved; not with the wind, but up, into a lumpy mass that grew while Tyrsa watched.

Keana relaxed her arm, the red-tipped lash resting against her thigh. She tilted her head first one way, then the other. "It's pretty, you know, the way the rain mixes with your blood, washing it away while more leaks out." Keana put a finger to her lips and tapped them. "The shreds of your gown have turned pink with it. A nice shade, I think."

Tyrsa pushed away thoughts of Lady Violet and her agony; she couldn't let the pain take control of her. She had to pay attention to the pool and what happened there, while feeding Lady Violet some of her remaining strength. It took all her concentration.

The water form grew until it reached Keana's height. Tyrsa thought the goddess might be as tall as Daric, but from her elevated level on the web, it was hard to say for sure. More water poured into the lump, from the rain and what lay on the ground. Soon, it stood much taller than Keana. Tyrsa wondered why the goddess didn't see it, then realized her attention lay with Lady Violet.

"I can feel how tired and weak you are, little insect." Keana swung the lash back and forth along her leg, making a swishing noise against the grass of her dress. "It will not be long now and my sister can have your soul to play with." She laughed again, a cackle that made Tyrsa shiver.

Can Shival take my soul? Tyrsa didn't know, but a stray thought from Lady Violet let her know just what a soul was.

Again the lash struck. The form behind the goddess took shape, human shape, with waterfall hair. With a rising horror, Tyrsa knew what it was…*Tailis*! Her heart sank and she waited for him to join in killing Lady Violet, and her, but he didn't. The god stood, staring at her, as if awaiting instruction.

Then Tyrsa remembered Lady Violet said she had his power. *I did this?* If her anger had created this Tailis, maybe she could control him.

"And now you die." Keana raised her arm, the look on her face one of vengeful glee.

Stop her! Tyrsa threw all her will into the command.

The water man grabbed Keana's wrist and spun her around.

"Tailis!" Keana cried. "How did you get your powers back?"

His other hand smashed into the goddess' face, spraying a thick rope of blood onto Lady Violet's torn gown, mingling with the red stains already streaking the pale fabric. A twist of his hand broke her wrist and she dropped the lash.

Keana cried out. "What are you doing?" She tried

to hit him with her left hand, but it passed right through, just as the Companions' efforts had done.

The water man punched her again, this time in the stomach. The goddess clutched her belly with her free hand. The stalks of grass surrounding Tailis' double grew and thickened. They wrapped themselves around the water man's legs and arms, but grabbed nothing, passing through as if he wasn't there.

"No! Tailis, stop!" Keana collapsed, held up by his grip on her wrist. He hit her face again. She screamed and raised her arm to protect herself.

How does it feel? Do you like being hit? Tyrsa's rage poured into the water man and he slammed his fist into her stomach.

The goddess, sobbing, dropped her arm. "I surrender! Let me go! Please!"

Hit her again! Tyrsa commanded.

No! her other self cried. *Do not become like her! Violence for the sake of violence is not acceptable. She has stopped.*

Lady Violet's words slapped her harder than the water man's fist did Keana's face. Tyrsa told him to stop. He stood, holding the goddess by the wrist. Keana hung her head, her body shaking with her sobs.

"You said you surrender." Lady Violet's words sounded a mere whisper. Her torn and bloody chest heaved, her breath coming in short pants. "Do you mean it?"

Keana nodded and lowered her head. "I will go back to Tai-Keth and will not return. Just, please, do not do to me what you did to Tailis. He is…not himself."

"Release me." The green web disappeared and Lady Violet fell to the ground, too weak to float. She pushed herself up so she half lay, half sat, though her arms shook with the effort.

Tyrsa told the water man to let go of Keana's wrist. She rested her wounded arm on her lap and, with her left hand, the beaten goddess reached for the lash.

"No." Lady Violet said. "That stays here."

Keana's head snapped up and she glared at Lady Violet. Tyrsa asked Tailis' double to reach for the goddess, but not to touch her. He held his open hand near the back of her neck. With a snarl, Keana shifted back into the shadows of the grass and vanished.

Tyrsa's relief turned to concern for her other self. They both hurt, though Lady Violet still held back most of the pain from her. More tired than she had felt in a long time, she could only imagine how bad it must be for Lady Violet.

How do we get you back to me? Tyrsa asked. No one could come and carry her, and Lady Violet wasn't capable of moving on her own. She could barely hold herself up. Nor could Tyrsa command the fake Tailis to carry her, she simply did not have the strength to control him for that long.

We need that lash, Lady Violet said. *It holds the power Keana used in Ardael. There should be enough energy for you to help me get home.*

Tyrsa thought a moment, then looked at the water man. He still stood, hunched over, as if to crush Keana's neck. *Bring me the lash.*

Lady Violet forced herself to sit upright. Before taking the lash from the water man, she removed the glowing white ball from her belly and let it float in front of her. She unravelled the ends of the weapon and separated the stalks. Pausing every few minutes to rest, Lady Violet broke the grasses into several small sections and, using what little strength Tyrsa could give her, squeezed them into a ball the same size as the one bobbing in front of her. It began to glow, green to Tyrsa's white. Lady Violet pressed the two together. The ball pulsed bright green, then, with one last flare, returned to its normal blazing white.

Her other self put the ball back and lay down, too weak to do anything else. *Keana's power over nature is now yours.*

How did I get Tailis' power? I don't remember you doing anything like that this morning.

Your orb was inside him and it absorbed Tailis' power when he exploded. Lady Violet closed her eyes a moment. *It is up to you now, Tyrsa. I know you are tired too. I should not have let you heal Cenith, but I had not expected trouble.*

What do I have to do?

You do not need your water man anymore and he is taking up strength. Just pull your thoughts away from him.

Tyrsa did as Lady Violet directed and the water man collapsed in a small flood.

I hate to do this to you. Prepare yourself. You are going to have to take the pain and feed me what's left of your strength so I can come home.

Tyrsa almost broke down in tears, but she had to be brave; she couldn't lose her other self. Lady Violet had taken her pain, now it was her turn. Squeezing the railing harder, Tyrsa grit her teeth and steeled herself against the coming agony.

What happens if I fall asleep from the pain? Like Trey and Jolin did? Tyrsa asked, her heart beating harder.

They did not fall asleep, they lost consciousness. Pray you do not, otherwise I will not be able to come home and I will die.

Tyrsa took a deep breath, then screamed with the pain.

* * * *

Cenith drifted through fog. Rough hands pulled and pushed at him, though he couldn't see anyone. A far-off voice, urgent and cajoling, shouted indistinguishable words. The fog thinned, revealing a single yellow light, beckoning him. He strode toward it and the light resolved itself into a flame.

The voice's words became clearer. "My Lord! Wake up! Please!"

Cenith knew that voice, though he couldn't place it. The fog peeled away. He blinked and peered through sleepy eyes at a lit candle on the table by his bed. The hands shook him again.

"My Lord! You have to wake up! It's Lady Orchid! She's hurt!"

Cenith tried to move his mouth. It felt glued shut. *Lady Orchid? Who's Lady Orchid?*

"Your wife is wounded, My Lord! Badly!"

My wife? Cenith's eyes flew open. "Tyrsa?" He tried to sit up. His head swam and his vision blurred, but now he recognized the voice. It belonged to the hands that helped steady him. "Ead. What do you mean she's hurt? She's right here." Cenith twisted and looked behind him at Baybee on the pillow and the empty place where Tyrsa should be. Panic gripped his heart like a vice. He leapt up and would have fallen if Ead hadn't still had hold of him. "Where is she?"

"In the other room, but you should put these on

143

first." The Companion handed him his pants.

Cenith tugged them on and did up the ties while stumbling into the sitting room, willing his vision to clear. Varth sat on the floor near the hearth, holding a small figure wrapped in a thick blanket. Wet black hair hung in stringy ropes from the top.

"Sit in your chair, My Lord," Ead said, guiding him there. "You're still wobbly from the potion Garun gave you." He took the other seat.

Varth stood and placed Tyrsa in Cenith's arms. The Companion pulled back the blanket, revealing the damage to her face.

Anger overwhelmed the fear in Cenith's heart. His stomach flipped when he discovered the full extent of her injuries. "These are lash wounds!" They were deep; some to the bone. Though all had stopped bleeding outright, some still oozed. "Who did this? *How?*"

Ead answered. "We don't know, My Lord. We heard nothing. I felt a draft coming from under the door and thought one of the balcony doors had blown ajar. When I came in, they were both open and had been for a while." He pointed to a large wet stain on the carpet in front of the now closed doors. "Lady Orchid was lying on the balcony, just as you see her. We checked for signs of an intruder, but could find nothing except for…a pool of blood. The rain has washed most of it away." The catch in Ead's voice mirrored the anguish on his face.

"I sent Dystan down to ask the guards on the main doors if they'd seen or heard anything," Varth said. "I told him she was sleepwalking, but just wanted to be sure. He should be back soon."

Cenith nodded, impressed with Varth's quick thinking.

"She said one word before she lost consciousness," Ead put in. "Keana. I guess she was praying, but I..."

"Keana!" Cenith's gaze whipped to the hearth. "I don't think she was praying. Look at the symbols." An empty space showed where the goddess' wheat sheaf should have sat.

Varth whistled and crouched near the fireplace, shifting his sheathed sword so it didn't catch on the carpet. "My lady defeated Keana? But we heard no sounds of a fight. Or anything else."

"Did you hear what happened earlier today?" Cenith asked.

"Yes, My Lord. Madin and Barit filled us in."

Cenith picked strands of hair away from the cuts. Three wounds crossed Tyrsa's face, three scars that would mar her sweet pixie features. The ridges on her back were easily hidden, but she would bear these openly the rest of her life. He could only hope they healed at least as fine as the others. He hadn't thought her pretty when he first saw her. Cleaned up, a little more weight and a healthier colour had made a world of difference, though she was more cute than truly beautiful.

A more urgent problem loomed ahead. How could Cenith explain her injuries without revealing what he'd tried so hard to keep quiet? "Did you send for Garun?"

Varth stood. "No, My Lord. You said you wanted her powers kept secret. Would you like me to?"

Cenith shook his head. "You did right. We'll take care of her ourselves. Varth, there's a jug of water and a basin in the privy. You'll find an old green shirt in the bottom of the chest at the foot of the bed. I'm going to take her to the bedroom and clean her up there." Varth strode off to fulfill Cenith's request.

A knock sounded at the door. Ead pulled it open and, using his body to shield the occupants of the room, spoke in low tones to someone in the hall, then closed it. "Dystan says the guards downstairs didn't see anything suspicious, My Lord, but they'll keep extra alert."

Cenith sighed. "It's a little late now, and besides, if it was Keana, I doubt there was anything they could have done. If a goddess doesn't want to be seen or heard, she isn't."

After a moment's silence, Ead said, "The water in the jug won't be enough, My Lord. I'll send for more."

"Have it heated. If anyone asks, keep up the sleep walking charade...and...she's soaked through because she opened the balcony doors. It'll explain the wet floor as well. Her wounds on the other hand…" Cenith shook his still fogged head. "We'll have to think of something." Perhaps the pounding rain would wash away the rest of the blood.

He shifted Tyrsa, stood up, and turned toward the bedroom.

Ead's voice stopped him. "My Lord! Your back!"

"What about my back?" Cenith tried to look over his shoulder, but with Tyrsa in his arms he couldn't see what had alarmed Ead.

"Your burns! They're gone!"

"I forgot all about them. She must have healed me before she fought Keana." Cenith sighed. "I asked her not to. If she hadn't been so tired she might have been able to fight off Keana better."

"Not to mention she'd already fought one battle today." Awe lit up Ead's narrow features. "She's an amazing girl, My Lord."

"She is that. I just wish she'd listened to me."

Cenith had to admit, he didn't miss the pain.

While Ead ordered the hot water, Cenith took Tyrsa to the bedroom and laid her on his side of the bed, closest to the door. Varth had already set the filled basin on the table and now rooted through the chest for the shirt. The only light came from the single candle on the bedside table. He glanced up at the boarded windows; with the dark storm raging beyond them, he doubted glass ones would have been a help.

"Got it, My Lord." Varth handed the shirt to Cenith and brought the wooden chair from the sitting room. "Do you need anything else?"

"A little more light would be appreciated."

After retrieving and lighting two more candles, Varth said, "I'll wait in the other room, unless…you need help?" The Companion's eyes roved everywhere but to Tyrsa and her shredded nightgown. Helping him clean her wounds appeared to be the last thing Varth wanted to do. Understandable since the tatters didn't hide much.

Cenith waved him away and made himself comfortable, tearing strips off the shirt. Tyrsa remained unconscious while he cleaned the cuts on her face. These didn't seem as deep as the ones Saulth had delivered or the ones on the rest of her body. He wished Daric were here, he might have a better idea as to how long they'd take to heal. With Tyrsa's naturally accelerated healing it would be faster than normal, but not quick enough to avoid questions and, of course, they'd leave unexplainable scars.

The hot water arrived, carried by a male servant and accompanied by a concerned Mara toting tea. Ead closed the bedroom door. Cenith covered Tyrsa with the sheet and crept to the door, curious as to how the

Companions would handle the maid.

"My lord and lady are not to be disturbed," Varth said.

"If you'll let me in, I can help m'lord clean her up," Mara said, her normally quiet voice stern and unyielding.

"Sorry, we have to follow orders. I'll take the tea in case she wants it, but you can't go in." Ead sounded as if he stood right in front of the door.

"Don't think I don't know about you two. And I'm not the only one." Mara's tone turned threatening.

That's an odd thing to say. Know what about those two?

Mara lowered her voice and Cenith had to strain to hear. "In case you hadn't noticed, m'lady is easily confused. I need to make sure she's all right."

Easily confused? Cenith could see her point, though he thought of Tyrsa more as just plain confusing.

"I don't care what you think you know. We're not disobeying our lord's orders," Varth said, his voice quiet, but deep with anger. "And I will not be threatened by the likes of you. You may think me a lowly guard, but I am still Master Zev's son and a nobleman."

The maid said nothing for a moment. "My apologies, *sir*. I will come back in the morning." Though her voice sounded stiff and formal, Cenith caught the underlying resentment.

"Come when you're called for." Varth's voice returned to its normal light banter. "I don't know when you'll be needed. I imagine my lady will sleep quite late. You can also inform Laron of my lord's wishes."

The outer door opened and closed, and Cenith hurried back to Tyrsa's side. Garun had left some salve for his burns on the bedside table; she probably didn't need it, but he had to do something. He picked up the jar just as

Ead opened the bedroom door, carrying a small tray.

Cenith applied a thick layer of the honey salve to a cut on Tyrsa's left cheek. The wound had stopped oozing. *Might be my imagination, but this looks better already.*

"I thought you might like the tea Mara brought." Ead set the tray on the table on Tyrsa's side of the bed.

"That would be nice, thank you."

Varth brought in a bucket of steaming water and put it on the floor. He took the basin and its pink tinged water to the privy.

Ead poured the tea and scooped some honey into it, keeping his eyes away from Tyrsa. "I've been thinking, My Lord, about Lady Orchid's wounds and your burns. I doubt you'll be able to hide any of it from Garun. He'll be by in the morning to inspect your back. He takes his responsibility to you as his life's work. I don't see how you can put him off."

Cenith sighed and spread salve on another of Tyrsa's face wounds. "You're probably right, but I'm worried about too many people knowing. Especially about Tyrsa's healing. Daric's right in that it could turn into one horrendous nightmare."

"Garun is a good and loyal man. I doubt he'd say anything." Ead set the steaming cup next to Cenith.

Varth returned and filled the basin with clean, hot water. "Ead has a point, My Lord. Garun wouldn't talk, especially if you ordered him not to."

Cenith had to face it, the Companions were right. Tyrsa's meddling with his burns, along with her wounds, left him no choice; he had to put more than his usual trust in the physician. He'd known the man all his life. Garun helped bring him into the world and had taken care of his cuts and broken bones, sneezes and coughs, for almost twenty years.

He set down the salve. "Tell the next shift I'll speak with Garun when he comes in the morning. They can also let Ors in. No one else…except Elessa." He'd kept nothing from her and Cenith could use her calm advice right about now, but wouldn't wake her. "Avina will probably want to see me as well. Just tell her the reports can wait until afternoon."

"Yes, My Lord," Ead said, giving him a half bow.

"You two might want to leave. I have to clean the rest of her wounds." If Varth hadn't wanted to stay to help, he doubted Ead would.

"We'll stay in the sitting room, just in case," Varth said, following Ead out the bedroom door. "Holler if you need anything, My Lord."

Cenith rubbed his eyes and shook his head. Garun's potion still clung to the cobwebs cluttering his brain. Cleaning Tyrsa's wounds gave him something to do while he organized his thoughts.

The list of things to discuss with Daric grew longer and longer. Cenith would need an entire day just to fill his councillor in, not to mention the story Daric would have to tell. With luck, he'd have Rymon with him and they could finally find out what the scroll said.

Apparently Tyrsa had to save the land from whatever was destroying it. According to Lady Violet, the gods were not responsible for the tornadoes and floods, but neither did they help. So why did the gods attack her? If they couldn't stop whatever caused the problem, why would they hinder Tyrsa?

This was their land. Why wouldn't they protect it? Cenith could see no reason for any of it, but then, he wasn't a god. Who knew their reasoning for anything? Too many times he'd seen an unworthy man granted his wish and a worthy one passed over. The gods had never made much sense to him; even less now that they wanted his wife dead.

Tyrsa had beaten two of them, Tailis and Keana. Cenith wondered what effect that would have on the sea-folk and those on the plains who worshipped them. *Probably not a lot, since they weren't doing anything anyway.* The more he thought about it, the better he liked the idea of saying nothing and letting people think the gods still watched over them. No one would notice. Another thought, if Tyrsa could beat the gods individually, why didn't they attack together? Tyrsa wouldn't stand a chance.

By the time Cenith finished with her wounds and got her into a clean nightgown, his head swam with more than thoughts of the gods and his strange wife. He swallowed the last of the now cold tea, stuffed the ruined nightgown into the wooden chest, crawled into her side of the bed, tucked Baybee in beside Tyrsa and let sleep take him.

Chapter Eight

Daric rubbed his eyes and shifted his stiff right leg, slow and careful, so as to not to make any noise. It hurt not just from the wound inflicted by the assassin, but from a severe injury long ago. He sat leaning against the tunnel-side fireplace bricks of Saulth's library, listening to Saulth complain about everything under the sun and the missing piece of the scroll in particular. He wished he knew what time of day it was, late morning if he guessed correctly, but in the darkness of the tunnel, it was impossible to tell.

He had slept here, in the dusty, stuffy corridor, until woken by the sound of Saulth entering the library. Snake's head remained in the corner of the tunnel under Saulth's chair; Daric refused to call it a throne. A rumble started at one end of his gut and ended at the other, the result of a skipped breakfast; he couldn't risk pulling food out of the pack near his feet in case the rustling announced his presence to Saulth. Despite training most days with the guard over the last twenty-two years, he'd grown soft in other ways—regular and tasty meals, for example. Though Elessa hadn't cooked since they moved into the castle several years ago, she'd done a damn fine job of it and Jarven had a special talent as well.

Heavy footsteps told Daric Saulth had resumed his pacing, just as he had most of the morning. A barely heard sigh indicated Rymon's thoughts on his lord's preoccupation. A soft thump preceded a shuffle-shuffle.

Rymon had finally moved. Listening to the two all morning, Daric had come to the conclusion that the old councillor was the only one standing between Saulth and total insanity.

The Lord of Bredun had raged about lazy, incompetent assassins, worthless advisors, complaining nobles, snotty-nosed young lords and mountain people in general. He'd even made a comment about a certain over-blown, dirty mercenary who didn't know his place. Daric had trouble stifling a laugh over that one. If this was how Saulth spent his time these days, then Lacus was correct in his opinion of his useless lord.

Daric squirmed again, this time to ease the pressure on his bladder. He'd used the tunnel that ended at Saulth's suite, hoping the odour would become another prick on the man's finger, but there'd been no opportunity to piss since waking.

"That is it!" Saulth's voice jolted Daric from his thoughts. "I cannot wait any longer. I *need* that piece of the scroll!"

"You…have a plan, My Lord?"

Daric caught the hesitation in Rymon's voice. If he were Saulth's councillor, he'd be just as concerned.

"If I do not get that piece of scroll, this country is doomed. We have only one choice. Attack Dunvalos Reach."

Daric jerked upright, prepared to abandon the scroll to get back to Cenith and warn him.

"Even with double guards at the station we will have no problem," Saulth continued. "We could play up a diplomatic visit, keeping most of our forces hidden, and then pounce on them before they can get a message away. We send a fake message declaring our good will, then sneak up Eagle's Nest Pass. They would never know until it is too late."

And run straight into the detachment we just set up at the end of the pass. How stupid do you think we are! Thirty bows could hold an army at that narrow pass long enough for reinforcements to come, but Daric would have to leave as soon as he could safely sneak away. Saulth would need a few days to gather his army and supplies, giving Daric time to get back to the station and send more men to the pass. His mind composed the message he would have to send Cenith by pigeon, devised alternate plans for attacking the rear of Saulth's army, trapping them in the pass…

"My Lord! You cannot! The other lords would never accept this!" Rymon cried.

"Damn the other lords! This is our country at stake!" Saulth spat.

"But that keep is set up to hold…" A knock at the door interrupted the rest of what Rymon intended to say.

"What is it?" The creaking of door hinges followed Saulth's words.

"Sorry to disturb you, My Lord." The deep voice must belong to one of the guards. "There's a young man here who says he has something you want."

A strained moment passed.

"Do…do we dare hope?" Rymon's words echoed Daric's thoughts.

"Send him in. And he had better be who I hope he is or I will gut him here on the spot," Saulth said.

"Y…yes, My Lord."

After an interminable wait, a young man's voice broke the silence. "I…I'm Artan, apprentice to Snake. I…I have the parchment you wanted."

"Give it to me!" Saulth snarled.

"Yes, My Lord!" A rustle of clothing indicated Artan's compliance.

Daric had the apprentice's name now…Artan…though he desperately needed a face to go with it. He wished Saulth's ancestor had put a peephole in here. Artan's pattern of speech indicated better breeding than most assassins. That, or Snake insisted his men lose their accents. Daric briefly wondered what had caused the young man to turn to Snake.

"Where is the girl? This is only part of the deal." The iron in Saulth's voice would surely have him shivering in his boots; the lad didn't sound like an experienced, confident assassin.

"We ran into trouble, My Lord. All the others are dead, except for Snake, I hope. I mean…I don't know where he is. He wasn't with the other bodies. I know the deal was one hundred gold for the parchment and…"

"Did Cenith find out it was I who sent you idiots?" Saulth interrupted.

"I…I don't think so, My Lord. The others all died in the attack, and…and even if Snake has been captured, he wouldn't say anything. I know he wouldn't! He'd die first!"

The conviction in Artan's voice almost made Daric laugh. His mentor had caved in quickly compared to others he'd tortured.

"I do not suppose you completed the other part of the deal…killing that pain in the ass mercenary of Cenith's?" Saulth snorted, indicating either his opinion of Daric or the assassins' lack of competence.

Daric raised his brows at Saulth's confirmation that his death was part of the plan. He took a grim pride in just how much he'd pissed off Saulth…and grinned at what was to come.

"My job was to get the parchment, My Lord, and that I did. But I…I know they didn't get the girl, and I don't think they killed the councillor."

Daric's grin vanished like warm breath on a cold day. *No, but you killed my son!*

He concentrated on building a picture of the young man in his mind, probably wearing simple clothing to blend in easily in a crowd, wringing his hands or clutching at his clothes, miserable at his companions' failure. Artan's voice told Daric much, but not what he looked like.

Wood scraping on wood and the clinking of coins meant Saulth had kept the assassins' money in his desk drawer. "Here, this is all you have earned. Take it and get out."

Judging by the sounds, Saulth threw the bag of coins to Artan. A door opened and quickly closed. Shuffling…murmurs Daric couldn't make out…and a gasp from Rymon.

"This says *her*! It is definitely her!"

"I see that Rymon, you do not have to point out the obvious." Saulth sounded annoyed. "What is more important is this part. If I am reading it correctly, it tells us where to be and when. All we need now is the girl."

"Yes, My Lord. The Jada-Drau." Rymon cleared his throat. "This first part also concerns me…"

The Jada-Drau? Daric remembered those words from what Tyrsa had written.

"Are you saying I made a mistake, Rymon?" The Bredun Lord's voice threatened, warned. "I did what I could with what I had at the time. How was I supposed to know?"

"My Lord, I am not accusing you of anything. I am merely concerned the girl may not know what she needs to know and…"

"Get out."

"But, My Lord…"

"I said get out! I need to think and I can *not* do it with you whining over my shoulder!" A fist pounded the desk.

"Yes, My Lord," Rymon said. This time the door opened and closed quietly. The tap-tap of Rymon's cane and shuffle of his feet on the wooden floor echoed in the hall.

Saulth muttered and grumbled to himself for a while. Daric sat, trying not to think of his bladder. Some interminable time later, the door opened and closed again and Saulth's voice, demanding lunch, could easily be heard through the closed door.

Daric sighed in relief, and, as he made his way to the tunnel outside Saulth's chambers, munched travel bread and sucked back some of the water from his canteen. It was almost gone and he'd have to be careful to make it last until he left the castle.

Saulth's discussion with Rymon had peaked Daric's curiosity over the scroll even more. Now, however, all he had to do was wait until tonight.

* * * *

Cenith awoke to Tyrsa's pixie face and bright blue eyes. He jerked back…and blinked. Her pale skin showed no sign of the cuts that had marred it the night before.

"Tyrsa! Your face!"

She frowned, touching her cheek with the hand she

157

wasn't leaning on. "My face?"

Cenith sat up and pulled the blankets off her. "Take off your nightgown!"

Tyrsa smiled and complied. "Do we have time before breakfast comes?"

He ignored the hopeful look on her face and stared at her smooth, unblemished skin. "This is impossible! Last night you had lash marks all over you!"

Tyrsa's face fell. "Oh. You know about that."

Cenith's brow furrowed. He put his hands firmly on her shoulders. "Who do you think cleaned you up and put you in bed?"

Tyrsa shrugged. "I don't know. You were asleep and I don't remember."

"Varth and Ead found you unconscious on the balcony, soaking wet and bleeding. They woke me. Now, tell me what happened."

With much frowning and long pauses as she struggled to find the right words, Tyrsa described the occurrences of the night before.

"Daric is all right?" Cenith asked, interrupting her.

"Yes, he hasn't got the scroll yet, but Lady Violet said it would be today."

"How does she know?"

Tyrsa shrugged again. "I don't know."

Cenith sighed. "Never mind, carry on."

He sat first in disbelief, then in horror while she described the battle with Keana. Cenith had expected the lashing, but he couldn't have imagined what had actually happened. When she finished, he held her close and kissed her head, tears blurring his vision when he thought of how close he'd come to losing her. He ran his hand up and down her back. Those scars were still there. *Strange.*

When Cenith regained control, he said, "None of that explains what happened to the lash marks." He ran a finger down her cheek, where one of the cuts had broken the skin. "There's not even a scar."

Tyrsa lifted her head from his chest. "I don't know. Maybe it's part of my new powers."

"Speaking of that, why didn't you tell me you gained Tailis' power?" That annoyed him.

"I didn't know what it was at first. Lady Violet told me when you were asleep and she said to practice with it when no one was around." No guile, no deception, at least not on her part. Lady Violet on the other hand…

"Tell Lady Violet we can't help if you two keep secrets. Daric and I need to know just what you're capable of."

Tyrsa reached for a cup of water from the bedside table. "I'll see what I can do."

Her frown of concentration almost made Cenith laugh…until a small stream of water crept up the side of the cup, about four inches from the rim. It spread out at the top, twisting and bulging, taking on a familiar shape—a perfect replica of a fairy orchid, made of clear water, the same flower the Companions used for her nickname. Tyrsa relaxed and smiled.

Cenith shook his head, disbelief once more taking control, though he couldn't deny what he saw with his own eyes. He took the cup from her and held it closer to his face, examining the minute detail of the water flower. A moment later it collapsed, showering him with its liquid remains.

Tyrsa let out a half giggle. "I guess I'm still tired."

Cenith tossed the cup aside and pushed her back on the bed. "You did that on purpose!" He covered her with his body so she couldn't sit up.

"No, I didn't!"

"You find that funny, do you? You need to be punished." Cenith kissed her, stopping her protests of innocence. A good tickling followed, degenerating into a quick lovemaking session.

Afterwards, Cenith held his wife tight, stroking her hair. He'd almost lost her, again. How much more of this could he take? Although he realized he could have done nothing to help her this time, other than catch her when she passed out, he had to make her understand that she couldn't keep these things from him. The more he knew, the better he could help her.

He lifted her chin so he could look into her eyes. "Promise me you'll tell me whenever you discover something new."

"I don't think Lady Violet is pleased, but I promise."

Cenith smiled and kissed her. A knock interrupted their cuddling. Cenith tossed Tyrsa her nightgown and pulled on his pants before answering it. Garun's grizzled features greeted him.

"I've come to check on your burns, My Lord." Garun pushed his way into the bedroom and set his bag on the bed. Tyrsa sat watching him, not saying a word.

"Ah…yes…my burns." Cenith could find no way out. Garun had to be told. He sat on the bed beside the healer's bag. "Do you trust me, Garun?"

The healer's clear brown eyes blinked. "Of course I do, My Lord. I aided your dear mother in your birth, watched you grow up." His grey brows greeted each other over his eagle nose. "Why would you ask such a foolish question?"

"Because I don't just need you to trust me, I need to trust you as well. And I believe I can."

"Out with it." Garun folded his arms across his chest and looked down at Cenith, like a stern father confronting an errant child. "Have you picked up a less than pleasant gift from those whores you frequent?"

"What is a 'whore'?" Tyrsa asked.

Cenith ignored her as his jaw dropped. "No! Of course not! I have a wife now and…and…why would you think I'd cheat on her?"

"I didn't suggest you had. Sometimes those things take time to come out. So, if it isn't that…" Garun's features softened. "…do you think your lady wife might be pregnant?"

Cenith couldn't stop the blush creeping up his face. "I'd like to think so, but that's not what I'm referring to. It would be easier to show you. But I have to have your word, Garun, that you will say nothing of this to anyone. I can't stress how important it is. Speaking of, did you say anything to the guards outside the door?"

Curiosity replaced Garun's fatherly look. "No, only that I needed to see you. I haven't discussed your treatments with anyone other than your father. Last night was the only exception, when I told Varth and Ead to make sure you used that salve I left. My tongue does not wag."

Cenith breathed a soft sigh and ran a hand through his tangled hair. "I didn't think you'd tell anyone, but I had to be sure you understood my position on this." He pointed at his back and twisted around to show Garun.

The healer gasped, then ran a gentle hand over the places where the skin had been blistered and red. Ever calm, Garun asked, "What happened?"

"Tyrsa." Cenith faced Garun again.

Tyrsa knelt behind him and put her arms around his neck. "What is a whore?" She sounded impatient.

Cenith patted her hand. "Later."

"Are you telling me your wife healed you?" A hint of doubt crept into Garun's quiet voice. He stared at Tyrsa; she returned his gaze without a flinch.

"That's exactly what I'm telling you. She has the god-given ability to heal not only herself, but others as well, though it takes a great deal of strength out of her to do it. Pull up a chair." Cenith went on to explain how they first discovered her talent, with her wounds and then Varth's and his own. Halfway through, Tyrsa scooted over to sit beside him, clung to his arm and swung her legs back and forth.

Garun scratched his balding head and harrumphed. "I'll admit, I'd wondered how you'd survived that." He poked the scar where the bandit's arrow had nicked Cenith's kidney. "From what Daric said, you should have died. A 'miracle' didn't sit with me."

Cenith repeated what Daric had told him about Tyrsa's healing of that wound, keeping Shival out of it. "The problem is, Tyrsa slept for five days afterwards. We were concerned she'd die."

Scratching his chin, Garun said, "I see your problem. And why you want this kept quiet. If word leaked out, there'd be no end of petitioners waiting to be healed and the lady's health would be a concern."

Cenith sighed in relief. "That's it exactly. And don't worry about your job, Garun, you will always be needed here. There's more trouble coming, though that's all I can say for now."

Garun laughed, something Cenith rarely heard him

do. "If it's more 'bandits', then I suppose I'd better stock up on bandages and splints."

Cenith thought a moment. "What's your opinion on the gods and their lack of aid in the recent troubles?"

Garun snorted. "Your father and I discussed that very topic the night before he left for that council meeting. The one he never returned from. I told him then that I'd seen too much bad happen to good people to believe in gods, especially those who don't care."

"Have you had breakfast?"

The healer shook his head.

Cenith grinned. "Then join us. Have I got a tale for you."

* * * *

Quiet as a sand gopher hiding from a desert cat, Daric, bootless, crept across the soft carpet of Rymon's bedroom, keeping to the shadows cast by the waning moon. Like Saulth's library, the entrance to the tunnel had been hidden behind a hinged bookcase and, to Daric's relief, the hinges just as well oiled. Other than avoiding two young guards 'visiting' with their girls in the tunnels, acquiring the scroll proved ridiculously easy. Watching the young lovers made him all too aware of how much he missed Elessa.

Loud snores rumbled from a pile of blankets on a bed that could only sleep one comfortably. Sweat trickled down Daric's face. Not from nerves, but from a room made too warm by a still active fireplace. How could the man stand the heat? The summer night was hot enough without adding a fire and a stack of blankets to it.

Daric wiped his brow and padded over to the bed.

Cautious, he peeled back the covers, revealing Rymon's thin, seamed, pale face. Quick as a cobra's strike, he covered Rymon's mouth with most of one hand and used the thumb and forefinger of that hand to close off his nostrils. With the other arm, he held Rymon down. The Bredun councillor's eyes flew open and he struggled to free himself.

"If you want to breathe," Daric whispered, close to Rymon's ear. "Promise me you'll make no noise. I intend you no harm, just so long as you remain quiet."

Rymon, his eyes bulging with the need to breathe, nodded. Daric removed his fingers, but kept his hand firmly over the man's mouth.

Keeping his voice low, Daric said, "Now then, I'm going to put a gag in your mouth and bind your arms. We're going to take a little trip. If you do as asked, you will be returned with no injury. Understood?"

Rymon nodded again and in no time Daric had him bound, gagged and standing on his feet; fortunately the old man wore a woolen nightshirt. He led the man out of the bedroom and to the bookcase. When he opened it, Rymon gave him a look that said 'So that's how you got in'. He said nothing, just guided Rymon into the corridor, picked up the torch from its holder and released the lever that closed the swinging bookcase.

Daric tugged on his boots before pulling the dagger from his belt. "Start walking. I'll tell you when to turn. That's a knife you feel at your back. Any sudden moves or noises and I'll cut you. Got it?"

A third time Rymon nodded, and limped forward. The man moved carefully, weaving like a drunk. Then Daric remembered he walked with a cane.

At this rate, we'll be all night just getting to the bolt

hole. Daric realized Buckam was correct in his assessment of the old man. He directed Rymon to another area of the tunnels.

When they finally arrived, Rymon breathing heavily and swaying to stay on his feet, Daric cut the man's bonds and let him sit on the stone floor.

Daric placed the torch in a bracket and crouched next to him. "I don't know how well you know these tunnels, but we're in a place that has thick stone walls, not the flimsy wood in your room. No one is near. No one will hear you."

Rymon nodded, struggling to regain control of his breathing.

"I'm going to remove the gag. We need to talk." Daric reached behind Rymon with one hand, putting the knife at Rymon's throat while he untied the knot in the cloth.

"And what would you like to discuss on this fine night, Councillor Daric?" Rymon said, a wry smile on his face, despite his discomfort. "You can put down that knife. I will not make a disturbance."

Daric slid his dagger into its sheath, though he kept his hand near it. "The scroll and the girl, among other things."

"Scroll?"

"Don't play innocent, Rymon. I know about the pieces of parchment Saulth keeps in his study and that they're related to our part, which Snake's apprentice stole."

Rymon sighed. "How did you find out?"

"Let's just say I have my sources." Daric wouldn't reveal Buckam. The lad probably had family in town and who knew what Saulth would do?

The old councillor nodded. "Just so you know where I stand, I did not agree with Lord Saulth on his treatment of the girl. If not for my intervention, she would already be dead."

Daric scowled. "Why would he keep her locked in a storeroom? How could he even think of killing his own daughter, and a special one at that?"

"Ah…you know about that, too?" Rymon looked genuinely surprised.

"A little bit of gold goes a long way. And…things have happened."

Rymon laced his fingers and rested them on his stomach. "Then we do have much to discuss. I hope this will not take too long. The cold is already seeping through my nightshirt, and I do not take chill well."

"Then speak quickly." Daric sat cross legged, facing him as well as he could in the narrow tunnel.

"I shall start at the beginning, then. Saulth came across the first part of the scroll when he was eighteen years old. He and I were wandering a market in eastern Cambrel when a little old man approached him. I remember the fellow well, he looked more like a small, gnarled tree than a human. The man offered Saulth a weathered scrap of old parchment. He wanted fifty gold coins for it, said it was a magical prophecy and that only a great lord like Saulth could make it come true." Rymon touched a finger to his temple to indicate he thought the man mad.

"At first Saulth brushed him off as an idiot, but the man persisted, waving his arms like branches in the wind, telling him he'd be a hero. I swear, after what I have seen and heard since, that little man put a spell on Saulth. One minute he protested a useless waste of money and the next he was planning on how to save the world, though he paid half what the man asked."

"What did that part of the scroll say?" Daric asked.

"It proclaimed the coming of the Jada-Drau and told of tornadoes and floods that would precede it. Damn me, if it has not come true." Rymon shook his head, as if he still couldn't believe it.

Daric rubbed his stubbled chin. "Jada-Drau. I saw that word on the scroll."

Rymon's head jerked up. "You have seen the scroll?" His expression turned hard. "You have it."

"Yes, but Tyrsa wrote it all down for us. Everything, except for the missing piece."

The old man held his hand up. "Tyrsa?"

"The girl…Cenith named her Tyrsa."

Rymon paused a moment. "Are you telling me she wrote the entire thing from memory? She cannot read or write!"

"I know. She couldn't read what she'd written, but from what I've seen of the real scroll, it looks accurate." Daric rested his arms on his knees. "I gather you've been able to translate it. What does Jada-Drau mean?"

"That little old man wrote the translation of the piece down for us. With that, and a few ancient books, we were able to manage the rest." Rymon rested his head against the wall. "I am not surprised you recognize a word or two. It is ancient Calleni. Jada-Drau means 'Choice Maker'. The man then told us there were four more parts to it, but we would have to find them on our own. It took five years and much travelling, but find them we did. All but yours. By the time we had translated the ones we had, and the girl was born, eleven years had passed."

"Choice Maker. I wonder what that's supposed to

mean." Daric tapped the fingers of his left hand against his knee.

"The scroll is not clear about that. As I said, the first part tells of the coming of the Jada-Drau. The second says the ritual, if followed correctly, will produce one of the Blood who will have powers, but does not tell us much about what those powers are." Rymon blew on his hands and rubbed them together. "The fourth, without really saying anything useful, discusses the choice and the fifth describes the ritual and prayers."

The Blood. Daric remembered stories of an ancient race of magical people who once roamed the wide prairies of a distant land. Could that land be Ardael?

"None of them told us the sex of the child and that is where Saulth's abuse of that poor girl started. Part of the second piece is torn and smudged. The word could have been either 'he' or 'she'. Saulth took it be 'he' since he could not imagine a woman capable of saving the land."

"What about the third one? Our piece?"

"It confirms the Jada-Drau is female and tells us where she needs to be to make this choice and when." A sad look crossed his face and he shook his head. "It also says the girl was to be raised by both parents in a loving home, learning both the old and new ways of Ardael. If only we had found that piece years ago, that poor child would not have suffered as she has."

Daric clenched his fists. "I don't care if he thought she was the Jada-Drau or not, there's no excuse for what he did to her."

"I will not argue that point," Rymon said, meeting Daric eye to eye. "I tried to stop him, but he would not listen. I feel lucky I was able to prevent him from killing her outright. But one thing you must understand. Right from the time his father died, Saulth was a good lord. He took care of his people and his lands. It has only been in the last couple of years that this prophecy has taken full control of him. He is convinced he is the only one who can save this country from the tragedy now afflicting it. I agree that his methods have been less than desirable, but the concern is genuine. He truly does wish to save Ardael."

It looked more to Daric like Saulth wished to be king, but he kept that thought to himself. "We have a problem. My lady has asked me to retrieve the scroll. And you."

"Me?" Rymon's thin white brows shot up. "Why me?"

"She wishes you to translate it for us. Tyrsa has no idea what the scroll says, only that she is connected to it somehow."

Rymon's face turned to stone. "I cannot come with you. I am not capable of travelling that far. Nor can I allow you to take the scroll. If it disappeared, I cannot predict what Saulth would do, but it would not be good. All out war would be the least of it."

Daric's heart sank. He had no desire to hurt the old man, but that's just what he'd do if he forced him to ride to Dunvalos Reach. And as for Saulth... After a moment's thought, he said. "There might be a way, if I can trust you."

"Tell me what you want and I will let you know if I can do it. You have trusted me so far, have you not?" Rymon had the right of that.

"If I promise to leave the entire scroll with you, will you translate it for me? Tonight?"

Rymon nodded. "Yes. Saulth can do nothing without the girl and you can do nothing without the information it contains. This country needs help and it does not matter who fixes the problem, just so long as it is fixed." He put his hands under his armpits. "There is parchment, quills and ink in the desk by my sitting room fireplace. Could I also ask you to bring me a couple of blankets?"

Daric nodded and stood. He put on his 'fierce' face. "Can I trust you to stay put?"

Rymon's teeth chattered. "I promise I will not move or make noise of any kind, as long as you promise to hurry…and bring me those blankets."

"Done."

Chapter Nine

Daric sat quiet while Rymon copied the scroll. He had no way to confirm if what he wrote was actually what was in the thing, he could only trust the old man meant what he said, that he wished to see his country saved, regardless of who did the saving.

He'd debated telling Rymon about the stashes and the guards' interesting use of the tunnels, but decided against it. Another nuisance for Saulth suited him fine.

Daric held the torch as close to the parchment as he dared, giving Rymon the light he needed. He resisted the urge to read as Rymon wrote, he'd only be in the way. Daric had brought a large book to use as a table, so Rymon didn't have to kneel and write on the stone floor. The Bredun councillor sat on one folded blanket and used the other as a shawl. Daric had also brought him his cane; it was a long way back up to his suite.

It seemed hours until the old man finished, but must, in reality, have been less than one. Rymon sat back and gathered the original pieces of the scroll, placing them carefully on top of Cenith's portion, still in its frame.

"As I told you earlier," Rymon said, rubbing his eyes. "The first part describes the coming of the Jada-Drau and the second tells of her bloodline. Those are not the parts we need to discuss. It is these…" He pointed to the third and fourth sections.

The entire thing took three pieces of parchment.

Daric picked up the second. Though shaky, Rymon's writing was legible.

"'The ones chosen as her parents will protect, nurture and cherish her, teaching her the ways of Ardael, old and new, equally, so she may wisely make the decision.' Saulth really messed up there. It must have galled him to read this." Daric didn't want to let on that he was listening when Artan brought the parchment.

Rymon grimaced. "He was not exactly happy, no. But that is not the important part, what is done is done."

Daric read on. "'When the time of choosing is at hand, a bright light will appear in the sky, to the west, on the First day of the eighth month in her sixteenth year."

Rymon put a hand up. "An important date that one, and not far off. It is when she turns sixteen, to the day. Less than a month away now."

Interesting, but not as compelling as the next part. "'It will look down on the place where the mountain lord breathed his last, to remain forever a symbol of what shall be. Find there, a door.'"

Did Daric dare ask the question? Rymon had been cooperative until now, how far would he go? "This part is obviously related to Ifan's death." He rose to a crouch, ignoring the pull of the knife wound, and stared straight into Rymon's eyes. "I have to know. Did Saulth have anything to do with it?"

Rymon looked away. He didn't have to say anything, his expression spoke volumes.

"How did he do it?" Daric tried hard to keep the anger out of his voice.

The old councillor gulped. "He…he sent men through the pass, Eagle's Nest Pass. They slipped through your guards. Easy enough to do, from what I've heard."

"We're working on that. Continue."

"From what the leader of the team said, they used shovels and pickaxes on a large ridge of snow near the top of the mountain. Once started, it picked up momentum." Rymon sighed and leaned back against the tunnel wall. "How they managed to time it right, I have no idea. Neither did they. They swore, to a man, that they had help from the gods. It would not budge, and then, with little effort from them, it did."

Daric couldn't see Ardael's gods having a hand in this, not if Tyrsa was meant to bring them down. He could do nothing about it. This didn't constitute proof enough for the lords, even if he could get Rymon to a Lord's Council meeting. Daric would have to be satisfied just knowing. "This door, do you know any more about it? I've been by there many times, before and after the avalanche. There's no door there, not even a cave." It was the same place Tyrsa had felt something in the rock. Coincidence? Not likely.

Rymon shook his head and put the stopper in the bottle of ink. "That part puzzled us as well. We figured we, well, Saulth and his men, would go there at the right time and hope all would be made clear." He put his hands over his face, muffling his voice. "After all these years, what we have strived for is about to happen and I cannot be there. I can have no part in it." When he removed his hands, two tears slipped from tired blue eyes.

"You've already played a large part, and not just in the translation," Daric said, switching the torch to his left hand. "You stopped Saulth from killing Lady Tyrsa. According to this scroll, she is the crux for everything. Don't delude yourself, you've done much just keeping Saulth under control and can do more if you can help me understand this."

Rymon sighed, and thought a moment. He sat up straight. "Then let us finish. It is getting late and we cannot risk the chance of someone finding you. You must get this information to Cenith. Though I have to say, as far as prophecies go, this is the strangest one I have ever heard."

Daric had to agree. He read on. "'Once inside, the Jada-Drau will go to the throne of the Old Ones. It is there the choice will be made. Be it also known, once the choice is done, it is final. All that is not chosen must be destroyed.' Daric paused a moment. If this was true, much more lay at stake than stopping tornadoes and floods. "That sounds ominous. Any idea what this choice involves?"

"None." Rymon scrubbed his tired face. "That is, I believe, why your section of the scroll was so important. She was supposed to learn the old and new ways from her parents to help her make this choice. Exactly what 'old' and 'new' refers to, I have no idea. Saulth and I have not had a lot of time to discuss this part, just a few hours this evening."

Because he kicked you out before you had time to really study it this morning. "What did you intend to do once you got to this throne?"

Rymon spread out his hands. "I have no idea. There is nothing to tell us, just that she has to be there on the first day of the eighth month of her sixteenth year. Saulth felt all would be made known to us at that time."

"Saulth doesn't strike me as one to put his faith in the gods."

"He is not, but as I said earlier, I truly believe a spell has been put on him to make him do the terrible things he has done. Those poor women…" Rymon's shoulders shook and Daric thought he'd break down in tears. The old man took a deep breath and sat straight. "Please, do not judge him by his recent actions. My lord is not…himself."

Why does he stay here? Daric had to know. "Tell me Rymon, it's obvious you don't agree with your lord's recent actions, and haven't for some time. Why don't you leave?"

Rymon sighed. "There are times when I wish I could, but I am sixty-three years old. I have spent my entire life in the castle. I have nowhere else to go, and even if I did, I could not leave. Someone has to try to keep a hand on Saulth. Without me, who knows what he would do?"

Daric nodded and returned his attention to the scroll. "'One will choose.' I assume that's Tyrsa. 'Twelve will guard. One will rule over all.'" *Twelve?* "It can't be!" Daric immediately regretted his outburst.

"What 'can't be'?" Rymon asked, leaning forward to look where Daric pointed.

Daric had to tell him. He'd hoped to keep the information flowing one way. "Twelve of our soldiers volunteered to form a new regiment, specifically to guard Tyrsa." He didn't need to mention who Tyrsa had chosen as the twelfth member.

"So that is what it means! Saulth and I puzzled over that passage for ages." Rymon sat back again. "It seems this prophecy is bound and determined to come true, regardless of what us foolish men have to say about it."

Daric blew out a long breath. *'One will rule over all.' So that's where Saulth got the idea of becoming king.* Perhaps it was Tyrsa who was meant to rule, not Saulth; but putting

175

the country in the hands of an innocent young girl who couldn't even read or write let alone deal with politics… That would be foolish.

Rymon waved his hand over the remainder of the translation. "The rest of this just tells us what to do for the Jada-Drau to be born and the prayers to go with it. You can read it later, once you are safely away. Time is running short."

That it was, and Daric still had one more deed to perform. "Can you find your way back to your rooms?"

"Many years ago, when I first found out about these tunnels from the previous councillor, I poked my nose around." Rymon shook his head. "But I am afraid you have me completely lost."

"I'll take you back far enough that you can find your own way, but then I must leave you. As you said, time is running out."

"That will do."

"Just a moment," Daric said. He took a clean sheet of parchment and tore off a portion. Using Rymon's quill and ink, he wrote a few words, blew it dry, then stuffed it in his pocket.

"What is that?" Rymon asked.

Daric shrugged and helped the old man to his feet. "Just something I needed to do." He gathered the parchments, old and new, and gave Rymon his quill, ink and book, wrapping them in the extra blanket. The new parchments he stuffed into his shirt and passed the old ones to Rymon.

They walked in silence a short while, then Rymon asked, "You mentioned earlier that you knew the girl was special. If you do not mind my asking, how did you find out?"

Daric thought a moment. He wouldn't tell Rymon everything, he still didn't trust him completely. "Tyrsa's lash wounds healed much faster than they should have."

Nodding, Rymon said, "I thought it might be that. We only found out about it shortly after Saulth had given her to Cenith. That is why he sent Tajik after you. If we had only known. But, perhaps it is better this way. Perhaps, despite what the scroll says, this is the way it was meant to be."

Daric almost told him about her ability to heal others, but decided the less Rymon knew, the better it was for their side. He had a question of his own. "Saulth still needs Tyrsa. Will he attack Dunvalos Reach to get her?"

Rymon sighed. "A few years ago I would have said never. Now…he probably would. Or at least try to. From what I have heard about your keep, he would have a hard time of it." He set his hand on Daric's shoulder. "I will do whatever I can to stop him."

"Thank you."

After a few minutes walking, Rymon cleared his throat. "Would you happen to know the fate of Snake?"

Daric's heart turned cold. "I do. I killed him."

Rymon nodded, his expression bland. "I thought as much. I cannot blame you. From what I have heard, many died in a raid that was supposed to be bloodless. You have my apologies. I am curious though, his apprentice, the one who brought us your piece of the scroll, said he was not among the dead."

Daric fought the urge to toss the torch aside and crush the man's throat. "He wasn't. I killed him six days ago, after torturing him for three. I'd tortured him before that as well."

Rymon's head whipped around so fast Daric

thought it might fall off. "Wh…why? I realize he was an assassin, but…"

"My son died in that raid!" Daric took two deep breaths to calm himself. None of this was Rymon's fault. This was all on Saulth's head. "The first time I tortured him was because I needed to find out for certain who'd sent him and why. He confirmed my suspicions. I tortured him a second time, then killed him, for the loss of my son and to ensure the bastard never killed again."

Rymon gulped. "I am truly sorry about your son. I…I had heard you had a dark past, but I had not imagined…"

Daric stopped and held the torch close to Rymon's face. The old councillor winced. "I stopped counting the men I've killed years ago," Daric said. "I had hoped to find peace here in Ardael, and I did, until the attack. Once this is done, I hope to find peace again."

"When…when what is done?" Rymon's voice cracked, his eyes screamed fear.

Daric turned and walked on. Rymon scrambled to keep up, the tick-tick of his cane matching the rhythm of Daric's heart. They travelled the rest of the way in silence.

* * * *

Jolin rubbed his eyes, trying to ignore the throb in his head. The letters in front of him swam like ducklings in a pond. He and Keev sat in his quarters, hunched over the writing desk. Now that he was a captain, he had a large room and more furniture than he could use.

"Give it up for tonight, yer only goin' t' make more mistakes," Keev said, cradling his broken arm. "Not to mention makin' yer head worse. Yer supposed t' be restin'.

Garun's orders."

"But I have t' finish this. Varth said copyin' books is th' fastest way t' learn. If Lord Cenith knew I couldn't read nor write, he'd never have made me captain. I don't want t' let him down."

Keev shook his head. "Took me a long time t' learn and I still don't know it all."

"I already know th' whole alphabet and I kin read easy stuff, if ye give me time. Now all I have t' do is learn th' harder words and how to write 'em all."

"Yer a stubborn fool."

"That's what my Da always says." Jolin bent his head over the parchment and scraped off the mistake he'd made with his fingernail. He carefully remade the letter, then the one next to it. "There. 'Wanted'."

He'd managed to keep his inability quiet since coming into his new rank. Trey volunteered to write his reports while he dictated, but Jolin needed to do them himself. Even Jayce had more learning than he did. Ead and Varth had offered to teach him to write, but they both had the night shift again tonight. Dathan, Trey and Buckam were asleep and the others were at Silk's enjoying the day off, so Keev took their place.

Jolin looked at the book, then set pen to parchment. "This word I know. 'To'." The scratching quill broke the silence. "This one's 'ride', and then "a"." The next one he had to sound out. It took a moment, but Jolin persevered. "Horse." Now all he had to do was write it.

Just as he set quill to parchment, a knock interrupted them. Jolin opened the desk drawer and shoved book and parchment into it before answering.

Ead and Varth stood in the hall, their faces expressionless.

"Ain't you two supposed t' be doin' guard duty t'night?" Jolin asked, touching his fingers to his aching head.

"We are. Lady Tyrsa would like to see you." Varth stepped back, allowing their lady access to Jolin's room. Keev jumped to his feet.

"M'lady!" Jolin's and Keev's voices sounded as one.

Lady Orchid waltzed in as if she always came to visit, a smile decorating her face, looking every bit the pretty flower they'd named her after. She wore a dark green dressing gown over an ivory nightdress. Her slightly tousled hair only made her more attractive. Jolin pushed his feelings away and joined Keev in giving her a bow.

He turned his chair around and offered it to her. "Tis well past midnight. Ye should be asleep."

She sat, her hands in her lap. "I needed to see you. You're hurt. I don't like that."

Ead closed the door, setting himself against it, Varth beside him. "She insisted she had to come now. It couldn't wait until morning. Trust me," the shorter Companion said, with a wry smile, "we tried to talk her out of it."

Jolin turned his attention back to Lady Orchid. "Does Lord Cenith know yer here?"

A little frown replaced the smile. "He's asleep. I didn't wish to wake him. He's tired from all that happened yesterday."

"We heard about yer experience with Keana, m'lady," Keev said, cradling his left arm once more. "Ye must be tired yerself."

"I'm fine. I won't have you hurt when you don't have to."

Jolin was the first to find the words. "Ye…ye want t' heal me? M'lady! No! I remember what happened when ye healed Lord Cenith at th' station!"

The frown turned into a glare. Jolin almost expected her to stomp her foot. "I have more power now. I have learned how to control the pain, so it's not so bad. Lady Violet says you are needed. All of you. I will do this. Now lie down."

Lady Tyrsa stood, determination highlighting her eyes. Jolin had no choice. He couldn't disobey his lady, and, he had to admit, getting rid of the pain and dizziness would be nice. He lay down on the bed.

Varth moved the chair to accommodate their lady and resumed his position in front of the door, though who he thought would come in at this time of night, Jolin had no idea. Keev took the same chair he'd occupied earlier, next to the writing desk. Lady Orchid sat down and he closed his eyes, putting himself completely under her care.

"This is the first time I have healed a person who is awake," Lady Tyrsa said, putting her hands on either side of his head. "I don't know what you will feel."

"Did you two know what she'd planned t' do?" Keev whispered.

Varth answered. "No."

Keev had another question. "Are we goin' t' git in trouble for this?"

"Probably," Ead said.

Lady Tyrsa's cool fingers probed his wound.

Jolin winced. "If you three don't shut yer traps, I'll put ye all on report. Lady Orchid needs t' concentrate."

Jolin cracked one eye open, expecting to see three glares from the Companions. Instead, he received only looks of curiosity as they watched their lady. He closed his eye and forced himself to relax, concentrating on Lady Tyrsa's soft touch and her clean, sweet scent. It made him think of the clover ridden mountain meadows of home, buttercups, irises and daisies in glorious profusion.

He pictured himself sitting on a blanket, picnic basket at hand, pouring a cup of wine for himself and Tyrsa. She smiled and took her cup, sipping it with laughing eyes. His lady still wore her nightdress and gown, which Jolin thought odd, but it was only a fleeting concern. He set down his cup and picked up a ripe strawberry, feeding it to her. Her blue eyes danced with merriment as she nibbled it.

A pain stabbed into the right side of his skull, as if she bit into him and not the strawberry. A crow screeched and dove at him again, pecking his head. Jolin tried to fend it off, keep it away from his lady. It was joined by another, a large one, almost the size of a raven. They pecked and stabbed at his wound.

Jolin cried out, waving his arms to shoo the birds away, but they dodged his useless efforts. All the while, Lady Tyrsa watched, sipping her wine, her lips blood red from the juice of the berry. She smiled, her eyes laughed. 'You fool! Nothing but a fool!' they seemed to say.

Once more the crows attacked. Blood streamed down Jolin's face, obscuring his vision, turning everything red. An explosion of pain sent him reeling into darkness.

* * * *

Daric released the catch on the bolt hole and carefully opened it. A brief check showed no guards nearby. He lifted himself partway out of the hole so he could look around Saulth's chair. The doors to the hall stood open, two guards standing just outside them. Daric spat a silent curse. He'd have to be extra careful.

He lowered himself back down into the tunnel. He waved away the flies trying to get into the double burlap sack and, bracing himself, reached in. His left hand found Snake's greasy hair, now coated with slime from days of decay. Wishing he'd brought a pair of gloves, Daric held his breath, trying not to look at, or smell, the disgusting object. Keeping it as far from him as he could, he pulled out the piece of parchment he'd put in his pocket earlier.

Maggots crawled over his hand and Daric found it hard to resist tossing the head away. He stuffed the paper in Snake's slack mouth. More maggots fell, wriggling in irritation.

Daric stood straight and placed the head behind him on Saulth's oak floor, dislodging more of the fat white worms feasting on the dead assassin. Wiping his hand on his old trousers, he ducked down, trying to find some clean air. Even without the head, the stink from the burlap bags and the hand he'd used to pick the thing up cloyed at him, sickly sweet, reeking of death.

Climbing through the hole once more, Daric crouched behind Saulth's chair, balancing on the edge of the bolt hole. Another quick peak showed the guards still facing the other way.

A slight breeze blew in the big doors, bringing blessedly fresh air with it. Daric breathed in deep. In one quick movement, he picked up the head and placed it on the gold velvet cushion adorning Saulth's pretend throne. Just as quick, he ducked back into the bolt hole and closed the door. Once again he wiped his hand on his trousers. He stared at his cloak, wishing he could bring it with him, but he doubted the odour could ever be removed. It would have to stay here with the burlap bags.

Shouldering his pack with his clean hand, he walked toward the barn exit, pondering ways to stop Saulth before the viper ever arrived at Tiras.

Chapter Ten

Saulth knotted his night robe as he strode down the hall to the stairs. "Just what is all this about, Corvin? You barely gave me enough time to get my trousers on."

"I'm not sure, My Lord. Sergeant Landis ordered me to get you, fast. Something about trouble in the Main Hall." The short guard almost ran to keep up with him. "My Lord?"

"What!" Saulth snapped.

"My...My Lord, the look on Sergeant Landis' face...I ain't never seen anyone look like that. Kinda green and like he was going to throw up."

What would make that tough old gizzard turn green? Saulth wondered if he should have brought his sword. "Am I going to be in danger if I show my face in the Hall?"

"I don't think so, My Lord. Sergeant Landis didn't say nothing about danger. His sword was still sheathed. But I can go in first, just to make sure."

Saulth almost laughed at the eager look on the young soldier's face. *So willing to die for me.* He stopped at the top of the stairs leading to the corridor behind the Main Hall and motioned for the guard to precede him. "You do that."

Corvin had his sword out in an instant, as if an entire army of Tai-Kethians awaited them. He had been one of the girl's guards before Cenith had taken her away. *I'll get her back. Somehow.*

Quick steps carried him down the corridor and through the Main Hall's rear door, Corvin struggling to keep in front of him. A chuckle escaped Saulth's lips. The guard just looked so funny with that eager look on his long face. Corvin glanced back, almost tripping over his own feet. Something else Saulth thought funny. The laugh died in his throat when he saw Landis and a young guard he didn't recognize standing near his throne.

Two ashen faces greeted him. Landis stared at the oak throne as if a dragon sat there, waiting to gobble them up. The other guard stood several feet away, doubled over. From the looks of the mess on the floor in front of him, he'd lost his dinner. *At least he missed the carpet.* Saulth sniffed, wrinkling his nose at an unexpected, and repulsive, odour.

"What is the problem, Landis, that you have to get me up before dawn? Could Tajik not have taken care of it?" He pointed to the other guard. "Did he have to do that? Is that what stinks in here? Now my floor will have to be scrubbed!"

"My Lord, I...I..." Landis lifted his hand and pointed to the throne.

Corvin moved in front of the big chair, dropped his sword and gagged. He stumbled back, his eyes wide.

A swirling draft from the open front doors bore a much stronger odour than the one that had greeted Saulth upon entering the room, one that brought tears to his eyes. "Siyon's sword and balls! What *is* that foul smell?"

"Death, My Lord," Landis said, turning away.

Saulth strode to the front of the throne and stopped. He covered his mouth as the full strength of the stench slammed into him. The object leaning against the padded arm turned his blood to ice. Despite the ravages of damage and decay, that face was unmistakable.

"Snake!"

"The assassin, My Lord?" Landis choked the words out.

"*Daric!*" It had to be that filthy Calleni. "He is here! In my castle!" Saulth spun, searching the shadows for the big mercenary. He backed himself into the corner formed by the fireplace and the stone wall.

"Who, My Lord?" Corvin's hand over his mouth muffled his words.

"He is here to kill me!" Fear strangled Saulth's heart. His stomach recoiled at the stench and the horrific sight in front of him. Bile burned his throat. "Rymon! Tajik! Bring them to me. Call out the guard! I want the castle searched!"

"Yes, My Lord!" Landis snapped to attention. "Corvin, awaken Councillor Rymon! Dash, get Guard-Commander Tajik and muster the castle guard!"

Corvin bolted for the stairs while the other young guard ran for the double doors.

Landis pulled his sword, then frowned at the rotting head. "My Lord, there's something in the mouth."

"Get it." Saulth said. He wished he could send someone to open the outside doors and let some fresher air in, but Daric could be waiting out there.

Landis screwed up his face and held his arm over his mouth. He approached the throne, sword out straight in front of him, as if the head could attack. He kept back as far as he could and used the weapon to dig a small piece of parchment from Snake's mouth. Maggots came out with it and Saulth retched. The paper fell to the floor. Landis used his sword to pull it closer to him. "There's words, My Lord."

Saulth wasn't sure he should let him read it, but he couldn't bring himself to lay a finger on the fouled parchment. "What does it say?"

"You want me to touch it?"

"*What does it say!*"

Landis used his sword and the toe of his boot to spread the piece out. "'There will only be one more visit.' What does that mean, My Lord?"

Saulth's gut sank to his toes. He slid down the wall and sat hard on the floor. "Tajik. Rymon," he said, his words a mere whisper. "Help me." Through the haze of fear, a thought forced its way forward. Saulth leapt to his feet. "My scroll!" He ran from the Hall.

* * * *

Once more, Artan bundled up his belongings. Now, however, instead of just his pack, he had two saddlebags as well. He'd never owned much, and everything fit in easily, including the new clothes he'd purchased two days earlier.

He'd finally come to the realization that Snake had to be dead. No sign of him, no word. Once others realized that, they'd be all over this place looking for treasure or just a better place to live.

Artan had already searched everyone's rooms. The gold and jewels he'd picked up fit nicely in one of the saddlebags. The larger items he placed in the storage space under the floor in Snake's room. The small trap door lay concealed under both the bed and a carpet. If someone found it, then that was Aja's wish. If not, he might have a use for it if he ever came back to Valda.

The decision to leave town had come in the middle

of a sleepless night. Everything had changed. No Snake, no Ice… The place was too quiet. Valda itself wasn't what it had been when he'd left. There'd been homeless in the streets then, but now a man couldn't turn around without running into a bedraggled child or starving woman looking for a handout. The alleys, one of the usual routes for the assassins, burst with hungry, anxious people. More than once he'd had to fight off a man who thought him easy pickings.

The guards had changed as well, more observant and far more likely to pull a man off the street for little reason. Men, women and children disappeared, taken away to the dungeons some said. Artan had put little stock in that rumour until he'd seen Lord Saulth for the first time in his life.

The man had squirrels storing nuts in his brain. He had a look to his eyes Artan had seen before in a woman who'd lived next door to his family when he was little. His mother told him to stay away from her and, as it turned out, for good reason. Her husband had come home one day to find her sitting on the floor in the middle of their common room, rocking back and forth, muttering. She held a bloody kitchen knife in her hand. A brief search of the house turned up all three of the children, their throats cut.

Artan shuddered just thinking of the madness in his lord's eyes. If a mere woman was capable of killing her own children, what would a man with his power do? He didn't want to stick around to find out.

With saddle bags over one shoulder and pack in hand, Artan bade farewell to the assassin's hideout. He opened the trap door leading to a set of stairs, another trap door, and a ladder. Artan locked both doors, but doubted

189

it would keep others out for long, provided they knew how to find the place. Ending up in a narrow, damp and smelly sewer, he sidled along the maintenance walk to the main conduit, down one tunnel and left at the next. A short walk brought him to yet another ladder, leading to a warehouse. Avoiding the lazy workers during the day proved only a minor delay. Artan slipped out a side door into a crowded alley. A few minutes to dodge the disgruntled families living there and he was out on the street, close to the livery where he'd stabled his horse.

The sun sat high as Artan left Valda by the south gate and meandered through the mess of sodden Docktown. The Asha River had calmed while he was away, though it still overflowed its banks. He crossed the newly rebuilt Town Bridge and now stood on Cambrellian soil, headed for Callenia. By all reports, it was a good place to learn the art of killing. He had a long ride ahead of him; the country Talend lay between Cambrel and Callenia.

A few yards past the bridge, a small Cambrellian garrison sat at the bottom of a hill. The guards on duty by the road asked him his business. Travelling, he said. They let him through.

At the top of the hill, Artan stopped his horse and looked back. *Valda.* The city of his birth. Other than his excursion into Dunvalos Reach, he'd never been anywhere else. Even from here, the once beautiful city looked tarnished and worn.

I hope things have improved by the time I come back…if I come back. Artan turned his horse's head south.

* * * *

Tyrsa stirred. Cenith jumped up from his chair

190

beside the bed and stared down at his errant wife, his anger flaring anew. She opened her eyes and smiled up at him, cooling some of that ire.

"Good morning," she said, as if nothing had happened.

"Good afternoon, you mean." Cenith folded his arms and Tyrsa lost her smile. "What did I tell you about keeping things from me?"

Tyrsa sat up. "Oh. You know about that?"

Cenith threw his hands up in the air and plunked himself back in the chair. "Yes, I know about that. Jolin screaming his lungs out well after midnight let a lot of people know something was up."

"Jolin screamed?" Tyrsa hugged her knees, huddling into a small ball. "I didn't hear him. I don't remember. Is he all right?"

Cenith ran his hand through his hair. "We don't know. He's still asleep." His anger loosened into frustration.

"I will go to him." Quick as a cat, Tyrsa rolled off the bed.

"No!" Cenith grabbed her and sat her in the chair. "Garun's watching him. You will explain to me why you healed him without telling me."

Without a hint of shame or remorse, as calm as a pool on a windless day, Tyrsa said, "Lady Violet told me to."

Cenith heaved a sigh and buried his face in one hand. *Lady Violet. I should have known.* He removed his hand and looked at her, all innocence and sweetness. "If Lady Violet told you to jump off a cliff, would you?"

"Lady Violet didn't tell me to jump off a cliff. You did."

Cenith almost groaned. "Wrong analogy."

"Wrong what?"

"Never mind." Cenith took her hand. "Let's go in the other room."

Tyrsa grabbed Baybee from the bedside table and clutched her tight. Cenith led her to his chair by the fireplace and sat her on his lap. "I asked you two not to keep things from me. Why didn't you tell me what you were going to do? Don't you think I have a right to know?"

"You said to let you know if we found anything new. This isn't new."

This time Cenith did groan. "All right. A new request." He took her head in his hands. "Please. *Please.* Tell me when you find out anything new *and* if you are going to use your powers in any way. Understood?"

Tyrsa nodded. "Lady Violet isn't happy."

"Lady Violet will just have to suffer." He removed his hands and studied her large blue eyes. "Is it possible to talk to Lady Violet? Maybe I can explain to her how important this is."

She shrugged. "I can ask her."

"Please do."

Tyrsa's eyes took on a faraway look, shimmered and turned violet. Now haughty, her head held high, she stood and placed Baybee in Cenith's lap. She sat in the other chair, both hands resting on the arms, regal, even in her nightgown, though her feet didn't touch the floor.

Cenith set Baybee down; he felt ridiculous holding the doll. "Lady Violet, I assume?"

She nodded once. "Cenith. I apologize if we caused any trouble. Tyrsa passed out and we were unaware of what happened." The words were spoken in an even tone, with very little emotion.

Cenith blinked. He hadn't expected an apology. "Fortunately, Varth and Ead used their heads and hid you when the guards came running. Keev told them Jolin had fallen asleep at his desk while catching up on reports and had a nightmare. He'd helped him to bed and Jolin had already fallen asleep again. Put it down to his head wound. When the guards left, they carried you up here and woke me." He sighed. "They told the guards on the stairs that you were sleep walking again."

"Then no harm was done."

Cenith clenched his fists. *This is Tyrsa.* And yet, she wasn't. "We were lucky this time. Your powers *have* to be kept secret. If people find out what you're capable of and what you intend…"

"And what do we intend, Cenith? You and Ors think we are here to destroy your gods. What if that is not the case? Both times, we were attacked. We did not do the attacking. How can you know what we are here for, when we do not?" Her peculiar eyes flared, the only sign of her anger.

Cenith leaned forward and stared at the god symbols on the hearth. Regardless of whether they'd intended it or not, two of the gods were gone, sent back to Tai-Keth, unable to return. "We were guessing. Maybe we're wrong and you're not here to destroy the gods, though they certainly seem intent on killing you." He looked at her, sitting like a child queen in the big stuffed chair. "We can't risk that, and not only because Tyrsa is my wife. That means keeping your powers secret. I know you don't understand people, either of you, but understand this…people, even those who owe their allegiance to me and seem kind and loyal, can become dangerous when faced with something they can't comprehend, something they're afraid will hurt them or their families, even if that hurt is only imagined.

"Please, Lady Violet, help us help you. You know we mean you no harm. Together we have a much better chance of discovering what your powers are and what you're supposed to do." Cenith leaned back, awaiting her response.

She watched him a moment, then nodded once.

"Good." He relaxed farther into the chair. "Now, why did you feel you had to heal Jolin? His injuries weren't that bad, he was in no danger of dying. Keev said you were in pain. There was no need to put Tyrsa through that."

"There is need. All the Companions must be fit and ready for what is to come. Tyrsa's pain was not that great. We will continue to heal those who are injured."

Cenith sat up. "What is to come? And what might that be?"

"I truly wish I could tell you, for then I would know as well, but I cannot. I am sorry it has to be this way, but that is the will of the Mother and Father." Lady Violet pushed herself off the chair and moved in front of Cenith. "I must go now and rest. Tyrsa will need my strength tomorrow, for she must heal Buckam." Quicker than a heartbeat, her eyes turned blue.

"Did that help?" Tyrsa asked, looking like she wanted to jump into his arms. She picked Baybee up off the floor.

Cenith motioned her onto his lap and held her close. "I think it did. There's just one thing I need to know. Could Lady Violet be lying to us?"

Tyrsa sat up. "No. I think I would know if she did."

"I thought so, but I had to be sure."

"You should be happy," she said, cupping Cenith's face with her hand.

"Other than having my lovely wife on my lap, why should I be happy?" Cenith pulled her closer and she settled her head on his shoulder.

"Because Daric is coming home."

He pushed her back, giving her a frown. "How do you know that?"

"Lady Violet told me." Tyrsa snuggled back into him again.

Cenith sighed. "Lady Violet. Why didn't she tell me when I was talking to her a minute ago?"

"She didn't know then. Now she does."

Cenith pinched the bridge of his nose between his fingers. "You two are giving me a headache. How does she find out these things?"

"I don't know. She just does."

The answer he'd expected; frustrating, although he felt nothing but relief that Daric was all right and heading home. *Ah, well. Maybe one day I'll understand it all.* He kissed her cheek. "Hungry?" He'd already eaten lunch, but felt in the mood for something sweet.

She straightened up. "Yes! Very!"

"Mara's probably waiting in the hall. Let her in and get dressed. I'll order up some food, then we'll go check on Jolin." While he waited for both food and wife, Cenith sat in his chair, thinking on what Lady Violet had said.

* * * *

Every muscle in Jolin's body ached. He groaned and opened his eyes, blinking away the blurriness.

195

"He's awake, My Lord." Varth's voice cut through the fog.

Varth. Ead. Keev. The memories trickled back…Lady Tyrsa, the healing, the dream…no, the nightmare; and the pain. "I feel like a herd o' cows ran o'er me," Jolin said, trying to sit up. His tongue felt thick and the room spun.

Lord Cenith pushed him back. "Don't get up, you're not ready yet. How's your head?"

Jolin settled back into his pillow, glad to do so. He touched his wound. A crusty scab covered it, as if it were five days old, not two. "I think my head is th' only part o' me that don't hurt. At least, not much."

His vision finally cleared and Jolin looked around the crowded room. Besides the three Companions, Lord Cenith, Lady Tyrsa and Garun all stared at him.

The healer grunted. "Wish I'd seen it. I might have been able to learn something."

Lord Cenith, seated beside Jolin's bed, twisted to look at Garun standing behind him. "Tyrsa plans on healing Buckam tomorrow. You'll have your chance then." His gaze turned back to Jolin. "Tell me about your nightmare. I find it odd that Varth had a pleasant dream…"

"It was pleasant only at the end, My Lord," Varth put in. "It wasn't fun being lost."

"Nonetheless, you didn't scream like Jolin did and I didn't dream at all, at least, not that I remember. So, was the nightmare because Jolin was conscious at the time?"

Screamin'? I don't remember screamin'. Not out loud, anyway. Jolin hoped he hadn't woken anyone. The last thing he wanted was to expose Lady Orchid's powers.

Lord Cenith thought a moment, his grey eyes

distant. "Tyrsa, was this healing any different for you than the other times?"

Lady Orchid sat beside her husband, dressed in a blue gown that matched her beautiful eyes. "I didn't feel much pain with Varth, not like I have since, but I didn't really do the healing." She placed her hand over her belly. "My power did it. I think it was showing me how. Or maybe it was the Mother and Father. That was the only thing that was different."

"So tell us yer dream, Jolin," Keev urged. "Wi' all that noise ye made, I'm not so sure I want t' git healed."

Jolin almost groaned. The guards must have heard him, yet no one seemed concerned. He scanned all their faces, interest and expectation highlighting each of them. Jolin couldn't tell them all of it. He just couldn't. "It started out peaceably enough. When Lady Orchid began her healin', I was reminded o' a favourite meadow back home. I was havin' a picnic, sippin' some wine. Then two crows attacked, one bigger than t'other. They kept peckin' at my wound 'til it bled. I remember th' pain, then nothin'. Did…did my screamin' alert th' guards?"

"Yes," Lord Cenith answered. "But don't worry about it. We told them part of the truth, you'd had a nightmare."

"Oh, good," Jolin said, with a sigh of relief. "I feel better now. Kin I sit up?"

Garun shrugged. "You have a little more colour than when you woke. It depends on how you feel."

Jolin sat, careful in his movements. Most of his muscles had settled down, but he wasn't sure his legs would hold him. Lady Tyrsa jumped up and fluffed his pillow for him. "M'lady! You don't have t' do that!"

"I want to. Mara does this for me sometimes."

Lord Cenith chuckled. "Don't argue. I've seen that look before." His face turned serious.

Jolin had always thought Lord Cenith had strong, personable features. He was the type of lord a man could look up to, worthy of respect and the full loyalty that naturally followed. The trip to Edara and back had given him the opportunity to learn more about his lord and had only confirmed his feelings. Pride flared in Jolin's breast, in his lord, Lady Orchid, and the best homeland a man could ask for. He would do whatever was required to protect all three.

"Lady Violet allowed me to speak with her this afternoon," Lord Cenith said, folding his arms across his chest. "Apparently there's more trouble coming, which is why she needs all the Companions healed."

"What kind o' trouble?" Keev asked.

"That we don't know. We need to be prepared for anything. She also told Tyrsa that Daric is on his way home."

Varth, Ead and Keev all joined Jolin in a whoop of joy. "Does she know if he was successful?"

"If she does, she didn't say. Prying information out of Lady Violet is like moving boulders. For every inch you gain, there's yards to go." Lord Cenith stood. "I don't think there's anything left to discuss. There's little we can do now until Daric gets back with Rymon and the scroll." He scratched his head. "I can't wait to hear that tale."

"Any chance o' us listenin' in, m'lord?" Jolin asked.

"It would be best if you all were there. It would save repeating everything."

Garun opened the door. "Jolin, you're to stay in bed for the rest of the day. I'll send to the kitchen for your dinner. I imagine you're hungry." He left.

"I think I could eat an entire cow, all by m'self." Jolin grinned and settled himself further into the bed, glad he didn't have to test his legs until later; although he'd have to dig the chamber pot out from under the bed before too long.

"If you're feeling better in the morning, Jolin, come find me. If there's going to be trouble, I'd like to discuss a few options with you and Ors, but there's no rush." Lord Cenith held out his arm to Lady Orchid. She took it and looked up at him, total adoration on her face.

Jolin's heart seized in his chest. "Aye, m'lord."

Varth held the door for them, all three Companions saluting their lord and lady.

Just before Varth closed the door, they heard, "You still haven't told me what a 'whore' is."

Lord Cenith heaved a heavy sigh. "I thought you'd forgotten about that."

Varth only just managed to close the door before he burst out laughing. Ead and Keev joined him. Jolin managed a chuckle, because he thought the others would expect it.

"I think we're going to go as well," Ead said, his grin fading. "We haven't had dinner yet and Varth and I are on night shift for the third night in a row." He made a face. "We slept this morning, but wanted to be here when you woke up. A little more sleep wouldn't hurt."

Jolin wondered if the two would actually sleep or intended to share a bed again. It didn't really matter. Truth was, he was just as glad they were leaving and even more so when Keev announced similar intentions…food and rest. Jolin didn't feel in the mood for talking. His nightmare troubled him and now he thought he knew what it might have meant.

When the other Companions left, Jolin folded his hands behind his head. His love for Lady Orchid had to end. It would lead only to trouble, for all three of them. The first crow he took to be Lord Cenith, the second Councillor Daric. Both would have severe objections if they learned his affection for Lady Orchid went beyond that a guard should have for his lady. The thought of hurting his lord like that didn't sit well with him, either.

But how kin I stop lovin' someone? Especially someone as sweet and special as m'lady? Perhaps a visit to Silk's would help. Some of the girls there were prettier than Lady Orchid and loved to see him come in, making it hard to choose. Now that he made more money, he sent more home to his parents to help out with his stricken older brother and his younger siblings. Maybe, this once, he could hold some back and not bother choosing.

Jolin closed his eyes. Pretty wasn't all there was to a girl. He tried to picture other attractive, and interesting, girls around the keep and town, but he couldn't hold their faces for long.

Chapter Eleven

Rymon sat in front of the library fireplace, wishing it was lit. A hot day, and he still felt cold. Saulth was perched in front of his beloved parchment, again. Four days had passed since Daric left Snake's head on Saulth's throne. The Lord of Bredun had spent most of the first day either in a rage or terrified he'd turn around to find Daric stalking him. He had put two guards on the scroll at all times unless he was in the room, then they waited outside with the others; he doubled the guards everywhere else.

"I still smell it, Rymon, especially when I am in my sitting room. It will *not* go away!" Saulth pounded the table, rattling the ink bottle and the glass protecting the parchments.

"We have done everything we can, My Lord. All the floors have been scrubbed. The furniture makers have taken the throne. With the doors open day and night, the smell is gone." Rymon sighed to himself. Two days before, he'd suggested removing the big chair to have it sanded, re-varnished and new padding made. It took most the day to finally convince his lord to relinquish his beloved throne for a short time.

"Then why can I still smell it!"

Rymon shook his head. "I do not know, My Lord." He had to put it down to paranoia. Neither he nor Tajik could detect anything; except in Saulth's sitting room. A disgusting odour permeated the place, despite having everything cleaned.

"Why did Daric not take the scroll?" Saulth demanded. A question he'd asked many times since that morning in the Main Hall.

To keep you from attacking Dunvalos Reach. Rymon did not enjoy lying to his lord, but for the sake of peace, it was necessary. He said the same thing he'd been saying for days. "Probably because he did not know about it. How would he find out? It has been kept here at all times, the guards sworn to secrecy."

Saulth stared at the scroll, ran his fingers over the glass. "Snake. He obviously told him who hired him. How else would Daric know where to bring the head?" His eyes widened.

Rymon couldn't blame him for his concern—Daric appeared to be capable of anything—but Saulth took concern to an entirely new level these days. "Snake was tortured, My Lord. Who knows what else was done to him besides his facial wound? Yes, he had to have told Daric who hired him. But Snake did not know about the rest of the scroll. You never brought him here, remember? He only knew about the portion you wanted him to steal."

Saulth's shoulders slumped. "Yes, you are right Rymon. My scroll is safe."

Rymon nodded. "Yes, My Lord, it is." *Thank Maegden! I think he finally believes me.* He glanced out the open window. "It is time for the meeting, My Lord. Your dukes await." Day two of hell. Char, the worst one.

Saulth scowled. "More whining and sniping. Do they not understand I am doing my best?"

"They are concerned for the people of their towns and villages. Many of them have lost much...family, fields, homes. If you would help them out with some gold, I am

202

sure…"

"Gold! They cannot eat gold."

"No, My Lord, but they can purchase grain from those least affected." Something had to be done. Why couldn't he see that? *Because all his attention is on the scroll and getting the girl back.* Rymon rubbed the left side of his chest and shoulder. The odd pain he'd felt there lately had increased since Daric left.

"Buy from whom? Mador, Kalkor, Amita and Sudara are all affected by the flooding, as is Cambrel."

Rymon leaned forward, resting his hands on his cane. "You can still send envoys to Cambrel, only a portion of their land along the Asha River has been flooded." *Too bad you ruined our relations with Dunvalos Reach. If we had use of their passes, we could have food here from the West Downs and Syrth before winter comes.*

Saulth grunted, an unusual action for him. "I could do that. Maybe it would keep those crows from pestering me."

"Have you decided how you are going to deal with the problem of the statues of Tailis and Keana? Many of the dukes will be expecting something." This was a puzzle Rymon simply could not figure out. First Tailis' idols, then Keana's had toppled over in all areas of the principality. Brother Dayfid had first brought it to their attention five days ago.

"The gods have deserted us. This is merely proof and if those idiots cannot accept it, that is their problem. Not mine."

Rymon closed his eyes a moment. Sometimes maintaining control took more energy than he possessed. "We must go, My Lord."

As they walked, Rymon thought hard about the

changes in Saulth, particularly over the past few months. There had been a time, not so long ago, when he could have predicted what Saulth would do under most circumstances. Not anymore.

Rymon hung his cane on the back of his chair and sat at Saulth's right, glad to do so. It took a few laboured breaths to settle the tightness in his chest. Tables had been set up in the Main Hall for the second day of the annual council meeting. Saulth sat in a regular chair at the head of the tables, mumbling about the smell and his missing throne. He pulled himself together and sat up straight, placing his hand on the papers in front of him.

"Let us get this over with, shall we?" Saulth said, scanning the pages before him. "To solve the problem of food shortages, I will send envoys to Cambrel. They are not as affected as Ardael."

Duke Therget of Willow Down stood. Past middle age and still a formidable warrior, he tended to speak for all the dukes. "An excellent idea, My Lord." The others nodded, muttering their approval. "We could also ask Lord Cenith for passage through his hills and purchase more from the West Downs."

The one fear Rymon had about his idea…someone else expanding on it.

"No!" Both Saulth's fists struck the table, startling the nobles.

"But…but why not?" Therget asked. "Now that he is your son-in-law there should be no problem." He sat back down, intent on what Saulth would say next.

Word had travelled fast after Saulth gave the girl to Cenith, though not one of the nobles said anything about him hiding her true identity, his treatment of her or the manner of her marriage…at least, not in public.

"He has a strange idea that I am responsible for his father's death. That is what led to the Lord Council's decision to join our families." Saulth's laugh sounded strange. "Is that not ridiculous? How could I possibly start an avalanche?"

The nobles responded with nervous laughter and half-hearted chuckles. It had become obvious they knew all was not right with their lord. Rymon saw it in their expressions, their mannerisms. *It is all falling apart. And not only because of the tornadoes and floods.* He lowered his eyes, not wishing to see the desperation on their faces.

"So," Saulth continued. "I have another plan to solve all our problems, but I cannot tell you what it is. You would not believe me anyway."

Rymon sat up straight. *What in Shival's hells is he doing?* Saulth had discussed no plan with him, other than obtaining food. Now the dukes appeared interested, but confused.

Duke Awin of Red Wing Creek stood. His holding was one of those hardest hit by the flooding Kalemi River. A small, timid young man, he wrung his hands as he spoke. "Perhaps…perhaps if you told us, My Lord…"

"I said you would not believe me and that is the end of it." Saulth stared Awin back into his chair. "I will be away from Valda for a while accompanied by six hundred soldiers. We leave at dawn the day after tomorrow. Guard-Captain Brindin and Rymon will be in charge. Therget, I would appreciate it if you would stay and help them out. Leave everything to me, gentlemen. I declare the Bredun Council Meeting for 426 over and done with."

The nobles could contain themselves no longer. The ones who didn't stand and demand an explanation sat with open mouths. Tajik stared at his lord, a deep frown almost hiding his dark eyes, indicating he knew nothing of this either. Protests of problems not yet dealt with and questions about what Saulth had planned abounded. One old Duke, in a loud voice, asked if the banquet was still on.

Saulth must have heard him. "The banquet will be moved up to tonight, so you may leave in the morning. Rymon, tell Lacus to speed up the preparations then you may come to the library. Tajik, follow me." He left by the main stairs, Tajik tagging behind like a faithful lap dog.

Rymon's heart pounded. The same squeezing sensation in his chest he'd felt for the last few days returned. He rubbed his left arm. That hurt as well, along with his jaw. *I hurt everywhere these days, but this is no time for illness.*

He stood and took his cane in hand, forcing himself to endure the pain and discomfort, leaving the nobles to settle down on their own. Talking to Lacus would take time and he needed to get to Saulth's study as quick as possible.

As he left for the kitchen, he had one thought in his head—warning Cenith, for he knew, deep down, Saulth had nothing but trouble in mind for the mountain lord. *Too bad Saulth released the Dunvalos Reach pigeons when all this began.* Rymon could really use one now.

* * * *

Saulth strode to the desk containing the scroll. "Close the door, Tajik, we have much to discuss."

The guard-commander complied then stood in front of the desk, his arms folded. "Are we going to attack Tiras? With only six hundred men?"

"Not Tiras itself, no. Wait until Rymon gets here. I

206

do not wish to repeat myself." Saulth scanned the third piece of the parchment. *'When the time of choosing is at hand, a bright light will appear in the sky, to the west, on the First day of the Eighth month in her sixteenth year. It will look down on the place where the mountain lord breathed his last, to remain forever a symbol of what shall be. Find there, a door.'* He tapped the glass. *Hmm…not much time left.*

Not much time to claim his throne. Four hundred and twenty-six years earlier, Rigen, the last king of Ardael, had broken the country into six principalities so his squabbling sons could each rule. It was the most idiotic thing the man could have done, especially since Saulth discovered he was descended from the eldest son. He should have ruled. Rigen hadn't even allowed his sons to call themselves princes and none of the lords over the last four hundred years had the balls to change it. Saulth's lip curled in disgust.

A knock announced Rymon's arrival. As usual, the first place he headed was the chair by the fireplace, huffing as he made his way. Saulth thought he should have died years ago, but the old man had a stubborn streak. Their many arguments over the years had shown that. Saulth waved Tajik to move his chair to the side so he could look directly at his councillor.

"My Lord," Rymon said, once he'd settled himself. "You cannot possibly be planning to attack Dunvalos Reach. Their…"

"Of course not, Rymon! Despite what you seem to think, I am not a fool." Saulth sat in his chair. "Why must you assume the worst?"

Rymon's face changed from worry to that insipid, condescending expression he always wore when disagreeing with him. *Maegden! I hate that look!*

"I am merely concerned…"

Saulth pounded the desk, careful to avoid the glass protecting the scroll. "As am I! But the only way we are going to solve our problems is by getting the girl back and taking her to that throne. I am well aware of how impenetrable Tiras Keep is. Ifan bragged about it on endless occasions." He sat back and took a deep breath. "Besides, we do not have time for an all out assault."

"What I plan is to take the guard station at the foot of Eagle's Nest Pass and use the people there as hostages. Those mountains fools are so over confident they allow women and children to live with the men. Once we have secured the station, we will send word to Cenith to bring the girl to me at an appointed place and time." A slow smile crept up Saulth's face. "Cenith is a weak fool. He will comply. I imagine he would be more than glad to be rid of that idiot girl."

Rymon opened his mouth then closed it again.

"If you have something to say, Rymon, say it." Probably twenty reasons why he shouldn't go through with his plan.

"Why attack the guard station, My Lord? Why not just send an envoy to Cenith?" Rymon actually looked hopeful as he rubbed his left arm.

Saulth sighed. "Because, my dear councillor, I do not have the time to waste on envoys running back and forth. It is eight days to Tiras at best, the same back. That will take us to the twenty-eighth, leaving us only three days to get ourselves to that mountain. We are running out of time."

Saulth looked to his guard-commander. "Now then, Tajik. I want all six hundred men handpicked. Only the best. We will take the station at night…"

"My Lord! You cannot! If you would only cooperate with Cenith, I…I am sure…" A look of pain and surprise flashed across Rymon's lined features. The councillor stood, weaving back and forth, using his cane for support. He took one step then collapsed to the floor. Rymon lay still.

"Tajik, see what is wrong with him then send one of the guards for the physician. I do not have time for this." Saulth glanced down at the scroll. *So much to do.*

Tajik knelt by Rymon, his eyes wide. "Lord Saulth! I…I think he's dead."

Saulth jumped to his feet, knocking his chair to the floor. "Dead! How can he die now? We have too much work to do!" He silently cursed Aja, Maegden, Shival and both Calleni gods, just for good measure. Taking a deep breath, he straightened his tunic and tugged on his cuffs. "No time. No time for this."

He picked up his chair and sat down. Since the birth of the girl, Rymon had been nothing but a sliver under his nail. In the early days, however, he had given good advice. "Have two of the guards take him to the physician for preparation. There is nothing we can do for him now."

Tajik nodded and headed for the door. Once Rymon's body was removed, he motioned for Tajik to join him at the desk. The guard-commander moved the small chair so it sat opposite Saulth.

"He has a cousin somewhere in town, does he not?" Saulth asked, setting a finger on the third portion of the parchment.

Tajik nodded. "If he's still alive. I'll send word as soon as we're done here."

"You will send word when all our preparations are

finished."

"Yes, My Lord."

If Tajik thought his request harsh, he showed no sign. *He has always been a good, loyal man.* Saulth tapped the reference to the mountain where Cenith's father died. "Do you know the spot where the avalanche hit Ifan?"

"I do, My Lord. The leader of the team told me." Tajik's expression remained bland, as usual. It didn't matter if one discussed dinner or the murder of a man, Tajik looked the same. "If you stand near the guard station, you can see the mountain. Apparently only on rare days is the entire thing visible. It's usually shrouded in cloud. A portion of Eagle's Nest Pass runs along it."

"That is where we need to be on the first of Eighth Month…with the girl. I want to take the scroll with me, so find a strong, weatherproof pouch to carry it."

"Yes, My Lord."

Saulth pulled a blank piece of parchment from his drawer. The money he'd set aside for the girl, and Daric's death, rattled. *Damned incompetent assassins.* Once the girl made her choice, whatever it was, he would rule Ardael. It said so in the scroll. 'One will rule over all'. *Then I will be done with Cenith and that foul mercenary. Traitors, the both of them.* He wrote 'bag for scroll' on the parchment.

Petrella had announced herself pregnant two days earlier. The only highlight from the previous day's meeting with the nobles was their toasting him and his lady. *I'll set Meric up as lord of Dunvalos Reach. That will remove him from my sight and my new son can take over for me as king. He shall be everything a son should be.*

As Saulth wrote out a list for Tajik, he dreamt of a future with himself on the throne of Ardael.

* * * *

Cenith watched Keev's light brown eyes close as Garun's potion took effect. The healer decided to try putting Keev to sleep to avoid the nightmares and pain both Jolin and Buckam had suffered when Tyrsa healed them. Two days had passed since the former Bredun guard had undergone Tyrsa's 'treatment'. He'd had trouble sleeping both nights, afraid the nightmare would return.

"Has Buckam told you about his dream yet?" Cenith asked Jolin, who stood nearby.

He sat close to the bed, next to Tyrsa. Garun had brought a chair with him so he'd be comfortable during the procedure, placing it near Keev's feet. Jolin leaned against the door. With the bed, a narrow wardrobe, clothes chest and two extra chairs for Cenith and Tyrsa, Keev's room couldn't hold much more. All the Companions wanted to attend, but space didn't allow it.

Jolin nodded. "I finally convinced him this mornin' that talkin' 'bout it would help. He said he dreamt he was back in Valda and Saulth had found out 'bout him turnin' t' our side. After beatin' him again, Saulth did t' him what he'd done t' that other guard, the one hangin' above the city gates when we went through."

Cenith suppressed a shudder. The Bredun guard had been tortured before Saulth ordered him nailed to the wall above the gates of Valda. It would be enough to frighten any man. "No wonder he can't sleep."

"I gave him a potion," Garun said. "He should be all right tonight, but I wouldn't recommend putting him on duty for another day or two." The physician shook Keev's bare foot then ran a finger down the bottom, toe to heel. No reaction. "He's ready whenever you are, My

Lady." He leaned forward, anticipation making him appear younger than his fifty-six years.

Tyrsa nodded and put her hands on Keev's broken arm. Fortunately the bed was situated so she didn't have to lean over him. She closed her eyes, just as she'd done with Buckam.

"I've asked the men t' spend more time with Buckam." Jolin kept his voice low. "I'm hopin' it'll make him feel more wanted here and the nightmares will stop."

"Good idea." Cenith didn't take his eyes off Tyrsa's hands.

After a few minutes, they glowed white, just as her entire body had the first night they'd made love. *The night Kian died.* He forced that thought from his head. Her hands had glowed the same way when she healed Buckam. The young Companion's thrashing and screams, though not as bad as Snake's, still disturbed him.

The glow spread to Keev's entire body. Tyrsa gasped and threw her head back. Cenith wanted to hold her, but stopped himself. She'd told him in the meadow that it would hurt him and he didn't want to test her statement. He kept his hands in his lap and concentrated on Keev. The Companion hadn't moved. It appeared as if Garun's potion did the trick. A few minutes more and the glow vanished. Tyrsa collapsed.

Cenith caught her. "In pain?"

She nodded, leaning against him. Tyrsa would now have to spend several minutes bringing that pain under control. As with Buckam, she hadn't passed out. That had to mean something.

Garun shook his head. "I have no idea how she does that."

"I don't think she does either," Cenith said, kissing

the top of her head.

The physician sat back and sighed. "Have you given any thought on how you plan to explain these suddenly healed injuries, My Lord?"

"Some. Buckam isn't a problem, he doesn't have any friends or family here. No one really knew about his broken ribs. Dathan and Trey's concussions are mild, so they won't be a concern. If anyone asks, they weren't as badly hurt as you thought. Sorry to put you in a bad position, but I'm not sure what else to do."

Garun waved his hand. "Not to worry. Much of the art of medicine is guess work anyway. We could say the same for Jolin, although pretending to have a headache for the next week wouldn't hurt."

"I kin do that. I spend most of my off duty time wi' th' Companions or doin' reports anyway. And I wasn't at Silk's afore m'lady healed me." Jolin indicated the guard on the bed. "Keev's goin' t' be th' difficult one. He has an uncle and cousin in town as well as friends in th' rest o' th' guard. I'm sure his girl knows 'bout it."

That had to be the girl Cenith had seen Keev with after Kian's funeral. He still found it amazing that the shy soldier would even talk to a noble's daughter, let alone court her. "That's going to be a problem. Do you know if he's spoken to his family since he was hurt?"

Jolin lifted one shoulder in a half hearted shrug. "If he has, he ain't said nothin' t' me. I suppose we should've asked him afore we put him out."

"When will he wake?" Cenith asked Garun.

"Not until morning, most likely."

Jolin straightened up, his gaze on his sleeping friend. "I hope he wakes up in a better mood. He's been kinda grumpy lately."

Grumpy? How can anyone tell? Keev rarely smiled, at least in Cenith's presence. "Why do you think he's grumpy?"

"He usually likes t' dice wi' us and has turned down several games since th' fight. Madin said he growled at him day afore yesterday when he asked him for some boot polish. He don't smile much around people unless he's really comfortable with 'em, but he likes Madin. I asked him 'bout it yesterday, but he just went to his room and locked the door."

Cenith didn't like the idea of one of the Companions having problems. They all needed to focus on their duty and any trouble that might be forthcoming. "Keep pressuring him, Jolin. If it turns out to be nothing serious, that's fine. But if it could affect his performance as a Companion, then I or Ors need to know."

"Aye, m'lord. I'll do my best."

An almost inaudible moan escaped Tyrsa's lips.

"Are you all right?" Cenith lifted her head enough to look at her face.

Tiny lines showed at the corners of her half-open eyes. "I have controlled the pain, but I'm tired. I think I might be doing this too much. I'm glad there is only one more to do."

"You're getting better, though. You're still awake." He stood and picked her up. "I'm taking her to our suite. Jolin, set up a rotation so one of the Companions is with Keev until he wakes."

Jolin nodded. "I'll take th' first shift."

Barit and Madin waited for them outside the door. They walked down the corridor to the Great Hall. Garun accompanied him.

"Have you been able to learn anything from

Tyrsa's abilities?" he asked the physician.

Garun sighed and shook his head. "I don't have any idea how she does it. It's too bad it causes her so much pain. I have some patients who could use her touch."

"You know we don't dare, Garun."

"Yes, and I understand why. I was only wishing."

Just as they reached the Grand Staircase, one of the master of the bird's messenger boys ran up, out of breath.

"Lord Cenith!" His head bobbed in a quick bow. "I've been looking for you everywhere, My Lord! Master Norbin said to get this to you as quick as I could." Damp, light brown curls stuck to the lad's forehead and neck. He must have run up and down the stairs several times. "He said to tell you it's from Councillor Daric." The boy kept glancing at Tyrsa, half asleep in his arms in the middle of the day. Nothing he could do.

"Can you take her?" he asked Garun.

The healer held his arms out. Once Tyrsa had been shifted, Cenith took the piece of parchment from the boy and sent him on his way.

He scanned the short message. "I think this is the trouble we've been waiting for." Cenith stuffed the parchment in a pocket and took Tyrsa back. "I need you to do me a favour."

"Of course, My Lord."

"I know you're not an errand boy, but I need Ors and Jolin in my sitting room as quick as possible. Join us if you wish. If this is what I think it is your input will be needed as well. Tell Jolin to find someone else to watch Keev."

"Yes, My Lord."

Cenith hurried up the main stairs as fast as his burden would allow, the Companions following. When they reached his suite, Madin and Barit stood next to the regular guards who'd remained behind when they went to Keev's room.

"Once Jolin, Ors and Garun arrive, we're not to be disturbed."

"Yes, m'lord," Madin said. Just a little shorter than Cenith himself, Madin had the build and muscles proclaiming the time spent in his father's smithy. Judging by Daric's message, they'd need those muscles in the days ahead. All four guards saluted him as he passed through the door, fist to chest. Barit closed it behind him.

Cenith laid Tyrsa in their bed, not bothering to put her in a nightgown. That could wait for later. She'd already fallen asleep. He poured himself a glass of white summer wine and downed it in one gulp, then sat waiting for the others.

When they'd arrived and settled themselves, Ors in the other big chair, Garun in a smaller one by the fireplace, Jolin standing behind him, Cenith spread the small piece of parchment across his knee.

"It says, 'Will leave station tomorrow with women and children. War probable. – D."

"War!" Garun stood up. "With who?"

"My guess would be Bredun." Cenith sat back and waved Garun to sit. "I was afraid it might come to this."

"Saulth needs m'lady, doesn't he?" Jolin said, his anger evident in both his eyes and his voice. "It's my guess he has every intention o' comin' for her."

"That would be my guess as well." Ors heaved a sigh of his own. "I suppose we could take another thousand from the west border and have the remaining soldiers continue the ruse Daric set up."

Cenith nodded. "Send word to the dukes. We

might need their levies and I'd like them here in case we do." He tapped the arm of the chair. "I think we should put more soldiers in Eagle's Nest Pass. It's the most logical place for him to attack. He can get more men up Black Crow Pass, but he has to go through part of Amita to do it. Somehow I doubt Urik will just let him march across his lands. Daric must think so as well, otherwise he wouldn't have evacuated the women and children at the station."

Ors and Jolin both agreed. "Most of the men at the pass are archers," Ors said. "If we can keep them supplied with arrows they could hold Saulth's entire army at bay indefinitely."

"Do it." Cenith picked up the piece of parchment. "There's twenty men there now, what's the maximum for that outpost? Fifty?"

Ors nodded. Cenith walked over to the desk by the balcony door and held the message over the candle flame until it lit. He carried the burning parchment to the cold fireplace and tossed it in. "Then send thirty more. I want that place full. Make sure they have supplies for a month and enough arrows to stop a horde of charging Tai-Kethians. Send more to Eagle's Nest station as well."

"Yes, My Lord." Ors stood. "If you will excuse me, I have much to do." With a salute to Cenith, he left.

"I'll have to stock up on bandages after all. I'll call in all the healers from the countryside that I can." Garun also took his leave.

"Jolin, alert the other Companions, but don't tell anyone else just yet."

"Aye, m'lord."

A moment later, Cenith sat alone with another glass of wine in hand, wondering how it had all come to this.

Chapter Twelve

Cenith strode down the hall, waving his right hand at Brother Hamm. "I don't have time. There are things that require my attention and can't wait."

"But I fear for your soul, My Lord. You haven't attended services since your father died." Brother Hamm hiked up his multicoloured robes to keep pace. "And there is more. I fear the entire principality has fallen out of favour."

That's a mild way of putting it. Cenith hadn't shared any of what Tyrsa had done to the gods with the priest, nor would he unless absolutely necessary. He hated destroying an entire religion, one he had believed in all his life; but if that's what had to be done to save the country, then so be it.

They reached the main staircase and, out of respect for the aging priest, Cenith tried not to take them down two at a time. "What makes you think we've fallen out of favour?"

"The statues of Tailis and Keana keep toppling over. It doesn't matter what we do, nails, glue, they just…fall."

Cenith stopped and Brother Hamm almost ran into him. *Interesting. I know why, but how? They're only statues.* "Could it be vandals?"

Brother Hamm shook his head so hard Cenith swore his little remaining hair would shake loose. "I have

218

seen it with my own eyes, as have the workmen who repaired the statues. And it's not just here, other temples are reporting the same thing, but only with Tailis and Keana. It's like those strange symbols on your hearth. They are the same two that disappeared."

Cenith folded his arms. "How did you know about those?"

"Servants love to gossip, but that is not all, My Lord." Creases added more wrinkles to Brother Hamm's already seamed face. "Word is spreading. The people are fearful that bad things will start happening to them, just like in the rest of the country. Maybe, if you put in an appearance? Just once or twice?"

Cenith put a hand on the old man's shoulder. "I'll see what I can do, but it won't be today. I really do have pressing matters that need attention." He ran a mental list through his mind. "Perhaps in the morning. Would that suffice?"

Brother Hamm smiled. "Yes, yes. That would do. Just to help reassure the people. Thank you, My Lord."

If it isn't one thing… Cenith sighed.

The priest took his leave and Cenith hurried to Trey's room, the last of the Companions to be healed. Fallan and Yanis had taken Tyrsa down without him. He'd had a few things to discuss with Ors regarding preparation of the principality for war.

Some of the dukes had arrived, levies in tow, and making room for all rapidly became a nightmare. He'd dispatched five hundred men to Black Crow Pass, just in case Saulth did try that route.

Cenith located Trey's room easily—Fallan and Yanis waited outside. The two could be brothers, with the same height, build and hair colour, except Fallan had grey eyes and Yanis' were blue. He acknowledged their salute and opened the door.

Trey sat on the bed, reclining against a pillow, his arms folded across his chest. His eyes appeared no sleepier than usual. Garun stood near him, potion bottle and spoon in hand. Tyrsa sat next to him, a puzzled look on her face, while Jolin leaned against the window frame, his hand over his face, trying not to laugh.

"I thought you'd be out cold by now," Cenith said to Trey.

Garun sighed. "He's refusing the medication."

Cenith's brow shot up. "Whatever in the world for? Do you like pain and nightmares?"

"Not particularly, My Lord, but I don't like nausea and lingering headaches either, both of which Keev and Dathan are suffering. They attribute it to the potion and not the healing since Jolin and Buckam don't have those problems, so..." Trey shrugged. "I've decided to get it over and done with."

"Well," Cenith ran a hand through his hair. "I suppose it's your decision." An empty chair waited for him next to Tyrsa. He sat and leaned his arms on his knees. "Let's get on with it then."

Trey wriggled down the bed, locked his fingers over his belly and closed his dark brown eyes. "Just give me a few minutes to fall asleep, if you don't mind, My Lady."

"I don't mind." She sat back, waiting.

"Will you go to sleep with all of us here?" Cenith asked.

Jolin laughed. "Trey kin fall asleep in a trice, My Lord."

"You're just jealous." Trey's smirk appeared then

220

disappeared just as quick.

All remained quiet. Trey's breathing slowed.

After only a few minutes, Jolin leaned down and whispered in his ear, "Trey, yer mother's sleepin' with th' butcher down the street and yer father's joinin' 'em for a threesome."

What the...! Cenith's head whipped around. "That's no way to talk in front of your lady." He struggled to keep his voice quiet.

"I apologize for my rudeness, m'lord, m'lady, but if Trey was still awake, he'd have come up swingin'." Jolin grinned. "I think you kin begin, m'lady."

Jolin resumed his place by the window, followed by Cenith's glare.

Tyrsa put her hand on Cenith's arm. "I don't understand what he said. It doesn't matter."

"It does to me," Cenith growled. He'd had a hard enough time explaining what a whore was, he didn't need to try to figure out a way to tell her about *that*.

Tyrsa's fingers glowed and she performed her magic. Trey remained asleep during the entire process. No pain, no screaming. Healing Dathan hadn't taken as much out of Tyrsa and they'd put it down to lesser severity of the wound. As with Dathan, Tyrsa finished quickly. Once done, regaining control of her pain didn't take as long either.

"Hmmm," Garun said, stroking his chin. "Lady Tyrsa passed out after healing you, My Lord, and Jolin, but not with the others, even though I'd consider Buckam's and Keev's wounds worse than his. Could it be because his was a head wound and the others merely broken bones? Though Dathan and Trey both had head wounds, but they weren't as bad. It might be a sign she's simply getting

221

better at healing, or it could be much more."

Cenith stroked Tyrsa's hair while she rested against him. "I wish I could answer your questions. I truly do."

Trey remained asleep through the conversation, a lock of his light brown hair resting on an unconcerned brow.

"He'll stay like that th' rest o' th' day if ye let him, m'lord. I've never met anyone as relaxed as Trey, he jus' don't git worked up over much o'anythin'." Jolin spoke in a normal tone of voice. Trey didn't stir. "Sometimes I think if he was any more relaxed, he'd be dead." Jolin punched Trey in the arm. "Hey! Wake up!"

Trey's eyes opened and he stared at everyone in confusion. "Oh, right." He touched his fingers to the wound above his right ear. "That feels much better. Thank you, My Lady."

Tyrsa, still leaning against Cenith, smiled. "You're welcome."

Garun stared at the Companion as if he'd just grown antlers. "You didn't feel any pain? No nightmares?"

Trey shook his head and sat up. "I feel fine, like I'd slept for twelve hours. I did have a dream though, I remember it quite clearly, which is odd. I don't usually remember my dreams."

"If you don't mind my asking," Cenith said. "What was it about?"

"I was laying by a stream on a nice summer day, My Lord. My head was in the lap of a very pretty girl." Trey leaned back, resting his head on his arms. A little smile played on his lips. "She was laughing and feeding me grapes. A sparrow came down and landed on her hand, singing a song. We listened to it for awhile and then the bird flew away. The girl was about to kiss me when 'someone' woke me up."

Jolin's grin reappeared. "I saved ye from bein' corrupted by a dream witch. Ye don't have t' thank me."

"I won't. You and your fairy people," Trey scowled, but it vanished as fast as it appeared. He sighed. "I don't know who she was, but I'd sure like to meet her."

The men laughed. Tyrsa still leaned against Cenith and he gave her a squeeze, his mood lifted for a brief moment.

"Strange," Garun said, one arm across his chest, chin in hand. "Varth had a dream where he was lost until Lady Tyrsa found him. Jolin had a nightmare about crows, Buckam one about Saulth catching him and Trey had a pleasant dream. Perhaps it depends on the personality of the person, and, maybe, the severity of the wound, or whether the patient is concerned, or perhaps fearful of something. I'll have to write all this down."

"I'm not afraid o' crows," Jolin put in. "But those ones sure didn't like me."

"Dreams are difficult to interpret at the best of times. Your crows may have represented someone you thought might not like something you're doing." Garun shrugged. "Or it could mean nothing, like Trey's dream."

"Nothing? She was pretty." Trey's lazy smile crept up one side of his face.

Once again everyone laughed but Tyrsa. Cenith wished he could find a way to make her laugh. Even when he tickled her, she only begged him to stop because it felt funny. That would have to wait. He had plenty to keep him busy. *I hope Daric shows up soon. I really need him now. Tomorrow, he should be here tomorrow.*

* * * *

Daric, where are you? It's almost dinnertime. Cenith sat in his study, going over the daily reports with Avina. The Calleni should have arrived home yesterday. He hoped nothing untoward had happened; with all the troops heading in his direction, how could it?

"Four more dukes arrived today with their levies, a total of one thousand eight hundred and fifty men," Avina said. "They're camped in the meadows near Canyon Falls. We're rapidly running out of room. And the dukes are demanding a meeting. They need to know what's happening."

Cenith sighed. "I know, but I have no idea what to expect. We might need all or none of those men, or maybe more." He threw his hands up. "I hate all this guessing!"

"If it's any consolation, Mother says Lady Tyrsa is coming along nicely with her manners and is participating more in some conversations."

He looked at the hopeful expression on her face. "Thank you, Avina, that's nice to know." Cenith felt a little guilty for not filling her in on all that had occurred. He would leave that to Daric, whenever his councillor felt it appropriate.

A knock interrupted them. The door opened at Cenith's request and Kindan stuck his head in. "A messenger arrived, My Lord. Councillor Daric is coming through the gates now."

"Well, finally!" Avina said, a small frown creasing her brow. "Mother's been worried sick."

"She has?" Cenith hadn't noticed, but then he didn't have time to pay much attention to anyone, even Tyrsa, something he'd have to rectify soon.

"Mother is very good at hiding things like that, unless you know what to look for."

Cenith turned his attention back to Kindan. "Tell Jolin to gather the Companions. I want them, Ors and Garun here as quickly as possible. And my wife. Also inform Morren he'll need to find rooms for the women and children who have no families in town." As if the chamberlain wasn't busy enough.

"Yes, My Lord." Kindan closed the door.

Avina gathered the parchments spread before them. "These can wait. I'm sure Father's tale will be long and eventful."

"If there's something that requires immediate attention, I trust your judgement. You've done very well while Daric's been gone."

The girl blushed, something she rarely did. "Thank you, My Lord."

Cenith frowned. "What did I say about calling me 'Cenith' in private? I hate all that 'my lord this' and 'my lord that' stuff. You never used to hesitate."

"We were kids then, this is…different. You're a lord now."

"And you're my councillor, even if it is temporary. Daric only uses my title in public, and so should you. We're friends after all, aren't we?"

Avina smiled and opened her mouth to speak, but a knock on the door stopped her.

"Enter." Cenith hoped it was Daric. It wasn't.

Ten of the Companions stuffed themselves into the room, filling the corners and leaning against the fireplace.

"That was fast," Cenith said.

Jolin grinned. "Keev saw Councillor Daric ride in on his way back from town. We figured you'd want t' see us."

Another knock brought Tyrsa, Buckam and Madin

into the room. The Companions shuffled to make way for them to pass. Cenith smiled and brought a chair around to his side of the desk. Before Tyrsa sat down, another knock announced Ors and Garun.

"Daric will be here in a moment, he just wanted to say hello to Elessa and the family first," Ors said. Only one empty chair remained; Ors waved Garun to it.

"I should go and see him as well," Avina said. She took her leave and the Companions made room once more.

Cenith had always felt a little sorry for Daric's oldest daughter. Avina took a chunk of her height, facial features and eye colour from her father, but had her mother's brown hair. While Daric's strong, rugged features looked good on him, they made Avina appear stern and cold—far from the truth.

Once she'd left, Cenith turned his attention to Keev. "Did Daric have Rymon with him?"

Keev shook his head. "I don't think so. I saw only women and kids."

"Well," he said to Tyrsa. "Let's hope he's got the scroll and some way of deciphering it."

"Doing what to it?" Tyrsa's brow dipped in a frown.

"Some way to read it."

"I hope so too." She smiled. Cenith's heart warmed. He would definitely have to make a point of spending more time with her. Lately she'd fallen asleep by the time he came to bed. Cenith dragged his thoughts back to the business at hand. "Did you visit your uncle?" he asked Keev.

The young man nodded and held up his still splinted arm. "I figured jus' not tellin' 'em I was healed would be best. I kin wear it 'til we leave. If we leave." He shrugged.

"Smart thinking." Cenith wondered again what bothered Keev. Jolin had no success in getting him to talk.

A few minutes later, the door opened and Daric strode in. He still wore his black riding leathers, covered in dust, and carried a handful of parchments. Nodding to both Cenith and Tyrsa, he said, "I must apologize, My Lady. I couldn't bring Rymon with me. Buckam was right, he's a sick man. I doubt he'll be in this world much longer."

Tyrsa's eyes shifted to violet. Garun gasped, reminding Cenith that the physician had only heard about Lady Violet.

"I assume you have what I requested?" Lady Violet indicated the parchments.

Daric passed them over and sat down, more tired than Cenith had ever seen him. "I bring you something just as good, a complete translation of the scroll."

Lady Violet frowned. "And what of the scroll itself?"

"I apologize once more. I felt it better to leave the scroll where it was, otherwise Saulth would have been right on my tail. This way we have some time." Daric went on to describe all that transpired since Lady Violet had visited him.

"And you're sure you can trust that Rymon wrote it accurately?" Cenith asked.

"Yes, My Lord. Rymon believes Saulth is mad. He needs Lady Tyrsa to complete the prophecy and will do anything to achieve his goal." Daric turned to Lady Violet. "Is this sufficient for your needs?"

She nodded. "Rymon has done well. I remember it

now. This is right." Lady Violet placed her finger on the first part. "'The land was stolen from us,'" she read. "'It bleeds under the abuse of the Others. One will be born to right the wrong, the Jada-Drau'. "

"According to Rymon it means Choice-Maker," Daric said.

Lady Violet gave him a nod. 'These are the signs when the Jada-Drau is needed: tornadoes and floods will destroy the plains; dissent amongst the progeny of a weak king, each working for themselves; storms and waves will steal the livelihood of the sea-folk; strange creatures will appear from the north, driven by hunger and cold; a mountain lord will find his death in snow. People will lose hope, for those they place it in will have grown weak and will desert them.'"

Silence echoed in the room. Finally, Cenith let loose the breath he'd held, stunned that the death of his father was part of the prophecy. "I...I assume the 'Others' are Ardael's gods? And 'us' are the people who were here first?"

Lady Violet nodded.

Garun slapped his knee. "That's incredible! Everything it says has happened."

"I'd prefer to think I'm not working just for myself," Cenith said, his head still spinning.

"No." Daric leaned back in the chair. "But you do work for your principality, negotiating the best trade deals that you can, making sure everything runs smoothly and no one goes wanting."

Cenith frowned. "Well, yes, but that's for Dunvalos Reach and her people, not for myself."

Ors shrugged. "It could still be taken that way since you aren't concerned about the other principalities."

"I suppose so, but I do worry about the country as a whole." Cenith tapped the parchment. "Where it says the land bleeds, is that the hurt Tyrsa felt when she touched the ground?"

"Yes. Shall I read on?" Lady Violet asked.

Cenith nodded.

"The rituals, sanctioned by Niafanna, sanctioned by Cillain, if followed exact, will produce one of the Blood, a true descendant of the Old Ones, but one with powers unknown by them. One sign of the Jada-Drau shall be love in the face of adversity, another shall be unnatural vigour. The Jada-Drau's full powers will appear at her coming of age." Lady Violet looked up at Cenith. "The part that refers to love in the face of adversity would be the love you have for each other. When you were first joined in marriage, neither of you was happy."

Cenith's thoughts drifted back to those first days. "That's true. I assume the unnatural vigour is her healing ability?"

"Yes, and I am sure you remember when she came of age."

Curious stares from Ors and Garun made Cenith's cheeks warm. He doubted he would ever forget that night. A subject change was in order. "What does it mean by 'the Blood'?"

"I remember stories from my youth," Daric said. "About a magical people who lived in a far off land. It could be them."

Jolin agreed. "I've heard those stories too, m'lord; but they lived here a long time ago, not in a far away land. I never heard them called 'th' Blood', though. We always included them wi' th' Old Ones."

Lady Violet continued. "This is the part you had.

'The ones chosen as her parents will protect, nurture and cherish her, teaching her the ways of Ardael, old and new, equally, so she may wisely make the decision. When the time of choosing is at hand, a bright light will appear in the sky, to the west, on the First day of the Eighth month in her sixteenth year. It will look down on the place where the mountain lord breathed his last, to remain forever a symbol of what shall be. Find there, a door.'"

Barit snorted. "Well that part isn't right. Lady Orchid certainly didn't grow up with nurturing parents."

"Saulth became quite touchy when he read that." Daric leaned on the desk. "Why this part of the prophecy failed to come true but other parts did is beyond me. I'm not an expert in the prophecy business."

"No one is," Garun said. "But I wonder…if Saulth had this piece all along, how it would have turned out? It says 'parents' and yet her mother died in childbirth."

"Things happen here that are not yet clear," Lady Violet said. "I hope that will change."

"I thought about that on the way home," Daric said. "And I can't help but wonder if Saulth would have made an effort to save the mother if he'd had the last piece."

"Possible. But he didn't try to get it until last year, which meant he didn't know where it was until then." Another problem bothered Cenith more. "The first day of Eighth month, that's only two weeks from now." He ran a hand through his hair. "And if Saulth is coming, that could pose a problem for getting Tyrsa there in time."

"We'll cut our way through if we have too, m'lord," Madin said, his gaze steady. The other Companions nodded their agreement.

Cenith couldn't fault their loyalty or bravery, but

he wouldn't waste them in what could be a pointless effort. "It says we'll find a door. I don't remember any door there."

Daric shook his head. "There isn't one. I checked thoroughly when I passed by." He smirked. "The women thought I was crazy."

"I guess that eliminates the thought of going early." Cenith turned his attention back to the parchments. "This last part sounds ominous."

"That's what I thought," Daric put in.

Lady Violet read on. "'Once inside, the Jada-Drau must go to the marble throne. It is there the choice will be made. Be it also known, once the choice is done, it is final. All that is not chosen must be destroyed. One will choose. Twelve will guard. One will rule over all.'"

"Choice?" Garun sat up straight.

"Destroyed!" Ors' jaw dropped.

Daric sat back and let out a long breath. "Rymon had no idea what kind of choice Tyrsa has to make. Lady Violet, do you know?"

"I do not, but I believe it will be made clear when the time comes. The Twelve must refer to the Companions."

"That's weird," Varth said. "It makes my spine crawl."

Jolin scowled. "I'm not sure I like bein' part o' a prophecy."

"You're not the only one." Yanis visibly shuddered. "We decided to guard Lady Orchid on our own, just the eleven of us."

Jayce nodded. "We didn't know 'bout any prophecy. We jus' wanted t' protect our lady."

Daric held his hands out. "There's no logical

explanation for any of this. We'll just have to make sure we have Lady Tyrsa at the appropriate place on the first of Eighth Month."

"Why?" Everyone looked at Ors. The guard-commander stood up. "You weren't here, Daric, when Lord Cenith was attacked by what Lady Violet says was Tailis."

"No, but I heard about it from her, when she came to visit." Daric turned to Tyrsa's other self. "I'm glad to see you're safe. You left in a bit of a hurry."

"That's another tale," Cenith said. "Ors, what's on your mind?"

"The same thing we discussed that night, My Lord. The scroll says Lady Tyrsa was supposed to learn both the old and new ways, so the choice can be made wisely. Then it says all not chosen will be destroyed. Is your lady wife here to wipe out our gods, and if so, what will be the aftermath?"

"Wipe out the gods?" Daric's eyebrow lifted. "I think I need to hear the entire story."

Cenith told most of it, with the Companions filling in from time to time; about Tailis, and Keana, as well as the disappearance of their symbols and the statues that wouldn't stay put.

When Cenith finished, Daric sat with his arms crossed, deep in thought. A quiet moment passed. "It's possible that is her mission, but as Cenith said, Tailis and Keana attacked her, not the other way around. The way I understand the scroll, it's Ardael's gods that are causing the problems, making the land hurt, as Tyrsa says, by their neglect, or perhaps by just being here. Is our duty to our country? Or to the gods?"

"Pardon my saying so, Daric," Ors said, his face

grim. "But that's an easy decision for you. Your gods are not the ones threatened."

"Not true. There is a decision to be made, between the old and new. Tyrsa may choose the new." Daric scanned the solemn faces of the others. "What does everyone else think?"

"I doubt it," Ors said. "Not after what Tailis and Keana did. Why would she choose those who tried to kill her?"

Jolin stepped forward. "If I may speak for all the Companions?" The others agreed. "We fought Tailis. We know what happened. I wish we'd been there t' help Lady Orchid when Keana attacked. All o' us have discussed this 'mongst ourselves. Even though we haven't actually spoken an oath t' our lady yet, we hold it in our hearts. If our gods choose t' fight her, we will stand in their way." A chorus confirmed Jolin's words. "And for myself, I will fight t' th' death t' git Lady Orchid where she needs t' be at th' right time, for I believe in her. Whatever it is, she will make the right choice."

"Well spoken," Fallan said. The others agreed.

Daric looked at Garun.

The healer cleared his throat. "As I told Lord Cenith just recently, I have trouble paying homage to gods who don't care about the people who believe in them. If Lady Tyrsa is here to destroy them, well, frankly I don't think anyone would notice."

Ors sank back in his chair, his face crinkled with worry.

Cenith folded his hands on his desk. "If you're not comfortable with this, Ors, you don't have to join us. As a matter of fact, I'll need someone here in case things go terribly wrong."

"It's not myself I'm concerned about, My Lord, but the rest of the people. They need the gods, need that support. Sometimes, just knowing there's someone watching over you helps you through the day."

"Which is fine," Daric said, "as long as those gods *are* watching over you. These ones are not."

Ors slumped further into his chair. "I'm afraid of a revolt if the people find out. I'm worried things will be said about my lady. That she, and Lord Cenith, may be in danger from the very people we are trying to protect."

Cenith sat back. "As I said that night, Ors, if we say nothing the people can keep on worshipping those gods. It wouldn't matter, they do nothing anyway."

The guard-commander's shoulders sagged and Cenith doubted he could sink any lower. "I suppose you're right, My Lord, but if someone talks, this could get very bad."

"Agreed," Daric said. "But if the choice Lady Tyrsa has to make has nothing to do with the destruction of the gods, then there's no need to worry. There's little we can do until the time comes, except keep her safe and get her to that mountain by the first of Eighth month. Shall we work for that and worry about the rest when we get there?"

Ors nodded, though he hardly appeared consoled.

Cenith leaned over the parchments once more. "As for this bit about one to rule, I see where Saulth got his idea of wanting to be king."

Daric nodded. "It seems he's more concerned about gaining a throne than fulfilling the prophecy. That's something else we'll just have to wait on."

Lady Violet spoke up. "The rest of this describes the ritual Saulth and his mistresses had to go through to produce the Choice-Maker." She looked up at Cenith. "I

234

would rather not read this. It is quite disgusting."

Cenith had already scanned that part. "I understand. I don't think it's necessary for what must be done."

Daric stretched his legs out under the desk. "The prayer is a standard one to Cillain and Niafanna still used today."

Ors shook his head. "I can't believe the man would forsake his gods just to gain a throne."

"Rymon believes a spell was put on him by the old man who sold him the first part of the scroll," Daric said. 'I doubt that's true, but Saulth has changed in the past year, significantly. He is, without a doubt, insane."

Garun rubbed his chin. "You say Saulth was involved with this scroll for eleven years before Lady Tyrsa was born?"

Daric nodded. "That's according to Rymon, who was there when Saulth bought the parchment."

"That's twenty-seven years in total." Garun sighed. "Sometimes obsession can rule a man. This appears to be a perfect example."

"Mad or not," Daric said. "My gut tells me Saulth's on his way. He needs Lady Tyrsa."

Every eye settled on Lady Violet. "There is nothing we can do until we arrive at the throne. Then all will be made clear." Her eyes changed back to Tyrsa's beautiful blue.

She hugged Cenith's arm. "I'm afraid. I don't want people to hate me."

Cenith pulled his arm from her grip and put it around her, holding her close. "We don't know if that's what will happen. There's no point in worrying about it now. Let's just wait."

She nodded.

"I see you've already made some preparations for war," Daric commented. "I told the men headed for the station to stay at the pass. They're camped in that large meadow east of the guard tower."

Cenith flashed him a questioning look. "Won't Aleyn need the support in case of an attack?"

"Saulth will attack, he has to, and he'll attack with a lot more than one hundred men. Don't worry about Aleyn. I told him to take the men and hide in the forest. He's to let Saulth through and then harry him from the rear. They can hide in the mountains and Saulth's plainsmen will have a demon of a time finding them. We brought the horses back with us and the men at the garrison put them in a meadow near the tower. At worst we'll lose some buildings and a few cows, pigs, chickens and goats."

"Sound thinking." Ors expression changed from worry to determination. This was a topic he could handle. "We put the word out to bring in the levies. Most of the dukes have arrived, so we've been storing bodies wherever we can. We sent five hundred to Black Crow Pass, figuring they could hold them off with bows until help comes. I've got everyone who can craft arrows filling boxes."

Daric nodded. "I'd thought the same thing about Eagle's Nest Pass, which is why I left a hundred men there. We can hold him no matter which pass he takes. It's getting Lady Tyrsa to Shadow Mountain that will be the problem. I just know Saulth will come by Eagle's Nest Pass. It's faster and time is running short."

"Then what do we do?" Cenith gritted his teeth.

"Just what we are doing," Daric said. "Gear up for

236

war and try to get Lady Tyrsa to that mountain in two weeks."

"We're going to have to tell the dukes everything." Cenith not only hated the thought, he feared it. Who knew how they'd react?

Daric nodded. "We have no choice. We can't lie to them about why we have a possible war on our hands."

"Will three days give you enough time to recover for the council?" Cenith asked. "If you don't mind my saying, you look terrible."

Daric grunted. "I didn't get much sleep the first two days out of the station. Too worried about attack from behind. A little rest and I'll be fine."

Cenith dismissed everyone and had Buckam and Madin return Tyrsa to Elessa. He leaned back in his chair, his feet up on the desk. *How in the three hells do I explain this to the dukes?*

* * * *

After a late dinner, Cenith and Daric retired to Cenith's suite for another long discussion. He sent Tyrsa to spend the time with Elessa. He didn't want her hearing any of what they had to discuss.

After Daric told the complete tale of his journey, Cenith stared at the symbols on the hearth, particularly the holes where two others had been, trying not to envision what his councillor told him. Another shudder ran down his spine. "I know Snake deserved everything you gave him, but I'm really glad I wasn't there."

Daric raised an eyebrow. "If I'd known you'd be this bothered, I never would have told you."

"No, I'm glad you did. It's reassuring, in an odd

sort of way, that you would do anything I asked you to." He glanced at Daric.

Daric nodded his head once. "Of course. You are my lord, and my friend."

Cenith managed to find a smile. "I wish I'd been there to see the look on Saulth's face when he found Snake's head."

"Me too, but I couldn't risk it. I had to return with the translation." Daric thought a moment. "I wish I could have brought Rymon back with me. He's a smart and sensible man, and the only reason Tyrsa is alive today. By the way, he also told me the first day of Eighth Month is Tyrsa's sixteenth birthday."

Cenith turned his gaze from the hearth to Daric. "Not a coincidence I assume."

"All part of the prophecy, strange as it is."

"A prophecy where some has come true, some has not, and the rest must wait." Cenith sighed. "I think that's the part I hate the most. The waiting."

Daric nodded and sipped his wine.

Another thought entered Cenith's head. "While I was tending Tyrsa's lash wounds, Mara said something that concerned me. She said she knew something about Varth and Ead, and that she wasn't the only one."

Daric smirked. "They hide it well, but, um..." The smirk disappeared and he shifted in his chair. "They're... lovers."

Cenith tried not to let his shock show on his face. He'd heard of such things—Kian had taken great pleasure in making jokes about it—but he'd never expected to run into it so close to home. Though it wasn't illegal, as in some countries, it certainly wasn't common. It explained Ead's reaction when Varth was hit by a rock during the tornado attack. "Oh." What else was there to say?

"They're not hurting anyone," Daric said. "And it hasn't caused problems in their performance of duty. It actually happens more than you'd think. I wouldn't worry about it."

Cenith looked back at the hearth. That was a subject best dropped. He let his thoughts drift back to Daric and how he'd exacted his revenge; Cenith couldn't get it out of his mind and hoped he didn't have nightmares over it. Most men should be afraid of the former mercenary, but Cenith felt sympathy. Daric wasn't only tired, a haunted look had come to his eyes since Kian's death.

He had hoped killing Snake would have removed it, but it appeared worse. What nightmares did Daric suffer? What dark memories chased him? Daric wasn't like Snake. The Calleni killed only when there was a purpose, not for money; at least, not anymore. Maybe that was it. Daric had discovered his heart, Snake hadn't, and it was that heart, his love for his family, that hurt him now. Then Cenith realized he was part of that family. 'You are my lord, and my friend.' A warmth spread through Cenith. It didn't matter what Daric had done in the past or what he might do in the future. It would be for the sake of peace in Dunvalos Reach, and in Ardael. Cenith slept better that night than he thought he would.

Chapter Thirteen

Flames leapt from windows and gaps where roofs had collapsed, lighting up the night and lending a malevolent cast to the faces of the men standing nearby.

Animals screamed and bellowed, caught in the deadly flames of the barns that had sheltered them. Chickens and goats squawked and bleated in their pens, seeking escape from the heat and smoke. Saulth closed his eyes and put his hands over his ears. The heat of a thousand suns slammed into his face. *This must be what Char is like. Shival, hear me! I only do this to protect our land! I must! I have to! Forgive me, Talueth! Maegden! I seek only to save what is yours!* Saulth opened his eyes. The dancing flames showed him an image of himself sitting on the throne of Ardael. His heart calmed. The gods sanctioned what he did.

He sat on his horse near the burning guard house, Meric next to him. The shadow of fire and smoke wove strange patterns on his son's face, revealing his fear, terror and revulsion. Saulth snarled. This was nothing compared to what should have occurred.

No one had come to challenge them. No faces screamed at the windows. No people ran through burning doorways. *Where have they gone? How could they have known?* One face flashed in his mind. *Daric!*

"My Lord!" Tajik stared up at him, his soot-covered features resembling one of Shival's demons. The roar of the fire and crashing of timbers almost drowned out his voice. "All the buildings have been searched and torched! No one is here!"

"Where? Where could they have gone!" Saulth leaned down closer to his guard-commander.

"Back to Tiras, perhaps? My guess would be the forest. If I were Daric, I would have told them to hide there, let us pass, then attack from the rear."

Saulth's eyes narrowed. "Then we will foil that little plan. Forget the buildings. Take five hundred soldiers and search the forest, leave the rest here to guard me. I want as many taken alive as possible."

"Shouldn't we wait until dawn? It will be difficult to…"

"No! They must start now. I want those men found!" Saulth wheeled his mount around and rode away from the heat, Meric following behind, silent for a change. Corvin's frightened face appeared out of the darkness.

"Corvin! I want our tents set up so the smoke from the fires does not disturb our sleep."

"Yes, My Lord." The young man vanished into the night.

Meric coughed. "You are going to sleep? After all this?"

"Of course. It is well after midnight. Something you will have to learn if you plan on becoming a lord is that sleep is essential. It helps you think clearly." Saulth waved his arm in the direction of the forest. "There are always others to take care of the details."

"I doubt I can sleep after this, Father. I mean…"

"Then force yourself! Pretend you are lying with one of your sluts if that is what it takes." Saulth located where the men set up their tents, dismounted and tugged off his gloves. Four soldiers worked on his tent, four more on Meric's. They'd be up in no time.

Meric almost fell off his horse. "I am still not sure why we are doing this. That whole business with the scroll is just too much to believe. I am still trying to get used to the idea that she is my sister. She is stupid and cannot even speak. How is she supposed to save the world?"

Saulth grit his teeth. "Country, Meric. Not the world." He'd told his son about the scroll, and the girl. Without Rymon, he needed someone with whom to discuss his plans. Tajik was too much a soldier; swing your sword and leave the diplomacy to someone else. Good for battle, but not for the more intricate aspects of strategy. Meric did have a brain, he just needed to learn how to use it.

Now Saulth regretted his decision. Meric had done nothing but argue every point of the scroll. He'd even dared suggest the entire thing was a hoax. A fist to the head had set him straight on that. At least, he thought it had. "The scroll is three thousand years old and yet it predicted the floods, tornadoes, everything. Why can you not understand that it is true?"

Two soldiers brought travel stools for them. Meric took his and plunked himself down. Another man brought a brazier and had a fire lit in a matter of minutes. Saulth flicked ash from his uniform tunic. Though it was the same shade of dark green as that of his men, it was made of better material and decorated with gold braid. He made a mental note to have Corvin give the uniform a proper brushing later. After all, a lord must always look his best.

"What I do not understand," Meric said, "is why you kept that girl in the storage room if you were supposed to have taught her…"

A smack to Meric's face put a stop to his blathering. "I explained that as well," Saulth said, through clenched teeth. "I did not have that part of the scroll until it was too late. I had expected a son, one who would be strong and smart enough to do what had to be done! Now stop whining and straighten up. Show you bear Bredun blood and not piss in your veins!"

The men nearby kept their faces turned away, pretending they saw nothing. Meric rubbed his face and scowled.

"Get some sleep. Tomorrow will be a long day." Saulth strode off to his tent.

* * * *

The next day proved longer than Saulth had anticipated. By nightfall, the Bredun soldiers had only found nine of the Dunvalos Reach men, at a cost of eighty of his own, but Aja tossed some of his luck their way. They'd captured the captain of the station and a lieutenant.

Saulth had beaten and kicked the captain bloody and he now knelt in front of him, held firm by Tajik. One eye had swollen shut, his lip bled, ribs were broken, but the man refused to say anything except his name.

"Bring the others," Saulth ordered. Meric stood beside him, looking like he'd throw up any minute.

Four of the guard brought the remaining prisoners, bound and gagged, and lined them up to Saulth's right. All bore signs of rough handling.

Saulth tucked his whip under his arm and inspected his gloves for damage. Blood spattered them and his uniform. He sighed; he would have to change when this was done.

The fire in the brazier spit and crackled. Leftover stew from dinner sent spicy tendrils of pepper and bay wafting on the night air. "Tajik, the next time this man fails to answer a question, kill the lieutenant."

Tajik nodded to Corvin, one of the guards with the prisoners. The young man drew his sword and placed it against the captive's neck. Fear flashed through the man's eyes, and was reflected in Corvin's.

"Now then, Aleyn, how many men are still out in the forest?"

Aleyn set his jaw and stared at the prisoners, his expression unreadable. A silent understanding passed between him and the man with the sword at his throat.

Saulth raised his hand.

The captain closed the eye not already shut, hung his head and mumbled something.

"What was that? I didn't hear you." Saulth kept his arm in the air.

"Fifty-one." Aleyn choked the words out.

Saulth chopped the air with his hand. Corvin hesitated only a moment. He swung, removing the prisoner's head. Aleyn and the remaining Dunvalos men cried out. Blood gushed from the lieutenant's neck, pumping in rhythm with the dying heart, spraying the soldiers—guards and prisoners alike. The body slumped forward. The head rolled close to Saulth, the now sightless eyes staring at a point just past him. A wet, retching noise came from just behind Saulth. He sneered at his son's weakness.

"Idiot!" Tajik spat. "When you cut someone's head off, lean them forward! How do you plan to clean your uniform out here?"

"My apologies, sir. I won't make the same mistake

again." Despite his calm words, Corvin's face turned a pale shade of grey.

"You bastard!" Aleyn cried. "You said if I answered, you wouldn't kill him!"

Saulth covered the distance between them in a moment and backhanded Aleyn, sending him sprawling to the ground. "Show some respect for your betters!" He grabbed the front of the captain's tunic and hauled him back to his knees. "You were not fast enough. Try again."

He let the captain go and resumed his position. "You said there are fifty-one still in the forest?"

Aleyn closed his eye again, struggling to stay upright, and nodded. Blood dripped down his chin from a new split in his lower lip.

About time he accepted his defeat. Stubborn fool. "You used to have only thirty. Why the increase? Look at me!"

The captain's good eye snapped open. "Lord Cenith and Councillor Daric were afraid you'd make another attempt at kidnapping Lady Tyrsa."

"Lady who?"

Confusion echoed in the captain's open eye. "Lady Tyrsa, Lord Cenith's wife. Your daughter."

Saulth spat on the ground in front of Aleyn. "He could not even give her a good Ardaeli name, the idiot. You mountain people had better watch it. If you are not careful you will all be speaking Calleni before long. Bowing down to pagan gods."

The captain glared, but said nothing. Meric stifled a cough.

"I assume that mercenary bastard told you to hide in the woods and pester us as we travel up the pass."

Aleyn licked blood from his split lip. "Yes."

"How did he know we were coming?"

245

"He didn't." Aleyn shook his head. "Councillor Daric only suspected you'd come and wanted to be prepared."

Too crafty for his own good. That Calleni has to go. Saulth paced back and forth in front of his captive before asking the next question. "What else did Daric do before he left?"

"He took our women and children with him. He…he also sent a message warning Lord Cenith." Aleyn pulled himself as straight as he could. "You won't succeed. They'll be ready for you. You'll never lay a hand on my lady again!"

Saulth pulled his whip from his belt and struck Aleyn on the side of the face, knocking him to the ground once more. The other prisoners fought against their bonds and Tajik ordered them subdued. The captain struggled to right himself and shook his head, glaring his defiance. More blood dripped from the new cut.

Maybe not quite defeated. "I *will* have her and you are going to help me." Saulth slapped the handle of the whip against his gloved hand. "Tajik, I think we will give Daric the same gift he gave us."

Corvin stepped forward. "Please allow me, My Lord."

Saulth nodded. The young man showed promise.

"What…what are you going to do? I answered your questions!" Aleyn tried to stand. Tajik pushed him down. The rest of the prisoners struggled and yelled. Saulth's men beat them quiet.

Corvin kicked Aleyn in the gut, forcing him to double over. A quick, steady swing, and the captain's head rolled on the ground. Tajik grunted his approval.

"Dispose of the bodies and put their heads in a

246

sack," Saulth ordered. "Tajik, I'm going to bed. Wake me at first light. That gives us twelve days to get the girl and find the throne."

"What should I do about them?" Tajik used his sword to point to the Dunvalos Reach men, now lying on the ground.

Saulth glanced in their direction. "They can stay there, just make sure they are watched."

"My Lord,' Tajik said, his heavy brows dipped in a frown. "If we continue, we'll face heavy losses from the soldiers that escaped."

"Are you suggesting we go home? If we are to save Ardael, we cannot leave! Losing men is all a part of war. Are you afraid to die, Tajik?" Saulth sneered. "And here I had thought you a braver man than that."

"No, My Lord, I am not afraid to die, as long as it's for a good cause."

"And saving the country is not a good cause?"

Tajik had no answer.

"Then I am going to bed."

* * * *

Saulth gritted his teeth as he listened to the sergeant's report.

"We just can't find the buggers, My Lord!" Landis said, anger turning his naturally reddish skin to that of a ripe apple. "They've it set up so someone's firing from different places at all times. With their long bows, we don't have a hope of answering even if we could see them. Over a hundred men are dead!"

The barrage had started that afternoon when they reached a narrow section of the path. No more than two horses could walk side by side.

"Are the idiots not using their shields?"

"Yes, My Lord, but they can't protect themselves and their horses too. The goat turds are deliberately hitting the horses in the flanks. They go berserk and fall off the cliff, taking their riders with them."

"How many are attacking?"

Landis shook his head. "We can't get an exact count. No one wants to stick their head up that far, but from what I could see, there could only be a couple dozen of them."

Saulth ground his teeth. "Where in the three hells are the rest?" No one offered an answer. The sounds of screaming men and horses rang in his ears. *Damn them to Shival's deepest hell!* He drummed his fingers on his thigh. "Tell the men to dismount and move in single file keeping themselves between their horses and the rocks. Make sure they put their shields over their heads."

"Yes, My Lord." Landis wove his way back to the rear guard, relaying the new orders as he went.

"I recommend we do the same, My Lord." Tajik slid off his horse as he spoke.

"Of course. Meric! Dismount!"

Saulth's son rode behind him with Corvin at his side, strangely silent for most of the trip.

"Corvin! Pass the word up the line," Tajik said.

Saulth had placed himself in the middle of the company, hoping the mountain men would think him at the front, where the prisoners walked. So far, the rear had taken the brunt of the attack. Once organized, Saulth ordered them to move, trying to catch up to the soldiers who had yet to hear the orders.

"Do we have any idea what is ahead?" he asked

Tajik, who walked in front of him.

"I've had no word. I wouldn't be surprised if our scouts are dead."

They carried on, hiding behind horse and shield. The screams of men and animals diminished, but didn't stop. Tajik proved right about the scouts. Their bodies were found on the path shortly before dinner time.

Saulth cursed. "We have to do something. Have the prisoners brought to the back. Maybe they will be reluctant to fire on their own men."

Tajik nodded and spoke to the soldier in front of him. It took a while for the prisoners to work their way back down the line; in the meantime, Saulth lost more men.

He and Meric accompanied Tajik to the rear guard, under severe protestations from his guard-commander. Saulth needed to see the extent of the damage to his small army and if there might be some way to stop the mountain men.

When Meric also protested the move, Saulth said, "Maybe you will learn something. I doubt it, but I have to try."

One of the prisoners suddenly lurched to his left, shoving his guard over the cliff.

"That man goes first!" Saulth cried. He glared at the prisoners. "Anymore of my men die by your nonsense and you will join them!"

Tajik took the mountain man guilty of killing the guard to the end of the line, using him as a shield as they approached the ambushers. Saulth stayed back with Corvin, protected by several men. Meric waited just behind, also shielded.

"We still have some of your men!" the guard-commander yelled. He pushed his captive in front of him. The arrows stopped. "Keep this up and they die!"

No response came from the rocks.

"There, you see Meric? All you have to do is show you are smarter than they are." Saulth remained hidden behind his and Corvin's shield.

Tajik suddenly dove to the ground. A thrum filled the air and arrows found their targets, each one a Bredun guard. The men around Tajik and the prisoners dropped like stones. The captive they'd used as leverage leapt to his feet, hands still bound behind his back, and ran down the path to the cheers of the other prisoners.

"Somebody kill that man!" Saulth picked Corvin up by his collar and used him as a full shield. Three arrows hit the young guard, almost jerking him out Saulth's grip. The man's eyes opened wide. He gasped, then hung limp.

Cursing the accuracy of the attackers, Saulth dropped Corvin's body and pushed Meric ahead of him as he struggled up the path. He shoved his way through, knocking several of his guards off balance. Some almost fell down the cliff.

When they arrived back to safety, Meric spun to face Saulth, eyes wide, his shaking hands trying to hold the shield above his head. "I definitely learned something Father," he spat. "Do *not* do a job someone else can do and do *not* yell out unless you want to be hit!"

Saulth backhanded Meric. His son's head snapped to the side, but he recovered quickly and glared defiance. Saulth paused a moment, shocked that his son showed some sign of the stones Maegden had given him. "Get going or I will toss you off the cliff!"

Tajik arrived a few moments later, cursing the air blue. "Landis put a crossbow bolt in the prisoner's thigh, but he disappeared around the bend before he could get another shot off. The bugger runs like a mountain goat."

"No mind, we still have six prisoners. We will carry on as fast as possible. With luck, we will find some shelter, a cave or something."

Not long after, Landis caught up with them. "The arrows have stopped, My Lord!"

"They must have run out," Tajik said. "At the rate they were firing, they had to eventually."

"Thank Aja for that!" Meric lowered his shield and slumped against the rock wall.

"Any estimate on how many we lost?" Saulth asked.

Tajik shook his head. "Not an accurate one, but I guess well over two hundred."

"That son of whore! Pig futtering, slimy, black hearted murderer!" Saulth paced the short distance between Meric and Tajik. "That stinking Calleni is responsible for this and he will pay! Soon!" He shook his fist in Tajik's face. "By my own hand!"

Saulth snatched the reins of his horse from the guard holding them and continued to use both animal and shield for protection, not trusting Tajik's assessment of the attackers' remaining arrows.

The sun vanished behind the mountains, a few clouds reflecting back its blood red glow. Soon, the path widened and they left the cliffs behind. The Bredun men now rode through an open forest, following a well used path. Before true dark fell, they found a wide meadow to spend the night.

Saulth ordered no tents set up, not wishing to pinpoint exactly where he and Meric slept. "I want half the men sleeping and half as sentries. They can rotate in the

251

middle of the night. Travel rations for dinner. No campfires permitted."

Tajik nodded and left to speak to Landis.

Meric watched him leave. "We have lost a lot of men, Father. Should we not just turn back?"

Saulth grabbed Meric by the hair. "Turn back? Are you that much of a coward that you will not stick with a mission to the end?" He threw his son to the ground. "We are not turning back! We still have more than enough men to accomplish our goal. If you want to leave, then do so, but you will do it alone!" Saulth spun and strode to his horse. "Corvin!"

"Corvin is dead, My Lord."

Saulth stared at the soldier who spoke. "Then you set up my bed. And find me some food." He unhooked his canteen from the saddle horn and drained it. "And more water." He tossed the empty container to the guard.

"Yes, My Lord." The man pulled Saulth's blankets from his horse.

Finding his stool already set up, Saulth sat. Tajik crouched beside him. "I am surrounded by fools and the biggest is my own son," Saulth said. He glanced over at Meric, who waited while a soldier set up his bed. His lip curled. "I see he decided not to leave after all."

The guard-commander made no comment.

"How are our prospects looking for tomorrow?"

"Provided the mountain men really have run out of arrows, good. We've lost a lot of men, but we're still on schedule. I figure we should arrive at the far end of Eagle's Nest Pass late tomorrow afternoon."

Saulth clasped his hands in front of him. "Excellent. Then we can eat and get some rest."

* * * *

Cenith stood and pounded the table with both fists, shocking the dukes to silence. "We have eleven days before we have to be at that mountain! I need to know if you back me or not!"

Duke Ramos of White Deer Valley stood. "How can we support something as tenuous as a prophecy? This might be an elaborate trap to kill you and Councillor Daric. The assassins didn't work, maybe this will." He sat down.

"I thank you for that concern, but Tyrsa is the one Saulth is really after. You've all read the parchments Daric brought back and I've told you about my wife and her other self. Believe me gentlemen, that was not easy." Cenith's hands throbbed and he resisted shaking them. He took his seat, his anger burning a hole in his gut. He glanced at Orman. The errant duke had yet to say a word.

"I can see why you didn't tell us about this earlier, My Lord." Duke Von of Bear Creek Valley leaned forward, his eyes riveted on Cenith. "It's difficult, if not impossible, to believe. Nonetheless, I feel you should have confided in us from the start." Murmurs of agreement echoed in the Hall.

Cenith heaved a long sigh and he glanced at Daric. The Calleni's face remained as stony as ever. Avina sat to his right, her features as stern as her father's. Daric had decided she needed to know. If something happened to him, Cenith would still have someone who understood the situation to help him with the paperwork.

"Perhaps you are right," Cenith said, "But to be honest, I never dreamt it would go this far. Most of what has happened in the last three months seems like a bad dream. I hate to say this, but maybe I should have followed Ors' advice and kept this from all of you."

The guard-commander's gaze remained on the table where it had sat for most of the meeting.

Timron of Sunset Vale spoke next. "No, My Lord. I, for one, am glad you told us. We need to know. Whether the people need to know is another matter." Some dukes nodded their approval, others voiced their objections loudly, while Orman remained quiet. Timron scanned the tables. "Lord Cenith is right. If this news leaks out, we could have a rebellion on our hands as well as war with Bredun. Do you want that?"

The dukes shook their heads and grumbled.

"Please be patient with us, My Lord," Timron continued. "You've had more time to assimilate this than us."

Cenith nodded. "That's why I wanted to tell you now. We need to be at Eagle's Nest Pass guard station by the thirty-first, and, if Daric is correct, we could easily have to plow through Saulth to do it. I need your men, and your support."

Ryler of Misty Vale cleared his throat. "The way I understand what's been happening, My Lord, your wife could possibly destroy our gods. Why do you think this is a good idea?"

"I never said it was, and our gods may not be destroyed." *Maegden's balls! How many times do I have to tell them!* "It all depends on this choice Tyrsa has to make. Surely you must realize that all the prayers and sacrifices don't work and haven't since long before this entire mess started. If there's a way to put an end to the suffering in Ardael, are we not obligated to pursue it?"

"Even to the extent of turning against our gods?"

Ryler asked.

Orman spoke before Cenith could answer. "By the looks of things, our gods have turned against us. According to Lord Cenith, and this…" He waved his hand in the air, "…Lady Violet, Tailis and Keana are gone. Have the rivers stopped flowing? Have the plants stopped growing?"

No one had an answer for that. Cenith gave Orman slight nod, acknowledgement of their agreement. He briefly wondered if the Duke of Warbler Ridge actually meant what he said, then decided it didn't matter.

"Can we agree that regardless of this business with the gods, we need to ensure we have enough men and supplies to attack Saulth if he stands in our way?" Cenith resisted the urge to cross his fingers.

"Saulth deserves everything we can throw at him," Von said.

Many were hesitant, but all the Dukes nodded. Cenith heaved a sigh of relief. "Then if you gentlemen don't mind, I'd like to end this meeting. It's lunch time and I'm sure everyone is hungry. And there are still preparations to be made for tonight's banquet."

Cenith had suggested the banquet to Daric, who'd agreed wholeheartedly. Besides the break from the tension, Cenith wished to formally introduce the Companions and have them swear their oaths before they left for Eagle's Nest Pass. Once again the dukes mumbled their agreement and Cenith took his leave.

Orman snagged him before he got very far and pulled him under the Grand Staircase. "Is this why you wanted my support?"

Cenith shook his head. "I knew something was up when I demanded it, but I had no idea what or to what extent. I just wanted to be sure of some kind of support for whatever the future held."

The duke nodded. "I would have sided with you in this matter regardless of our agreement. I have five daughters and I love every one of them. I don't understand how anyone could treat that poor girl the way he did. Saulth needs to pay for this. I'll speak to the others and try to convince them as well."

Now there's a surprise. Cenith set his hand on the duke's shoulder. "Thank you."

Orman nodded and Cenith flew up the stairs to meet with Daric and Ors.

Chapter Fourteen

Buckam stood with the rest of the Companions lined up before Lord Cenith and Lady Tyrsa. His stomach churned and he tasted bile at the back of his throat. He'd rehearsed what he intended to say over and over, but felt sure he'd forget something. Buckam needed this to be perfect.

Lady Tyrsa looked lovely in a gown of midnight blue, matching Lord Cenith's outfit. Her large eyes sparkled every time she looked at her husband. Buckam hadn't realized how pretty she was when he guarded her. She was just a sickly looking idiot girl. Just a job.

He glanced down the line of Companions, decked out in their new armour, tabards and shields. Their helmets had nose guards and side pieces to protect the cheeks while a full, white horse hair plume fell like a tail from the top, the tips tinged purple. The orchid emblem on the round shields matched the one on their breasts. Impressive didn't begin to describe them. Buckam hoped he looked just as good. He still couldn't believe he was one of them.

The shield felt heavy on his left arm; he'd never used one before. He doubted he would now, not with the two long knives strapped to his back, but Ors had issued it, so he bore it.

Lord Cenith and Lady Tyrsa stood on a dais several feet in front of the Companions. The mountain nobility waited behind with some of the other Companions' families. Buckam's stomach roiled. At a nod from Ors, Buckam cleared his throat and stepped up to the Lord and Lady of Dunvalos Reach. As youngest, he had the dubious honour of being the first to swear the oath. Buckam removed his helmet and tucked it under his arm. He dropped to one knee, thanking Aja that he didn't fall over, then rebuked himself for invoking a god who had turned against his people.

Buckam looked up into blue eyes, then farther up into grey ones. "Lord Cenith, Lady Tyrsa. I wish to say something before I take my oath."

Curiosity crossed Lord Cenith's handsome features. Lady Tyrsa smiled.

"First, I must apologize to Lady Tyrsa. It was my fault Saulth beat her that day. It is a shame I must live with for the rest of my life."

Lord Cenith opened his mouth to say something.

"Please, My Lord," Buckam said. "Let me finish. Second, I would like to thank both you and Councillor Daric for your willingness to give me a chance to prove myself. Councillor Daric made me realize that Saulth is a lord unworthy of respect and honour. You have shown me what a lord should be to his people. My eyes have been opened. For that I thank you."

Lord Cenith's smile grew. "You're welcome."

Buckam blew out a quiet breath. The rest was just recitation. His oath would be twofold, one to Lord Cenith, the other to Lady Tyrsa. The rest of the Companions had sworn their oath to their lord when they first joined the guard.

"Lord Cenith, I do solemnly, sincerely and duly swear upon all I hold dear that I will honour, obey and protect you and your heirs to the best of my ability, laying down my life if it is required. I swear to uphold the laws of Dunvalos Reach, my heart and my home. Please accept my oath as I have sworn it."

Lord Cenith changed the last line from the original oath to Maegden. None felt it appropriate under the circumstances.

"Buckam, formerly of Valda, now of Tiras, I accept your oath. In return, I promise to respect your vow and provide for you and yours to the end of your days." Cenith offered his hand, palm down, and Buckam kissed his signet ring.

Now for Lady Tyrsa. No one had ever sworn an oath to a Lady of Ardael, so the Companions made one up based on the vow to Lord Cenith, approved by their lord and Councillor Daric.

Buckam took a deep breath. "Lady Tyrsa, I do solemnly, sincerely and duly swear upon all I hold dear that I will honour, obey and protect you to the best of my ability, laying down my life if it is required. I will guard both you and your children, may you be blessed with many. Please accept my oath as I have sworn it." The official oath ended there. "And, please My Lady, accept my deepest apologies."

Tyrsa smiled, and no sweeter smile had Buckam seen. "I do accept your oath, Buckam of Tiras." She leaned closer and said, for all to hear, "And…I do forgive you, with all my heart. If things didn't happen the way they did, I wouldn't have met Cenith. Thank you."

She held out her hand. Buckam took it and touched it to his forehead for a moment before kissing it. Tears blurred his vision as he made his way back to the line of Companions, praying he didn't stumble.

Yanis leaned down. "You did well. That was a nice

touch." He stepped forward to say his vow.

"Thank you." Buckam hoped he heard. Yanis had been obvious in his dislike for him. Perhaps things had changed.

After Yanis, the rest of the Companions took their turn, with the officers last. By the time Jolin had sworn his vow, Buckam's stomach had settled enough to remind him he hadn't eaten much that day. The odours emanating from the kitchen promised a marvellous feast…and he didn't have to clean any pots.

Lord Cenith's voice jolted Buckam's thoughts from his hunger. "I would like everyone to welcome our newest regiment, The Lady's Companions."

The crowd cheered and hooted as the Companions turned as one to face them. Buckam's heart swelled. He could never have dreamt of a moment more wonderful than this. *Father, wherever you are, I hope you are proud of me.*

Once the Companions had removed their armour, the servants brought out dinner. The food proved to be as delicious as it smelled. Three different kinds of soup started the meal. A wonderful array of beef, chicken, pork, mutton and fish in sauces ranging from a dark, rich gravy to a light, delicate cream. Mounds of potatoes, green beans, peas, carrots and whole roasted onions with garlic sat among platters piled high with breads ranging from white to dark. An assortment of cheeses rounded out the meal.. Another table groaned under the weight of wine and punch bowls. All simple food, not like the fancy dishes Saulth preferred, but Buckam didn't care, everything looked delicious.

He filled his plate to overflowing and found a quiet corner to sit. The Companions had declined a formal dinner, preferring to mix and mingle while they ate. To his surprise, Yanis came and sat with him. Half a foot taller than Buckam, Yanis seemed to enjoy looking down on him. Not now. He smiled and clapped Buckam on the back, making him almost drop his plate.

"You did a fine job up there and, from what Councillor Daric says, an excellent one on the map of the tunnels."

"Thank you. I was surprised to hear the other guards are using them for their own gain. I had thought they were better than that."

Yanis stuffed a chunk of beef dripping with gravy into his mouth. He hadn't quite finished chewing when he asked, "What does your father do? Won't your family miss you?"

Buckam swallowed his cheese. "He was a captain for Saulth, and a good man."

"I don't doubt that. There's good and bad men everywhere and it tends to show in their blood." Yanis' blue eyes flashed with amusement.

"He is gone now, so is my mother. I have two older sisters, but they are both married with families of their own. They do not worry about me too much." Buckam hadn't seen them since he'd joined Saulth's guard, right after his mother died. He doubted they'd miss him terribly much, especially once they found out he was a traitor.

"I'm sorry to hear about your parents. My father keeps a tavern on Stone Street, near the bottom of Keep Hill. We can go there after this nonsense is over if you'd like; unless you want to go to Silk's." Yanis stuffed more food into his mouth. Barit, Fallon and Madin wandered over to join them, all with full plates. Yanis filled them in on the discussion.

Buckam was glad for the reprieve. It gave him a

moment to think and try to cool his cheeks. The first, and last, time he'd been to Silk's he'd received a real education in how to make love to a girl. He hadn't realized he was so inadequate. "No, not tonight. A quiet ale sounds nice. Thank you."

Yanis looked at him sideways. "Have you a girl in Valda?"

Buckam nodded. "Her name is Lina." A long time had passed since thoughts of her crossed his mind. He wondered why he felt no guilt.

"You could send her money to come here if she wished," Barit said, pulling a chair over for himself.

Then Buckam realized why Lina had slipped from his thoughts. He shook his head. "She is pretty enough, and quite willing." That received a chuckle from the men. "But she is also bossy and demanding. I think I would rather leave her where she is."

Madin grinned and put a hand on his shoulder. "Well, there's plenty o' pretty girls 'round here. The mountain air is great for 'em. Makes 'em frisky. Yer a right lookin' lad, ye shouldn't have no trouble." The others laughed. Buckam even managed a chuckle.

Barit grinned. "Just wait until winter when there's practically nothing to do. The wind's so cold it would freeze the nuggets right off a man. But the girls feel the cold too, and they love to keep warm."

Buckam laughed with everyone else. Cold didn't worry him, the prairies could freeze a man good and solid as well.

"You're a mountain man now, Buckam," Fallon put in. "We're going to have to do something about that formal speech of yours. No offence, but you sound kind of stuffy. You'll probably have better luck with the girls if you relax a little."

Buckam smiled, his heart warm. "I will…I'll try. Maybe after that ale with Yanis, I'll go to Silk's after all."

They laughed and Buckam knew he'd found a place worthy to call home.

* * * *

Cenith took a sip of the light white wine chosen for the occasion. If he brought out what remained of the Cambrel they'd brought back from Edara, it would disappear in mere minutes. He stood with Daric near the south fireplace, the only location offering a small pretence of privacy. Tyrsa sat with the children surrounding the Story Teller, while Elessa occupied a chair nearby, one of the younger twins on her lap. The Story Teller had become a fixture in Tiras during recent years, relating tales of the Old Ones Cenith had never heard before. The old man always had different ones to tell mixed in with the favourites. Though still not comfortable in crowds, Tyrsa loved listening to his stories. Cenith just had to get her to realize the Lady of Dunvalos Reach shouldn't sit on the floor.

"Everyone appears to be enjoying themselves," he said.

"They do, including Buckam." Daric pointed out the young man, seated with some of the other Companions in the opposite corner of the room.

"It's nice to see him finally fitting in. Did what he said to Tyrsa surprise you as much as me?"

"It did," Daric said, with a smile. "It was admirable, not to mention brave. Admitting one's mistakes in a roomful of people takes a great deal of courage."

263

Cenith nodded. "I'm also proud of the way Tyrsa handled the unexpected exchange. We spent a large part of this afternoon rehearsing her response, but she took the surprise very well." Perhaps there was hope she'd make a proper Lady someday; then again, Lady Violet may have had a hand in it.

Jolin strode toward them, his expression dark.

"Trouble?" Cenith asked, setting his wine on a nearby table.

"Not the kind ye're worried about, m'lord. I took Keev outside and he finally told me what's bin botherin' him." Cenith motioned for Jolin to continue. "The day afore we had that fight with Tailis, his girl's father told him not t' see her anymore. Said he wasn't 'suitable'." Jolin almost spat the word. "Keev's a good man. Better than a lot o' these nobles."

"Where's Keev now?" Daric asked.

Jolin indicated a solitary figure almost hidden under the Grand Staircase. He pointed in the opposite direction. "His girl's over there."

Cenith remembered her from Kian's funeral, a pretty girl with auburn hair. She stood with her parents, staring in Keev's direction when they weren't watching. The look of longing on her face tugged at Cenith's heart.

He scowled once he recognized her father. "That's Elden."

Daric nodded. "The only reason he's allowed to call himself a noble is because his wife is a cousin of Duke Von," he explained to Jolin.

"I really hate pretentious people." Cenith turned to Jolin. "What's the girl's name?"

"Breena."

"Thank you for telling me," Cenith said. "I think

we might be able to help."

Jolin bowed. "I appreciate it, m'lord. I know Keev needs t' keep his head in what's happenin', but he's my friend too and I hate t' see him hurt for no good reason." He strode away, in Buckam's direction.

Cenith and Daric sauntered over to the main doors, where Elden and his family stood chatting with Duke Von and his wife. He apologized for interrupting and took Elden by the arm. "Might I speak with you a moment?"

The small man's grin almost split his face. With dark hair, thin features and a beak nose, he reminded Cenith of a crow. How he managed to produce a pretty daughter, Cenith couldn't imagine.

"Of course, My Lord! What do you wish to discuss? We have some fine silks and brocades coming in from Syrth next week, I'm sure your lovely wife would…"

"I didn't come to talk business. Actually, Daric and I would like to speak to you about your daughter."

Elden's narrow eyes lit up. "Are you looking for a match? Breena is just the perfect age, though…" His wide brow dipped in curiosity. "You're already married." He glanced at Daric. "I believe now that…uh…well, I don't think any of Councillor Daric's sons are old enough."

Cenith wished the man would shut up. "We're referring to Keev. It's obvious the two are in love."

Elden glowered. "That backwoods bumpkin? He's not good enough for Breena. She deserves someone who can give her the things she's used to, fine clothes and jewellery, and…and…" Cenith moved closer to the little man, so did Daric. Elden looked up at them. "Uh…"

Daric crossed his arms, giving Elden a black look. "Keev is fine young gentlemen. No, he's not of noble birth, but then, neither are you. Or me."

Elden shrank.

Cenith took over. "Keev is one of twelve very special men. Not just anyone has the skill to be a Companion. Lady Tyrsa is quite fond of him. Just think of the parties Breena would be invited to, the social status. Everyone would want to attend their wedding."

The little man's eyes glazed and Cenith thought he might pass out. He stifled a laugh. *Probably tallying up the cost of the nuptials.*

"Not a one of the Companions is married," Daric said. "There would be great honour in being the father-in-law of the first."

"I…I think I see your point, My Lord, Councillor." Elden clasped his shaking hands together. "Perhaps I should relent. After all…" He gave a nervous laugh. "…they are in love."

Cenith put his hand on Elden's shoulder. "Good man. I knew I could count on you. And remember, I need all the Companions to have clear, untroubled minds and hearts in these desperate times. You would be doing the principality a favour."

"Yes, yes of course, My Lord." Elden pointed at his daughter. "I'll…uh…just go tell her the good news."

"You do that." Once the little man had left, Cenith let loose a snort of derision. "Snotty goat turd. If he was genuinely concerned for Breena's happiness, I wouldn't have pushed so hard."

Daric chuckled. "We're doing the girl a favour by removing her from his household."

"That's provided Keev *wants* to get married."

They both laughed. Cenith and Daric knew the instant Elden told Breena he'd changed his mind. Her face lit up like Maegden's Lights on a clear night. She almost ran to the Grand Staircase. The pair disappeared into the shadows.

Cenith sighed. A normal courtship with Tyrsa would have been nice. *But then, would I have chosen a tiny little sprite with large eyes and a pixie face?* He doubted it, though when he thought about her and Lady Violet, who she was supposed to have been, he was glad Tyrsa was who she was.

Daric's eyes narrowed and Cenith followed the line of his gaze. Jolin had left the crowd around Buckam and now sat with Jennica. The two had their heads quite close together. He looked askance at Daric. The Calleni's jaw tightened. Cenith burst out laughing.

"Don't tell me Jolin's not good enough for Jennica!"

Daric growled. "No man is."

Just then Elessa appeared and slid her arm through Daric's. Tyrsa smiled up at Cenith and took his hand. The Story Teller had finished his tales and the musicians readied their instruments.

"Now what's got you so upset?" Elessa asked. "You look like someone just tried to take your favourite horse."

"No. My daughter." Daric nodded in Jennica's direction.

"Oh, that's wonderful!" Elessa pulled her arm away from Daric and clasped her hands together. "It's about time. She's been trying to catch his eye for over two months."

Ever since I brought Tyrsa home, I bet. Cenith kept his snicker to himself.

"Daric," Elessa warned. "You leave those two alone. You knew she'd grow up one day."

Daric's shoulders slumped and the glare lost some

of its intensity. "Yes, I know. I just didn't think it would be so soon."

"Even if she's successful in nabbing Jolin, she's not going anywhere," Cenith said, trying to be helpful. "She'll only move down a floor."

"I like them together. It feels right." Tyrsa's eyes shone. Was that a flicker of violet he saw?

Cenith studied her a moment, but Lady Violet didn't put in an appearance. "Is there something you know that we don't?"

Daric and Elessa both turned their attention to Tyrsa. She shrugged. "No, it's just a feeling."

The innocence in her eyes pulled at Cenith's heart. "If you'll excuse us, Daric, Elessa. It's been a long day." He didn't take his eyes off his wife.

"But the dancing is about to start," Elessa said.

He squeezed Tyrsa's hand and tore his gaze from her eyes. "That's all right. Tyrsa still has trouble dancing. This is the Companions' night anyway. Just make sure you keep an eye on him." Cenith pointed at his still glowering councillor.

Daric grunted. Elessa laughed and took hold of his arm again. "I'll keep him in line, and we'll see you in the morning."

When Cenith reached the main staircase, he scooped Tyrsa into his arms and took the stairs as quick as he could. Two regular guards followed since Cenith had given all the Companions the day off.

"What are we doing?" Tyrsa asked.

"Hush."

He reached their suite and, stopping only long enough to bolt the door, headed straight for the bedroom. Cenith kissed her, devoured her. His need banished all thought from his mind. Within moments, he had Tyrsa out of her clothes and she had him out of his.

Cenith lay on the bed and pulled Tyrsa on top of him. She preferred this position; she had control and Cenith didn't need to worry about hurting her.

Tyrsa settled herself, holding him tight with her body. She kissed him, her lips sweet and moist, overpowering him with her sensuality. Cenith struggled to maintain control.

"I want to go to the cliff tonight." Tyrsa's breath warmed Cenith's cheek, sending a shiver through him.

He wrapped his arms around her as tight as he dared. "So do I." *For two reasons.* The first time she'd used her powers to take him to the cliff he thought he'd die for certain. Now it was their special place, a place no one else in the world could visit.

Cenith's vision twisted and warped. Tyrsa and their bedroom shifted to the grey stone of Shadow Mountain. She tugged on his hand, pulling him to the edge of the cliff, though they weren't there in reality, only in Tyrsa's mind. Soft clouds hid whatever lay below the cliff while a gentle fog enclosed them in this private world.

"Not just yet." Cenith ran his free hand over the stone, looking for tiny lines or fractures, something that might hint at a door.

Tyrsa frowned. "I thought you wanted to jump off the cliff."

"I do, but Daric said he couldn't find anything that looked like a door. I thought maybe we might be able to." Cenith placed Tyrsa's hand on the stone. "Do you still feel something in the rock?"

Tyrsa rested her cheek against it and closed her eyes. "Yes. I feel sadness and anger, but there is something else now too. It's like…it's waiting for something to happen, something good." She opened her eyes and looked up at Cenith. "Lady Violet says 'hope' is the word."

Cenith's head spun as he realized he wasn't making love to one woman, but two. He tried to force that thought aside. "Where is it strongest?"

Tyrsa wandered several feet to the right, trailing her hand along the stone, then did the same to the left. She came back to where she'd started. "It's here."

The same place she brings me when she wants to fall off the cliff…just above where they found my father's body. Cenith searched again, but could only find partial cracks—until Tyrsa set both hands on the stone.

A pale light formed a perfect rectangle, incorporating some of the cracks Cenith had found. He pushed on the now revealed door, then set his shoulder to it. "It won't open."

"Maybe it has to be that day the scroll said."

Cenith cupped Tyrsa's face. "And probably in the real world. Regardless, I can't waste any more time on this. You're driving me insane." He leaned down and kissed her, closing his eyes.

The scene that greeted him almost made him climax on the spot. A fine sheen of sweat glistened on Tyrsa's sweet face as she rode him. The look of rapture swelled his heart. She held him fast, body and soul. He opened his eyes, forcing himself to maintain control. "I love you Tyrsa, more than I ever thought I could."

Then he realized that he meant it as more than just something he should say to his wife, that he truly meant what he'd said to her after she'd banished Tailis; they weren't just words to help her ease the pain. This was the love he'd hoped for and thought he'd never find. This was the love his parents had felt, what Daric and Elessa knew. Cenith's heart soared to the heavens.

Tyrsa's sweet smile thrilled him. "I think I love you too."

The upward flight of his heart lurched to a halt. "You think?"

"I only remember Rani and what I felt for her. What I feel now is like that, but a lot more. I don't ever want you to go away." She hugged him tight. "Especially like Rani did."

All he had to do was look in her bright eyes and he knew she felt the same way he did. "I won't, my love. I promise." Cenith led her to the cliff's edge, and, with a whoop of delight, dove into ecstasy.

* * * *

Saulth guided his horse along the trail. Once again they rode in a place too narrow for more than two horses to walk abreast and the late morning sun in their faces didn't help. Sheer rock bordered the left while the right dropped off into a chasm. Meric rode beside him, Tajik behind. "I do not understand these mountain men," Saulth said. "Can they not build better roads? How can they stand picking their way along like this?"

"If I remember my lessons correctly," Meric commented. "That is why they usually use Black Crow Pass. It is much wider and easier to travel."

Saulth kicked his son in the leg. "I am aware of that, you idiot. Despite a better pass, they still use this one, otherwise they would not bother with a guard station at the bottom. I know for a fact that Cenith and his father before him preferred this pass to the other."

"There are two reasons I can think of," Tajik said. "It's faster, and they're like mountain goats, born knowing how to travel these rocks and crags." Tajik held up his hand and tilted his head. "I thought I heard something."

They stopped. Saulth raised his shield over his head. Meric did the same. Those in front who didn't hear Tajik carried on. A rumble sounded from ahead, rapidly turning into a roar.

Tajik stood in his saddle and twisted around. "Back! Turn back! Landslide!"

Men tried to turn horses unused to mountain paths on too narrow trails. Once again the cries of men and horses filled Saulth's ears. Not just the ones behind, but ahead as well, those about to be caught in the rush of rock, dirt and broken trees. The crash of falling stone mingled with the dying screams of man and beast. Frightened animals in front panicked, their riders unable to control them. Many were lost over the edge. Small rocks and debris pummelled Saulth's shield, forcing him to use both hands to steady it. Unable to back up fast enough, Saulth closed his eyes and cursed.

Seeming hours later, the last of the rocks crashed onto the trail and off the cliff, a shower of smaller stones following it. Dust shrouded the air, clogging throats, eyes and noses. Saulth coughed and peered through watery eyes at the devastation before him.

An entire section of the mountain side had given way, blocking the path and burying the front riders. Hoping to confuse the attackers, Saulth rode with three quarters of his men in front of him. The rest, along with the prisoners, travelled behind. As Saulth scanned the devastation ahead, he thanked every god in Ardael that he'd chosen this position. Ten men separated him from instant death.

The only sound came from the whinny of nervous mounts and rubble tumbling from the hillside. Everyone stared at the destruction. Finally, birds resumed their summer songs and Saulth shook his head. Dirt flew out. Dust covered Meric's and Tajik's uniforms. Saulth looked down at himself. He fared no better.

"We have to go back." Meric's voice sounded dead.

"Ridiculous!" Saulth's mind worked past this new problem. "We just need to clear the path."

"Clear it!" Meric cried. "This will take days! We will have to sleep sitting on our horses or we could roll off in the dark! Aja has deserted us!"

Saulth slapped him once, then again. "Straighten up! You are supposed to be my son, capable of taking over Bredun in the event of my death. Right now, you could not guide a whore to your bed!"

He turned to his guard-commander. "Tajik, move your horse back behind us so more men can come forward. They will have to work in shifts, one hour each, that way we will always be working with fresh men. Fortunately we have most of the day to clear this."

Tajik nodded and dismounted. Using both hands and voice to calm the beast, he succeeded in moving his horse back far enough to allow passage. Working four at a time, the Bredun men tossed rocks off the cliffs, using uprooted small trees as leverage when needed. While they waited, Tajik had Landis do a head count. Of the six hundred soldiers that left Valda, one hundred and sixty-five remained, plus Saulth, Meric and Tajik.

By nightfall, much of the rubble still lay before them. It proved to be deeper than Saulth had originally thought. When some of it was removed, debris farther up shifted causing smaller slides. Five more men died.

Meric had proved right in one thing. They had to sleep on their horses that night. Landis reported grumbling from the men behind—fear over what would happen next and declarations that the gods didn't approve of one lord attacking another and had deserted them. "I'm afraid some of them might do like the gods and disappear," the sergeant said.

Saulth ground his teeth before responding. "Send your most trusted men to the rear. Tell them to kill anyone who tries to desert. As incentive, tell them I will double their pay." *If they survive this.*

"Yes, My Lord."

Saulth used his arms as a pillow against his horse's bony neck and pretended to sleep.

Chapter Fifteen

Sweat dripped down Saulth's face. He wiped it from his brow, then slapped a glove against his thigh, giving rise to a small dust cloud. With a scowl, he tugged the glove back on. He'd like nothing more than a long bath and a longer visit with his wife. Since that wasn't possible, he gazed at the supposedly empty tower in front of him, then at the arrow in the ground at his horse's feet. He grunted. *More delays.*

Clearing the landslide had wasted an entire day. Some of Saulth's own men had deserted during the night of the clearing, despite the promise of gold, but Tajik had their names and once they arrived back in Valda, there would be retribution. Saulth promised quadruple pay, just to keep the soldiers he had.

The mountain men had returned with their pesky arrows, killing most of the rest of his soldiers. Then they'd quit for no apparent reason. Saulth, and what remained of his guard, had travelled a wider portion of the pass in relative peace, riding two abreast, the prisoners walking between the guards' horses. Then they'd arrived at another narrow section and could only travel in single file. It was a harrowing journey, but they'd made it without any further loss of life.

With so few men left, Saulth had to change his plans and instructed Landis to make a peace staff, a strip of white cloth on a long branch. Tajik carried it like a banner, fully expecting to run into Dunvalos Reach men well before they arrived at Tiras; and now they had.

"No one from Bredun is welcome here!" The voice came from the third floor of the squat tower.

Tajik walked his horse a few paces forward and planted the peace staff in the ground before returning to Saulth's side. An attack now would mean shame for either principality.

Saulth studied the tower again. Sunlight glinted off arrowheads showing at every window. He leaned close to his guard-commander. "Tell the mountain bastards we only wish to talk."

Standing in his stirrups, Tajik waved his arms to show he held no weapon. "Ho, the tower! We wish to speak with someone!"

"So speak!"

"Stupid goat turds," Saulth muttered.

Tajik cupped his hands to his mouth. "We need to speak to someone here! We have something for you!"

Moments later, an older man, dressed in the uniform of a Dunvalos captain, strode out the door, fifteen archers following him. "Say what you need to and leave our mountains."

Saulth nodded at Landis. The sergeant slid off his horse and removed the sack containing the lieutenant's head from the saddle horn. He took a deep breath and stepped forward. Opening the bag, he threw the contents on the ground. The head landed a few feet from the captain. Landis also tossed the sack then almost ran back to the shelter of horses and men. He gasped in another deep breath. Meric gagged. Saulth moved his horse away from his son. It would be just like the idiot boy to shame him by throwing up.

Some of the Dunvalos Reach men turned away, but kept their arrows nocked. Others couldn't take their eyes off the disgusting object. Though not as offensive as Snake's head, after three days in the heat, it hadn't fared well.

The captain flashed them a dark look. "Am I supposed to be afraid now?" When he received no answer, he said, "So who's this supposed to be?"

With the beating the man had taken before he died, added to the decay, his mother wouldn't recognize him.

Tajik sneered. "Fine captain you are if you can't recognize one of your own men."

Saulth chuckled, the low throaty sound a result of too much dust and too little sleep.

"Despite what you lowlanders may think," the captain said, pointing his sword at Tajik. "Our numbers are not so few that everyone knows everyone else." He lowered his weapon to indicate the head. "I assume you're telling me he was one of our men?"

Tajik nodded. "A lieutenant from the station at the foot of the pass, or rather, what used to be the station. Oh, by the way, as you can see, we also have six prisoners. If anything should happen to us, something worse will happen to them." Twelve swords pointed at six necks.

The captain glared at Tajik. Arrows strained at bowstrings, all pointed at Saulth and Tajik.

"Careful," Saulth said quietly. "We do not want anyone getting excited. We are under the peace staff. They will not fire."

"Yes, My Lord."

"What is it you want?" the captain asked, his voice almost a growl.

Saulth leaned closer to Tajik. "Tell him we want a

message sent to Cenith requesting a meeting between him and myself. He is to bring that girl with him."

Once the message had been relayed, the captain nodded his agreement and spoke to one of his men. The soldier disappeared into the tower. Tense moments passed before a bird flew from a window at the top of the guard tower.

The captain aimed his sword at Tajik again. "The message has been sent. It should be two to three hours, depending on how long Lord Cenith takes to respond. Are you waiting here for your answer?"

Saulth sat back in his saddle. "Tell him we'll move back down the trail. I do not wish to be stuck by some young buck with nervous fingers."

When that had been related, Tajik ordered the men to turn around. Once they'd reached a safe distance, he had Saulth's newest field valet, a young man named Leonas, set up a brazier and make some tea. Some of the lords of Ardael allowed their men wine and brandy when on campaign. Saulth was not so stupid. His men needed to be in full control of their senses. Especially now.

Meric sat on the ground and clasped his shaking hands together. "I thought I was afraid during the attack and landslide. I have never been as scared as I am now."

Saulth glanced at his son's crotch. "At least you had the stones not to piss yourself." He signalled for his chair then settled in it to wait for Cenith's answer. *Nine days until I have to be at that throne. Maegden! This had better work.*

*   *   *   *

Cenith rode next to Daric with Garun, Von and

Timron just behind. They led sixteen regiments, eight hundred men. Two days travel hadn't calmed his anger. At least one man had died and from what Captain Renys relayed, probably more. They'd left the city as soon as possible, leaving Tyrsa behind under the care of the Companions. Cenith couldn't risk her safety. If things worked out, plenty of time remained to retrieve her. The group rounded a bend and the tower came into view. Captain Renys waited outside with the sentries.

"Where's Saulth?" Cenith asked.

"Camped on the other side of Shadow Mountain, in the Painted Caves. One of the Bredun men stayed here. When I heard of your arrival, I sent him off to inform Lord Saulth. He should be here soon." Cenith and Daric dismounted while the captain continued his report. "Lieutenant Turis and some of the men from the station have been keeping an eye on them."

"How many escaped?" Daric asked.

"Fifty one initially, one more since then." Renys ushered them into the tower, directing them to chairs surrounding a large table. Cenith's chair groaned when he sat down. It also wobbled. He'd never seen the inside of the old garrison.

The stone walls showed signs of leakage in the past, though it appeared the men had done what they could to stop it. The furniture and staircase hadn't fared much better. If they intended to keep this post manned, major repairs would have to be made, and soon.

"The men at the station did as Councillor Daric requested," Renys said, his arms folded across his stomach. "Saulth guessed what was up and searched the forest. Nine men were caught, including Captain Aleyn."

Cenith's heart thudded. "Aleyn's one of the

prisoners?"

Renys shook his head. The look on his face twisted Cenith's gut. "The man who escaped said Aleyn had been tortured and killed along with Lieutenant Swen the night they burned the station. They still hold six."

"Great gods!" Timron exclaimed. "Saulth burned the entire station?"

"Yes, Your Grace. He struck after midnight five days ago."

"Aleyn is…dead." Cenith clenched his fists. *How do I tell Mareta and the children?* His belly burned, and not from the travel rations he'd eaten for two days. A fist hit the table. "That bastard is going to pay."

"He is," Daric said, his eyes as cold as stone. "Saulth is responsible for the deaths of too many Dunvalos Reach men."

"If it's any consolation, My Lord, we buried what we got back of Swen in a quiet place not far from here and Turis killed a lot more of their men than they did ours." Renys' eyes lit up. "Some attacked from the rocks. Remember that spot we've been worried about letting go?" Cenith nodded. "The others went ahead and helped it along. The landslide worked better than expected. When they ran out of arrows, they headed back here for more. Then so few of the Bredun men remained they had to be careful so as not to hit the prisoners. Turis harassed them until Shadow Mountain got in the way." The steep cliffs of the mountain didn't provide any cover.

Pride surged in Cenith's breast. Crawling around the rocks and hills for several days wasn't easy, living off whatever they were able to carry with them when they left or the little those few who dared live in that barren area could give them.

"Lord Saulth came trotting up here two days ago like he owned the place. If I was him, I'd have put my tail between my legs and gone home." Renys snorted. "Stubborn bastard. I've never seen the man, but I picked him out with ease. He thought he'd be smart and have someone else do his talking for him, but the oaf he used had to keep leaning over for instructions. Didn't have the bearing of a lord either."

A smirk lightened Daric's dark expression. "A big man with greying hair and a face like a sheep's asshole?"

Renys, Garun and the dukes laughed. "Yes, that would be him," Renys said.

Cenith and Daric said the name at the same time. "Tajik."

Renys nodded. "I thought as much. I've heard about him, but with all the dust on his uniform I couldn't make out the insignia. There was another with Saulth, a young man who looked a lot like him."

Cenith looked at Daric. "Sounds like he brought Meric."

Daric nodded. "He must be mad to bring his only heir to war."

The captain explained the finer details of Saulth's visit, including his 'gift'. "I swear to Maegden, My Lord. I didn't recognize Swen and I've known him since we were boys. He'd been beaten and…" He couldn't continue.

Garun folded his hands on the table. "I can imagine what he looked like. I'm sorry."

Cenith felt nothing but sympathy for Renys, but he needed more information. "How many of Saulth's men are left?"

He lifted his head. A sparkle returned to his dark eyes. "Turis says they started with six hundred men.

Between the arrows and the landslide, including Saulth, fifteen."

Von whistled. "They did an incredible job."

"They did." Daric's expression had turned as stony as his eyes. "But Saulth still holds six men prisoner. He must want them for some reason or he'd have killed them by now."

"What would that reason be?" Timron asked.

"The only thing I can think of," Daric said, his voice frigid as ice. "He asked for Tyrsa to come, he must want to trade." The same reason he'd mentioned in Tiras.

Cenith leapt to his feet. "No! I don't want any more men to die, but I can't give my wife to Saulth!" More than the love of his life, he didn't dare let Saulth have access to Tyrsa's powers.

Daric motioned for Cenith to sit. "I've had time to think during our ride. I have an idea."

* * * *

Cenith tugged on his riding gloves. He sat astride Windwalker, Daric beside him on Nightwind. Von, Timron and Garun also sat on larger steeds than they'd ridden for the past two days. Cenith would willingly leap into Char before he'd let Saulth look down on him. Cenith glanced back at the soldiers behind him. With the hundred sent here a few days ago and the men from the garrison, they numbered almost a thousand. Hardly needed now, but useful for keeping Saulth in his place.

The Bredun troop came into view, the prisoners between two guards each. Cenith clenched jaw and fists. As they came closer, he could see bruising and dried blood on all of them. Saulth stopped a few paces before the peace staff. Cenith motioned his group to a similar distance on their side. His army stayed put, but were well within Saulth's line of vision and arrow fire.

"I see you brought a few friends," Saulth said, his eyes on the Dunvalos Reach men.

Cenith gave him a cocky smile. "So did you. Too bad you left most of them behind."

Saulth eyes narrowed. "What I do not see is the girl."

"What girl? Your message didn't specify which one." Cenith sat back and crossed his leg over the saddle horn.

"You bastard son of a whore futtering goat! You damn well know which girl! Your wife!"

"She has a name. Tyrsa. Now you see," Cenith said, waving a finger at Saulth. "I was really having trouble trying to figure out why you'd want her back so soon after giving her to me. A change of heart? I decided no. You didn't care about her while she was growing up. As a matter of fact, you went out of your way to make her life as miserable as possible. In all consciousness, I couldn't return her. And I can't now."

"I need her!" Spittle flew from Saulth's mouth. "You have no idea what will happen if I do not get her back! You will be responsible for destroying our country!"

"But I do know."

Cenith's words stopped Saulth cold, his mouth half open.

Tajik filled in for him. "That's impossible!"

The Bredun lord looked at Daric. "Son of a whore! You read my scroll! How dare you invade my castle!"

"You invaded us first," Daric said, his entire body stiff with rage. "Your assassins killed twenty-six of our guards, including my son! I didn't kill anyone, nor did I steal anything. Feel lucky I only pissed in the tunnel next to your rooms and didn't strangle you in your sleep!"

"Pissed in my…" Saulth snapped his mouth shut.

Tajik nodded to someone. The man, a sergeant, brought forward a burlap sack and dumped its contents at the foot of the peace staff. A head. Five days of decay added to the bruising and cuts on the face and it took a moment for Cenith to recognize Aleyn. A lump in his throat prevented him from speaking. Von and Timron turned their heads in disgust. Garun swore. Daric sat like an angry rock.

"We appreciated your gift so much we thought we'd give you a similar one. If you don't turn over the girl," Tajik said. "We will kill these men." The soldiers guarding the prisoners raised their swords.

Cenith found his words, though he couldn't keep his eyes off what remained of Aleyn, a good kind man and a respected soldier. "You'll break the peace truce and we'll be free to kill you where you stand." He raised his fist and his archers stepped forward, ready to fire. "It seems we are at an impasse."

"I can take your men back down the road and kill them there." Saulth sounded like a petulant child.

Cenith gave the archers the signal to hold position. "Yes, you could, but you still won't have Tyrsa. And you'd have to go through my army to get to her. Trust me. This is only a small portion of what's waiting for you in Tiras." He unhooked his leg from the saddle horn and leaned back as he stretched, ignoring Saulth's string of curses.

By the time the Bredun lord finished, he appeared on the verge of passing out.

Once Saulth had calmed down, Cenith cleared his

throat. "We have another proposal."

"And what might that be!"

"According to the scroll, Tyrsa has to be at the throne on the first of Eighth Month. We take her there for you, you free our men, turn around and go home. Everyone's happy."

"No!" Saulth almost jumped out of his saddle. "I have to be there! The scroll says so!"

"It does not," Daric said. "Not only have I read it, I have a copy."

Tajik had to restrain Saulth. Meric sidled his horse away from his father.

"One shall rule! It says so in the scroll!" Saulth divided his glare between Cenith and Daric. "Esryn is too weak, the other lords are too old and you are too young! I am the only lord alive who fought in the Tai-Keth war fifteen years ago! None of you have any idea how to rule an entire country!"

"And you do?" Cenith's quiet words set Saulth off again.

"Your mother futtered a pig to spawn you, demon-blooded son of slug-kissing pustule! May Maegden take your balls, then your eyes and force you to eat them! I will kill these men and come back with a bigger army! And keep coming back until I wear you down!"

"Now he's spouting nonsense," Timron said, out of the side of his mouth. "He hasn't got a hope of getting reinforcements by the end of the month let alone subduing us. We should just fill them full of arrows and go home."

Cenith spat in disgust. "Except that peace staff is in our way. Saulth placed it there; he or his representative has to remove it. Until then, we can't kill the bastard unless he attacks us. Somehow I doubt he'll just go away."

Cenith and Daric both suspected Saulth wouldn't agree to their first proposal. Time for the second. "Then how about this, Saulth," Cenith said. "We all go together. You have twelve guards. You can bring them along with Tajik and Meric. I'll bring Daric, my healer and twelve guards. You free my men as we go in."

Tajik leaned close to Saulth and the two conferred. Cenith could just imagine the schemes they discussed.

"Strange how that worked out." Daric had a point.

"Two sets of twelve? Weird." Cenith leaned on his saddle horn. "What's your answer Saulth? I don't have all day. The sun's almost down and we've ridden a long way. I'd like to get some sleep."

The man snarled. "Accepted. But I keep the prisoners until then and no more of my soldiers die!"

Cenith nodded, though he hated leaving his men in Saulth's hands for even one more minute. "Agreed, although if one of your men dies by snake bite or bear attack, it's not my fault."

"You know what I mean!" Saulth snarled. "Just make sure you have the girl here by dawn on the first of Eighth Month!" Saulth jerked his horse around and rode back down the path, his troop—and the prisoners—following. Cenith watched them until the last had disappeared, then gave the signal for the archers to stand down.

"I see what you meant by the man is mad, Councillor Daric," Timron said.

Von tsked. "He seemed fine when I saw him two years ago, or as fine as Saulth ever got."

"Hmmmm…" Garun scratched his chin. "That rabid look in his eyes supports my theory of obsession."

"Rymon thinks he's under a spell," Daric said.

"Whatever the cause, he's been nothing but trouble for us and I don't expect it to get better." He turned to Cenith. "I don't like the idea of bringing him along, My Lord. He could try anything."

Cenith sighed. "I know, but we have no choice, not if we're to free those men and have Tyrsa where she needs to be in six days. Von, dismiss the men and see they're set up for the night. That meadow back down the road should be big enough. You, Garun and Timron can stay with them while Daric and I ride to Tiras."

"Yes, My Lord." The Duke of Bear Creek Valley wheeled his horse and rode back to the troops.

"Timron, though there isn't much of him left, Aleyn needs a decent burial. Could you please arrange a detail to dig a grave? We'll hold the service as soon as that's done." Timron nodded and followed Von. "Daric, Garun, I need a drink." Cenith turned Windwalker's nose toward the tower.

Chapter Sixteen

Saulth had proved stubborn in his conviction to see the prophecy to its end. Tyrsa shared that stubborn blood; convincing her to come with them turned out to be harder than Cenith thought. While he and Daric were gone, she'd fretted and worried so much Elessa ended up spending the nights in their bed so she could sleep.

"I'm afraid. I don't want to see him." Her beautiful blue eyes shimmered with tears.

"Why now?" he asked. "You never said anything before. We all thought you were fine with this."

Tyrsa's lower lip quivered. "I didn't know Saulth would be there. It seemed so far away. And now it's here."

"Don't worry." Cenith tilted her chin up. "Daric, the Companions and I won't let anything happen to you. I won't even let him get near you. I promise."

"I don't want to go!" Tyrsa ran into their bedroom and closed the door. It took Daric and Elessa's help to coax her out from under the covers. Then she sat on his lap for over an hour before she finally admitted what really troubled her.

"I don't want people to hate me." Tyrsa had a death grip on Baybee as two tears slid down her cheeks. "I know they will if I have to make their gods go away."

The people in Tyrsa's life in Valda had ignored or hurt her. Now she'd found some who talked to her and taught her things. Her fears were understandable.

"The people who truly know what you're doing, and why, won't hate you, Tyrsa," Elessa said, from where she crouched beside them. "Most probably won't even know and the others don't matter. We will still love you. All of us, and the Companions."

Tyrsa buried her face in Cenith's shoulder and sobbed. It tore his heart. He wanted to keep her safe, protect her from every hurt. Instead, he had to find a way to get her to Eagle's Nest Pass, force her to face the man who'd tormented her for so many years and deal with the choice apparently only she could make.

Then she jerked upright and looked at him out of different eyes. Lady Violet stood and placed Baybee on Cenith's lap. She requested a handkerchief and wiped her eyes before straightening her dress.

Elessa rose from her crouch, fascination highlighting her light brown eyes. "I don't believe we've met. I'm Elessa, Daric's wife."

Lady Violet nodded her greeting. "Tyrsa thinks well of you." She turned her eyes on Cenith. "I have talked with Tyrsa. She will listen now. Baybee must also come. And I know you would like nothing better than to run Saulth through with your sword, but it is necessary that he be there. Events have worked out as they should." Before Cenith could say one word, Tyrsa's eyes turned blue and she dove onto his lap, hiding her face once more.

The two days back to the guard station passed and Cenith couldn't even coax a smile out of his wife. He and Daric rode with Tyrsa between them, Baybee crushed in the crook of her arm. She spoke little, but he could tell riding a horse on her own for that long bothered her and she still fretted over her upcoming duty.

The evening sky had turned a dusty orange by the

time the Eagle's Nest Pass garrison crept into view. Tomorrow Tyrsa would open the door and make her choice, whatever it was.

Cenith stood straight in his stirrups, hoping to ease his strained muscles and bring some life back into his arse. Murmurs and laughter from behind told Cenith the trip hadn't bothered the Companions much, despite wearing full armour most of the day.

As they passed the meadow where the Dunvalos Reach army camped, nine hundred men and officers cheered. It lifted Cenith's spirits and he pumped his arm, spurring on more shouts. Von and Timron mounted their horses for the short ride to the garrison.

Both Renys and Garun waited for them outside the keep, a young Bredun soldier nearby. "Welcome back, My Lord, My Lady, Councillor Daric." Renys bowed. "This here's Leonas. Saulth's had him running back and forth all day to see if you'd arrived yet. He just got here, again."

Sweat dripped from the young man's face. "I'll tell my lord you have arrived."

"You can also tell him not to bother coming tonight," Cenith said. "My wife refuses to see him and it will only cause problems we don't need. Let her rest and perhaps she'll be in a better frame of mind in the morning. You can inform Saulth that she's here, as promised."

"I will." Leonas took a steadying breath and loped down the trail.

Renys bowed to Tyrsa again. "My Lady, I apologize for our lack of appropriate accommodations. We cleaned up the Lord's room as best we could when Lord Cenith was here before. I'm afraid it isn't much better now."

"I'm sure it'll be fine." Those were the most words

she'd uttered at one time since Lady Violet put in her appearance. He hoped the little surprise he had for her tomorrow would improve her mood.

Cenith dismounted and lifted her off her horse. She stumbled, but his firm grip prevented her from falling. Not trusting her legs, Cenith picked her up. "I think we'll eat in our room, Renys."

Saulth showed up an hour later with Tajik and five other men. Cenith and Daric both refused to see him and he finally left, yelling about useless, tit-fed lords and murderous, dog-futtering Calleni. Daric wondered how many men Saulth would lose trying to manoeuvre the narrow path along Shadow Mountain in the evening gloom.

Hours later, Cenith remained awake, still holding Tyrsa. She'd cried herself to sleep. He thought it must be about midnight and wished his eyes would close. A light appeared at his window, growing brighter with each passing moment. He leapt out of bed and, using the shirt he'd worn that day, wiped some of the grime from the cheap glass; his men were good soldiers, but terrible housekeepers. He couldn't make out much through the dirt and distortion.

Just as the scroll predicted, a light gleamed high over the darkness that had to be Shadow Mountain. Cenith checked to make sure Tyrsa still slept then threw on his pants. He ran down the creaky stairs, ordering Buckam and Madin to stay with Tyrsa. Daric and Renys were already outside with several of the guard, Companions included. Renys and his men pointed at the light, speculating on what had caused it. Cenith hadn't told him about the scroll.

Trey scratched his head. "Well, send me to Char.

The scroll got one more thing right."

"This is incredible," Garun said, his eyes almost as bright as the light. "I feel like I'm standing in the doorway to something wondrous!"

Jolin had only two words to say. "It's started."

Cenith stared at the light, hanging high in the sky like a little sun. "Are we supposed to go now?"

The Calleni shook his head. "I wouldn't. It's too dark along the path. The scroll only said Tyrsa had to be there on the first, not what time. I think the choice can wait until morning."

"I'd prefer it. Tyrsa's asleep and I don't want to wake her." He headed back to bed.

* * * *

Cenith let Tyrsa sleep in late, then kissed her awake. She still didn't smile. He strode to his pack and pulled out a small, long box. "Today isn't just prophecy day," he said. "It's your sixteenth birthday."

"Birthday?"

"It means you were born sixteen years ago on this day, the First of Eighth Month. It's tradition to receive gifts on your birthday. This is from me, to you." He held the box out to her.

A look of wonder replaced the fear and worry that had lived there over the past few days. She opened the box. "Oh! This is beautiful!"

Almost reverent, she picked up the string of sapphires encircled with glittering diamonds—the wedding gift intended for Iridia, Saulth's other daughter, the one he'd thought he was supposed to marry. The necklace had sat in the drawer in his study desk since they'd arrived in Tiras a month and a half ago. Tyrsa had no jewellery; this was her first piece.

"This is a necklace," Cenith said, removing the gift from its box. "Turn around."

He placed it around her neck and snapped the clasp shut.

"I've seen other women wearing things like this." She touched it. The necklace hung down to the top of her breasts. A nice fit.

"Now you can too. And this is just the start. My mother had several necklaces, as well as rings and brooches. I doubt the rings will fit you, but we can have that fixed. My wife deserves pretty things and she shall have them. Happy birthday, my love." He kissed her.

For the first time in days, Tyrsa smiled. Cenith's heart soared.

* * * *

Flecks of mica and other minerals glinted in the sheer granite face of Shadow Mountain, reflecting back the late morning sun. After a leisurely breakfast, Cenith had taken his time organizing the men; more to spite Saulth than for any other reason. The strange light had faded with the stars. The scroll said it would remain as a sign, but perhaps only at night.

The wind tossed Cenith's hair and blew dust in his face as he led the procession to the place of prophecy. Part way there they ran into Saulth and his men. A quick head count told him the Bredun lord hadn't lost any men on the trek back to the Painted Caves. *Too bad.*

"Where have you been!" Saulth demanded. He held a protective arm over a leather pouch hanging from his shoulder. "You were supposed to have been here at dawn." His eyes narrowed. "You have more men than we agreed upon."

Tajik stood beside him, dangerously close to the cliff's edge. They both wore the same scowl.

Cenith had brought an extra dozen men, including two healers who would tend to the prisoners. "Yes, I do," he said. "They're here to ensure my men remain safe. Once we are all in the cave, they'll take them back to the garrison." The prisoners, tied together by rope, stood behind the Bredun guards. If one fell, they'd all go. Cenith opened and closed his fists, trying to control his anger. "I agreed to have Tyrsa at the garrison by dawn today. Not here. She was tired from the journey and I let her sleep."

Saulth sputtered, but Cenith couldn't make sense of anything he said. He twisted to glance at Tyrsa. She stood behind Daric, Jolin and Trey, hugging Baybee, her eyes wide. She wore a plain grey summer dress with half sleeves, decorated with her new necklace. Tyrsa resembled a terrified rabbit with nowhere to run.

He sighed. Saulth continued to rant until he could take it no more. "Shut…up!" Cenith's words stunned Saulth into silence, echoing off the rock and down into the canyon below. "If you want to do this, you'll all have to back up. The place is farther ahead."

"How do you know where it is?" Saulth demanded.

"The scroll says it's the place where my father died." He glared at Saulth, silently daring him to say one word. "I happen to know where that is."

Saulth grumbled, but instructed his men to turn back. Shortly after, they reached the place where Tyrsa had found the rock that hurt, the place they jumped off the cliff when making love, where his father lost his life. Cenith looked down at the broken trees, scraped hillside and shattered rock, remembering the man who had carried him on his shoulders, taken him fishing and hunting, played soldiers with him. The one responsible for Ifan's death now stood beside him. How easy it would be to just reach over and push. Daric rested his hand on Cenith's shoulder.

"Stop day dreaming!" Saulth peered at the stone wall. "There's no door!"

His words pierced Cenith's ears. He glared at the Bredun lord a moment, tempted to accuse him, make him face what he'd done; but then he'd have to reveal how he knew and that could put Rymon in danger. "Jolin, Trey, Jayce, Dathan. I want you to stand to the left of the door." Cenith used one finger to trace dirt filled cracks, then faced Saulth. "This door. That means that you'll have to back up some more to make room."

Saulth shook his fist. "What are trying to pull? I am going through that door if I have to push your pretty soldiers out of the way!"

"Yes, you are. For some strange reason my lady insists on it," Cenith replied, already tired of the man. "But I am *not* letting you near her. And would you please keep your voice down, you're scaring her." Cenith flashed him a cold smile. "She really doesn't like you."

Saulth made a rude noise, but did as Cenith asked. Daric and Garun flattened themselves against the rock wall to make room for the Companions to pass. Once they'd formed a shield to the left of the door, Cenith motioned Tyrsa forward. She gave Baybee to him, then with a worried glance in Saulth's direction, placed her hands on the outline they'd found. For a moment he feared it wouldn't work, but then a soft glow formed along the cracks.

Daric leaned close to him. "How did you find it?"

"Long story. I might even find the nuggets to tell you one dark, cold winter night when I've nothing better to do. If you ply me with enough wine." *And provided we survive this.* "Try pushing on it, Tyrsa."

She did. Without a sound, the stone moved back then slid to the left. Nothing but darkness lay beyond. Daric would have to duck to enter and some of the Companions would have to remove their helmets, but the rest of them would fit with little trouble.

Six of the Companions slung their shields over their backs and took a torch from Daric. The Calleni lit one before entering. He disappeared into the gloom. After several minutes, he returned. "There's a tunnel that goes quite a ways in. It's wide enough to walk three abreast." A wry smile twisted his mouth. "And I don't have to duck."

With Tyrsa between them, Cenith and Daric led the way. Garun and the Companions followed, Saulth and his men behind. The Bredun lord had insisted on taking point. Cenith put a stop to that and now Saulth's inane mutterings echoed up the tunnel.

Daric carried a lit torch, as did half the Companions, Tajik and six of Saulth's men. Water dripped down the walls and pooled in the center of the floor, forming a trickle that grew as they walked. Damp earth and wet rock filled Cenith's nostrils, and the smell of something else.

He sniffed. "What is that odour? It's like old, wet leather. I've been in caves and mines all over the principality and I've never smelled this before."

"Neither have I," Garun put in. He took a deep whiff. "There's a touch of brimstone in that."

Daric shrugged. "I imagine we'll find out when are supposed to find out."

Whatever that means.

"Keep your eyes open," the Calleni said. "A door where there is no door is odd, but I have a feeling it's only the first layer of the quicksand."

Pleasant thought. They travelled steadily down a gentle slope, the trickle of water growing into a tiny creek. To keep their feet reasonably dry they split into two columns, one down each side of the stream. Tyrsa walked behind Cenith, strangling Baybee and holding his hand so tight she squished his fingers. The tunnel itself was quite spacious, with plenty of head room for everyone.

Mutterings and murmurs surrounded him, bouncing off the walls in front and behind, stretching Cenith's already tight nerves to the breaking point. "Saulth! Would you please shut up!"

"It's not me, you idiot!" After a brief pause, "I thought it was you."

Cenith raised his hand and the column came to a stop. He glanced at Daric. The flames of the torch danced over the Calleni's face, highlighting the angles and planes, making him seem a part of the rock wall.

"Jolin, have any of the Companions been talking?" Cenith faced the long column. When Jolin asked the question, helmets shone in the torch light and horse tails swished as the Companions shook their heads.

Jolin and Jayce put their heads together a moment. "If ye want our opinion, m'lord," Jolin said. "Jayce and I think it's th' Old Ones. There's stories 'bout whispering caves back home."

Jayce nodded. "I heard it m'self, when I was a boy. I got lost in a cave and there was no one but me, and I heard 'em. Scared th' britches right off me. I ran so fast I kept bashin' into walls. That's how I broke my nose. Lucky I ran in the right direction."

"Are we just going to stand around chatting all day?" Saulth yelled.

Cenith grimaced. "Can everyone hear me?" The Companions answered smartly, but he could make no sense of the grumbles emanating from the back of the line. "I want no talking. None! Understood?" Again, the Companion's responses were clear, but not Saulth and his men.

He leaned closer to Daric. "I've heard some of the old stories and if they're true, we've good reason to be worried. I'll be honest. I've got shivers up my spine." Cenith glanced at Tyrsa, who now clutched his arm. The waves of her terror washed over him, adding to his discomfort.

Daric nodded. "I, too, have heard stories, on my mother's knee and from battle hardened men. I always thought them imaginings of an over active mind. I suggest we hurry, but keep our eyes and ears open."

Cenith motioned for the column to continue. He ignored Saulth's exclamation of 'About time', listening instead for the whispers and rustles of things not seen.

Sparkles and the glint of something yellow on the walls caught Cenith's eye. He ran his hand over a line of quartz glittering with gold. "I wonder how deep this vein runs? Maybe I should have the mine master check it out." The murmurings grew louder. Though he couldn't understand the actual words, their intent was obvious…anger. "Maybe on second thought, I won't bother." The noise subsided.

Cenith shivered and Tyrsa flung her arms around

his waist, which made walking difficult since she was behind him. He pulled her to his side, though it meant he now had to walk with one boot ankle-deep in the stream. Eventually they could hear more water rushing past stone on its journey to only the gods knew where.

The murmurings continued until the end of the passageway, then stopped; the sound of water didn't. Cenith's shiver returned. The sides of the tunnel fell away from the light of Daric's torch. Nothing showed but a rough stone floor. The stream vanished somewhere beyond. A hint of a breeze whiffed past his cheek. There was an opening somewhere, but no light made it through.

Cenith held his wife tighter while Daric took several steps forward. He joined him and the Companions surrounded them, blocking Tyrsa from Saulth. Garun placed himself to the left of the circle of Dunvalos guards, peering into the darkness. Saulth grabbed the torch from Tajik and pushed his way past the Companions.

When all the men, Dunvalos Reach and Bredun, had entered the cavern, the combined light of the torches revealed several five foot tall stone figures lining the stream. Each statue was carved to resemble a man in primitive garb Cenith didn't recognize. They held a tall, fat candle in one hand, a shield in the other, a helmet hiding their features. They faced something in the distance. Whoever had carved them had done a marvellous job. Cenith could swear there were eyes behind the slits in the helmets.

Garun let loose a long, low whistle. Approaching the first, he said, "Absolutely incredible. They look like they could breathe."

"Jolin," Daric said, his voice an echoing rumble in the darkness of the cave. "Help me light these candles."

The wicks sputtered from the dust, but caught, adding their illumination to that of the torches.

Saulth didn't wait and strode past them, on the right side of the statues, Tajik, Meric and their soldiers in tow. When Saulth reached the end of the figures he gasped. "The throne!"

The Bredun lord's torch showed a white stone chair perched on a circular dais of the same material. The stream split in two just before the throne and rushed to a wide river flowing behind, starting and ending in darkness. A thin pillar rose from the back of the chair, ending in a stone hand with fingers curled like claws around a dark glass orb.

Saulth shoved the torch back at Tajik and strode to the throne. Daric and Jolin caught up to him, lighting the last of the candles. With only a moment's hesitation, Saulth sat, wedging his arse in the narrow space between the arms.

"No!" Jolin shouted.

Beams of white light flashed from the slits of the statues' helmets, twelve in all, striking Saulth in the chest as a boom reverberated in the cavern, rattling the globe above the throne. Garun stumbled back from the figure he studied, his eyes wide. The beams of light pulled Saulth out of the chair. He flew between Daric and Jolin and landed in the stream. The light disappeared, leaving only spots in front of Cenith's eyes. Meric snickered.

Daric laughed, a deep rumble resembling the last echo of the roar that accompanied Saulth's exodus from the chair. "I don't think that throne was meant for you."

Cenith could tell that just from looking at it. It appeared more for an older child than an adult. He studied his slender wife, then the throne. It would fit her perfectly.

300

Daric and Jolin strode past Saulth to where Cenith and Tyrsa stood at the start of the line of figures. Cenith looked at the statues, the Companions and those who accompanied Saulth. "Twelve to guard. Does that mean the Companions, the statues or the soldiers?"

Daric shrugged. "Maybe all three. I think Lady Tyrsa should try sitting on the throne. Perhaps then we'll find out."

Tajik tried to help Saulth out of the water. The Bredun lord pushed him away and picked himself up, trying to smooth his wet uniform. "That is my throne!"

"I don't think so," Cenith said. "Not only do we not like you, it doesn't either. You could try again if you want. We enjoyed the entertainment."

Daric, Garun and the Companions laughed. Saulth approached the throne again, just touching it with a finger. The slits in the helmets of the statues lit up and he jerked his hand away. The helmets dimmed.

"I thought it was the throne of Ardael you wanted, not this one," Daric said, amusement lightening his eyes.

Saulth ignored him. He scowled and stepped back to the right side of the stream. Tajik and Meric flanked him. They muttered amongst themselves.

Daric scanned the vast darkness beyond the revealing light of the candles and torches. "Do you know what's strange about this place?"

Cenith blinked. "You mean besides weird statues that shoot beams of light and a throne with no king or queen, hidden behind a secret door only Tyrsa can open?"

"Yes, besides that."

"Tell me. I think I might be prepared. 'Strange' seems to be my way of life these days."

"There are no insects." Daric indicated the statues,

the chunk of wall they could see, the floor. "Not a worm or centipede in sight. Nor can I hear them. There wasn't any the entire way through the tunnel. Not even near the opening."

Another shiver crawled its way down Cenith's spine and lodged in his tailbone. Every cave had insects. He looked around as far as the torch and candlelight would let him. Nothing moved, or looked like it had in a very long time.

"Do you think something ate them?" Garun asked, though he appeared more interested in the statues than the lack of bugs.

The Calleni shrugged. "Possible. But if that's the case, it finished eating them a long time ago. If it's still alive, it must be very hungry."

Cenith decided to ignore the fear creeping into his gut. This was even too much for the butterflies he'd put up with in Edara all those weeks ago.

"Look here, My Lord," Barit said, pointing to an object barely visible in the darkness. "There's posts with brackets for the torches."

While the Companions and Saulth's men placed the torches, Cenith turned to Jolin. "Why did you try to stop Saulth from sitting in the chair?"

"There's a tale my grandma used t' tell 'bout th' throne o' th' Old Ones. It belonged t' their queen and no one not o' her line could sit on it. Grandma described it as white marble with th' Orb o' Truth above it."

Cenith frowned. "I don't remember that story."

"Neither do I," Daric said.

"Grandma said it was old and not many knew it anymore. She also said that when th' queen died, she had no heir," Jolin continued. "The queen predicted a true child o' her line would be born far in th' future. Her twelve guardians gave up their lives t' protect th' chair from any who would usurp it, callin' on th' power o' th' land t' help them."

Cenith let loose a low whistle. "It appears to be more than just a story."

"I've bin tryin' t' tell ye, m'lord," Jolin said, with a grin. "Th' Old Ones are real."

Cenith grimaced. "So you have. Any other stories you think we should know?"

"Plenty. But I doubt we have time for them now." Jolin waved at the marble chair. "I believe th' throne awaits its new queen." He bowed to Tyrsa.

She tried to hide behind Cenith. "I don't want that to happen to me."

"I see you taught her to talk," Saulth said, his lips set in a sneer. "That was a big mistake."

His men laughed. The Companions set their hands on their weapons. Cenith waved them down; Saulth wasn't worth the effort.

Jolin fell to one knee in front of Tyrsa. "Ye are th' true queen, m'lady. I know it in my heart. Th' throne will not hurt ye." He removed his gauntlet and held out his hand to her.

Hesitant, Tyrsa took it, then let go of Cenith. Her captain rose and led her between the statues. The other Companions followed.

A twinge of guilt crept into Cenith's heart. *I should be the one leading her, not Jolin.* Yet he made no move to stop him.

Daric must have read his mind. "Jolin believes. You don't. There's still doubt in your heart."

Cenith couldn't argue the point. Despite all he'd

seen and experienced, it still seemed a very long, very weird, dream.

"There's doubt in mine too." Daric's eyes narrowed. "Look at her feet. She's walking on the water."

Garun crouched to get a better view. "Remarkable!"

Cenith's eyes widened. Tyrsa's gown should have been wet from walking in the stream on their way here. It was dry, as were her shoes. Daric was right, her feet didn't even make a ripple in the stream. The Companions' boots splashed, tossing droplets to either side. Not a one touched Tyrsa. Cenith motioned Daric and Garun to join him by Tyrsa's side, conscious of Saulth's silent glare.

Tyrsa stood before the stone chair. With a nervous hand she touched it. Nothing happened.

Jolin smiled. "See m'lady? The throne is meant for ye."

Tyrsa sat, one hand resting on an arm, the other holding Baybee on her lap. It fit her perfectly. Her feet even touched the ground. She closed her eyes and her hands began to glow. The radiance spread to the throne, lighting it up from inside like a candle through a thin layer of alabaster. The orb shifted from dark to white, lighting up more of the cavern. The ceiling still lay somewhere in the stygian darkness above while the rest of the cave vanished into ebony shadows.

Garun and the Bredun guards gasped.

"When did she get her powers!" Saulth demanded.

Should I tell him? He doesn't deserve to know. Then the right words came to him and a slow smile spread across his face. "When she became my wife." *My wife in truth.*

Saulth opened his mouth, but Daric silenced him with a gesture and grabbed Cenith's arm. "Listen!"

Muttering, scrabbling and rustling sounded from the darkness, along with a ticking noise, like someone tapping rock with a stick. The shadows moved.

The Companions spread out, circling the throne. "Look, My Lord!" Varth pointed at his feet.

Cenith stepped over the stream, careful not to touch the throne. The wide dais surrounding the iridescent marble chair glowed with the same life as the throne. Varth moved back to reveal footprints…twelve sets of them embedded in the stone, in the shape of a horseshoe with the chair in the middle. As each Companion took his place, the footprints molded themselves to a perfect fit. Before Cenith could utter a word, a beam of light stabbed from the invisible roof and struck the orb, sending waves of illumination in all directions.

Light bathed the cavern, and still the far walls and ceiling couldn't be seen. What it did reveal were strange lights in the shadows. When Cenith's vision settled down, his heart took up the rhythm of fear. The new lights were the reflection of hundreds of eyes.

Chapter Seventeen

Out of the shadows came creatures Cenith had only heard about in the tales of the Old Ones. Others came, too; some he couldn't have thought of in his worst nightmare.

Thin branches with the faces of old men and arms like twigs walked on skinny wooden legs, the tips clicking on the stone. Short, well muscled, hairy creatures with leather-like faces loped hunched over, using their hands to balance themselves. Slender men and women of a similar height as the statues rode small, delicate horses less than four feet high. Each steed sported a spiral horn in the middle of its forehead. Tiny flying women with wings like butterflies flew around little brown men only six inches tall. Horned men with goat's feet appeared next to a large heavyset man carrying a club studded with spikes. The man had to reach at least ten feet. His bald head, long face and heavy jowls made him appear an idiot.

Cenith didn't think he'd bother telling him that. His eyes scanned creatures that couldn't exist—birds with animal feet and animals made of parts of others, dryads, pixies, men more bear and wolf than human. Naiads, mermen and mermaids poked their heads up from the river along with another creature that appeared to be half horse and half fish. The Old Ones.

"Talueth!" Garun exclaimed. "Never have I seen the like!" Daric grabbed the healer before he could walk into the midst of the strange creatures.

The Old Ones filled the left side of the cavern. Behind them shadows hinted at something much larger, and far more sinister. Saulth and Tajik backed away from the throne. Meric and the rest of the Bredun guard headed for the exit, their eyes wide with panic. Cenith understood how they felt, but he had to protect Tyrsa. He and Daric took up positions at the foot of the dais, completing the circle of protection around her.

"Father!" Meric cried. "Come away or we are doomed!"

"You coward!" Saulth shook his fist. "I *will* get my throne and you *will* stay and help me!"

Tajik raised his sword over his head. "Men of Bredun! Stop pissing yourselves and protect your lord!"

Eight men stopped, the others, Meric included, made for the tunnel.

"No." Tyrsa raised her hand and a thin line of light shot from her palm. A shimmer formed in the entrance to the tunnel. One of Saulth's men ran straight into it and bounced back, falling hard on the floor.

Two others pounded the invisible shield, with no effect. "Let us out! Please! Maegden hear us! Help!"

Cenith's heart thumped in his chest. Somehow his sword found its way into his hand. Daric held his weapon before him. The hiss of metal sliding from sheaths came from Tyrsa's direction. Cenith tore his eyes off the creatures long enough to confirm the Companions stood ready to protect their lady. Tyrsa sat calm on the throne, looking every bit the queen she apparently was; then he saw the violet eyes and realized that command hadn't come from his wife.

Saulth pointed at her, his hand shaking. "Her…her eyes! She's supposed to have blue eyes!"

"It's her power," Daric said. As good an answer as any.

The creatures didn't appear in a rush as they plodded walked, or flapped their way toward him. Cenith found his balance and picked his first opponent, one of the slender, pale-faced men. He carried a short spear and a wooden shield, both adorned with feathers and strange runes. Silver hair, braided and then braided again, brushed shoulders cloaked in wolf-skin. Two thin braids framed his lined face. Rough leather trousers covered his bottom half. His feet were bare, as was his chest. From his haughty demeanour, Cenith judged him a leader. All the men were dressed and armed much the same, as were the women who also wore sleeveless leather vests. The clothing was similar to that worn by the statues.

"No." Again Lady Violet's command echoed in the cavern and another glimmering shield materialized several yards past the line of torches, blocking the creatures' advance and extending through the river to prevent the water people from approaching. The man Cenith had chosen to fight scowled. He glared at Cenith out of bright blue eyes, the same as Tyrsa's.

"Put your weapons away," Lady Violet said. "All of you." Echoes whispered back her words, some of them from the hoard behind the shield.

The slender man lost his scowl and tilted his head toward her. "But it is the time of choosing, my queen." He spoke with a mountain lilt stronger than Cenith's own, though not as pronounced as Jolin's.

Lady Violet met his gaze and kept it until he looked down. "The time of choosing, yes. The time for war, no. Not yet. Perhaps never. You will hold position."

The man bowed, his right hand spread over his

heart. "It is as ye command, my queen."

"Queen? She is no queen!" Saulth took one step. The Companions pointed their weapons at him. The Old Ones rattled theirs and he stopped.

The slender man raised his spear high over his head, then slowly lowered it. He thumped his shield three times before placing the spear with others in a wooden quiver on his saddle. The rest of the creatures put their weapons away, if they had them, the giant resting his club on the ground in front of him. He shoved a griffin to one side then settled himself on the floor, legs crossed. The griffin snarled, clacking its eagle beak, but made no attempt to reclaim its position. The giant grinned, showing uneven, but sharp, teeth. Cenith wasn't sure if the big man prepared himself for entertainment or suffered from a bad case of gas.

Cenith sheathed his sword and instructed Daric and the Companions to do the same. He wouldn't be responsible for breaking a truce, however tenuous it appeared.

The Companions kept their weapons pointed at Saulth. "I'm sorry, m'lord," Jolin said, standing at Tyrsa's right hand, on one end of the horseshoe. "We can't until they do."

Cenith faced the Bredun lord. "Put your sword away and tell your men to do the same."

"And be attacked by those things? Or you? Do you think I'm crazy?"

Yes, I do. Cenith pointed to the creatures. "They're behind a shield. They can't get to you. You've seen the power here. Do you really think your swords would make a difference if Tyrsa chose to hurt you?"

Saulth's glance shifted from him to the creatures, to

Tyrsa, then back to him, his mutters barely audible. "Sheath your swords," he spat, but held onto his until last.

The Companions put their weapons away.

"Look!" Trey pointed at one of the stone figures.

Silvery wisps arose from each one and flew toward the Companions. Before any could react, the thin fog disappeared into their mouths. The Companions jerked, then pulled their weapons once more, both hands on crossguards, sword tips resting on the ground. Madin loaded his crossbow, but pointed it at the floor. Buckam held his two long knives crossed over his breast. Each one of the Companions now had bright blue eyes. Garun, his fascination with the Old Ones forgotten, rushed to stare up at Jolin.

Cenith rounded on Lady Violet. "What happened to my men!"

She regarded him with cool eyes. "Worry not. Your men are still here. They are aided by those who guarded our throne. They are now more than mere men and will insure the peace is kept. Others are coming who might not abide a truce."

Jolin stopped Garun from removing his helmet, then looked at Cenith, his face expressionless. "I'm still here, m'lord. There's another wi' me, and I kin see into his heart. He means only well for m'lady." The rest of the Companions nodded. "This must be how Lady Orchid feels with Lady Violet."

Cenith took a deep breath. *This has to be a dream.* He glanced over at the creatures on the other side of the shield. *It has to be!*

* * * *

Buckam stood behind Lady Orchid's throne, trying to get used to someone else in his head. *Who are you?*

I am one of the Queen's Souls, those who guard her and her throne. His voice sounded deeper than Buckam thought it should.

Queen's Souls?

Yes, the strange voice answered. *We are called such because the queen owns us, body and soul.*

But...but that's slavery!

The man, or what was left of him, chuckled. *No, it isn't. We all volunteered, knowing full well we might have to give our lives for our queen. I'm proud to be one of the few so honoured.*

Buckam felt that pride swelling in his breast. *Do you have a name?*

I was known as Chay.

Was? Aren't you still?

Chay chuckled again, his amusement washing over Buckam, easing his tension. *In reality, I'm dead. I have been for many centuries.*

Buckam found it hard to imagine, encased in stone all that time, alive, and yet not alive. *Are you of the same race that rides those small horses?*

I am.

He looked at Saulth. The lord hadn't moved and Buckam realized his entire conversation with Chay had taken mere seconds. Buckam had more questions, but Saulth put an end to that.

"We're all here. Now make your choice so I can claim my throne!" Saulth drew his sword again.

Respond! Chay cried.

As one, Buckam and the Companions on Saulth's side of Lady Violet aimed their weapons at him. Saulth's

311

jaw dropped as he stared at the Companions. Buckam turned his face, praying his former lord didn't spot him. *I thank whatever god will listen that the armourers put cheek plates on the helmets!* He watched the strange beings behind the shield for two reasons—interest mixed with fear and it kept his face away from Saulth.

Thank Niafanna and Cillain. They are the only ones who will listen, Chay said. *I see and understand your fear, but ye must not turn away from those who threaten our queen.*

The man didn't chastise, only advised, and Buckam faced Saulth once more.

Ye're young, Chay said. *Ye'll learn and I can help ye. Ye're nimble and bright, though my reflexes and knowledge are greater than yours. Together we will be good.*

"Sheath your weapon!" Jolin's voice, though the same, sounded even more commanding.

Daric chuckled. "Keep it up. You'll find yourself skewered in no time."

Saulth snarled, but obeyed. As one, Jolin and the Companions resumed their positions, the rattle of their armour and clank of boots on stone echoing in the cavern.

"The choice will be made when the time comes." Lady Violet stared in disdain at Saulth. He flinched. "There is other business to attend to first. We await the Others. They refuse our command to appear, but are weakening. They will come." Her violet eyes flashed. "We require the scroll."

Saulth grabbed the bag hanging at his right side. "It is mine! Bredun guard to me!"

His men recovered their senses and ran to their lord, though they didn't pull their swords. Meric stayed by the door. Buckam realized Saulth was a bigger idiot than he ever could have imagined. He'd just let everyone know that he carried the scroll, and where.

Ye know what ye must do. Chay couldn't actually touch Buckam, but somehow he nudged him into action. *Ye know where your loyalty truly lies.*

Buckam slid his knives back into their sheaths and removed his helmet. He set it on the floor, stepped off the dais and strode toward Saulth, his heart pounding so hard he thought it would burst out of his chest.

"Buckam!" Councillor Daric took a step forward. "What are you doing?"

Ignore him, Chay said.

Buckam stopped in front of Saulth.

The lord's eyes almost popped from his head. "You…you're alive!"

"Yes. I recovered from my wounds."

Tajik glared. "What are you doing in that ridiculous armour? You look like a daisy."

Buckam swallowed his fear and clenched his fists, afraid his hands would shake. "I was captured. I have done what I needed to do."

"Buckam!" Lord Cenith cried.

Saulth laughed. "Once a Bredun man, always a Bredun man." He put his hand on Buckam's shoulder. "Good work, son. I am sure you have much to tell me."

Buckam bowed, leaning just close enough to grab the pouch with both hands. He yanked hard, snapping the strap, spun and ran back to Lord Cenith, more nimble than he believed possible in full armour. Buckam didn't see Saulth's reaction. He could hear it, though. The man screamed obscenities that would make a whore blush. Councillor Daric stood with his arms crossed, daring Saulth to attack. All the remaining Companions now had their weapons aimed at the Bredun Lord. Saulth bellowed, but made no move to retrieve the pouch.

Lord Cenith smiled at Buckam. "You had me scared for a moment. Well done."

Buckam saluted and grinned. "Once a Dunvalos man, always a Dunvalos man."

Lord Cenith laughed and slapped him on the shoulder.

Buckam took the step up to the dais and bowed to Lady Violet. "My Lady. I believe these are yours." He removed the parchments from the leather bag, passed them to her and tossed the pouch on the floor on the other side of the dais from Saulth, just missing the stream.

Lady Violet nodded once. "Thank you, Buckam. You have done well."

His chest burst with pride, his own this time. He turned to face Saulth. "Lord Cenith has taught me what a lord should be. You have much to learn."

Lord Cenith and Councillor Daric laughed. Buckam returned to his position behind the throne, replaced his helmet and drew his weapons. He added his glare to that of the Companions, facing Saulth with a freedom and lightness of heart he hadn't felt since the banquet.

Chay chuckled. *Ye did well, lad. Very well.*

Buckam was surprised to find that praise meant almost as much to him as those received from Lady Violet and Lord Cenith. Despite the grim situation, he smiled.

* * * *

Cenith's brain raced to make some sense of everything he saw and heard. He glanced at the creatures on the other side of the shield. They merely watched, making no comment on the proceedings. Lady Violet now had the parchments, thanks to Buckam's bravery. It must have taken a great amount of courage to face his nightmares head on in order to procure the scroll.

Lady Violet laid the parchment sections on her lap, Baybee under one arm which surprised Cenith. Usually she set the doll down or gave it to him.

She looked up into the immeasurable darkness, her pixie face calm and regal. "Niafanna, Mother of all. Cillain, Father of all. I have the scroll for you."

The beam of light brightened. Lady Violet set Baybee on her lap next to the scroll, holding her up with both hands. A pulse of light moved from the orb, down through her arms, and into the doll. Now Baybee sat on her own.

Cenith blinked as the doll turned her head toward him. "We thank you, Cenith of Tiras, Daric of Callenia and Tiras, for your help in these matters." Two voices came from the doll's mouth. One male, one female. Lady Violet spoke the same words, at the same time. Garun, still close to Jolin, almost fell over backwards.

Daric bowed deeply, hand over heart. "You are most welcome, Mother and Father of all. I am, as always, your servant."

How Daric managed to keep his composure, Cenith had no idea. He floundered for words. "You…you're welcome noble Niafanna and Cillain. I'm glad I could help." *I think.*

"One wonder piled on another!" Garun reached out to touch the doll, then thought better of it. He reminded Cenith of a child in a candy shop.

"Rest your heart, Daric," the doll said. "Kian is with us. His is a good soul. He will be born again soon."

Daric closed his eyes a moment before nodding his

thanks. The doll faced the Bredun company. "Thank you Saulth of Valda, for following the ritual that produced our daughter." Baybee's yarn mouth frowned. "However, we are not pleased with your treatment of her."

Saulth's mouth hung open. He snapped it shut before replying. "It is not my fault! I did not have that part of the scroll!" He pointed his finger at Cenith. "They did! And they refused to give it to me!"

"That is no excuse. Did you treat your other children that way? You are not worthy to be called her father."

Cenith had never imagined a simple cloth doll could exude such majesty, or contempt. Lady Violet sat with her eyes on the doll, speaking Niafanna and Cillain's words.

"It is not my fault!" Saulth repeated, his eyes wild.

"We will agree the fault is not entirely yours." Niafanna/Cillain waved a cloth arm and the pieces of parchment floated in front of the doll. Garun's incredulous eyes followed it. A brief flash sealed the torn edges and the scroll became one. After a moment, the doll spoke again. "We see the problem. Abbatar!"

From the ranks of the strange creatures came a man who could only be called ancient. His face resembled gnarled wood and the brown woollen robes he wore appeared at least as old as him. He hobbled forward using both hands to lean on a wooden staff. Niafanna/Cillain waved their arm and a small section of the shield disappeared. The man shuffled his way through and the shield closed.

Saulth pointed at the man, his hand shaking. "You! You are the one who sold me the scroll! How can you still be alive?"

Abbatar ignored him. "Mother, Father, ye called me?" The man spoke with the same lilt as the leader of the small people though his voice quavered and sounded dry as dust.

The doll indicated the scroll. "We instructed you to make up the prophecy. We trusted you to complete it as we ordered. You deliberately disobeyed us."

Abbatar scratched his nose. "Well, umm, ye see, Mother, Father. I thought on what ye'd requested and it seemed too open, too…" He waved a hand in the air. "Too risky. Yes, that's the word. Risky."

The doll stared at Abbatar, obviously expecting more of an answer. The old man picked at his thin white hair, then examined what he'd found. Niafanna and Cillain waited patiently for him to continue. Cenith supposed if he were that old, a few minutes wouldn't matter.

He leaned close to Daric. "You don't seem bothered by all this. Aren't you even a little surprised by any of it? Those things on the other side of the shield? Meeting your gods?"

Daric gave him a half smile. "I must admit, those creatures disturb me. But as for Niafanna and Cillain, I am a little surprised for they don't usually show themselves. The difference between us is that I have always believed in my gods. You have not, not deep down in your heart. I am thrilled to my soul to meet Niafanna and Cillain."

His councillor spoke true; Daric's eyes gleamed. He rejoiced in seeing his gods. Cenith was terrified to meet his, for he was sure that's who Niafanna and Cillain were waiting for.

"Ye see, Mother and Father," Abbatar continued. "I saw holes in your prophecy. There was too much room for something to go wrong. The whole idea was for the choice to go our way, wasn't it?"

"No, Abbatar, it was not." Niafanna/Cillain spoke as if Abbatar was an errant child. "It was to determine whether our time here was done or if we were ordained to continue. The choice must be unbiased and you changed that. You kept her gender hidden and your selfish act has resulted in much torment for our daughter."

Ordained? Did that mean there was a higher power than even the gods? Cenith found that thought difficult to wrap his head around.

"Well, ummm…" Abbatar pointed at Cenith. "I see ye made amends. Ye've fixed the problem, so everything's all right. Right? Heh, heh." He blinked bright blue eyes.

The doll frowned. "This…ritual. Blood was required, yes, but only a drop from the sire and dame. This is disgusting."

Abbatar held up a finger. "But quite entertaining."

Saulth's jaw dropped. "You…you *watched* me?"

Abbatar examined his nails and smiled.

Bredun's lord set his hand on his sword hilt. The Companions made a subtle move towards theirs. Tajik grabbed Saulth's arm and whispered in his ear. Saulth grimaced, but removed his grip on the weapon.

Daric bowed to Tyrsa and the doll. "Mother, Father, if I may speak?"

Niafanna/Cillain nodded.

"Abbatar," Daric said. "I heard that you may have put a spell on Saulth. Is that true?"

"What are you talking about, Calleni?" Saulth demanded.

Daric ignored him and the doll turned its head toward Abbatar. "Is it true?"

"Well, ye see, Mother, Father." He put his forefinger and thumb together. "'Twas only a tiny spell, just enough to make him buy the scroll. He wasna' going to, ye know, and that would have ruined everything."

The doll sighed. "It ruined everything anyway, Abbatar." Niafanna/Cillain looked at Saulth. "That little spell grew. He is now not just obsessed with the scroll, he is insane. There is nothing we can do."

"My apologies." Abbatar bowed. Cenith wasn't sure if was to the doll or Saulth.

"I am not insane!" Saulth spat. "Make the choice and we will be done with this!"

The doll faced Cenith and Daric. "In all fairness, we should explain to you what has happened. Three thousand years ago, a great war was fought in this land. Maegden and his offspring attacked from Tai-Keth." Niafanna/Cillain bowed their head a moment. "They caught us when we were weak."

Images slammed into Cenith's head. Twenty-foot tall beings, who could only be Maegden and his brood, strode alongside the mounted Tai-Keth, wreaking havoc amongst strange creatures like those standing on the other side of the shield. Maegden tossed thunderbolts, scattering a small army of griffins and hippogryphs, while Siyon's mighty sword sliced through tree people and giants alike. Dark shapes, large and small, fell from the sky.

"The peoples of this land fought hard," the doll continued. "But could not match the forces Maegden brought to bear. They retreated to these mountains, hiding in the caves, the forests, and waters. Maegden followed those who fled to this place and destroyed them." As the Calleni gods spoke, the images in Cenith's head flowed to match them. He watched the final battle that took place in this very throne room, resulting in the sacrifice of the queen's twelve loyal guards. The lone survivor, the queen, died a horrible death, but not before she placed a spell on the souls of the dead guards. "Most of the surviving Blood fled to the lands now known as West Downs, Syrth, Cambrel, Talend, and Callenia. Eventually, they mated with humans there, so their blood would carry on. The rest bided their time in the mountains, finally making their way here when it was safe.

"The Tai-Keth wished to take more than just Ardael," the gods continued. "But by that time we were able to stop them at Ardael's borders, though we could not remove them. The invaders settled down and became farmers, fishermen, and miners. They became your people."

The images in Cenith's head vanished. He glanced at Saulth.

"That's impossible!" the Bredun Lord cried. "My people have always been here."

Cenith leaned closer to Daric. "Did you just see images in your head?"

Daric nodded, all his attention on the throne.

Niafanna/Cillain smoothed the wrinkles from Baybee's dress. "The land cried for its lost people, for the blood shed on its soil. It has cried ever since."

"Are you listening to me?" Saulth started toward the throne. The Companions stirred and Tajik yanked him back.

'It has cried ever since.' Cenith thought a moment. "Tyrsa said the ground hurt."

"Yes," Niafanna/Cillain said. "We had to do something. At that time, however, Maegden and his children were more powerful than us. We saw that would

320

change and prepared for it."

Niafanna/Cillain glared at Abbatar. "Or at least, we thought we had. Time passed and the war was forgotten by humans. The land continued to weep and, finally, to fight back. The land rejected Maegden. He and his spawn had to struggle to keep what they had taken. Eventually, they wore down to the point where they had to keep returning to Tai-Keth, the land of their birth, to renew their flagging strength. They still refused to relinquish control of a land that hated them. That is when the tornadoes and flooding began. You must remember, you may have occupied Ardael for three thousand years, but the land still considers you invaders."

"Mother, Father," Daric said. "We were attacked by three tornadoes while bringing Tyrsa to Dunvalos Reach. She said the ground helped her stop them. If the land is responsible for the tornadoes, why did it save us?"

Niafanna/Cillain folded their hands on their lap, or as much as hands with no distinct fingers could. "Those tornadoes were sent by Maegden to destroy the Jada-Drau. The land would never attack her."

Maegden! "He tried to kill us even then?" Cenith's mind reeled.

The doll nodded. "Cenith, Saulth, your people pray to gods who are worthless and no longer have the strength to maintain the nature of things. They quarrel endlessly amongst themselves. Despite all this, they resist. They will not give up. Your gods are like a festering sliver in the flesh of Ardael. A decision must be made. Our child was born to make this choice. She will choose who will stay and who will go. Once the choice is made, the land will accept the decision."

Daric cleared his throat. "Excuse me, Mother,

Father. The scroll says all not chosen will be destroyed."

"Yes." The doll looked at them with sympathy, if button eyes could be said to show emotion. "If Tyrsa chooses Maegden and his ways, the Old Ones and the Blood will vanish from this land. If she chooses the Blood, Maegden and all those not of the Blood will disappear. Daric, you need not worry. You and your children belong to us."

Daric glanced at Cenith. "I'm not worried for myself, Mother, Father, but those I care for."

Cenith choked as the bottom fell out of his world. "Disappear?" *Lady Violet! She tricked us! After all we've done to get Tyrsa here!* Then he remembered she'd said she didn't know what choice Tyrsa had to make. Had she lied to him? Though Tyrsa said she'd know if Lady Violet lied. All he'd been through over the last several weeks…*For this?*

"Disappear! You mean I sired that brat so she could destroy my people? The scroll says she is to save them!" Saulth strode toward the throne, sword once more in hand. Tajik and the guard followed, some more hesitant than others. "I will kill her now and end this myself!"

"Stop!" Jolin's voice rang out. The Companions' blue eyes glowed as the guard quickly formed a double row of protection between Tyrsa and Saulth.

Madin fired his crossbow, sending a bolt at the lord's feet. It skidded on the stone floor. He reloaded in the blink of an eye. Saulth swore and shook his sword, but he stopped.

Cenith's mind reeled. He'd expected the choice to involve the gods, but *this*? "Niafanna, Cillain! I beg you! Don't destroy my people! They had nothing to do with this. It happened so long ago!"

The doll raised its hand. "In view of the changes in the prophecy, each side will be given the opportunity to make their plea. Abbatar will speak for the Blood and the Old Ones. You, Cenith, for your people and gods."

Me? Cenith couldn't move, couldn't breathe. A clamour arose from the strange creatures on the other side of the shield.

"No! It must be *me*! He is only a boy!" Saulth leapt, not at Tyrsa, but at Cenith.

Daric's sword appeared out of nowhere and he stepped in front of Cenith, meeting Saulth's weapon with a loud clash of steel. Cenith skipped back, giving them room. Daric met each of Saulth's frenzied blows with a calm ease. His eyes shone with cold fury. Cenith sincerely hoped Daric could finally exact the last of his revenge.

Cenith turned to the doll. "Mother! Father! Please forgive Daric for breaking the truce."

They smiled. "Daric did not break the truce, Saulth did. He is defending his lord, which is as it should be."

Cenith took a deep breath. "Would you forgive me if I drew my sword?"

Niafanna/Cillain nodded. "As long as it is in defence of our daughter, yourself or one of those in your care."

Cenith eyed Tajik. The guard-commander watched his lord intently and Cenith expected him to come to Saulth's aid if it looked like Daric might win. Tajik waited until the combatants had traded places, circling for advantage before he struck. Cenith leapt, blocking the blade.

* * * *

Daric silently blessed Cenith for keeping Tajik off his back. He twisted to one side to avoid a slash and spotted one of Saulth's men sneaking up on him.

"No interference," Niafanna/Cillain said. "This is as must be." Another shield formed in front of the Bredun men. That left only Meric free, and he still cowered near the entrance.

Sweat covered Saulth's face. He'd proved a more formidable foe than Daric expected. Perhaps his madness lent him strength, or perhaps he was simply stronger than he'd anticipated. Daric avoided a slash aimed at his chest, using one of the statues as a shield. Saulth gouged out a chunk of stone with his strike, then ducked away from Daric's response.

Around and through the statues they moved, the clash of their swords ringing alongside those of Cenith and Tajik. Daric prayed to the pair inhabiting Baybee's body that Cenith would defeat the Bredun guard-commander. He couldn't stop worrying. Older and more experienced, Tajik had the advantage.

A slash to Daric's right shoulder brought his attention back to the fight at hand. He dropped and rolled, coming up in a fighter's crouch, avoiding the worst of the damage. His shoulder stung, but he'd long ago trained himself to ignore simple wounds. Saulth tried to stay behind one of the end statues while attempting to remove Daric's head, but Daric ducked and his sword snaked up and around the stone figure, sliding between Saulth's ribs. The Bredun lord fell back.

"Father!" Meric cried, but he made no move to help.

Saulth stared at the blood pouring from the wound. "Impossible!"

Daric kicked the sword out of Saulth's hand. Transferring his own weapon to his left hand, he punched Saulth in the face. Blood and spit flew from the lord's mouth. Daric hit him again, in the stomach. Saulth dropped to his knees. One more blow laid him flat on his back. The clash of swords told Daric Cenith still fought. He straddled Saulth and rested the tip of his blade against his throat.

Wild panic filled Saulth's brown eyes. "You cannot kill me! I am king!" He laughed, crazy, maniacal, then coughed up blood. "I am king of Ardael! The prophecy says so!"

"You killed my son." Daric pushed down on the sword. "You are dead."

Saulth's ranting turned to gurgles. His body jerked one last time, his wide eyes staring somewhere up above into the darkness. Daric's revenge was finally complete. This was the man who'd hired the assassins responsible for Kian's death. He thought he'd feel momentary joy at taking the man's life, as he had when he killed his mother's murderer, but he only felt relief. Perhaps now the nightmares would end.

"No!"

Meric's cry echoed in Daric's ears. After making sure Meric stayed put, he whirled and ran to where Cenith and Tajik fought, near the creatures' shield. They both bore injuries. Many of the Old Ones pumped fists and cheered on one combatant or the other.

They stood at an impasse, swords locked. Cenith pushed hard, but Tajik pushed harder. Then, quick as a flash, Cenith pivoted, dodging Tajik's long sword, putting the Bredun guard-commander off balance. He stumbled, but couldn't recover and went down. Cenith slashed the falling man. If he'd planned a killing blow, he missed, catching him in the upper arm instead. Gulping in air, Cenith put the tip of his blade against the side of Tajik's neck.

Daric stepped in and set his sword to the man's gut. He twisted Tajik's weapon out of his hand and tossed it away. "Saulth is dead." He nodded in Meric's direction. "Go protect your new lord, unless you wish to join your old one."

Tajik glanced at his sword, well out of reach, then at Daric's blood covered blade, pointed at his belly. He growled. "Bredun guards! To Lord Meric!"

Daric and Cenith both lowered their weapons and Tajik rose to his feet, his arms spread wide in surrender. The new shield disappeared and Saulth's men followed their guard-commander to Meric, setting up a better ring of protection than they'd given their former lord.

The creatures beyond the shield cheered. It appeared they didn't care who'd won. Daric bowed to Tyrsa and her doll. "Mother, Father, My Lady, I apologize for the disturbance."

The doll nodded. "We understand. The time of choosing draws near." Niafanna/Cillain closed their eyes.

A tense moment passed while Lady Violet fought some sort of internal struggle. Finally, she let out a slow breath. "The Others come."

The two gods waved their arm and the shield returned. It appeared thicker. Shapes took form behind it. Maegden, and what remained of his brood, had arrived.

Chapter Eighteen

Cenith sheathed his sword and crouched near the dais, catching his breath, preparing for the next round of strange happenings. Blood dripped from a cut on his hand. He'd parried a blow and Tajik's weapon slid along the blade, slicing into the web of flesh between the thumb and forefinger of Cenith's sword hand before he could back away. It took a moment to realize how much it stung.

Garun appeared in front of him and studied the cut. "A few stitches will take care of this."

Cenith shook his head. "Not now."

The healer pulled a clean bandage from the bag hanging from his shoulder and wrapped it around Cenith's hand.

As Cenith steadied his breathing, he looked up at Daric. "Thanks, for the help."

"You're welcome..." Daric tugged a strip of cloth from one of his many pockets and wiped Saulth's blood off his sword. "...though you didn't need it."

"Any other wounds I should worry about?" Garun asked.

Cenith shook his head. "A few nicks and scrapes. Nothing serious."

The healer turned to Daric. "You?"

The mercenary-turned-councillor shook his head. "My shoulder can wait, but you might want to direct your attention to the next act in the performance." He indicated the right side of the cavern. "I believe your gods are putting in an appearance."

Meeting Daric's gods had unnerved Cenith. The prospect of meeting the ones he'd only half believed in shook him to the roots of his soul.

The forms behind the shield solidified. Four of the five measured the same height as Tailis, while the other, a female, stood a few feet shorter, none as tall as the images Cillain and Niafanna had put in his head. Perhaps it was a manifestation of their loss of power. They might be smaller than when they took over Ardael, but each of them appeared extremely angry, and it was dangerous to defy an angry god, let alone five of them.

The first had to be Maegden, though he looked nothing like Cenith had imagined nor did the beatific sun that was his usual representation seem appropriate. Maegden's black hair and beard hung down to his chest. Storms flashed in his dark eyes. He held a massive sword shaped to resemble a jagged lightning bolt. It reminded Cenith of the scar on his left shoulder. The day of the bandit attack seemed very far away.

Next to Maegden could only be Ordan, giant hammer in hand, his red hair flickering around his face like flames. Cenith dragged his eyes away from the dancing fire to see what had to be Aja, one side of his face deathly pale, the other dark, almost black, like the people Daric said lived to the south of Callenia. He tossed a pair of dice in the air, catching them with ease, a mocking smile on his strange face. Cenith's eyes riveted on the dice, the spots shifting, forming familiar patterns, there and then gone. He blinked. More deception.

Siyon came next, wearing furs of red. Instead of the golden spear his statues bore, he held a sword almost as tall as himself, a curved, beastly thing that looked like it could cut a man in half with little effort; it was same sword Cenith had seen in the images Niafanna/Cillain had put in his head.

Last was the lone female. Judging from Tyrsa's descriptions of Shival, this wasn't her. It had to be Talueth, although, again, she looked nothing like the idols his people worshipped. Though still beautiful beyond compare, she wasn't pregnant and her eyes held a calm he'd never seen in anyone. It brought back the only really vivid image he had of his mother—the night she rocked him while he sweated out a fever. She'd caught the same fever shortly after, but couldn't fight it.

"My Lord?" Daric set his hand on Cenith's shoulder.

Cenith shook his head and leapt to his feet. "Damn! I almost fell for her tricks!"

"I thought that might be the case."

"Where is Shival?" Niafanna/Cillain asked.

Maegden snorted, a rude noise that boomed throughout the cavern. "I do not know, nor do I care. Why have we been dragged here?" His voice resembled the rumble of distant thunder. He scanned the cave. "This is the place we finally defeated that imp queen of yours. Have you come to surrender?"

The doll regarded Maegden with cool button eyes. "You have come to meet your fate. The time of choosing is at hand."

Maegden frowned. "Speak clearly. You make no sense."

Abbatar snorted. "They mean, ye big ugly idiot, that our new queen will decide whether ye remain in Ardael or not."

"Abbatar!" Niafanna/Cillain's and Lady Violet's voices snapped in the cool air of the cavern.

"Your new queen?" Aja laughed. "This little insect and her doll?"

Yes, the same little insect who defeated your brother and sister. Cenith said nothing, however, not wanting to draw their attention. He'd fought one battle today and didn't really want to fight another, especially against a god or five. That barrier didn't look particularly thick and the memory of Tailis sat far too fresh in his mind.

No sooner had the thought entered his head, than Siyon swung his mighty sword, rending the shield. The doll jerked on Tyrsa's knee. Lady Violet steadied it while Niafanna/Cillain mended the tear, but not before Siyon slipped through. The creatures on the other side of the cavern screamed, yelled, howled, begging for Niafanna and Cillain to drop their barrier.

"Let's see how it handles a true warrior!" Siyon, God of War, bellowed.

The Companions leapt to the attack. Cenith and Daric unsheathed their swords, Cenith hissing at the pain in his hand, and took up places to Tyrsa's left, the last line of defence.

In identical armour and helmets, the Companions were difficult to tell apart. Jolin and Madin were the two tallest. The captain stood with what looked like Dathan and Yanis, taking Siyon's blows on their swords while Madin pumped crossbow bolts into the god at an amazing rate until Siyon resembled a porcupine. Buckam's double knives flashed in a blurry haze as he darted between Siyon's legs, hacking and slashing, only just dodging the giant sword. The others harried the immortal warrior with nips and jabs.

The white horsetails on the Companions helmets flipped and whirled as they performed their deadly dance. One of the Companions sliced Siyon's left arm. Blood dripped onto the floor, splattered the new tabards. The god laughed and sucked on the wound while fighting with his other hand. More blood turned his arms and legs a bright red, but none of the wounds weakened him.

Garun stared, his eyes bulging from his head like a fish. "Incredible! If I were to write this in a journal, no one would believe me. The gods! I'm actually seeing the gods!"

"If the Companions lose, you might see them a little closer than you wish," Cenith said.

Madin tossed his crossbow to one side, the bolts spent, drew his sword and attacked, his weapon a blur. All the Companions moved with unimaginable speed, especially for men in heavy armour. They twisted and ducked, dodged and spun. Siyon's free hand caught one of them, Cenith thought it might be Fallon, and flung him against the shield. The Companion bounced back to his feet, shook his head and re-joined the fray.

"How are the Companions able to fight like that?" Cenith asked Daric.

He shrugged.

"They are aided by the Queen's Souls."

Cenith glanced at Niafanna/Cillain. *The Queen's Souls?* "Are those the wisps that entered my men?"

"Yes. They are of the Blood and are adding their unique abilities to those of your Companions. But they are weakening much faster than Siyon. That one killed many thousands of our children. The blood he drinks from his own wounds renews his strength. I am afraid our daughter will have to step in." The doll looked up into Lady Violet's passive eyes before returning its gaze to the battle.

"Must she? Tyrsa suffers so much from the pain." Cenith couldn't hold her while she sat in the chair.

"Daughter, pass us to Daric, he will care for us."

Daric held Niafanna/Cillain in the crook of his left arm, like he would a small child.

Lady Violet did as asked and Tyrsa's eyes turned blue. She gasped. Fear drained what little colour she had in her cheeks. Cenith wanted to hold her, tell her everything would be fine, but if he did, he might brush up against the chair.

"You may touch the throne, Cenith," the gods said. "Our daughter wishes it, and so it shall be."

Cenith picked Tyrsa up, holding her close. "It's all right, love. I'm here. Your Companions need you."

"I don't understand! I don't know what all this is! Lady Violet says you might die and Shival was here but now she's gone!"

He sat on the dais, cradling her in his arms. If he found all this unbelievable, he could imagine what she must be suffering. "You don't have to understand everything right now, Tyrsa. All you need to worry about is that the Companions are in trouble. They need your help." *Shival was here?* He'd have to remember to talk to her about it later.

Tyrsa sucked in a shuddering breath and nodded. "I can do this."

"Yes, you can. You've done it before." Cenith placed her so he didn't interfere with her ball of power. She reached inside herself and pulled it out.

Holding it between her hands, the white orb grew brighter and bigger. It flew toward Siyon. The God of War grabbed it. Smoke rose from his hand and he howled in pain, then tossed it back to her. Tyrsa caught it before it

332

could touch Cenith, then left it to float in the air. The other gods laughed.

"That didn't work."

Cenith kissed the top of her head. "Try something else." All the Companions still fought, but their armour bore rents, some red with their own blood. Cuts marred their white and purple tabards.

"I like you holding me," she said. "But I need to sit in the chair. I have more power there."

He wished she'd said so in the first place. Cenith set her on the throne, careful not to touch the white globe floating near her, and stepped to one side. Daric moved behind the chair, to the left of the pillar holding the Orb of Truth.

Tyrsa's features crinkled in concentration. From the river came thick ropes of water. They snaked out, deftly avoiding the Companions, and wrapped themselves around Siyon's arms and legs. The god stumbled, then fell, roaring his pain and fear. His hand continued to smoke. The Companions took advantage of the opportunity. Three stabbed his chest while two hacked at his neck. Once again Tyrsa threw her orb. It sunk deep into Siyon's body. When the god stopped thrashing, she ordered the Companions back. His body swelled, bloating with Tyrsa's power.

In a flash of red heat, the God of War disappeared, leaving only a glowing crimson orb that soon turned to white. Tyrsa called it back to her, then sank down in the chair, shaking like a leaf on a windy autumn day. Cenith crouched beside her, holding her hand.

"That wasn't so bad," she said, giving Cenith a tired smile. "It's easier here."

"Now then," Niafanna/Cillain said, from the protection of Daric's arm. "Shall we stop this nonsense and proceed with the choosing?"

Maegden scowled. "And if we attack again? Your little knights look worn out."

Talueth stepped to his side and set her hand on his arm. Maegden shrugged it off. She shot him a nasty look and pointed to the creatures raging behind the other shield. "They do not."

"Daughter." The doll looked at Tyrsa. "You know what to do."

She gave a weary nod. "Companions."

Her guard limped to their positions around the throne, leaning on their weapons, or each other, for support while Daric took up his former position at the foot of the dais. The Companions' once pristine tabards were torn and splotched red with blood, theirs and Siyon's.

Tyrsa closed her eyes and the white glow emanating from the throne surrounded the Companions, Cenith and Daric. Blood stopped flowing, metal creaked as dents and tears disappeared and holes vanished. Cenith flexed his injured hand. The wound was gone, as were all his cuts and bruises. A few moments later, the glow faded and the soldiers stood straight, proud and whole once more. Cenith unwrapped his bandage. Not even a scar remained.

Garun watched all of it, his eyes darting from one Companion to another. He shook his head. "I must be dreaming. What I could do with such power."

"They are healed," Niafanna/Cillain said. "Daric, you may put us back."

Once he'd done as ordered, he resumed his place at the foot of the dais. One look at Tyrsa showed violet eyes. Maybe it was for the best.

"Is your wound healed?" Cenith asked Daric.

The Calleni nodded. Cenith wished Tyrsa could heal like this all the time. Perhaps she could take some of that power with her when they left the cavern. If they left.

The remaining gods glared at the doll on Lady Violet's lap. Talueth shook her head. "It is pointless, Father. Two of your sons and a daughter have been forced back to Tai-Keth because of this child queen. She now has Siyon's power as well as Tailis' and Keana's, and, for some puzzling reason, we are not what we once were. Perhaps it is time we went home."

"No. I will not give up what I have won without a fight!" Maegden shook his fist. He slammed his sword into the shield. It shimmered, but held. Ordan lifted his hammer and added his blows to his father's. Aja used his fists. Maegden added lightning bolts to the weapons slamming the barrier. When they hit the shield, it sounded as if all the thunder that had ever resounded in the world boomed through the cavern. Cenith clapped his hands to his ears. So did Daric and Garun. The Companions and Lady Violet seemed unaffected, as did Talueth, who stood back from the rest of her family, a bored expression on her face.

Niafanna/Cillain set a cloth hand to their brow, head dipped in concentration. Lady Violet closed her eyes and her hands glowed. From behind Maegden's shield, three strands of water, as thick as a man's thigh, slid along the ground. In an instant, each one wrapped itself around the gods' legs, pulling them to the ground. The thunder and lightning storm behind the shield stopped, though Cenith's ears still rang.

"What is this?" Ordan kicked his legs, but the water rope held strong.

"Do you give up now?" Niafanna/Cillain asked.

Maegden spat. "Have your choosing then. But the decision had better be fair, or I will see you all dead!"

Niafanna/Cillain nodded their head. Lady Violet released the ropes and the gods leapt to their feet. The doll motioned for Meric and his guards to come forward. In all the fuss, Cenith had forgotten about them. Meric hesitated.

"Come," Niafanna/Cillain said. "We will not hurt you. If you have something to say on your people's behalf, then speak it to Cenith so he may relate it to the Jada-Drau."

Meric crept forward like a frightened child, stopping between the first pair of statues, Tajik and his guard around him. He looked first at his father's body, then at Cenith, his face one of abject misery. "I would not know what to say. I leave it to you."

The doll lifted one arm. "The time of pleas has come."

Cenith's heart pounded. What could he say in favour of his gods, especially after they'd tried to kill Tyrsa? How could he blame her if she chose the Blood? One look at the slender people behind the shield told him what race she actually belonged to, despite her parents. For most of her life she'd suffered pain and loneliness because of one of his kind. He leaned closer to Daric. "I suppose it's too late to convert now."

Daric's face remained impassive, but his eyes showed his worry. "I imagine it is."

* * * *

Jolin watched Cenith, Daric and Garun walk to the far end of the statues to join Abbatar and Meric. Memories of recent pain and unaccustomed exertion tugged at him.

Though Lady Orchid had healed the wounds, his joints felt stiff, as did the muscles in his arms, from fending off Siyon. None bothered him as much as the scene unfolding before him.

Lady Orchid had to choose between the man she loved and the creatures unjustly driven from their land. Jolin had to wonder where he and the Companions fit into this. They had sworn oaths to lord and lady. How could they protect both if Lady Orchid chose the Blood? What would happen to the Companions? Would they disappear along with the Ardaeli people? If she chose in Cenith's favour, would she vanish with the rest of the Old Ones? His heart ached at the thought of never seeing her again.

Stop worrying lad! Ye're giving me a headache. Rierden had hardly shut up since he'd joined with Jolin.

Hmmm, what's this now? the Queen's Soul said. *I think ye love our queen a little too much.*

I know I do.

Rierden sighed. *I understand what ye suffer. I loved one I couldn't have. As one of the Queen's Souls, we weren't permitted families. It was thought they would divide our loyalty and duty. I fell in love with one of Queen Ashling's hand maids, but I had already sworn my vows, so I could do nothing but stand and watch my love serve our queen. To be honest, I think we both need a drink. Or several.*

Jolin's longing combined with Rierden's; it was almost too much to bear. An image flashed before his eyes, black hair falling in thick, rippling waves, dark brown eyes flashing with amusement. A sweet mouth just made for kissing. *Jennica!*

Rierden's interest picked up. *Now there's a pretty one. Tall, well-shaped.* He laughed. *If I wasn't dead, I'd have a go at her myself.*

A rush of defensive jealousy surged through Jolin, surprising him. *Ye'll not touch her! I thought ye were in love wi' someone else.*

I am, but she died three thousand years ago. Besides, I don't have hands anymore.

Jolin felt a pang of longing, a deep grief that wasn't his.

Nonetheless, Rierden chuckled. *Jealous, are ye? Well, ye should be. That one is a prize. And better suited for ye than our queen.*

Jolin scowled. *I'm not sure I like ye in my head, lookin' into my thoughts, my life. Why don't ye be quiet for a while so I kin listen to what's happenin'?*

Rierden snorted. Abbatar hobbled up the left side of the aisle formed by the statues, holding up his robe so it didn't trail in the stream.

I can't believe that buffoon is still alive, Rierden commented. *I thought someone would have stuck a knife in his gut ages ago. The only reason Queen Ashling kept him around was because he is her son by some oafish human she favoured for awhile...no offence.*

Jolin sighed. *None taken, now hush. He's 'bout t' speak.*

Abbatar spread his arms, his gnarled walking stick resembling a writhing serpent he'd just captured. "Great Queen, our Jada-Drau, Choice Maker, she for whom we have waited so long. It is with great admiration that I come before you."

Cillain's balls! Rierden spat. *What a load of troll dung!*

Jolin ignored him, mostly because he agreed.

Lowering his stick, Abbatar gave Lady Violet a deep bow. "Look there, my queen." He pointed to the creatures standing behind the shield. Those that could bore

338

scowls, the rest bared teeth.

Jolin frowned. *They're goin' to scare my poor lady if they keep doin' that.*

Nobody likes Abbatar.

Then why did Niafanna and Cillain choose him t' speak for them?

Rierden chuckled. *Because he is the one least likely to kill any o' ye.*

Jolin focused on Abbatar, not the claws, teeth, spears and clubs that waited beyond the shield.

"The Shanadar, the Blood, your people, stand on the other side of that barrier with the Old Ones, ready to protect and serve ye. What's left of them, that is. What Maegden and his followers did…" Abbatar indicated the opposite side of the cavern, Lord Cenith, Meric and the Bredun men. "…was nothing less than the murder of yer true family and those under their care."

Maegden and his remaining sons bellowed and pounded the shield. Talueth remained silent, observing the proceedings with piercing eyes.

Lord Cenith did nothin'! Jolin wanted to set the little man straight. Straight into the river.

Settle lad. Rierden sent out calming thoughts. *Your lord will have his say. It is your duty to stand and protect. Leave the rest to Cenith.*

"For over three thousand years, the remnants of your people have hidden in these hills, in this mountain, barred from the rest of the land they were born in." Abbatar covered his heart with one hand. "For millennia they have suffered, some not seeing the light of day in all that time. This land is theirs, rightfully given to them by the Mother and Father, yer true Mother and Father, the ones who love you. I beseech you, my dearest queen, to choose justice. Choose yer people. The Shanadar and Old Ones will never hurt ye, but honour and cherish ye for the rest of yer long days." Abbatar gave Lady Orchid another deep bow, then made his way back to the first pair of statues.

He said nothin' 'bout his part in m'lady's sufferin'! If he hadn't changed that scroll...

Again Rierden snorted. *Abbatar doesn't want to draw attention to the fact that he's as responsible for her hard life as that egotistical, throne-seeking buffoon who helped sire her. That wouldn't help his cause.*

Lord Cenith moved in front of the dais with none of the confidence Abbatar displayed. "I know you are in control, Lady Violet. Is it you who will make the choice or Tyrsa?"

"Tyrsa will make the choice. She listens while I explain things she does not understand."

Cenith swallowed. "Tyrsa, I know this is hard for you. I wouldn't wish to be in your place for anything." He glanced at his gods. "You know I don't agree with what Maegden and his brood did to your people. If it were today, I wouldn't follow him. I could not, in all conscience, destroy another people simply for the land they possessed.

"All I ask is that you think of the innocent folk of the mountains, plains, forests and shores of Ardael, the people you have met since we married. Those who love you, who have befriended you. Those who have taught you the words you love so much, and the men who gave their lives to protect you. None of them were responsible for the suffering of your people."

Cenith fell to his knees. "There is but one thing I ask. If you choose the Old Ones, then please, take my life first, for I am a coward and I cannot watch those I care for die."

He hung his head a moment then rose to his feet to join Daric. The look on his face tore at Jolin. Rierden whistled, a strange buzzing in the back of Jolin's head.

Why didn't he speak o' their love? Wouldn't that help sway her? Jolin asked.

He didn't have to. Can't ye feel their love when they look at each other? The air is thick with it.

Through Rierden, Jolin felt the remnants of a love so profound, it almost hurt. He had no chance of competing with that kind of devotion. He could only wish he would find it someday.

He's good, you know," Rierden said. *"That sounded like it came right from the heart.*

Jolin stiffened. *It did! Lord Cenith is a decent, honest man!*

Relax. I never said he wasn't. Rierden paused a moment. *Yer loyalty is to be commended. What will ye do if the queen chooses us and yer noble lord has to die?*

Won't I die with him? Aren't we the people you blame for a tragedy three thousand years gone? Jolin clenched his fist.

Actually, Rierden said. *The Queen's Souls now inhabit ye and your Companions, making ye part of the Blood. Ye won't die.*

Small comfort. Jolin's heart pounded. Lord Cenith dead? *This has to be a nightmare!*

Sorry, lad. It's real. So were the waves of sympathy emanating from Rierden. *What will ye do? I'm not intending to be nasty, ye understand. This is something ye have to think about. Now.*

If Lord Cenith died, it would be by Lady Tyrsa's hand. It was her choice. Jolin had sworn to protect them both, but how could he defend Lord Cenith if Lady Tyrsa chose the Blood? If she chose for Lord Cenith, then she might die and Jolin couldn't protect her. Either way, he was foresworn. Reluctantly, he came to the conclusion that there could be only one answer to Rierden's question. *If my lord is dead, and there is nothing I can do to stop it, then I have to protect my lady. I swore an oath.*

Good lad! I knew ye'd make the right choice.

Despite Rierden's words, Jolin's heart sunk down to his toes. *I can't speak for t' others.*

Ye don't have to, ye are their captain. They will listen to ye, and to the Queen's Souls within them.

The doll on Lady Violet's lap raised one hand. "Our daughter will now make the choice."

* * * *

I don't want to! Tyrsa cried.

Lady Violet closed her eyes. *You have to. It is the will of the Mother and Father. You heard the pleas. Now is the time to weigh what Abbatar said against what Cenith said, and choose who has the right to live in Ardael.*

Tyrsa tried to ignore Lady Violet's stern words. *I don't understand why I have to choose! Why can't everyone stay the way they are?*

Is it fair for the Shanadar, your people, to continue living here, under the mountain? Away from the sun and fresh air of the land that belongs to them? Is it fair for the Old Ones to hide in fear for their lives? Lady Violet sighed. *The Mother and Father gave you life. They protected you while you grew up, so you would not go mad from Saulth's cruelty. If you make the wrong choice, the Shanadar and Old Ones will cease to exist, after all these centuries of suffering. You bear the blood of both races. No matter your choice, you will not die. But, if you run, and do not make the choice, Maegden will destroy you. He dare not let you live. And they will not come at you one at a time, they will set their animosity for each other aside and attack all at once. Even you and your Companions will not win.*

Tyrsa's chest hurt, the same as when she thought Cenith would die. *That is true.*

Then you choose the Blood? Lady Violet couldn't hide the hope in her voice.

But if I do, Cenith will die and I will be alone again. I don't want to be alone!

No. You will not. The Shanadar will revere you and love you as their queen. The creatures they protect, the fairies, pixies and the rest, will be your friends. You will never be alone again.

I don't know them! I love Cenith! I want to be with him! Tyrsa wanted to cry.

Lady Violet's voice hardened. *Then you choose Cenith and his violent gods?*

Tyrsa tried to scream. Nothing came out. She understood that the funny looking creatures behind the shimmering wall had suffered as much as she had. Tyrsa hurt for them, but she hurt for Cenith too, and all the others who would die with him. *If...if I choose the Blood, will...will it hurt when Cenith dies?*

Lady Violet's gentle words slid across her thoughts. *No. He will feel no pain, no discomfort. He will simply cease to be. I am sure the Mother and Father can erase all memory of him for you, then you will not suffer his loss.*

Did she want to forget about him? All the nice things he did for her, even though he didn't have to? The nights spent just holding each other and the special times they shared bodies...and the cliff?

Tyrsa remembered what the Mother and Father

343

said that night on the cliff about the history of Queen Ashling and her fight to save her throne; about the brave Queen's Souls who gave up their lives to protect that throne when all was lost. How could she abandon the hope they had held in their hearts for so long?

Look inside your heart, Lady Violet said. *You know which choice to make.*

Cenith! The Blood! Tyrsa's head whirled until she looked deep inside herself and something she hadn't seen; something the Mother and Father had told her that night on the cliff, only just remembered. She took control of her body once more and cried out her decision. It was the only choice that felt right.

"I choose…the Blood!"

Chapter Nineteen

Cenith couldn't move, couldn't believe what his ears told him. He closed his eyes and waited for the end. A moment passed, then another. Cenith risked a peek. All remained the same. Maybe he wouldn't die until his gods left for Tai-Keth. The Old Ones, silent until now, shifted feet, ruffled feathers, cocked their heads, oddly subdued. Meric and his guards stood in shock, their faces pasty white.

Maegden bellowed and hammered the shield with sword and lightning bolts. Ordan joined in. Once again the Companions shifted, forming the double row between Tyrsa and Maegden, weapons drawn. Were those tears he saw in Jolin's eyes?

The Old Ones resumed their howls and yells. The Shanadar banged spears against shields, crying for blood. The doll sat serenely on Tyrsa's lap, showing little of the struggle the two gods must be enduring to keep the shield intact. Had Tyrsa's decision given them more strength?

A mighty roar rocked the cavern, followed so closely by another it could only have come from the throat of a second creature of the same species. Though he tried to peer past the Shanadar, trolls and other strange beings, Cenith couldn't see what made those monstrous cries.

Tyrsa's brow furrowed in concentration and the thick ropes of water reappeared, wrapping themselves around the gods' legs, jerking Maegden, Aja and Ordan off their feet.

"The choice has been made. We are ordained to continue here. You are not," Niafanna/Cillain said. "Shall we lower the shields? Shall we turn loose those whose land you stole? Or will you depart quietly, leaving us the power you hold in this land." The orb above Tyrsa's head grew brighter, sending out tendrils of light. The air vibrated with power.

Talueth folded her hands in front of her. "Father, it is time to go."

"She is right," Aja said, a sly smile sliding across his face. "But this is not all."

"What does he mean by that?" Cenith asked Daric.

"Shival isn't here. It might be her he refers to."

According to Tyrsa, Shival *had* been here, but had left. How?

Maegden struggled to his feet, still held by the ropes of water. Without warning, he bellowed and threw his lightning sword at Tyrsa. It shattered the shield and shot toward the throne. Jayce and Fallan caught it on their blades and it flew up into the light cast by the orb. The shining globe sucked it in. Maegden's shoulders sagged in defeat. Aja scowled and threw his dice at the orb. They vanished in the pulsating light. Ordan's hammer went next, accompanied by a cry of rage from the God of Fire. His hair flared in a whoosh of anger.

All eyes turned to Talueth. "Perhaps we were wrong to take this land," she said. "We thought we could create something good here, something better than what our people have in Tai-Keth. And we did, for a while." She reached into her belly and pulled out a glowing ball like Tyrsa's, only yellow.

She set it adrift. It floated toward Tyrsa who redirected it up to the giant orb where it blended with the white light.

Maegden shook his fist. "As Aja said, this is not all. We will return and you will suffer more than you can imagine!"

The gods faded, Ordan's final cry of rage echoing off the unseen walls and ceiling. The Companions returned to their places. With horror in his heart, Cenith watched his hands. They didn't fade. His heart still beat, though at a rapid pace.

Tyrsa pulled her ball of power from inside her and with deft movements, separated the red sphere representing Siyon's power. She sent it up with the others before replacing her own globe within her. Tyrsa looked at Cenith. The longing in her eyes tore his heart.

Garun patted himself. "I'm still here." He looked at Cenith. "So are you. I'm confused."

Cenith had to agree. "Mother, Father, why are we not gone along with our gods?"

The doll smiled. "Our daughter made the right choice. As we said earlier, many of the Shanadar travelled to other lands bordering Ardael and took mates from the humans living there. Over the centuries, some of those people travelled back into Ardael, spreading the Blood here. Very few remain without a portion of the Blood in them, especially in your mountains." The doll closed its eyes a moment. "A total of three hundred and twenty four people in Ardael have died, all in the north, the few who remain of pure Tai-Kethian blood."

Meric collapsed, tears wetting his cheeks. "I thought for sure I was going to die, the way Father treated her…"

Tajik hauled him to his feet, disgusted, though Cenith could see relief in his eyes as well. Tyrsa stood and

347

set Baybee carefully on the throne, then ran between the rows of statues and threw herself in Cenith's arms. The doll sat on her own, her hands folded one atop the other.

He picked Tyrsa up and buried his face in her hair. The remnants of the soap she used mixed with dried sweat, leather and horse. She smelled wonderful. "I thought I'd never hold you again."

"I was scared and I didn't know what to do. I couldn't let you die!"

"You made the right choice, my love. I'm so proud of you." Though he felt sorry for those who'd died, and those who loved them, he couldn't help but feel relief that they were both alive.

"We are also proud of you, daughter," the doll said, "although your choice has caused problems that must be resolved. The Shanadar and the Old Ones still need a proper home. They are your people now and look to you for answers."

Cenith set Tyrsa on her feet. She stared up at him, her eyes wide with fear. "I don't know what to do!"

"That's not the only problem," Daric said. "There's still the part of the scroll that says 'One will rule'."

"And Shival," Cenith said. He turned to Tyrsa. "You said she was here."

Tyrsa nodded, her eyes wide. "She took Saulth's soul. The Mother and Father tried to hold her, but she escaped. Lady Violet said she is stronger than she should be."

"We also can't forget the people who worship her family," Garun put in.

Ors came to mind. Cenith ran a hand through his hair. "And here I thought once Tyrsa had made her choice, our troubles would be over. They've only just begun." He

348

kissed the top of Tyrsa's head. "Perhaps you should go back to your throne until this is settled."

Tyrsa nodded and walked to the marble chair, her feet floating on the stream. She sat, Baybee on her lap once more. The Shanadar man Cenith had picked out for battle struck his shield with his spear twice before replacing the weapon in its quiver.

The doll nodded. "You may speak Kyr, Battle Chief of the Shanadar."

"Mother, Father, although it doesna' make me happy, our queen has the right of it," the Shanadar said. His voice wasn't deep, nor loud, with a pleasant timbre to it and could easily be heard in the cavern.

"Bah!" Abbatar shook his stick. "They should be gone!"

"Then ye would be gone, too!" Kyr countered. "For ye only have partial Blood." He turned back to Niafanna/Cillain. "Cenith's people have some of the Blood in them. I see that now. Choosing who should live and who should die would prove difficult. I understand the way it must be. Cenith has a great deal of our blood, more than the one who sired our queen." The Shanadar warrior turned his blue eyes on Cenith. "How is this so?"

Cenith took a step forward. "My mother, grandmother, and great-grandmother were all Syrthian, and others of my ancestors have married Syrthian or West Downs women."

"Even so, we canna accept ye as king." Kyr said. "I have serious doubts about ye as consort, but, though the marriage between ye and our queen is not according to our traditions, it is, nonetheless, binding and true."

"I don't wish to be king," Cenith said. "I only want to rule my principality in peace, as my forefathers have before me. And your queen has a name. It's Tyrsa."

Kyr studied him a moment before responding. "Peace is a thing of the future, if it can be achieved at all. By her choice, our queen…Queen Tyrsa, has asked us to live side by side with those now inhabiting Ardael. Yer people won't accept us or the passing of yer gods easily. Nor will those who rule beside ye accept one ruler, as is decreed by the scroll."

"He's right," Daric said, out of the side of his mouth. "The Lords' Council proved that."

Niafanna/Cillain looked up at the scroll, still hanging in the air. "There can only be one ruler. This division of the land is not productive. There are too many squabbles between your leaders. Still, this is something that can wait. With the Others gone, the land will heal."

The Old Ones resumed their shouts and howling.

The doll held an arm up and they quit. "The one who will rule has yet to be born. Tyrsa carries a child, a son of both peoples."

Kyr frowned. "Only a daughter is acceptable."

Cenith's heart thumped. He blinked. "Son?"

"We're deciding the fate of the country here, My Lord, I don't think you should stand with your mouth hanging open," Daric said, adding a smirk.

Cenith closed it, still trying to work around the sudden news of his impending fatherhood.

Niafanna/Cillain placed one cloth hand over the other. "This is Tyrsa's first child. There will be more."

Groans from the Shanadar and the Old Ones echoed in the massive cavern. "Then we must wait to take our place in the world," Kyr said. "For though we love her dearly, Queen Tyrsa isna' suitable to rule, thanks to Saulth…and Abbatar." The battle chief's cold stare found the old man who'd caused much of Tyrsa's problems. Abbatar pretended to find something interesting in the darkness above.

I'm going to be a father? Cenith shook his head, struggling to bring his thoughts to the matters at hand. "Won't our son be acceptable? As the Mother and Father have said, he is of both peoples." *My son. A son of my own. I hope I'm ready for this.*

Kyr shook his head. "The Shanadar only have queens. Is it not yer way that ye only accept sons as heirs? Going so far as to give land to someone else than let a daughter have it?"

"Yes, it is so." Cenith's words brought sniggers and giggles from the ranks of the Old Ones, though he couldn't see the perpetrators, except for Abbatar, whose smirk took over the lines on his face.

"Problem is," the little old man said. "Ye canna really be sure of the son's parentage. A queen produces a daughter who is obviously hers."

Though Cenith knew he was Ifan's son, he had to grudgingly admit Abbatar had a point.

"Mother, Father, will Lady Tyrsa have a daughter?" Daric asked the doll.

"Yes."

A son and a daughter. Conflicting emotions ran through Cenith, joy and pride over his soon-to-be children, relief that Tyrsa would bear them and live, and worry over how to sort all this out. "Then I suggest we find a place in Dunvalos Reach for the Shanadar and Old Ones to live in comfort while we wait for her birth. This would also give us time to resolve the problems now facing us."

Kyr's blue eyes bored into his. "Though we prefer the plains to raise our unicorns, that would be acceptable, for now."

The remainder of the Shanadar nodded their heads. The Old Ones were strangely silent. Garun still stood nearby, his eyes flitting from one of the creatures to another. The mixture of curiosity and wonder on the physician's face forced a small smile to Cenith's lips.

"If ye don't mind my speakin' up, m'lord." Jolin took a step forward. "There's a valley behind Shadow Mountain that ain't bein' used, least, last time I looked. It's bin a few years since I've been through there."

Jolin should have green eyes, not blue. I wonder if it's permanent. A movement to Cenith's left turned his attention that way.

Meric squared his shoulders and stepped forward. "If you give me time, I might be able to find room in Bredun for the Shanadar. They are not quite so...obviously different as the others. My people will accept them, if I tell them to."

Cenith tried hard to keep his jaw from dropping. Daric raised both eyebrows. Tajik glowered at his new lord.

"Keep your scowl to yourself, Tajik. What happened three thousand years ago was wrong. What my father did..." Meric glanced at Saulth's body, anguish on his face, "...was also wrong. I regret his death, but perhaps he will find peace now." Meric's shoulders slumped. "I regret many things. The least I can do is help right that wrong." He turned to Kyr. "How many of your people are there?"

"We were once many thousands. Now we are two hundred and twenty four." The Shanadar battle chief held his head proud, though pain darkened his eyes.

"With all the recent troubles, there should be more

than enough land for you."

Kyr nodded. "We would like to be near the mountains, but not in the scrubland, if that's possible."

"I'm sure we can find something." Meric stepped back to Tajik's side.

"Good," Niafanna/Cillain said. "I believe everyone else would prefer to remain in the mountains, away from most of your people, but out in the open, in the sunlight and fresh air, with their cousins, the pixies, fairies and brownies. The valley would suffice."

Jolin's words rang in Cenith's head. *'I've bin tryin' t' tell ye, m'lord. Th' Old Ones are real.'* Damned if he wasn't right. "I gather they've been living amongst us all along," Cenith said. "I doubt my people would notice a few more. Um...how many giants are there?" They could be a definite problem.

Kyr took a moment to answer, keeping his cool gaze locked on Cenith. "Chock is the last, all the others died in the war. The Tree People, naiads and dryads are already amongst ye, as are the fairies, pixies and brownies." He indicated those Cenith thought of as walking sticks, then pointed to the river creatures. "The merfolk and hippocamps will return to the secret coves they've been hiding in all these centuries. They dinna like humans."

Cenith glanced at the half horse-half fish creatures in the river, their front hooves resting on the stone bank, damp manes hanging limp. They had to be the hippocamps Kyr mentioned.

The Shanadar man waved a hand at the short hairy men. "The trolls can share the valley with the others. The griffins and hippogryphs prefer high mountain tops, where yer people don't go, but they do need to come down to hunt. The chimera actually enjoy living down here. The satyrs would like to go where the dryads and naiads are. They'll run a risk of discovery."

Cenith cast his gaze over all the fairy tale folk staring back at him, unable to absorb what he saw. "Apparently many of my people believe they all exist anyway." He glanced at Jolin, still standing at attention on the dais. "I think if they just stay away from the towns and bigger villages, they shouldn't fare too badly. I suppose you could let me know if there's any trouble."

Kyr agreed. "The only ones I can see really posing a serious problem are Greythorne, Grimtag and the shivers."

"Shivers?" Cenith didn't like the sound of that.

Four indistinct shapes slipped from the cavern's gloom. Floating black shadows, at first they appeared man-like then changed to amorphous blobs before shifting back into men. Garun gasped, his eyes widening further.

"M'lord!" Jayce cried. "Beware o' them! Tis said they eat a man's shadow 'til he sickens and dies!"

Kyr thumped his shield with his fist. "Stories! Passed down by frightened people who dinna understand! Yes, shivers eat shadows, but they rarely eat those of humans. And they never kill. They are not evil. Merely different."

"Wouldn't they prefer the darkness of the caves, then?" Daric suggested.

"No." Kyr moved his horned pony closer. "In darkness there are no shadows, there must be light for shadow to exist. And the shadows they eat must belong to living things."

"I'm not sure I'd like them running amok amongst my people," Cenith said. "I have nothing against them myself, but mountain folk are superstitious and trying to convince them the shivers mean no harm will take time."

Kyr's eyes blazed. The shivers moaned, a strange sound, reminiscent of a breeze passing through dead trees. "These are all that are left. We will keep them with us, on the plains," the Shanadar battle chief said. "They can feed off the shadows of our unicorns." He turned his attention to Meric. "Though they willna' kill, we will ensure they stay away from yer people."

Meric nodded, the look on his face passing from horror to worry to stoic conviction. "I said you could have the land. As long as my people are safe, they may live there."

Kyr almost smiled. He gave the new Bredun lord a half bow. "We thank ye. Perhaps we can learn to live in peace."

"Who are this Grimtag and Greythorne you spoke of?" Daric asked.

Kyr raised his voice. "Grimtag! Greythorne!"

The Old Ones shifted farther down the cavern, a lot farther. From out of the deepest shadows crawled two creatures whose size dwarfed the massive cave. Claws longer than daggers adorned each lizard-like foot. Great reptilian heads sat on elongated, ridged necks. What looked like folded leather wings hugged their bodies. Long, spiked tails vanished into the darkness from which they'd come. In the flickering lights of the cavern, their scales appeared a shimmering dark green. One whiff told Cenith these were the source of the odd smell he'd detected in the tunnel.

Daric's eyebrows lifted and his eyes widened to the point where Cenith thought they'd pop right out, imitating Garun's. "Dragons! I thought they'd disappeared millennia ago!"

A deep, powerful voice sounded in Cenith's head. *We are the last.* By the look on Daric's and Garun's faces, they heard it as well.

We offer our assistance in the search for peace, so we may bear offspring. This voice had a distinctly female tone to it.

Meric half hid behind Tajik. "I think I am *very* glad I chose to help your side."

A wry smile tipped the edge of Kyr's mouth. He pointed to the larger of the dragons. "This is Grimtag. His mate is Greythorne. These two will strike fear into the hearts of many who dinna agree with us. Their kind killed many of our enemies and did it with joy in their hearts. Be assured, they don't eat people, but those who oppose us need not know."

What sounded like a sniff echoed in Cenith's head. *Humans are too stringy and bitter tasting,* Grimtag said. *Perhaps, once we are free, a tender cow or two sheep each could be arranged? We only need eat once every ten days. The Shanadar have brought us food, and we appreciate it, but it was insufficient and we have grown weak.*

Cenith tried to take in what his eyes and ears insisted stood there. It took a couple of tries before he could find the words. "I'm sure we could manage something."

Garun took a few steps toward the dragons before Daric hauled him back.

"Cenith." Niafanna/Cillain's button eyes rested on him. "As consort, you are now War Chief of the Shanadar. You have a great chore ahead of you. Approach and receive our blessing."

Cenith walked the length of the statues to the throne, followed by Daric and Garun. He was unsure of what to expect, but glad that he was alive to feel that trepidation.

"Kneel before us Cenith, consort of Queen Tyrsa, War Chief of the Shanadar, Lord of Dunvalos Reach." They held out a small cloth hand.

Cenith obeyed and Niafanna/Cillain touched his forehead. He closed his eyes. A warmth spread through him. Comforting memories rushed to his head...his mother holding him, singing a Syrthian lullaby; his father standing beside him, pride on his face as Cenith brought down his first deer. Calm replaced the confusion, worry, fear and lingering anger that he'd placed all his people at risk.

Two voices sounded in his head. *Tyrsa is our daughter, you are our warrior. You must use the skills you have learned, and those you have yet to learn, to find peace for this troubled land. Shival's absence disturbs us. We are unable to locate her. She will make trouble in the future and the fight will not be an easy one. Make use of those around you. Some have unexpected talents. The Old Ones and the Shanadar will also help. Use their skills and wisdom. They will be needed. Trust them. Despite their ferocity, they are loyal to us and will work for the peace we wish to have in this land. We wish you luck, for no matter how much you plan, fate and destiny always have a part to play.*

Mother, Father, I will do as you ask. The god and goddess removed their touch and Cenith opened his eyes. Tyrsa, his Tyrsa, gazed at him, happiness shining in her sweet face. He stood and placed his hands on her shoulders. "Are you really pregnant?"

"I don't feel it, but Lady Violet says I am."

Cenith grinned, the peace of Niafanna and Cillain's blessing joining with the joy in his heart. He stepped back, resuming his former position at the base of the throne.

Tyrsa's doll cast its gaze over all present. "Our job here is finished. It is now up to you to plan how to accomplish what must be done for peace in this land." With that, the life left the button eyes and Baybee fell over. A pulse of light ran up the beam emanating from the orb and disappeared into the darkness. The light in the orb dimmed then vanished along with the beam. The shields across the door and in front of the creatures disappeared and the scroll, hanging in the air all this time, fluttered down to land on Tyrsa's lap. She folded it and tucked it beside her. Darkness crept to the edge of the glow cast by the torches.

The Shanadar guided their horned ponies into the light. Fairies flew like fireflies around their heads. The trolls, Tree People, griffins and the rest of the Old Ones followed. The giant stood and shook himself. Tyrsa shrank back in the throne, her happiness gone in an instant.

"They are your people, love," Cenith said. "They won't hurt you." He knew that for certain now. They could hurt her no more than himself or the Companions.

Still terrified, Tyrsa hugged Baybee. Tiny fairies fluttered past the torches, careful of the flames, and clung to her hair, giggling and whispering to her. Tyrsa's blue eyes widened, but she seemed to calm at their quiet words.

Garun took a step toward the Old Ones. "May I...um...I mean...I have never seen..."

A twitter of laughter erupted from some of the creatures. A female pixie, no more than half a foot high beckoned to him. Her tiny voice, though quiet as a moth's wings, was heard by all. "Please, come. Join us. We're all friends now."

Garun didn't wait for further encouragement and in moments was surrounded by the strangest collection of beings Cenith had ever seen. Kyr guided his small horse closer to Cenith, his head held high, a fierce glower in his eyes.

Daric touched the hilt of his dagger. Cenith put his hand on his councillor's arm and shook his head. Along with the warmth of the blessing, Niafanna and Cillain had instilled in him a trust of these unusual people. For all their posturing, he knew they wouldn't hurt him.

"I am Battle Chief, one rank below ye," Kyr said. "The only reason I didna fight to the death in the war was because Queen Ashling commanded me to take some of our people into hiding and protect them, so our race wouldna die." The short warrior seemed a bit prickly on the subject. "The Mother and Father gave us the long lives necessary to accomplish this, though we will age naturally now."

Cenith blinked. Kyr was that old? "A noble cause," he said. "I think you, Daric, Jolin and I have much to discuss, but not here. It's been a long, strenuous day." He looked back at Meric. "Despite all that's happened between our families, you should talk with us as well. I imagine some hot food and a comfortable bed wouldn't hurt either."

Meric nodded. Tajik scowled.

Daric glanced at Saulth's body, then back at Meric. "Perhaps Rymon might have some suggestions."

Both Meric and Tajik gave him a blank stare. "Oh, you would not have heard," Meric said. "Rymon died several days ago. He was trying to talk Father out of attacking you and just fell over. Dead."

Daric gave him a half bow. "My sympathies. Rymon was a good man."

"He was the only one who could make Father see

reason these last few years." Meric clenched his fists. "I did not know Father was responsible for the death of your son. I am sorry." He paused a moment, staring at Saulth. "Strange. I miss the man my father used to be, when I was young. I do not miss the man he had become."

"I'm sorry about Rymon." Though he'd met him, Cenith didn't really know the man, but had heard much about him. "And your father. It's unfortunate it came to this. From what Niafanna and Cillain said, it wasn't entirely his fault." Everyone looked at Abbatar, who suddenly found something interesting underneath his fingernails.

"It's time to go," Kyr said. "We have lived in this mountain long enough. We wish to feel the sun on our faces, the wind in our hair."

Cenith nodded and held his hand out to Tyrsa. The fairies flitted away when she moved, their giggles like chimes in the wind. As soon as she stood, the light of the throne dimmed, then vanished. The Companions picked up torches and followed them to the tunnel entrance, an unusual crowd behind them, Garun babbling in their midst. Tajik ordered two of the Bredun men to carry Saulth's body before joining Meric at the entrance to the tunnel, torch in hand.

Cenith took a last look at the cavern, the throne and the creatures it held.

"I still think this has to be a dream," he said to Daric. His councillor chuckled. Cenith wished they could take the now dark throne with them. It held power they might need.

His gaze settled on the dragons, their necks entwined in an embrace. "Those two won't fit in the tunnel," he said to Kyr. Chock would have to bend over and still might have trouble fitting through the door.

"They got in three thousand years ago." Kyr pointed up. "They'll get out the same way."

Cenith and Tyrsa, Baybee and scroll in hand, led the odd procession, Kyr and Meric right behind.

"Why did you give up Siyon's power?" he asked his wife. They needed all the help they could get.

"Lady Violet said it was too much for me right now. I have to learn to use what I have better. She said we might be able to get it back in the future."

Cenith hoped it wouldn't be too far in the future. When they arrived at the door, a quarter moon hung in a twilight sky and the strange light hanging above Shadow Mountain cast its eerie glow on the ruined slopes below. *This mess took most of the day?* His stomach growled.

"So much for the sun on my face," Kyr said, with a sigh. "Ah well, tomorrow will do." He stared up at the stars with such joy on his face it made Cenith want to weep for what he and the others had endured.

Tyrsa's quiet voice pierced the ensuing silence. "I have to use the privy."

Cenith groaned. Everyone else laughed. "I think we all do, love."

When Jolin stepped from the tunnel, the Companions grabbed their heads and, as one, sank to their knees, each with a cry of pain.

As suddenly as the cries started, they stopped. Cenith slid past Tyrsa, entrusting her safety to Daric. Jolin knelt, doubled over, panting while Cenith crouched beside him.

Jolin put his hand on his forehead. "Th' Queen's Souls left us. They…they've passed on, as they should have ages ago." With Cenith's help, he stood. All the

361

Companions struggled to their feet. Jolin shook his head and frowned. "I feel...strangely alone. I think I miss th' little bugger." His eyes were green once more.

"At least you're back to normal," Cenith said, "or as normal as we seem to get."

"Maybe not, My Lord." Varth clenched his gloved fist. "I still feel just as strong as when Laith was in me."

Cenith turned to Daric. "A parting gift?" Could this be what Niafanna and Cillain meant by 'unexpected talents'?

The Calleni shrugged. "Perhaps. If it is, it's a generous one."

They spread out along the path to the garrison, the flying creatures taking wing, performing loops and dives with obvious joy before disappearing into the twilight, although a few fairies flitted around Tyrsa before landing on her hair.

"There's much in our future that's unknown," Daric said, watching them go. "Besides helping the Shanadar and the Old Ones fit in, we have to find a way for your daughter to rule the country. It's the only path to peace with these people, and, apparently, with our own."

Cenith sighed. "And deal with Shival." He lifted his face to the cool evening air. A daunting task lay before him. "But that can wait for another day." He took a deep breath. "I'm really going to be a father, aren't I?"

Daric just laughed.

Chapter Twenty

The tenth of Fifth Month, 427, a special day in Cenith's life. This was the day his son turned one month old, the day the new heir would be presented to the people of Tiras.

Cenith stood in front of the mirror in his bedroom while Laron adjusted his midnight blue and silver tunic. This was the third state outfit made for him in the past several months. His growth had taken a turn toward the strange. He now stood almost as tall as Daric, a height he'd never thought to attain, but the one aspect of his new self that had everyone scratching their heads was the width of his shoulders and chest. If they'd changed at all, they should have grown broader, instead, they'd narrowed. Cenith now stood taller and leaner than he had before entering the cave of the Old Ones, yet his strength and agility matched that of the Companions.

Niafanna and Cillain had blessed him with more than just their best wishes and the additional changes stared back at him from the mirror. His face had also narrowed, losing most of its gentle roundness, picking up angles and planes that tended to lend him a sterner visage. Even the ends of his ears had lengthened, though they weren't quite the pointy ears of the brownies and pixies. His once grey eyes now had distinct tones of the bright blue of the Shanadar.

The Calleni gods said Cenith must use the skills he

possessed, as well as those he would learn, to find peace, but he'd never imagined those skills would match those of the enhanced Companions. Before Cenith met Tyrsa, he'd never beaten Daric in a one-on-one sword match, now he had to be careful he didn't go too far. He wondered if he'd ever get used to his new self.

He brushed a stray thread from the crest of Dunvalos Reach, three purple-blue mountains, topped with snow, on a sky-blue background, standing clear and proud on his breast. Ardael may have to become one in the future, but for now Cenith ruled here and he was content to do so.

"That's got it, My Lord," Laron said, with a smile. "You look magnificent."

"I think so too." Tyrsa stood near one of the windows, their son in her arms, wearing a dress in the same colours as Cenith's outfit and sporting a huge smile. She hadn't laughed yet, but it was only a matter of time.

She was the only one who'd protested the changes to Cenith's body, complaining that she now had to look farther up to see him and it made her neck hurt. He returned her smile and joined her at the window, bending to kiss her cheek, then that of his son. The little boy didn't stir. He slept like his mother, as solid as the rock surrounding Tiras Keep.

Baybee sat in a place of honour on a shelf above their bed, along with Tyrsa's book. She needed the doll during her pregnancy and labour, but hadn't touched it since, much to Cenith's relief.

He glanced out the window. The courtyard overflowed with the citizens of Tiras and surrounding areas. All his dukes were there, most with their families.

Laron opened the bedroom door and gave him a

bow. Daric, Elessa, Jolin, Trey, Jayce, Meric, Kyr and two of the Shanadar's friends waited in the sitting room, the Companions resplendent in their full armour. The rest of the Companions stood below with the dukes.

Kyr bowed to Tyrsa, then gave Cenith a half one. "I must admit, I approve of the changes the Mother and Father made in ye, though why they made ye even taller I canna imagine. Ye'll never be able to ride a unicorn like a proper Shanadar." He and his friends laughed. Cenith couldn't help but join them.

The past year had been stranger than Cenith could ever have imagined, especially the days following Tyrsa's choice. The Shanadar lived a nomadic life not far from the newly restored guard station at the foot of Eagle's Nest Pass. By all reports, the locals accepted them as the magical people they were; it seemed not only mountain folk were superstitious. Lieutenant Turis, the man responsible for organizing the attacks on Saulth, had been promoted to captain and now took Aleyn's place. Cenith had set up the dead captain's widow with a pension, enough to keep her and the children in food, shelter and clothing.

Meric was the biggest surprise. He seemed to hold no grudge against Daric for the death of his father and, by all reports, had completely turned around from the drunken rake he used to be. Perhaps this was his real personality, allowed to show through now that he was out from under Saulth's thumb.

Bredun's lord caressed the soft baby skin of the newborn as Tyrsa passed by. "I see my nephew is still asleep," he said, a wisp of a smile on his lean face. "Will I be able to hold him when this nonsense is over?"

Tyrsa beamed. She loved showing off her baby. "Yes." She also enjoyed having a sibling who acknowledged her. Iridia was another matter.

Petrella, Saulth's wife, lost her child in her fourth month and went back to Syrth. Meric had yet to marry and didn't seem in a rush.

"It's time," Daric said, standing next to his wife near the fireplace. Cenith's eyes slid to the hearth and the remaining symbols, that of Niafanna and Cillain, the ones representing the Old Ones and the heart that stood as a reminder that Shival still existed in Ardael; but that worry was for the future.

Jolin opened both doors to the balcony. The sun shone bright and warm, a good omen. Cenith took Tyrsa by the arm and led her out, the others behind them. Cheers greeted their arrival.

Another surprise had been the people of Dunvalos Reach. The country folk took the appearance of the Old Ones who chose to show themselves in stride, with many "I told you so's'. The townspeople took longer since they'd never seen any of the creatures, especially when it came to the dragons.

Grimtag and Greythorne soared over the mountains from time to time, searching for wild game, sometimes coming in view of the city. At first they'd startled the residents of Tiras, but they were almost used to them now. The dragons had promised not to eat the livestock, so Cenith gave them his portion of the cattle from the Amita mine deal. He could live with less beef in his stomach if it meant peace in the principality.

When the noise died down, Cenith took a deep breath to steady himself, then rested his hands on the iron railing. "People of Dunvalos Reach." He projected his voice and it echoed off the stone curtain walls of the fortress. "This has been a strange and difficult year, with many surprises, good and ill. But we have come through with not only a new lady for our principality, but a new heir as well." More cheers erupted. People waved coloured cloths and tossed flowers at the balcony.

When peace settled once more, Cenith continued. "One of the best surprises was the addition of the Old Ones to our home. They grace the skies, forests, fields and rivers with a magic this land has not seen in millennia. We welcome them." He turned and bowed to Kyr and his companions. Kyr bowed back and the crowd cheered anew.

Though Meric`s people were adapting to the Old Ones, how the rest of the country welcomed them remained to be seen. Messages had been sent by horse to the other lords explaining Saulth's death, but he had yet to attend a Lord's Council meeting since leaving the cavern. Out of necessity, many of the details were omitted.

Of the three hundred and twenty four people who had died that day, most were Ardaeli nobles, including Jylun and all his immediate family, throwing the other principalities into confusion. Kalkor was in total disarray. Cenith would have to face the lords, and soon, but not today.

Some of his own people opposed the arrival of the Old Ones, strongest were the priests of Maegden and his brood. Attendance at services for the gods dropped dramatically after people realized the Old Ones were real and walking amongst them. Cenith had said nothing of the defeat of the gods, nor Tyrsa's part in it. No one who had been in the cavern that day had, some because they believed the time was not yet right; others, those from Bredun, because Meric had convinced them people would think they'd gone insane. All the idols to the old gods had gone the way of Tailis' and Keana's, they simply wouldn't remain standing no matter how securely they were fastened; all but one, Shival's. The priests had taken it for an evil omen and removed her statue themselves. They now performed the services without idols. Some even said the gods themselves had deliberately removed the statues so people would worship them instead of idols. Whatever made the priests happy was good enough for Cenith.

The people themselves had decided the Old Ones were responsible for the end of the aberrant weather, not the fickle gods. Autumn had seen a better harvest than expected, winter was shorter than previous years and the people were happy. They still believed in Maegden and his lot, but Cenith saw no point in causing trouble in that area. He even attended services from time to time to keep Brother Hamm content, though the priest almost had a fit when Cenith told him the new heir would be raised in the Calleni religion.

Ors knew the truth of it all. He remained Cenith's guard-commander, but wasn't a happy man. Garun on the other hand, pestered Jolin, Jayce, Madin and Keev for information on his new interest, the Old Ones, and plied Daric for knowledge of the ways of Niafanna and Cillain.

Cenith turned to Tyrsa and took his son in his arms. With help from Daric, he removed the blankets surrounding his tiny body. "My beloved people, I present to you my son, Kian of Tiras, your new heir."

He held the naked babe up for all to see, whole and healthy. Little Kian awoke and bellowed a greeting to the throng below, who shouted back to him their wishes for a long life and good health. The little boy had inherited his mother's lungs and Cenith swore his cry outdid theirs.

Daric and Elessa had taken Cenith's choice of name

for the child for the honour intended. Both stood beside him, their smiles wide, as proud as if the boy was their own Kian. Daric had even gone so far as to suggest he was. After all, Niafanna and Cillain had said Kian would be born again soon. Maybe it was so. It was a nice thought.

Shouts of joy turned to cries of wonder. The people below pointed to the sky. Cenith looked up just as two tremendous roars echoed through the valley. Dark shadows soared against the azure blue sky. Grimtag and Greythorne sent their best wishes to the screaming child. From out of nowhere an army of colourful wings filled the air near the balcony...fairies, their giggles and laughter audible even through Kian's cries.

He is strong and healthy, Greythorne said.

Her mate cut loose with another bellow. *He will be your daughter's protector as well as brother. A warrior to be proud of. His war cry will be heard all over Ardael.*

Warmth and pride filled Cenith's heart. Tyrsa tugged on his tunic, worry on her face. She didn't like to hear her child cry. He lowered his son and wrapped him in his blankets once more before passing Kian to his mother.

Tyrsa still had trouble adjusting to her new life. Not only was she wife and lady, she now had the duties of a mother to fill. Her pregnancy had been both exciting and difficult as she progressed through the stages. The birth itself was painful, but swift. Garun assisted, along with the help of Elessa and two visiting Shanadar women. All went well enough. Tyrsa didn't like the hurt, but once Kian was born, she forgot all about it. As for Lady Violet, though she was still in Tyrsa's head, not a word had been heard from her since that day in the cavern. At least, that's what his wife said and Cenith had to believe her.

He raised his arms for quiet. "I am proud of my

son. I know he will be a good man, for he will be raised not just by us, but by all of you as well. No one knows what the future holds, but this I can say for sure. Today is special for more than one reason. This is the dawning of a new age, with new friends. Let us work together to find the peace and prosperity we all deserve." He held his arms wide, the signal for the servants to bring out platters of food to the tables waiting below. "Let us celebrate this new age."

Cenith bowed to his cheering people before turning to his wife. He passed little Kian to Meric, who's smile grew, and picked up Tyrsa. He kissed her, full on the mouth, in front of the entire city. The roaring crowd approved. Life was good.

Watch for the third book in The Jada-Drau trilogy, The Angry Sword, coming soon!

Excerpt from The Angry Sword

Eleventh Month, the year 432, Ardaeli Reckoning

Snow lay thick on the gentle hills surrounding the city of Ys, yet the sun shone as bright as possible for winter. It reflected off the metal tip of the temple spire rising high above the grey and white buildings. Bells rang in the clear air, calling the inhabitants to worship. Esryn, Lord of Sudara, should be leading the procession as he usually did most Maedgen Days. Most, that is, until two months ago. He wrapped his robe tighter around him and turned from the bedroom window. The air felt as cold as his heart. His beloved Meira lay under the frozen ground in the cemetery set aside for the ruling family.

Esryn left the chilly bedroom and held his hands out to the fire burning brightly in his sitting room. It was spacious, filled with expensive furniture, rugs, tapestries and trinkets, yet it held no more warmth than the lonely bedroom.

Two chairs sat in front of the stone fireplace, his and Meira's. This was where they'd talked for hours about matters concerning both the family and the principality. This was where they'd chosen their children's names, all three of them.

A knock sounded. "Breakfast, My Lord."

"Send it away. I'm not hungry."

The guard's muffled voice responded with something that sounded like, 'Yes, My Lord', but could have been anything for all Esryn cared.

Two months had passed since his beloved wife had slipped into a coma, then away from him entirely. It had been a long, painful illness and he should have felt relief that she was finally at peace and sitting in Maegden's Hall, for surely a soul as sweet, loving and gentle as hers deserved a special place.

His eyes slid from the dancing fire to the bottle of apple brandy sitting on a nearby table. Drink dulled the pain, helped him to forget. Payden, his councillor, had chastised him more than once for drunkenness. Esryn no longer cared. He strode to the table and picked up the bottle.

"You don't need that," said a voice, a woman's voice, low and silky.

Esryn almost dropped the brandy. He spun, then did drop it. The glass shattered, spraying broken glass and alcohol over the patterned carpet on the floor. It was of little consequence. What mattered was the person who stood by his balcony doors.

She was all black, except for her pale skin. Her ebony hair waved in a non-existent breeze, floating around her like an ethereal mist. The snug-fitting dress matched her hair exactly. Esryn's eyes followed the curve of her breasts to her hips, then to the floor. She had no feet, at least none that he could see. Then he realized that the dress didn't stop at the floor, it continued into it. She held out her hand and his eyes rose. The ragged sleeves of the dress also moved in a breeze that he couldn't feel.

"Who…who are you? How did you get in here?" He should call for the guards, but something prevented it.

"You know who I am." Her quiet, seductive voice slid through him, gripped his heart, and he knew.

About the Author

Sandie Bergen lives on an island in the Pacific; Vancouver Island to be exact, idyllic and perfect in its own way. She lives with Charlie, her husband of thirty-three years, and three muses, otherwise known as cats, MacDuff, Harmony, and Molly. She has two grown children, Amanda and Aaron. Sandie has been writing for years, mostly for personal enjoyment. The Jada-Drau is her first published novel though she had two ghost stories with Whispering Spirits Digital Magazine, as well as stories published with Worlds of Wonder Magazine and Flash Me Magazine.

Visit me at:

www.sandiebergen.com
www.sandiebergen.ca

On Facebook at: Sandie Bergen, Author

About the Cover Artist and Designer

Stephen Blundell lives in Brisbane , Australia with his wife Joanne and their sons, Michael and Daniel. His illustrations have graced many book covers and interiors from horror to historical fiction. His is still working on his zombie illustrated novel "No Sound Before Dying", as well as his art book. His art can be found at djdyme.deviantart.com and can often be found on Facebook where he regularly posts new images and music.

The Still Life of Hannah Morgan by Lora Deeprose

"The longer you choose to play it safe, the more miserable your life will become. The universe rewards risk my dear; you know what you need to do."

Hannah Morgan's life is at a standstill. Her dreams of becoming an artist vanished with the sudden death of her grandmother and mentor. To appease her distant and disapproving mother, Hannah gets a respectable job at a high-end day spa.

Instead of painting masterpieces, Hannah spends her days painting nails and giving facials to wealthy women. Her dreams for the future have become a hideous nightmare. And, it just keeps getting worse. She catches her boyfriend cheating, loses her job and has to watch from the sidelines as her best friend Jasmine Blue goes after her own dreams of owning her own salon.

When she meets Aaron, a working artist, Hannah finds a kindred spirit. And, to her surprise, she finds the courage to follow her dreams.

When circumstances beyond her control threaten to destroy both her relationship with Aaron and her dreams of a bright future, Hannah fears her mother was right; that some dreams aren't meant to come true.

The Piper by S.L. Partington

It is agreed then. The piper will enter Duntrune and spy out their garrison...

With those words, a man's fate is decided.

It is the year 1642. Colla Coitach, Chieftan of Clan Donald of Colonsay, seeks to wrest his ancestral home from his enemy, the Campbells. Duncan MacArthur, Colla's personal piper, is sent to spy out the enemy garrison in advance of Colla's impending raid. Young and inexperienced, tossed out into a dangerous world where every word from his mouth is either a complete or a mangled half truth, Duncan strives to keep suspicious Campbell eyes from his true purpose while he seeks to do his master's will.

Aided by Eileen Murdoch, the lovely highland woman who pretends to be his love, Duncan must overcome his fear and self-doubt and find the courage to discover the information Colla has asked him to retrieve. Sent to accomplish an impossible task, Duncan finds himself torn between his love for Eileen and the knowledge that oaths, once spoken, are binding forever.

Duty. Honor. Love.

Sometimes a man must choose the harder road...

Beyond The Wizard's Threshold by Loretta Sylvestre

Lucky wants to explain away as a bizarre accident his involvement in sword fights, magic, and inter-world travel. He wants to say that ice-breathing dragons and fire-breathing eagles are a mistake, or a dream, or a bad practical joke. But the truth is this unlikely life belongs to him.

He's fourteen, homeless, and hunted. Yet Behliseth's mystic Key sparks at his touch. Past and future, wizard's and warriors, magic and monsters... What will Lucky find, what will he do, once he steps *Beyond the Wizard's Threshold?*

Huntress by Karina Kantas

When Sofi learns of the pain her family's suffered at the hands of the cruel leader of a motorcycle club, she vows to get revenge. With her journalistic skills she infiltrates the club, finding surprises of her own. Karina Kantas takes us deep into the heart of the most feared motorcycle club in London.

Demonocalypse by Melinda S. Reynolds

In an effort to regain his lost title as the Prince of Hell, Lucifer recruits four demons to masquerade as the Four Horsemen of the Apocalypse: Famine, Pestilence, War, and Death.

Archangel Michael, Angel Warriors Mihdael and Liftheon, and Angel Aleilah form the Heavenly Task Force sent to stop the Fake Four.

Bound by their human forms, the Angels try to survive long enough on Earth to destroy the phony Horsemen, and defeat the powerful, unholy leader of the Old Ones taking on the mantle of Death.

Join the Heavenly Task Force as they pursue the Fake Four from Texas, to Kansas, to Kentucky as they try to prevent an apocalyptic catastrophe: a Demonocalypse!

Days End: A Better Fiction Anthology

From the saving grace of a child's beloved rag doll to a world where degenerate rich pay to experience the minds of the dying, we present nine mesmerizing works of fiction and poetry, tales of Man's ultimate folly.

The Knightens Quest by Diana Cacy Hawkins
Coming April 2012 in Kindle format

A magician, Dithron, has escaped the Void the Druid Mage Kerix imprisoned him in 200 years ago, and is using the Forbidden Magic again. Already damaged, the world's magic can't survive this abuse, and neither can the gods. The world's survival, and that of the very gods, depends on Taun and Dagan.

First, they must bring back the Knightens and restore the Knightens magic to the world. No one knows where they are, or who has them. With their friends, they follow the clues left by prophecy.

But time is running out. Will they find them before it's too late, or will all be lost?

http://www.marionmargaretpress.com

CPSIA information can be obtained at www.ICGtesting.com
Printed in the USA
LVOW061313250812

295851LV00001B/9/P